John Griffith London (born **John Griffith Chaney**; January 12, 1876 – November 22, 1916) was an American novelist, journalist, and social activist. A pioneer in the world of commercial magazine fiction, he was one of the first writers to become a worldwide celebrity and earn a large fortune from writing. He was also an innovator in the genre that would later become known as science fiction. His most famous works include The Call of the Wild and White Fang, both set in the Klondike Gold Rush, as well as the short stories "To Build a Fire", "An Odyssey of the North", and "Love of Life". He also wrote about the South Pacific in stories such as "The Pearls of Parlay" and "The Heathen". London was part of the radical literary group "The Crowd" in San Francisco and a passionate advocate of unionization, socialism, and the rights of workers. He wrote several powerful works dealing with these topics, such as his dystopian novel The Iron Heel, his non-fiction exposé The People of the Abyss, and The War of the Classes. (Source: Wikipedia)

Literary works:
The Cruise of the Dazzler (1902)
A Daughter of the Snows (1902)
The Call of the Wild (1903)
The Kempton-Wace Letters (1903)
The Sea-Wolf (1904)
The Game (1905)
White Fang (1906)
Before Adam (1907)
The Iron Heel (1908)
Martin Eden (1909)
Burning Daylight (1910)
Adventure (1911)
The Scarlet Plague (1912)
A Son of the Sun (1912)
The Abysmal Brute (1913)
The Valley of the Moon (1913)

THE JACKET
(STAR-ROVER)
&
THE
KEMPTON-WACE LETTERS

JACK LONDON

PRINCE CLASSICS

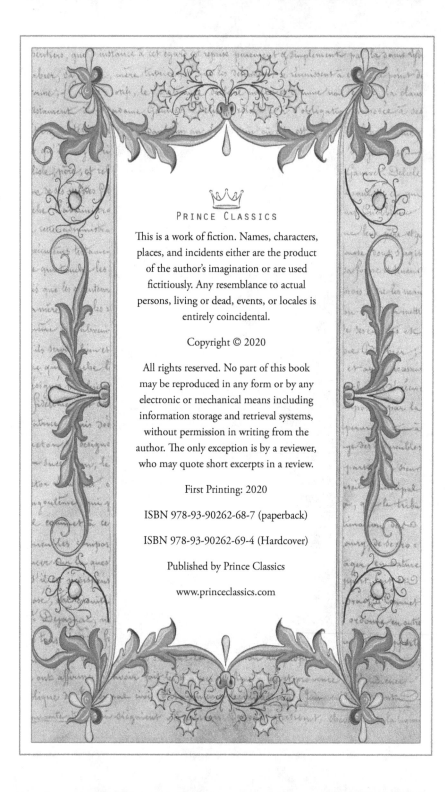

PRINCE CLASSICS

First Printing: 2020

ISBN 978-93-90262-68-7 (paperback)

ISBN 978-93-90262-69-4 (Hardcover)

Published by Prince Classics

www.princeclassics.com

Contents

THE JACKET
(STAR-ROVER)
&
THE
KEMPTON-WACE LETTERS

THE JACKET (STAR-ROVER)

CHAPTER I

All my life I have had an awareness of other times and places. I have been aware of other persons in me.—Oh, and trust me, so have you, my reader that is to be. Read back into your childhood, and this sense of awareness I speak of will be remembered as an experience of your childhood. You were then not fixed, not crystallized. You were plastic, a soul in flux, a consciousness and an identity in the process of forming—ay, of forming and forgetting.

You have forgotten much, my reader, and yet, as you read these lines, you remember dimly the hazy vistas of other times and places into which your child eyes peered. They seem dreams to you to-day. Yet, if they were dreams, dreamed then, whence the substance of them? Our dreams are grotesquely compounded of the things we know. The stuff of our sheerest dreams is the stuff of our experience. As a child, a wee child, you dreamed you fell great heights; you dreamed you flew through the air as things of the air fly; you were vexed by crawling spiders and many-legged creatures of the slime; you heard other voices, saw other faces nightmarishly familiar, and gazed upon sunrises and sunsets other than you know now, looking back, you ever looked upon.

Very well. These child glimpses are of other-worldness, of other-lifeness, of things that you had never seen in this particular world of your particular life. Then whence? Other lives? Other worlds? Perhaps, when you have read all that I shall write, you will have received answers to the perplexities I have propounded to you, and that you yourself, ere you came to read me, propounded to yourself.

* * * * *

Wordsworth knew. He was neither seer nor prophet, but just ordinary man like you or any man. What he knew, you know, any man knows. But he most aptly stated it in his passage that begins "Not in utter nakedness, not in entire forgetfulness. . ."

Ah, truly, shades of the prison-house close about us, the new-born things, and all too soon do we forget. And yet, when we were new-born we did remember other times and places. We, helpless infants in arms or creeping quadruped-like on the floor, dreamed our dreams of air-flight. Yes; and we endured the torment and torture of nightmare fears of dim and monstrous things. We new-born infants, without experience, were born with fear, with memory of fear; and *memory is experience.*

As for myself, at the beginnings of my vocabulary, at so tender a period that I still made hunger noises and sleep noises, yet even then did I know that I had been a star-rover. Yes, I, whose lips had never lisped the word "king," remembered that I had once been the son of a king. More—I remembered that once I had been a slave and a son of a slave, and worn an iron collar round my neck.

Still more. When I was three, and four, and five years of age, I was not yet I. I was a mere becoming, a flux of spirit not yet cooled solid in the mould of my particular flesh and time and place. In that period all that I had ever been in ten thousand lives before strove in me, and troubled the flux of me, in the effort to incorporate itself in me and become me.

Silly, isn't it? But remember, my reader, whom I hope to have travel far with me through time and space—remember, please, my reader, that I have thought much on these matters, that through bloody nights and sweats of dark that lasted years-long, I have been alone with my many selves to consult and contemplate my many selves. I have gone through the hells of all existences to bring you news which you will share with me in a casual comfortable hour over my printed page.

So, to return, I say, during the ages of three and four and five, I was not yet I. I was merely becoming as I took form in the mould of my body, and all the mighty, indestructible past wrought in the mixture of me to determine what the form of that becoming would be. It was not my voice that cried out in the night in fear of things known, which I, forsooth, did not and could not know. The same with my childish angers, my loves, and my laughters. Other voices screamed through my voice, the voices of men and women aforetime, of all shadowy hosts of progenitors. And the snarl of my anger was blended with the snarls of beasts more ancient than the mountains, and the vocal madness of my child hysteria, with all the red of its wrath, was chorded with the insensate, stupid cries of beasts pre-Adamic and progeologic in time.

And there the secret is out. The red wrath! It has undone me in this, my present life. Because of it, a few short weeks hence, I shall be led from this cell to a high place with unstable flooring, graced above by a well-stretched rope; and there they will hang me by the neck until I am dead. The red wrath always has undone me in all my lives; for the red wrath is my disastrous catastrophic heritage from the time of the slimy things ere the world was prime.

* * * * *

It is time that I introduce myself. I am neither fool nor lunatic. I want you to know that, in order that you will believe the things I shall tell you. I am Darrell Standing. Some few of you who read this will know me immediately. But to the majority, who are bound to be strangers, let me exposit myself. Eight years ago I was Professor of Agronomics in the College of Agriculture of the University of California. Eight years ago the sleepy little university town of Berkeley was shocked by the murder of Professor Haskell in one of the laboratories of the Mining Building. Darrell Standing was the murderer.

I am Darrell Standing. I was caught red-handed. Now the right and the wrong of this affair with Professor Haskell I shall not discuss. It was purely a private matter. The point is, that in a surge of anger, obsessed by that catastrophic red wrath that has cursed me down the ages, I killed my fellow professor. The court records show that I did; and, for once, I agree with the court records.

No; I am not to be hanged for his murder. I received a life-sentence for my punishment. I was thirty-six years of age at the time. I am now forty-four years old. I have spent the eight intervening years in the California State Prison of San Quentin. Five of these years I spent in the dark. Solitary confinement, they call it. Men who endure it, call it living death. But through these five years of death-in-life I managed to attain freedom such as few men have ever known. Closest-confined of prisoners, not only did I range the world, but I ranged time. They who immured me for petty years gave to me, all unwittingly, the largess of centuries. Truly, thanks to Ed Morrell, I have had five years of star-roving. But Ed Morrell is another story. I shall tell you about him a little later. I have so much to tell I scarce know how to begin.

Well, a beginning. I was born on a quarter-section in Minnesota. My mother was the daughter of an immigrant Swede. Her name was Hilda Tonnesson. My father was Chauncey Standing, of old American stock. He traced back to Alfred Standing, an indentured servant, or slave if you please, who was transported from England to the Virginia plantations in the days that were even old when the youthful Washington went a-surveying in the Pennsylvania wilderness.

A son of Alfred Standing fought in the War of the Revolution; a grandson, in the War of 1812. There have been no wars since in which the Standings have not been represented. I, the last of the Standings, dying soon without issue, fought as a common soldier in the Philippines, in our latest war, and to do so I resigned, in the full early ripeness of career, my professorship in the University of Nebraska. Good heavens, when I so resigned I was headed for the Deanship of the College of Agriculture in that university—I, the star-rover, the red-blooded adventurer, the vagabondish Cain of the centuries, the militant priest of remotest times, the moon-dreaming poet of ages forgotten and to-day unrecorded in man's history of man!

And here I am, my hands dyed red in Murderers' Row, in the State Prison of Folsom, awaiting the day decreed by the machinery of state when the servants of the state will lead me away into what they fondly believe is the dark—the dark they fear; the dark that gives them fearsome and superstitious fancies; the dark that drives them, drivelling and yammering, to the altars of their fear-created, anthropomorphic gods.

No; I shall never be Dean of any college of agriculture. And yet I knew agriculture. It was my profession. I was born to it, reared to it, trained to it; and I was a master of it. It was my genius. I can pick the high-percentage butter-fat cow with my eye and let the Babcock Tester prove the wisdom of my eye. I can look, not at land, but at landscape, and pronounce the virtues and the shortcomings of the soil. Litmus paper is not necessary when I determine a soil to be acid or alkali. I repeat, farm-husbandry, in its highest scientific terms, was my genius, and is my genius. And yet the state, which includes all the citizens of the state, believes that it can blot out this wisdom of mine in the final dark by means of a rope about my neck and the abruptive jerk of gravitation—this wisdom of mine that was incubated through the millenniums, and that was well-hatched ere the farmed fields of Troy were ever pastured by the flocks of nomad shepherds!

Corn? Who else knows corn? There is my demonstration at Wistar, whereby I increased the annual corn-yield of every county in Iowa by half a million dollars. This is history. Many a farmer, riding in his motor-car to-day, knows who made possible that motor-car. Many a sweet-bosomed girl and bright-browed boy, poring over high-school text-books, little dreams that I made that higher education possible by my corn demonstration at Wistar.

And farm management! I know the waste of superfluous motion without studying a moving picture record of it, whether it be farm or farm-hand, the layout of buildings or the layout of the farm-hands' labour. There is my handbook and tables on the subject. Beyond the shadow of any doubt, at this present moment, a hundred thousand farmers are knotting their brows over its spread pages ere they tap out their final pipe and go to bed. And yet, so far was I beyond my tables, that all I needed was a mere look at a man to know his predispositions, his co-ordinations, and the index fraction of his motion-wastage.

And here I must close this first chapter of my narrative. It is nine o'clock, and in Murderers' Row that means lights out. Even now, I hear the soft tread of the gum-shoed guard as he comes to censure me for my coal-oil lamp still burning. As if the mere living could censure the doomed to die!

CHAPTER II

I am Darrell Standing. They are going to take me out and hang me pretty soon. In the meantime I say my say, and write in these pages of the other times and places.

After my sentence, I came to spend the rest of my "natural life" in the prison of San Quentin. I proved incorrigible. An incorrigible is a terrible human being—at least such is the connotation of "incorrigible" in prison psychology. I became an incorrigible because I abhorred waste motion. The prison, like all prisons, was a scandal and an affront of waste motion. They put me in the jute-mill. The criminality of wastefulness irritated me. Why should it not? Elimination of waste motion was my speciality. Before the invention of steam or steam-driven looms three thousand years before, I had rotted in prison in old Babylon; and, trust me, I speak the truth when I say that in that ancient day we prisoners wove more efficiently on hand-looms than did the prisoners in the steam-powered loom-rooms of San Quentin.

The crime of waste was abhorrent. I rebelled. I tried to show the guards a score or so of more efficient ways. I was reported. I was given the dungeon and the starvation of light and food. I emerged and tried to work in the chaos of inefficiency of the loom-rooms. I rebelled. I was given the dungeon, plus the strait-jacket. I was spread-eagled, and thumbed-up, and privily beaten by the stupid guards whose totality of intelligence was only just sufficient to show them that I was different from them and not so stupid.

Two years of this witless persecution I endured. It is terrible for a man to be tied down and gnawed by rats. The stupid brutes of guards were rats, and they gnawed the intelligence of me, gnawed all the fine nerves of the quick of me and of the consciousness of me. And I, who in my past have been a most valiant fighter, in this present life was no fighter at all. I was a farmer, an agriculturist, a desk-tied professor, a laboratory slave, interested only in the soil and the increase of the productiveness of the soil.

I fought in the Philippines because it was the tradition of the Standings to fight. I had no aptitude for fighting. It was all too ridiculous, the introducing of disruptive foreign substances into the bodies of little black men-folk. It was laughable to behold Science prostituting all the might of its achievement and the wit of its inventors to the violent introducing of foreign substances into the bodies of black folk.

As I say, in obedience to the tradition of the Standings I went to war and found that I had no aptitude for war. So did my officers find me out, because they made me a quartermaster's clerk, and as a clerk, at a desk, I fought through the Spanish-American War.

So it was not because I was a fighter, but because I was a thinker, that I was enraged by the motion-wastage of the loom-rooms and was persecuted by the guards into becoming an "incorrigible." One's brain worked and I was punished for its working. As I told Warden Atherton, when my incorrigibility had become so notorious that he had me in on the carpet in his private office to plead with me; as I told him then:

"It is so absurd, my dear Warden, to think that your rat-throttlers of guards can shake out of my brain the things that are clear and definite in my brain. The whole organization of this prison is stupid. You are a politician. You can weave the political pull of San Francisco saloon-men and ward heelers into a position of graft such as this one you occupy; but you can't weave jute. Your loom-rooms are fifty years behind the times. . . ."

But why continue the tirade?—for tirade it was. I showed him what a fool he was, and as a result he decided that I was a hopeless incorrigible.

Give a dog a bad name—you know the saw. Very well. Warden Atherton gave the final sanction to the badness of my name. I was fair game. More than one convict's dereliction was shunted off on me, and was paid for by me in the dungeon on bread and water, or in being triced up by the thumbs on my tip-toes for long hours, each hour of which was longer than any life I have ever lived.

19

Intelligent men are cruel. Stupid men are monstrously cruel. The guards and the men over me, from the Warden down, were stupid monsters. Listen, and you shall learn what they did to me. There was a poet in the prison, a convict, a weak-chinned, broad-browed, degenerate poet. He was a forger. He was a coward. He was a snitcher. He was a stool—strange words for a professor of agronomics to use in writing, but a professor of agronomics may well learn strange words when pent in prison for the term of his natural life.

This poet-forger's name was Cecil Winwood. He had had prior convictions, and yet, because he was a snivelling cur of a yellow dog, his last sentence had been only for seven years. Good credits would materially reduce this time. My time was life. Yet this miserable degenerate, in order to gain several short years of liberty for himself, succeeded in adding a fair portion of eternity to my own lifetime term.

I shall tell what happened the other way around, for it was only after a weary period that I learned. This Cecil Winwood, in order to curry favour with the Captain of the Yard, and thence the Warden, the Prison Directors, the Board of Pardons, and the Governor of California, framed up a prison-break. Now note three things: (a) Cecil Winwood was so detested by his fellow-convicts that they would not have permitted him to bet an ounce of Bull Durham on a bed-bug race—and bed-bug racing was a great sport with the convicts; (b) I was the dog that had been given a bad name: (c) for his frame-up, Cecil Winwood needed the dogs with bad names, the lifetimers, the desperate ones, the incorrigibles.

But the lifers detested Cecil Winwood, and, when he approached them with his plan of a wholesale prison-break, they laughed at him and turned away with curses for the stool that he was. But he fooled them in the end, forty of the bitterest-wise ones in the pen. He approached them again and again. He told of his power in the prison by virtue of his being trusty in the Warden's office, and because of the fact that he had the run of the dispensary.

"Show me," said Long Bill Hodge, a mountaineer doing life for train robbery, and whose whole soul for years had been bent on escaping in order to kill the companion in robbery who had turned state's evidence on him.

Cecil Winwood accepted the test. He claimed that he could dope the guards the night of the break.

"Talk is cheap," said Long Bill Hodge. "What we want is the goods. Dope one of the guards to-night. There's Barnum. He's no good. He beat up that crazy Chink yesterday in Bughouse Alley—when he was off duty, too. He's on the night watch. Dope him to-night an' make him lose his job. Show me, and we'll talk business with you."

All this Long Bill told me in the dungeons afterward. Cecil Winwood demurred against the immediacy of the demonstration. He claimed that he must have time in which to steal the dope from the dispensary. They gave him the time, and a week later he announced that he was ready. Forty hard-bitten lifers waited for the guard Barnum to go to sleep on his shift. And Barnum did. He was found asleep, and he was discharged for sleeping on duty.

Of course, that convinced the lifers. But there was the Captain of the Yard to convince. To him, daily, Cecil Winwood was reporting the progress of the break—all fancied and fabricated in his own imagination. The Captain of the Yard demanded to be shown. Winwood showed him, and the full details of the showing I did not learn until a year afterward, so slowly do the secrets of prison intrigue leak out.

Winwood said that the forty men in the break, in whose confidence he was, had already such power in the Prison that they were about to begin smuggling in automatic pistols by means of the guards they had bought up.

"Show me," the Captain of the Yard must have demanded.

And the forger-poet showed him. In the Bakery, night work was a regular thing. One of the convicts, a baker, was on the first night-shift. He was a stool of the Captain of the Yard, and Winwood knew it.

"To-night," he told the Captain, "Summerface will bring in a dozen '44 automatics. On his next time off he'll bring in the ammunition. But to-night he'll turn the automatics over to me in the bakery. You've got a good stool there. He'll make you his report to-morrow."

Now Summerface was a strapping figure of a bucolic guard who hailed from Humboldt County. He was a simple-minded, good-natured dolt and not above earning an honest dollar by smuggling in tobacco for the convicts. On that night, returning from a trip to San Francisco, he brought in with him fifteen pounds of prime cigarette tobacco. He had done this before, and delivered the stuff to Cecil Winwood. So, on that particular night, he, all unwitting, turned the stuff over to Winwood in the bakery. It was a big, solid, paper-wrapped bundle of innocent tobacco. The stool baker, from concealment, saw the package delivered to Winwood and so reported to the Captain of the Yard next morning.

But in the meantime the poet-forger's too-lively imagination ran away with him. He was guilty of a slip that gave me five years of solitary confinement and that placed me in this condemned cell in which I now write. And all the time I knew nothing about it. I did not even know of the break he had inveigled the forty lifers into planning. I knew nothing, absolutely nothing. And the rest knew little. The lifers did not know he was giving them the cross. The Captain of the Yard did not know that the cross know was being worked on him. Summerface was the most innocent of all. At the worst, his conscience could have accused him only of smuggling in some harmless tobacco.

And now to the stupid, silly, melodramatic slip of Cecil Winwood. Next morning, when he encountered the Captain of the Yard, he was triumphant. His imagination took the bit in its teeth.

"Well, the stuff came in all right as you said," the captain of the Yard remarked.

"And enough of it to blow half the prison sky-high," Winwood corroborated.

"Enough of what?" the Captain demanded.

"Dynamite and detonators," the fool rattled on. "Thirty-five pounds of it. Your stool saw Summerface pass it over to me."

And right there the Captain of the Yard must have nearly died. I can actually sympathize with him—thirty-five pounds of dynamite loose in the prison.

They say that Captain Jamie—that was his nickname—sat down and held his head in his hands.

"Where is it now?" he cried. "I want it. Take me to it at once."

And right there Cecil Winwood saw his mistake.

"I planted it," he lied—for he was compelled to lie because, being merely tobacco in small packages, it was long since distributed among the convicts along the customary channels.

"Very well," said Captain Jamie, getting himself in hand. "Lead me to it at once."

But there was no plant of high explosives to lead him to. The thing did not exist, had never existed save in the imagination of the wretched Winwood.

In a large prison like San Quentin there are always hiding-places for things. And as Cecil Winwood led Captain Jamie he must have done some rapid thinking.

As Captain Jamie testified before the Board of Directors, and as Winwood also so testified, on the way to the hiding-place Winwood said that he and I had planted the powder together.

And I, just released from five days in the dungeons and eighty hours in the jacket; I, whom even the stupid guards could see was too weak to work in the loom-room; I, who had been given the day off to recuperate—from too terrible punishment—I was named as the one who had helped hide the non-existent thirty-five pounds of high explosive!

Winwood led Captain Jamie to the alleged hiding-place. Of course they found no dynamite in it.

"My God!" Winwood lied. "Standing has given me the cross. He's lifted the plant and stowed it somewhere else."

The Captain of the Yard said more emphatic things than "My God!" Also, on the spur of the moment but cold-bloodedly, he took Winwood into his own private office, looked the doors, and beat him up frightfully—all of which came out before the Board of Directors. But that was afterward. In the meantime, even while he took his beating, Winwood swore by the truth of what he had told.

What was Captain Jamie to do? He was convinced that thirty-five pounds of dynamite were loose in the prison and that forty desperate lifers were ready for a break. Oh, he had Summerface in on the carpet, and, although Summerface insisted the package contained tobacco, Winwood swore it was dynamite and was believed.

At this stage I enter or, rather, I depart, for they took me away out of the sunshine and the light of day to the dungeons, and in the dungeons and in the solitary cells, out of the sunshine and the light of day, I rotted for five years.

I was puzzled. I had only just been released from the dungeons, and was lying pain-racked in my customary cell, when they took me back to the dungeon.

"Now," said Winwood to Captain Jamie, "though we don't know where it is, the dynamite is safe. Standing is the only man who does know, and he can't pass the word out from the dungeon. The men are ready to make the break. We can catch them red-handed. It is up to me to set the time. I'll tell them two o'clock to-night and tell them that, with the guards doped, I'll unlock their cells and give them their automatics. If, at two o'clock to-night, you don't catch the forty I shall name with their clothes on and wide awake, then, Captain, you can give me solitary for the rest of my sentence. And with Standing and the forty tight in the dungeons, we'll have all the time in the world to locate the dynamite."

"If we have to tear the prison down stone by stone," Captain Jamie added valiantly.

That was six years ago. In all the intervening time they have never found that non-existent explosive, and they have turned the prison upside-down a thousand times in searching for it. Nevertheless, to his last day in office Warden Atherton believed in the existence of that dynamite. Captain Jamie, who is still Captain of the Yard, believes to this day that the dynamite is somewhere in the prison. Only yesterday, he came all the way up from San Quentin to Folsom to make one more effort to get me to reveal the hiding-place. I know he will never breathe easy until they swing me off.

CHAPTER III

All that day I lay in the dungeon cudgelling my brains for the reason of this new and inexplicable punishment. All I could conclude was that some stool had lied an infraction of the rules on me in order to curry favour with the guards.

Meanwhile Captain Jamie fretted his head off and prepared for the night, while Winwood passed the word along to the forty lifers to be ready for the break. And two hours after midnight every guard in the prison was under orders. This included the day-shift which should have been asleep. When two o'clock came, they rushed the cells occupied by the forty. The rush was simultaneous. The cells were opened at the same moment, and without exception the men named by Winwood were found out of their bunks, fully dressed, and crouching just inside their doors. Of course, this was verification absolute of all the fabric of lies that the poet-forger had spun for Captain Jamie. The forty lifers were caught in red-handed readiness for the break. What if they did unite, afterward, in averring that the break had been planned by Winwood? The Prison Board of Directors believed, to a man, that the forty lied in an effort to save themselves. The Board of Pardons likewise believed, for, ere three months were up, Cecil Winwood, forger and poet, most despicable of men, was pardoned out.

Oh, well, the stir, or the pen, as they call it in convict argot, is a training school for philosophy. No inmate can survive years of it without having had burst for him his fondest illusions and fairest metaphysical bubbles. Truth lives, we are taught; murder will out. Well, this is a demonstration that murder does not always come out. The Captain of the Yard, the late Warden Atherton, the Prison Board of Directors to a man—all believe, right now, in the existence of that dynamite that never existed save in the slippery-geared and all too-accelerated brain of the degenerate forger and poet, Cecil Winwood. And Cecil Winwood still lives, while I, of all men concerned, the utterest, absolutist, innocentest, go to the scaffold in a few short weeks.

* * * * *

And now I must tell how entered the forty lifers upon my dungeon stillness. I was asleep when the outer door to the corridor of dungeons clanged open and aroused me. "Some poor devil," was my thought; and my next thought was that he was surely getting his, as I listened to the scuffling of feet, the dull impact of blows on flesh, the sudden cries of pain, the filth of curses, and the sounds of dragging bodies. For, you see, every man was man-handled all the length of the way.

Dungeon-door after dungeon-door clanged open, and body after body was thrust in, flung in, or dragged in. And continually more groups of guards arrived with more beaten convicts who still were being beaten, and more dungeon-doors were opened to receive the bleeding frames of men who were guilty of yearning after freedom.

Yes, as I look back upon it, a man must be greatly a philosopher to survive the continual impact of such brutish experiences through the years and years. I am such a philosopher. I have endured eight years of their torment, and now, in the end, failing to get rid of me in all other ways, they have invoked the machinery of state to put a rope around my neck and shut off my breath by the weight of my body. Oh, I know how the experts give expert judgment that the fall through the trap breaks the victim's neck. And the victims, like Shakespeare's traveller, never return to testify to the contrary. But we who have lived in the stir know of the cases that are hushed in the prison crypts, where the victim's necks are not broken.

It is a funny thing, this hanging of a man. I have never seen a hanging, but I have been told by eye-witnesses the details of a dozen hangings so that I know what will happen to me. Standing on the trap, leg-manacled and arm-manacled, the knot against the neck, the black cap drawn, they will drop me down until the momentum of my descending weight is fetched up abruptly short by the tautening of the rope. Then the doctors will group around me, and one will relieve another in successive turns in standing on a stool, his arms passed around me to keep me from swinging like a pendulum, his ear pressed close to my chest, while he counts my fading heart-beats. Sometimes twenty minutes elapse after the trap is sprung ere the heart stops beating. Oh, trust me, they make most scientifically sure that a man is dead once they get him on a rope.

I still wander aside from my narrative to ask a question or two of society. I have a right so to wander and so to question, for in a little while they are going to take me out and do this thing to me. If the neck of the victim be broken by the alleged shrewd arrangement of knot and noose, and by the alleged shrewd calculation of the weight of the victim and the length of slack, then why do they manacle the arms of the victim? Society, as a whole, is unable to answer this question. But I know why; so does any amateur who ever engaged in a lynching bee and saw the victim throw up his hands, clutch the rope, and ease the throttle of the noose about his neck so that he might breathe.

Another question I will ask of the smug, cotton-wooled member of society, whose soul has never strayed to the red hells. Why do they put the black cap over the head and the face of the victim ere they drop him through the trap? Please remember that in a short while they will put that black cap over my head. So I have a right to ask. Do they, your hang-dogs, O smug citizen, do these your hang-dogs fear to gaze upon the facial horror of the horror they perpetrate for you and ours and at your behest?

Please remember that I am not asking this question in the twelve-hundredth year after Christ, nor in the time of Christ, nor in the twelve-hundredth year before Christ. I, who am to be hanged this year, the nineteen-hundred-and-thirteenth after Christ, ask these questions of you who are assumably Christ's followers, of you whose hang-dogs are going to take me out and hide my face under a black cloth because they dare not look upon the horror they do to me while I yet live.

And now back to the situation in the dungeons. When the last guard departed and the outer door clanged shut, all the forty beaten, disappointed men began to talk and ask questions. But, almost immediately, roaring like a bull in order to be heard, Skysail Jack, a giant sailor of a lifer, ordered silence while a census could be taken. The dungeons were full, and dungeon by dungeon, in order of dungeons, shouted out its quota to the roll-call. Thus, every dungeon was accounted for as occupied by trusted convicts, so that there was no opportunity for a stool to be hidden away and listening.

Of me, only, were the convicts dubious, for I was the one man who had not been in the plot. They put me through a searching examination. I could but tell them how I had just emerged from dungeon and jacket in the morning, and without rhyme or reason, so far as I could discover, had been put back in the dungeon after being out only several hours. My record as an incorrigible was in my favour, and soon they began to talk.

As I lay there and listened, for the first time I learned of the break that had been a-hatching. "Who had squealed?" was their one quest, and throughout the night the quest was pursued. The quest for Cecil Winwood was vain, and the suspicion against him was general.

"There's only one thing, lads," Skysail Jack finally said. "It'll soon be morning, and then they'll take us out and give us bloody hell. We were caught dead to rights with our clothes on. Winwood crossed us and squealed. They're going to get us out one by one and mess us up. There's forty of us. Any lyin's bound to be found out. So each lad, when they sweat him, just tells the truth, the whole truth, so help him God."

And there, in that dark hole of man's inhumanity, from dungeon cell to dungeon cell, their mouths against the gratings, the two-score lifers solemnly pledged themselves before God to tell the truth.

Little good did their truth-telling do them. At nine o'clock the guards, paid bravoes of the smug citizens who constitute the state, full of meat and sleep, were upon us. Not only had we had no breakfast, but we had had no water. And beaten men are prone to feverishness. I wonder, my reader, if you can glimpse or guess the faintest connotation of a man beaten—"beat up," we prisoners call it. But no, I shall not tell you. Let it suffice to know that these beaten, feverish men lay seven hours without water.

At nine the guards arrived. There were not many of them. There was no need for many, because they unlocked only one dungeon at a time. They were equipped with pick-handles—a handy tool for the "disciplining" of a helpless man. One dungeon at a time, and dungeon by dungeon, they messed and pulped the lifers. They were impartial. I received the same pulping as the rest. And this was merely the beginning, the preliminary to the examination each man was to undergo alone in the presence of the paid brutes of the state. It was the forecast to each man of what each man might expect in inquisition hall.

I have been through most of the red hells of prison life, but, worst of all, far worse than what they intend to do with me in a short while, was the particular hell of the dungeons in the days that followed.

Long Bill Hodge, the hard-bitten mountaineer, was the first man interrogated. He came back two hours later—or, rather, they conveyed him back, and threw him on the stone of his dungeon floor. They then took away Luigi Polazzo, a San Francisco hoodlum, the first native generation of Italian parentage, who jeered and sneered at them and challenged them to wreak their worst upon him.

It was some time before Long Bill Hodge mastered his pain sufficiently to be coherent.

"What about this dynamite?" he demanded. "Who knows anything about dynamite?"

And of course nobody knew, although it had been the burden of the interrogation put to him.

Luigi Polazzo came back in a little less than two hours, and he came back a wreck that babbled in delirium and could give no answer to the questions showered upon him along the echoing corridor of dungeons by the men who were yet to get what he had got, and who desired greatly to know what things had been done to him and what interrogations had been put to him.

Twice again in the next forty-eight hours Luigi was taken out and interrogated. After that, a gibbering imbecile, he went to live in Bughouse Alley. He has a strong constitution. His shoulders are broad, his nostrils wide, his chest is deep, his blood is pure; he will continue to gibber in Bughouse Alley long after I have swung off and escaped the torment of the penitentiaries of California.

Man after man was taken away, one at a time, and the wrecks of men were brought back, one by one, to rave and howl in the darkness. And as I lay there and listened to the moaning and the groaning, and all the idle chattering of pain-addled wits, somehow, vaguely reminiscent, it seemed to me that somewhere, some time, I had sat in a high place, callous and proud, and listened to a similar chorus of moaning and groaning. Afterwards, as you shall learn, I identified this reminiscence and knew that the moaning and the groaning was of the sweep-slaves manacled to their benches, which I heard from above, on the poop, a soldier passenger on a galley of old Rome. That was when I sailed for Alexandria, a captain of men, on my way to Jerusalem . . . but that is a story I shall tell you later. In the meanwhile . . . .

CHAPTER IV

In the meanwhile obtained the horror of the dungeons, after the discovery of the plot to break prison. And never, during those eternal hours of waiting, was it absent from my consciousness that I should follow these other convicts out, endure the hells of inquisition they endured, and be brought back a wreck and flung on the stone floor of my stone-walled, iron-doored dungeon.

They came for me. Ungraciously and ungently, with blow and curse, they haled me forth, and I faced Captain Jamie and Warden Atherton, themselves arrayed with the strength of half a dozen state-bought, tax-paid brutes of guards who lingered in the room to do any bidding. But they were not needed.

"Sit down," said Warden Atherton, indicating a stout arm-chair.

I, beaten and sore, without water for a night long and a day long, faint with hunger, weak from a beating that had been added to five days in the dungeon and eighty hours in the jacket, oppressed by the calamity of human fate, apprehensive of what was to happen to me from what I had seen happen to the others—I, a wavering waif of a human man and an erstwhile professor of agronomy in a quiet college town, I hesitated to accept the invitation to sit down.

Warden Atherton was a large man and a very powerful man. His hands flashed out to a grip on my shoulders. I was a straw in his strength. He lifted me clear of the floor and crashed me down in the chair.

"Now," he said, while I gasped and swallowed my pain, "tell me all about it, Standing. Spit it out—all of it, if you know what's healthy for you."

"I don't know anything about what has happened . . .", I began.

That was as far as I got. With a growl and a leap he was upon me. Again he lifted me in the air and crashed me down into the chair.

"No nonsense, Standing," he warned. "Make a clean breast of it. Where is the dynamite?"

"I don't know anything of any dynamite," I protested.

Once again I was lifted and smashed back into the chair.

I have endured tortures of various sorts, but when I reflect upon them in the quietness of these my last days, I am confident that no other torture was quite the equal of that chair torture. By my body that stout chair was battered out of any semblance of a chair. Another chair was brought, and in time that chair was demolished. But more chairs were brought, and the eternal questioning about the dynamite went on.

When Warden Atherton grew tired, Captain Jamie relieved him; and then the guard Monohan took Captain Jamie's place in smashing me down into the chair. And always it was dynamite, dynamite, "Where is the dynamite?" and there was no dynamite. Why, toward the last I would have given a large portion of my immortal soul for a few pounds of dynamite to which I could confess.

I do not know how many chairs were broken by my body. I fainted times without number, and toward the last the whole thing became nightmarish. I was half-carried, half-shoved and dragged back to the dark. There, when I became conscious, I found a stool in my dungeon. He was a pallid-faced, little dope-fiend of a short-timer who would do anything to obtain the drug. As soon as I recognized him I crawled to the grating and shouted out along the corridor:

"There is a stool in with me, fellows! He's Ignatius Irvine! Watch out what you say!"

The outburst of imprecations that went up would have shaken the fortitude of a braver man than Ignatius Irvine. He was pitiful in his terror, while all about him, roaring like beasts, the pain-racked lifers told him what awful things they would do to him in the years that were to come.

Had there been secrets, the presence of a stool in the dungeons would have kept the men quiet, As it was, having all sworn to tell the truth, they talked openly before Ignatius Irvine. The one great puzzle was the dynamite, of which they were as much in the dark as was I. They appealed to me. If I knew anything about the dynamite they begged me to confess it and save them all from further misery. And I could tell them only the truth, that I knew of no dynamite.

One thing the stool told me, before the guards removed him, showed how serious was this matter of the dynamite. Of course, I passed the word along, which was that not a wheel had turned in the prison all day. The thousands of convict-workers had remained locked in their cells, and the outlook was that not one of the various prison-factories would be operated again until after the discovery of some dynamite that somebody had hidden somewhere in the prison.

And ever the examination went on. Ever, one at a time, convicts were dragged away and dragged or carried back again. They reported that Warden Atherton and Captain Jamie, exhausted by their efforts, relieved each other every two hours. While one slept, the other examined. And they slept in their clothes in the very room in which strong man after strong man was being broken.

And hour by hour, in the dark dungeons, our madness of torment grew. Oh, trust me as one who knows, hanging is an easy thing compared with the way live men may be hurt in all the life of them and still live. I, too, suffered equally with them from pain and thirst; but added to my suffering was the fact that I remained conscious to the sufferings of the others. I had been an incorrigible for two years, and my nerves and brain were hardened to suffering. It is a frightful thing to see a strong man broken. About me, at the one time, were forty strong men being broken. Ever the cry for water went up, and the place became lunatic with the crying, sobbing, babbling and raving of men in delirium.

Don't you see? Our truth, the very truth we told, was our damnation. When forty men told the same things with such unanimity, Warden Atherton and Captain Jamie could only conclude that the testimony was a memorized lie which each of the forty rattled off parrot-like.

From the standpoint of the authorities, their situation was as desperate as ours. As I learned afterward, the Board of Prison Directors had been summoned by telegraph, and two companies of state militia were being rushed to the prison.

It was winter weather, and the frost is sometimes shrewd even in a California winter. We had no blankets in the dungeons. Please know that it is very cold to stretch bruised human flesh on frosty stone. In the end they did give us water. Jeering and cursing us, the guards ran in the fire-hoses and played the fierce streams on us, dungeon by dungeon, hour after hour, until our bruised flesh was battered all anew by the violence with which the water smote us, until we stood knee-deep in the water which we had raved for and for which now we raved to cease.

I shall skip the rest of what happened in the dungeons. In passing I shall merely state that no one of those forty lifers was ever the same again. Luigi Polazzo never recovered his reason. Long Bill Hodge slowly lost his sanity, so that a year later, he, too, went to live in Bughouse Alley. Oh, and others followed Hodge and Polazzo; and others, whose physical stamina had been impaired, fell victims to prison-tuberculosis. Fully 25 per cent. of the forty have died in the succeeding six years.

After my five years in solitary, when they took me away from San Quentin for my trial, I saw Skysail Jack. I could see little, for I was blinking in the sunshine like a bat, after five years of darkness; yet I saw enough of Skysail Jack to pain my heart. It was in crossing the Prison Yard that I saw him. His hair had turned white. He was prematurely old. His chest had caved in. His cheeks were sunken. His hands shook as with palsy. He tottered as he walked. And his eyes blurred with tears as he recognized me, for I, too, was a sad wreck of what had once been a man. I weighed eighty-seven pounds. My hair, streaked with gray, was a five-years' growth, as were my beard and moustache. And I, too, tottered as I walked, so that the guards helped to lead me across that sun-blinding patch of yard. And Skysail Jack and I peered and knew each other under the wreckage.

Men such as he are privileged, even in a prison, so that he dared an infraction of the rules by speaking to me in a cracked and quavering voice.

"You're a good one, Standing," he cackled. "You never squealed."

"But I never knew, Jack," I whispered back—I was compelled to whisper, for five years of disuse had well-nigh lost me my voice. "I don't think there ever was any dynamite."

"That's right," he cackled, nodding his head childishly. "Stick with it. Don't ever let'm know. You're a good one. I take my hat off to you, Standing. You never squealed."

And the guards led me on, and that was the last I saw of Skysail Jack. It was plain that even he had become a believer in the dynamite myth.

* * * * *

Twice they had me before the full Board of Directors. I was alternately bullied and cajoled. Their attitude resolved itself into two propositions. If I delivered up the dynamite, they would give me a nominal punishment of thirty days in the dungeon and then make me a trusty in the prison library. If I persisted in my stubbornness and did not yield up the dynamite, then they would put me in solitary for the rest of my sentence. In my case, being a life prisoner, this was tantamount to condemning me to solitary confinement for life.

Oh, no; California is civilized. There is no such law on the statute books. It is a cruel and unusual punishment, and no modern state would be guilty of such a law. Nevertheless, in the history of California I am the third man who has been condemned for life to solitary confinement. The other two were Jake Oppenheimer and Ed Morrell. I shall tell you about them soon, for I rotted with them for years in the cells of silence.

Oh, another thing. They are going to take me out and hang me in a little while—no, not for killing Professor Haskell. I got life-imprisonment for that. They are going to take me out and hang me because I was found guilty of assault and battery. And this is not prison discipline. It is law, and as law it will be found in the criminal statutes.

I believe I made a man's nose bleed. I never saw it bleed, but that was the evidence. Thurston, his name was. He was a guard at San Quentin. He weighed one hundred and seventy pounds and was in good health. I weighed under ninety pounds, was blind as a bat from the long darkness, and had been so long pent in narrow walls that I was made dizzy by large open spaces. Really, mime was a well-defined case of incipient agoraphobia, as I quickly learned that day I escaped from solitary and punched the guard Thurston on the nose.

I struck him on the nose and made it bleed when he got in my way and tried to catch hold of me. And so they are going to hang me. It is the written law of the State of California that a lifetimer like me is guilty of a capital crime when he strikes a prison guard like Thurston. Surely, he could not have been inconvenienced more than half an hour by that bleeding nose; and yet they are going to hang me for it.

And, see! This law, in my case, is *ex post facto*. It was not a law at the time I killed Professor Haskell. It was not passed until after I received my life-sentence. And this is the very point: my life-sentence gave me my status under this law which had not yet been written on the books. And it is because of my status of lifetimer that I am to be hanged for battery committed on the guard Thurston. It is clearly *ex post facto*, and, therefore, unconstitutional.

But what bearing has the Constitution on constitutional lawyers when they want to put the notorious Professor Darrell Standing out of the way? Nor do I even establish the precedent with my execution. A year ago, as everybody who reads the newspapers knows, they hanged Jake Oppenheimer, right here in Folsom, for a precisely similar offence . . . only, in his case of battery, he was not guilty of making a guard's nose bleed. He cut a convict unintentionally with a bread-knife.

It is strange—life and men's ways and laws and tangled paths. I am writing these lines in the very cell in Murderers' Row that Jake Oppenheimer occupied ere they took him out and did to him what they are going to do to me.

I warned you I had many things to write about. I shall now return to my narrative. The Board of Prison Directors gave me my choice: a prison trustyship and surcease from the jute-looms if I gave up the non-existent dynamite; life imprisonment in solitary if I refused to give up the non-existent dynamite.

They gave me twenty-four hours in the jacket to think it over. Then I was brought before the Board a second time. What could I do? I could not lead them to the dynamite that was not. I told them so, and they told me I was a liar. They told me I was a hard case, a dangerous man, a moral degenerate, the criminal of the century. They told me many other things, and then they carried me away to the solitary cells. I was put into Number One cell. In Number Five lay Ed Morrell. In Number Twelve lay Jake Oppenheimer. And he had been there for ten years. Ed Morrell had been in his cell only one year. He was serving a fifty-years' sentence. Jake Oppenheimer was a lifer. And so was I a lifer. Wherefore the outlook was that the three of us would remain there for a long time. And yet, six years only are past, and not one of us is in solitary. Jake Oppenheimer was swung off. Ed Morrell was made head trusty of San Quentin and then pardoned out only the other day. And here I am in Folsom waiting the day duly set by Judge Morgan, which will be my last day.

The fools! As if they could throttle my immortality with their clumsy device of rope and scaffold! I shall walk, and walk again, oh, countless times, this fair earth. And I shall walk in the flesh, be prince and peasant, savant and fool, sit in the high place and groan under the wheel.

CHAPTER V

It was very lonely, at first, in solitary, and the hours were long. Time was marked by the regular changing of the guards, and by the alternation of day and night. Day was only a little light, but it was better than the all-dark of the night. In solitary the day was an ooze, a slimy seepage of light from the bright outer world.

Never was the light strong enough to read by. Besides, there was nothing to read. One could only lie and think and think. And I was a lifer, and it seemed certain, if I did not do a miracle, make thirty-five pounds of dynamite out of nothing, that all the years of my life would be spent in the silent dark.

My bed was a thin and rotten tick of straw spread on the cell floor. One thin and filthy blanket constituted the covering. There was no chair, no table—nothing but the tick of straw and the thin, aged blanket. I was ever a short sleeper and ever a busy-brained man. In solitary one grows sick of oneself in his thoughts, and the only way to escape oneself is to sleep. For years I had averaged five hours' sleep a night. I now cultivated sleep. I made a science of it. I became able to sleep ten hours, then twelve hours, and, at last, as high as fourteen and fifteen hours out of the twenty-four. But beyond that I could not go, and, perforce, was compelled to lie awake and think and think. And that way, for an active-brained man, lay madness.

I sought devices to enable me mechanically to abide my waking hours. I squared and cubed long series of numbers, and by concentration and will carried on most astonishing geometric progressions. I even dallied with the squaring of the circle . . . until I found myself beginning to believe that that possibility could be accomplished. Whereupon, realizing that there, too, lay madness, I forwent the squaring of the circle, although I assure you it required a considerable sacrifice on my part, for the mental exercise involved was a splendid time-killer.

By sheer visualization under my eyelids I constructed chess-boards and played both sides of long games through to checkmate. But when I had become expert at this visualized game of memory the exercise palled on me. Exercise it was, for there could be no real contest when the same player played both sides. I tried, and tried vainly, to split my personality into two personalities and to pit one against the other. But ever I remained the one player, with no planned ruse or strategy on one side that the other side did not immediately apprehend.

And time was very heavy and very long. I played games with flies, with ordinary house-flies that oozed into solitary as did the dim gray light; and learned that they possessed a sense of play. For instance, lying on the cell floor, I established an arbitrary and imaginary line along the wall some three feet above the floor. When they rested on the wall above this line they were left in peace. The instant they lighted on the wall below the line I tried to catch them. I was careful never to hurt them, and, in time, they knew as precisely as did I where ran the imaginary line. When they desired to play, they lighted below the line, and often for an hour at a time a single fly would engage in the sport. When it grew tired, it would come to rest on the safe territory above.

Of the dozen or more flies that lived with me, there was only one who did not care for the game. He refused steadfastly to play, and, having learned the penalty of alighting below the line, very carefully avoided the unsafe territory. That fly was a sullen, disgruntled creature. As the convicts would say, it had a "grouch" against the world. He never played with the other flies either. He was strong and healthy, too; for I studied him long to find out. His indisposition for play was temperamental, not physical.

Believe me, I knew all my flies. It was surprising to me the multitude of differences I distinguished between them. Oh, each was distinctly an individual—not merely in size and markings, strength, and speed of flight, and in the manner and fancy of flight and play, of dodge and dart, of wheel and swiftly repeat or wheel and reverse, of touch and go on the danger wall, or of feint the touch and alight elsewhere within the zone. They were likewise sharply differentiated in the minutest shades of mentality and temperament.

I knew the nervous ones, the phlegmatic ones. There was a little undersized one that would fly into real rages, sometimes with me, sometimes with its fellows. Have you ever seen a colt or a calf throw up its heels and dash madly about the pasture from sheer excess of vitality and spirits? Well, there was one fly—the keenest player of them all, by the way—who, when it had alighted three or four times in rapid succession on my taboo wall and succeeded each time in eluding the velvet-careful swoop of my hand, would grow so excited and jubilant that it would dart around and around my head at top speed, wheeling, veering, reversing, and always keeping within the limits of the narrow circle in which it celebrated its triumph over me.

Why, I could tell well in advance when any particular fly was making up its mind to begin to play. There are a thousand details in this one matter alone that I shall not bore you with, although these details did serve to keep me from being bored too utterly during that first period in solitary. But one thing I must tell you. To me it is most memorable—the time when the one with a grouch, who never played, alighted in a moment of absent-mindedness within the taboo precinct and was immediately captured in my hand. Do you know, he sulked for an hour afterward.

And the hours were very long in solitary; nor could I sleep them all away; nor could I while them away with house-flies, no matter how intelligent. For house-flies are house-flies, and I was a man, with a man's brain; and my brain was trained and active, stuffed with culture and science, and always geared to a high tension of eagerness to do. And there was nothing to do, and my thoughts ran abominably on in vain speculations. There was my pentose and methyl-pentose determination in grapes and wines to which I had devoted my last summer vacation at the Asti Vineyards. I had all but completed the series of experiments. Was anybody else going on with it, I wondered; and if so, with what success?

You see, the world was dead to me. No news of it filtered in. The history of science was making fast, and I was interested in a thousand subjects. Why, there was my theory of the hydrolysis of casein by trypsin, which Professor Walters had been carrying out in his laboratory. Also, Professor Schleimer had similarly been collaborating with me in the detection of phytosterol in mixtures of animal and vegetable fats. The work surely was going on, but with what results? The very thought of all this activity just beyond the prison walls and in which I could take no part, of which I was never even to hear, was maddening. And in the meantime I lay there on my cell floor and played games with house-flies.

And yet all was not silence in solitary. Early in my confinement I used to hear, at irregular intervals, faint, low tappings. From farther away I also heard fainter and lower tappings. Continually these tappings were interrupted by the snarling of the guard. On occasion, when the tapping went on too persistently, extra guards were summoned, and I knew by the sounds that men were being strait-jacketed.

The matter was easy of explanation. I had known, as every prisoner in San Quentin knew, that the two men in solitary were Ed Morrell and Jake Oppenheimer. And I knew that these were the two men who tapped knuckle-talk to each other and were punished for so doing.

That the code they used was simple I had not the slightest doubt, yet I devoted many hours to a vain effort to work it out. Heaven knows—it had to be simple, yet I could not make head nor tail of it. And simple it proved to be, when I learned it; and simplest of all proved the trick they employed which had so baffled me. Not only each day did they change the point in the alphabet where the code initialled, but they changed it every conversation, and, often, in the midst of a conversation.

Thus, there came a day when I caught the code at the right initial, listened to two clear sentences of conversation, and, the next time they talked, failed to understand a word. But that first time!

"Say—Ed—what—would— you—give—right—now—for—brown— papers—and—a—sack—of—Bull—Durham!" asked the one who tapped from farther away.

I nearly cried out in my joy. Here was communication! Here was companionship! I listened eagerly, and the nearer tapping, which I guessed must be Ed Morrell's, replied:

41

"I—would—do—twenty—hours—strait—in—the—jacket—for—a—five—cent—sack—"

Then came the snarling interruption of the guard: "Cut that out, Morrell!"

It may be thought by the layman that the worst has been done to men sentenced to solitary for life, and therefore that a mere guard has no way of compelling obedience to his order to cease tapping.

But the jacket remains. Starvation remains. Thirst remains. Man-handling remains. Truly, a man pent in a narrow cell is very helpless.

So the tapping ceased, and that night, when it was next resumed, I was all at sea again. By pre-arrangement they had changed the initial letter of the code. But I had caught the clue, and, in the matter of several days, occurred again the same initialment I had understood. I did not wait on courtesy.

"Hello," I tapped

"Hello, stranger," Morrell tapped back; and, from Oppenheimer, "Welcome to our city."

They were curious to know who I was, how long I was condemned to solitary, and why I had been so condemned. But all this I put to the side in order first to learn their system of changing the code initial. After I had this clear, we talked. It was a great day, for the two lifers had become three, although they accepted me only on probation. As they told me long after, they feared I might be a stool placed there to work a frame-up on them. It had been done before, to Oppenheimer, and he had paid dearly for the confidence he reposed in Warden Atherton's tool.

To my surprise—yes, to my elation be it said—both my fellow-prisoners knew me through my record as an incorrigible. Even into the living grave Oppenheimer had occupied for ten years had my fame, or notoriety, rather, penetrated.

I had much to tell them of prison happenings and of the outside world. The conspiracy to escape of the forty lifers, the search for the alleged dynamite, and all the treacherous frame-up of Cecil Winwood was news to them. As they told me, news did occasionally dribble into solitary by way of the guards, but they had had nothing for a couple of months. The present guards on duty in solitary were a particularly bad and vindictive set.

Again and again that day we were cursed for our knuckle talking by whatever guard was on. But we could not refrain. The two of the living dead had become three, and we had so much to say, while the manner of saying it was exasperatingly slow and I was not so proficient as they at the knuckle game.

"Wait till Pie-Face comes on to-night," Morrell rapped to me. "He sleeps most of his watch, and we can talk a streak."

How we did talk that night! Sleep was farthest from our eyes. Pie-Face Jones was a mean and bitter man, despite his fatness; but we blessed that fatness because it persuaded to stolen snatches of slumber. Nevertheless our incessant tapping bothered his sleep and irritated him so that he reprimanded us repeatedly. And by the other night guards we were roundly cursed. In the morning all reported much tapping during the night, and we paid for our little holiday; for, at nine, came Captain Jamie with several guards to lace us into the torment of the jacket. Until nine the following morning, for twenty-four straight hours, laced and helpless on the floor, without food or water, we paid the price for speech.

Oh, our guards were brutes! And under their treatment we had to harden to brutes in order to live. Hard work makes calloused hands. Hard guards make hard prisoners. We continued to talk, and, on occasion, to be jacketed for punishment. Night was the best time, and, when substitute guards chanced to be on, we often talked through a whole shift.

Night and day were one with us who lived in the dark. We could sleep any time, we could knuckle-talk only on occasion. We told one another much of the history of our lives, and for long hours Morrell and I have lain silently, while steadily, with faint, far taps, Oppenheimer slowly spelled out his life-story, from the early years in a San Francisco slum, through his gang-training, through his initiation into all that was vicious, when as a lad of fourteen he served as night messenger in the red light district, through his first detected infraction of the laws, and on and on through thefts and robberies to the treachery of a comrade and to red slayings inside prison walls.

They called Jake Oppenheimer the "Human Tiger." Some cub reporter coined the phrase that will long outlive the man to whom it was applied. And yet I ever found in Jake Oppenheimer all the cardinal traits of right humanness. He was faithful and loyal. I know of the times he has taken punishment in preference to informing on a comrade. He was brave. He was patient. He was capable of self-sacrifice—I could tell a story of this, but shall not take the time. And justice, with him, was a passion. The prison-killings done by him were due entirely to this extreme sense of justice. And he had a splendid mind. A lifetime in prison, ten years of it in solitary, had not dimmed his brain.

Morrell, ever a true comrade, too had a splendid brain. In fact, and I who am about to die have the right to say it without incurring the charge of immodesty, the three best minds in San Quentin from the Warden down were the three that rotted there together in solitary. And here at the end of my days, reviewing all that I have known of life, I am compelled to the conclusion that strong minds are never docile. The stupid men, the fearful men, the men ungifted with passionate rightness and fearless championship—these are the men who make model prisoners. I thank all gods that Jake Oppenheimer, Ed Morrell, and I were not model prisoners.

CHAPTER VI

There is more than the germ of truth in things erroneous in the child's definition of memory as the thing one forgets with. To be able to forget means sanity. Incessantly to remember, means obsession, lunacy. So the problem I faced in solitary, where incessant remembering strove for possession of me, was the problem of forgetting. When I gamed with flies, or played chess with myself, or talked with my knuckles, I partially forgot. What I desired was entirely to forget.

There were the boyhood memories of other times and places—the "trailing clouds of glory" of Wordsworth. If a boy had had these memories, were they irretrievably lost when he had grown to manhood? Could this particular content of his boy brain be utterly eliminated? Or were these memories of other times and places still residual, asleep, immured in solitary in brain cells similarly to the way I was immured in a cell in San Quentin?

Solitary life-prisoners have been known to resurrect and look upon the sun again. Then why could not these other-world memories of the boy resurrect?

But how? In my judgment, by attainment of complete forgetfulness of present and of manhood past.

And again, how? Hypnotism should do it. If by hypnotism the conscious mind were put to sleep, and the subconscious mind awakened, then was the thing accomplished, then would all the dungeon doors of the brain be thrown wide, then would the prisoners emerge into the sunshine.

So I reasoned—with what result you shall learn. But first I must tell how, as a boy, I had had these other-world memories. I had glowed in the clouds of glory I trailed from lives aforetime. Like any boy, I had been haunted by the other beings I had been at other times. This had been during my process of becoming, ere the flux of all that I had ever been had hardened in the mould of the one personality that was to be known by men for a few years as Darrell Standing.

Let me narrate just one incident. It was up in Minnesota on the old farm. I was nearly six years old. A missionary to China, returned to the United States and sent out by the Board of Missions to raise funds from the farmers, spent the night in our house. It was in the kitchen just after supper, as my mother was helping me undress for bed, and the missionary was showing photographs of the Holy Land.

And what I am about to tell you I should long since have forgotten had I not heard my father recite it to wondering listeners so many times during my childhood.

I cried out at sight of one of the photographs and looked at it, first with eagerness, and then with disappointment. It had seemed of a sudden most familiar, in much the same way that my father's barn would have been in a photograph. Then it had seemed altogether strange. But as I continued to look the haunting sense of familiarity came back.

"The Tower of David," the missionary said to my mother.

"No!" I cried with great positiveness.

"You mean that isn't its name?" the missionary asked.

I nodded.

"Then what is its name, my boy?"

"It's name is . . ." I began, then concluded lamely, "I, forget."

"It don't look the same now," I went on after a pause. "They've ben fixin' it up awful."

Here the missionary handed to my mother another photograph he had sought out.

"I was there myself six months ago, Mrs. Standing." He pointed with his finger. "That is the Jaffa Gate where I walked in and right up to the Tower of David in the back of the picture where my finger is now. The authorities are pretty well agreed on such matters. El Kul'ah, as it was known by—"

But here I broke in again, pointing to rubbish piles of ruined masonry on the left edge of the photograph.

"Over there somewhere," I said. "That name you just spoke was what the Jews called it. But we called it something else. We called it . . . I forget."

"Listen to the youngster," my father chuckled. "You'd think he'd ben there."

I nodded my head, for in that moment I knew I had been there, though all seemed strangely different. My father laughed the harder, but the missionary thought I was making game of him. He handed me another photograph. It was just a bleak waste of a landscape, barren of trees and vegetation, a shallow canyon with easy-sloping walls of rubble. In the middle distance was a cluster of wretched, flat-roofed hovels.

"Now, my boy, where is that?" the missionary quizzed.

And the name came to me!

"Samaria," I said instantly.

My father clapped his hands with glee, my mother was perplexed at my antic conduct, while the missionary evinced irritation.

"The boy is right," he said. "It is a village in Samaria. I passed through it. That is why I bought it. And it goes to show that the boy has seen similar photographs before."

This my father and mother denied.

"But it's different in the picture," I volunteered, while all the time my memory was busy reconstructing the photograph. The general trend of the landscape and the line of the distant hills were the same. The differences I noted aloud and pointed out with my finger.

"The houses was about right here, and there was more trees, lots of trees, and lots of grass, and lots of goats. I can see 'em now, an' two boys drivin' 'em. An' right here is a lot of men walkin' behind one man. An' over there"—I pointed to where I had placed my village—"is a lot of tramps. They ain't got nothin' on exceptin' rags. An' they're sick. Their faces, an' hands, an' legs is all sores."

"He's heard the story in church or somewhere—you remember, the healing of the lepers in Luke," the missionary said with a smile of satisfaction. "How many sick tramps are there, my boy?"

I had learned to count to a hundred when I was five years old, so I went over the group carefully and announced:

"Ten of 'em. They're all wavin' their arms an' yellin' at the other men."

"But they don't come near them?" was the query.

I shook my head. "They just stand right there an' keep a-yellin' like they was in trouble."

"Go on," urged the missionary. "What next? What's the man doing in the front of the other crowd you said was walking along?"

"They've all stopped, an' he's sayin' something to the sick men. An' the boys with the goats 's stopped to look. Everybody's lookin'."

"And then?"

"That's all. The sick men are headin' for the houses. They ain't yellin' any more, an' they don't look sick any more. An' I just keep settin' on my horse a-lookin' on."

At this all three of my listeners broke into laughter.

"An' I'm a big man!" I cried out angrily. "An' I got a big sword!"

"The ten lepers Christ healed before he passed through Jericho on his way to Jerusalem," the missionary explained to my parents. "The boy has seen slides of famous paintings in some magic lantern exhibition."

But neither father nor mother could remember that I had ever seen a magic lantern.

"Try him with another picture," father suggested.

"It's all different," I complained as I studied the photograph the missionary handed me. "Ain't nothin' here except that hill and them other

48

hills. This ought to be a country road along here. An' over there ought to be gardens, an' trees, an' houses behind big stone walls. An' over there, on the other side, in holes in the rocks ought to be where they buried dead folks. You see this place?—they used to throw stones at people there until they killed 'm. I never seen 'm do it. They just told me about it."

"And the hill?" the missionary asked, pointing to the central part of the print, for which the photograph seemed to have been taken. "Can you tell us the name of the hill?"

I shook my head.

"Never had no name. They killed folks there. I've seem 'm more 'n once."

"This time he agrees with the majority of the authorities," announced the missionary with huge satisfaction. "The hill is Golgotha, the Place of Skulls, or, as you please, so named because it resembles a skull. Notice the resemblance. That is where they crucified—" He broke off and turned to me. "Whom did they crucify there, young scholar? Tell us what else you see."

Oh, I saw—my father reported that my eyes were bulging; but I shook my head stubbornly and said:

"I ain't a-goin' to tell you because you're laughin' at me. I seen lots an' lots of men killed there. They nailed 'em up, an' it took a long time. I seen— but I ain't a-goin' to tell. I don't tell lies. You ask dad an' ma if I tell lies. He'd whale the stuffin' out of me if I did. Ask 'm."

And thereat not another word could the missionary get from me, even though he baited me with more photographs that sent my head whirling with a rush of memory-pictures and that urged and tickled my tongue with spates of speech which I sullenly resisted and overcame.

"He will certainly make a good Bible scholar," the missionary told father and mother after I had kissed them good-night and departed for bed. "Or else, with that imagination, he'll become a successful fiction-writer."

Which shows how prophecy can go agley. I sit here in Murderers' Row, writing these lines in my last days, or, rather, in Darrell Standing's last days ere they take him out and try to thrust him into the dark at the end of a rope, and I smile to myself. I became neither Bible scholar nor novelist. On the contrary, until they buried me in the cells of silence for half a decade, I was everything that the missionary forecasted not—an agricultural expert, a professor of agronomy, a specialist in the science of the elimination of waste motion, a master of farm efficiency, a precise laboratory scientist where precision and adherence to microscopic fact are absolute requirements.

And I sit here in the warm afternoon, in Murderers' Row, and cease from the writing of my memoirs to listen to the soothing buzz of flies in the drowsy air, and catch phrases of a low-voiced conversation between Josephus Jackson, the negro murderer on my right, and Bambeccio, the Italian murderer on my left, who are discussing, through grated door to grated door, back and forth past my grated door, the antiseptic virtues and excellences of chewing tobacco for flesh wounds.

And in my suspended hand I hold my fountain pen, and as I remember that other hands of me, in long gone ages, wielded ink-brush, and quill, and stylus, I also find thought-space in time to wonder if that missionary, when he was a little lad, ever trailed clouds of glory and glimpsed the brightness of old star-roving days.

Well, back to solitary, after I had learned the code of knuckle-talk and still found the hours of consciousness too long to endure. By self-hypnosis, which I began successfully to practise, I became able to put my conscious mind to sleep and to awaken and loose my subconscious mind. But the latter was an undisciplined and lawless thing. It wandered through all nightmarish madness, without coherence, without continuity of scene, event, or person.

My method of mechanical hypnosis was the soul of simplicity. Sitting with folded legs on my straw-mattress, I gazed fixedly at a fragment of bright straw which I had attached to the wall of my cell near the door where the most light was. I gazed at the bright point, with my eyes close to it, and tilted upward till they strained to see. At the same time I relaxed all the will of me and gave myself to the swaying dizziness that always eventually came to me. And when I felt myself sway out of balance backward, I closed my eyes and permitted myself to fall supine and unconscious on the mattress.

And then, for half-an-hour, ten minutes, or as long as an hour or so, I would wander erratically and foolishly through the stored memories of my eternal recurrence on earth. But times and places shifted too swiftly. I knew afterward, when I awoke, that I, Darrell Standing, was the linking personality that connected all bizarreness and grotesqueness. But that was all. I could never live out completely one full experience, one point of consciousness in time and space. My dreams, if dreams they may be called, were rhymeless and reasonless.

Thus, as a sample of my rovings: in a single interval of fifteen minutes of subconsciousness I have crawled and bellowed in the slime of the primeval world and sat beside Haas—further and cleaved the twentieth century air in a gas-driven monoplane. Awake, I remembered that I, Darrell Standing, in the flesh, during the year preceding my incarceration in San Quentin, had flown with Haas further over the Pacific at Santa Monica. Awake, I did not remember the crawling and the bellowing in the ancient slime. Nevertheless, awake, I reasoned that somehow I had remembered that early adventure in the slime, and that it was a verity of long-previous experience, when I was not yet Darrell Standing but somebody else, or something else that crawled and bellowed. One experience was merely more remote than the other. Both experiences were equally real—or else how did I remember them?

Oh, what a fluttering of luminous images and actions! In a few short minutes of loosed subconsciousness I have sat in the halls of kings, above the salt and below the salt, been fool and jester, man-at-arms, clerk and monk; and I have been ruler above all at the head of the table—temporal power in my own sword arm, in the thickness of my castle walls, and the numbers of my fighting men; spiritual power likewise mine by token of the fact that cowled priests and fat abbots sat beneath me and swigged my wine and swined my meat.

I have worn the iron collar of the serf about my neck in cold climes; and I have loved princesses of royal houses in the tropic-warmed and sun-scented night, where black slaves fanned the sultry air with fans of peacock plumes, while from afar, across the palm and fountains, drifted the roaring of lions and the cries of jackals. I have crouched in chill desert places warming my hands at fires builded of camel's dung; and I have lain in the meagre shade of sun-parched sage-brush by dry water-holes and yearned dry-tongued for water, while about me, dismembered and scattered in the alkali, were the bones of men and beasts who had yearned and died.

I have been sea-cuny and bravo, scholar and recluse. I have pored over hand-written pages of huge and musty tomes in the scholastic quietude and twilight of cliff-perched monasteries, while beneath on the lesser slopes, peasants still toiled beyond the end of day among the vines and olives and drove in from pastures the blatting goats and lowing kine; yes, and I have led shouting rabbles down the wheel-worn, chariot-rutted paves of ancient and forgotten cities; and, solemn-voiced and grave as death, I have enunciated the law, stated the gravity of the infraction, and imposed the due death on men, who, like Darrell Standing in Folsom Prison, had broken the law.

Aloft, at giddy mastheads oscillating above the decks of ships, I have gazed on sun-flashed water where coral-growths iridesced from profounds of turquoise deeps, and conned the ships into the safety of mirrored lagoons where the anchors rumbled down close to palm-fronded beaches of sea-pounded coral rock; and I have striven on forgotten battlefields of the elder days, when the sun went down on slaughter that did not cease and that continued through the night-hours with the stars shining down and with a cool night wind blowing from distant peaks of snow that failed to chill the sweat of battle; and again, I have been little Darrell Standing, bare-footed in the dew-lush grass of spring on the Minnesota farm, chilblained when of frosty mornings I fed the cattle in their breath-steaming stalls, sobered to fear and awe of the splendour and terror of God when I sat on Sundays under the rant and preachment of the New Jerusalem and the agonies of hell-fire.

Now, the foregoing were the glimpses and glimmerings that came to me, when, in Cell One of Solitary in San Quentin, I stared myself unconscious by means of a particle of bright, light-radiating straw. How did these things come to me? Surely I could not have manufactured them out of nothing inside my pent walls any more than could I have manufactured out of nothing the thirty-five pounds of dynamite so ruthlessly demanded of me by Captain Jamie, Warden Atherton, and the Prison Board of Directors.

I am Darrell Standing, born and raised on a quarter section of land in Minnesota, erstwhile professor of agronomy, a prisoner incorrigible in San Quentin, and at present a death-sentenced man in Folsom. I do not know, of Darrell Standing's experience, these things of which I write and which I have dug from out my store-houses of subconsciousness. I, Darrell Standing, born in Minnesota and soon to die by the rope in California, surely never loved daughters of kings in the courts of kings; nor fought cutlass to cutlass on the swaying decks of ships; nor drowned in the spirit-rooms of ships, guzzling raw liquor to the wassail-shouting and death-singing of seamen, while the ship lifted and crashed on the black-toothed rocks and the water bubbled overhead, beneath, and all about.

Such things are not of Darrell Standing's experience in the world. Yet I, Darrell Standing, found these things within myself in solitary in San Quentin by means of mechanical self-hypnosis. No more were these experiences Darrell Standing's than was the word "Samaria" Darrell Standing's when it leapt to his child lips at sight of a photograph.

One cannot make anything out of nothing. In solitary I could not so make thirty-five pounds of dynamite. Nor in solitary, out of nothing in Darrell Standing's experience, could I make these wide, far visions of time and space. These things were in the content of my mind, and in my mind I was just beginning to learn my way about.

CHAPTER VII

So here was my predicament: I knew that within myself was a Golconda of memories of other lives, yet I was unable to do more than flit like a madman through those memories. I had my Golconda but could not mine it.

I remembered the case of Stainton Moses, the clergyman who had been possessed by the personalities of St. Hippolytus, Plotinus, Athenodorus, and of that friend of Erasmus named Grocyn. And when I considered the experiments of Colonel de Rochas, which I had read in tyro fashion in other and busier days, I was convinced that Stainton Moses had, in previous lives, been those personalities that on occasion seemed to possess him. In truth, they were he, they were the links of the chain of recurrence.

But more especially did I dwell upon the experiments of Colonel de Rochas. By means of suitable hypnotic subjects he claimed that he had penetrated backwards through time to the ancestors of his subjects. Thus, the case of Josephine which he describes. She was eighteen years old and she lived at Voiron, in the department of the Isère. Under hypnotism Colonel de Rochas sent her adventuring back through her adolescence, her girlhood, her childhood, breast-infancy, and the silent dark of her mother's womb, and, still back, through the silence and the dark of the time when she, Josephine, was not yet born, to the light and life of a previous living, when she had been a churlish, suspicious, and embittered old man, by name Jean-Claude Bourdon, who had served his time in the Seventh Artillery at Besançon, and who died at the age of seventy, long bedridden. *Yes*, and did not Colonel de Rochas in turn hypnotize this shade of Jean-Claude Bourdon, so that he adventured farther back into time, through infancy and birth and the dark of the unborn, until he found again light and life when, as a wicked old woman, he had been Philomène Carteron?

But try as I would with my bright bit of straw in the oozement of light into solitary, I failed to achieve any such definiteness of previous personality. I became convinced, through the failure of my experiments, that only through death could I clearly and coherently resurrect the memories of my previous selves.

But the tides of life ran strong in me. I, Darrell Standing, was so strongly disinclined to die that I refused to let Warden Atherton and Captain Jamie kill me. I was always so innately urged to live that sometimes I think that is why I am still here, eating and sleeping, thinking and dreaming, writing this narrative of my various me's, and awaiting the incontestable rope that will put an ephemeral period in my long-linked existence.

And then came death in life. I learned the trick, Ed Morrell taught it me, as you shall see. It began through Warden Atherton and Captain Jamie. They must have experienced a recrudescence of panic at thought of the dynamite they believed hidden. They came to me in my dark cell, and they told me plainly that they would jacket me to death if I did not confess where the dynamite was hidden. And they assured me that they would do it officially without any hurt to their own official skins. My death would appear on the prison register as due to natural causes.

Oh, dear, cotton-wool citizen, please believe me when I tell you that men are killed in prisons to-day as they have always been killed since the first prisons were built by men.

I well knew the terror, the agony, and the danger of the jacket. Oh, the men spirit-broken by the jacket! I have seen them. And I have seen men crippled for life by the jacket. I have seen men, strong men, men so strong that their physical stamina resisted all attacks of prison tuberculosis, after a prolonged bout with the jacket, their resistance broken down, fade away, and die of tuberculosis within six months. There was Slant-Eyed Wilson, with an unguessed weak heart of fear, who died in the jacket within the first hour while the unconvinced inefficient of a prison doctor looked on and smiled. And I have seen a man confess, after half an hour in the jacket, truths and fictions that cost him years of credits.

I had had my own experiences. At the present moment half a thousand scars mark my body. They go to the scaffold with me. Did I live a hundred years to come those same scars in the end would go to the grave with me.

Perhaps, dear citizen who permits and pays his hang-dogs to lace the jacket for you—perhaps you are unacquainted with the jacket. Let me describe, it, so that you will understand the method by which I achieved death in life, became a temporary master of time and space, and vaulted the prison walls to rove among the stars.

Have you ever seen canvas tarpaulins or rubber blankets with brass eyelets set in along the edges? Then imagine a piece of stout canvas, some four and one-half feet in length, with large and heavy brass eyelets running down both edges. The width of this canvas is never the full girth of the human body it is to surround. The width is also irregular—broadest at the shoulders, next broadest at the hips, and narrowest at the waist.

The jacket is spread on the floor. The man who is to be punished, or who is to be tortured for confession, is told to lie face-downward on the flat canvas. If he refuses, he is man-handled. After that he lays himself down with a will, which is the will of the hang-dogs, which is your will, dear citizen, who feeds and fees the hang-dogs for doing this thing for you.

The man lies face-downward. The edges of the jacket are brought as nearly together as possible along the centre of the man's back. Then a rope, on the principle of a shoe-lace, is run through the eyelets, and on the principle of a shoe-lacing the man is laced in the canvas. Only he is laced more severely than any person ever laces his shoe. They call it "cinching" in prison lingo. On occasion, when the guards are cruel and vindictive, or when the command has come down from above, in order to insure the severity of the lacing the guards press with their feet into the man's back as they draw the lacing tight.

Have you ever laced your shoe too tightly, and, after half an hour, experienced that excruciating pain across the instep of the obstructed circulation? And do you remember that after a few minutes of such pain you simply could not walk another step and had to untie the shoe-lace and ease the pressure? Very well. Then try to imagine your whole body so laced, only much more tightly, and that the squeeze, instead of being merely on the instep of one foot, is on your entire trunk, compressing to the seeming of death your heart, your lungs, and all the rest of your vital and essential organs.

I remember the first time they gave me the jacket down in the dungeons. It was at the beginning of my incorrigibility, shortly after my entrance to prison, when I was weaving my loom-task of a hundred yards a day in the jute-mill and finishing two hours ahead of the average day. Yes, and my jute-sacking was far above the average demanded. I was sent to the jacket that first time, according to the prison books, because of "skips" and "breaks" in the cloth, in short, because my work was defective. Of course this was ridiculous. In truth, I was sent to the jacket because I, a new convict, a master of efficiency, a trained expert in the elimination of waste motion, had elected to tell the stupid head weaver a few things he did not know about his business. And the head weaver, with Captain Jamie present, had me called to the table where atrocious weaving, such as could never have gone through my loom, was exhibited against me. Three times was I thus called to the table. The third calling meant punishment according to the loom-room rules. My punishment was twenty-four hours in the jacket.

They took me down into the dungeons. I was ordered to lie face-downward on the canvas spread flat upon the floor. I refused. One of the guards, Morrison, gulletted me with his thumbs. Mobins, the dungeon trusty, a convict himself, struck me repeatedly with his fists. In the end I lay down as directed. And, because of the struggle I had vexed them with, they laced me extra tight. Then they rolled me over like a log upon my back.

It did not seem so bad at first. When they closed my door, with clang and clash of levered boltage, and left me in the utter dark, it was eleven o'clock in the morning. For a few minutes I was aware merely of an uncomfortable constriction which I fondly believed would ease as I grew accustomed to it. On the contrary, my heart began to thump and my lungs seemed unable to draw sufficient air for my blood. This sense of suffocation was terrorizing, and every thump of the heart threatened to burst my already bursting lungs.

After what seemed hours, and after what, out of my countless succeeding experiences in the jacket I can now fairly conclude to have been not more than half-an-hour, I began to cry out, to yell, to scream, to howl, in a very madness of dying. The trouble was the pain that had arisen in my heart. It was a sharp, definite pain, similar to that of pleurisy, except that it stabbed hotly through the heart itself.

To die is not a difficult thing, but to die in such slow and horrible fashion was maddening. Like a trapped beast of the wild, I experienced ecstasies of fear, and yelled and howled until I realized that such vocal exercise merely stabbed my heart more hotly and at the same time consumed much of the little air in my lungs.

I gave over and lay quiet for a long time—an eternity it seemed then, though now I am confident that it could have been no longer than a quarter of an hour. I grew dizzy with semi-asphyxiation, and my heart thumped until it seemed surely it would burst the canvas that bound me. Again I lost control of myself and set up a mad howling for help.

In the midst of this I heard a voice from the next dungeon.

"Shut up," it shouted, though only faintly it percolated to me. "Shut up. You make me tired."

"I'm dying," I cried out.

"Pound your ear and forget it," was the reply.

"But I *am* dying," I insisted.

"Then why worry?" came the voice. "You'll be dead pretty quick an' out of it. Go ahead and croak, but don't make so much noise about it. You're interruptin' my beauty sleep."

So angered was I by this callous indifference that I recovered self-control and was guilty of no more than smothered groans. This endured an endless time—possibly ten minutes; and then a tingling numbness set up in all my body. It was like pins and needles, and for as long as it hurt like pins and needles I kept my head. But when the prickling of the multitudinous darts ceased to hurt and only the numbness remained and continued verging into greater numbness I once more grew frightened.

"How am I goin' to get a wink of sleep?" my neighbour, complained. "I ain't any more happy than you. My jacket's just as tight as yourn, an' I want to sleep an' forget it."

"How long have you been in?" I asked, thinking him a new-comer compared to the centuries I had already suffered.

"Since day before yesterday," was his answer.

"I mean in the jacket," I amended.

"Since day before yesterday, brother."

"My God!" I screamed.

"Yes, brother, fifty straight hours, an' you don't hear me raisin' a roar about it. They cinched me with their feet in my back. I am some tight, believe *me*. You ain't the only one that's got troubles. You ain't ben in an hour yet."

"I've been in hours and hours," I protested.

"Brother, you may think so, but it don't make it so. I'm just tellin' you-you ain't ben in an hour. I heard 'm lacin' you."

The thing was incredible. Already, in less than an hour, I had died a thousand deaths. And yet this neighbour, balanced and equable, calm-voiced and almost beneficent despite the harshness of his first remarks, had been in the jacket fifty hours!

"How much longer are they going to keep you in?" I asked.

"The Lord only knows. Captain Jamie is real peeved with me, an' he won't let me out until I'm about croakin'. Now, brother, I'm going to give you the tip. The only way is shut your face an' forget it. Yellin' an' hollerin' don't win you no money in this joint. An' the way to forget is to forget. Just get to rememberin' every girl you ever knew. That'll eat up hours for you. Mebbe you'll feel yourself gettin' woozy. Well, get woozy. You can't beat that for killin' time. An' when the girls won't hold you, get to thinkin' of the fellows you got it in for, an' what you'd do to 'em if you got a chance, an' what you're goin' to do to 'em when you get that same chance."

That man was Philadelphia Red. Because of prior conviction he was serving fifty years for highway robbery committed on the streets of Alameda.

He had already served a dozen of his years at the time he talked to me in the jacket, and that was seven years ago. He was one of the forty lifers who were double-crossed by Cecil Winwood. For that offence Philadelphia Red lost his credits. He is middle-aged now, and he is still in San Quentin. If he survives he will be an old man when they let him out.

I lived through my twenty-four hours, and I have never been the same man since. Oh, I don't mean physically, although next morning, when they unlaced me, I was semi-paralyzed and in such a state of collapse that the guards had to kick me in the ribs to make me crawl to my feet. But I was a changed man mentally, morally. The brute physical torture of it was humiliation and affront to my spirit and to my sense of justice. Such discipline does not sweeten a man. I emerged from that first jacketing filled with a bitterness and a passionate hatred that has only increased through the years. My God—when I think of the things men have done to me! Twenty-four hours in the jacket! Little I thought that morning when they kicked me to my feet that the time would come when twenty-four hours in the jacket meant nothing; when a hundred hours in the jacket found me smiling when they released me; when two hundred and forty hours in the jacket found the same smile on my lips.

Yes, two hundred and forty hours. Dear cotton-woolly citizen, do you know what that means? It means ten days and ten nights in the jacket. Of course, such things are not done anywhere in the Christian world nineteen hundred years after Christ. I don't ask you to believe me. I don't believe it myself. I merely know that it was done to me in San Quentin, and that I lived to laugh at them and to compel them to get rid of me by swinging me off because I bloodied a guard's nose.

I write these lines to-day in the Year of Our Lord 1913, and to-day, in the Year of Our Lord 1913, men are lying in the jacket in the dungeons of San Quentin.

I shall never forget, as long as further living and further lives be vouchsafed me, my parting from Philadelphia Red that morning. He had then been seventy-four hours in the jacket.

60

"Well, brother, you're still alive an' kickin'," he called to me, as I was totteringly dragged from my cell into the corridor of dungeons.

"Shut up, you, Red," the sergeant snarled at him.

"Forget it," was the retort.

"I'll get you yet, Red," the sergeant threatened.

"Think so?" Philadelphia Red queried sweetly, ere his tones turned to savageness. "Why, you old stiff, you couldn't get nothin'. You couldn't get a free lunch, much less the job you've got now, if it wasn't for your brother's pull. An' I guess we all ain't mistaken on the stink of the place where your brother's pull comes from."

It was admirable—the spirit of man rising above its extremity, fearless of the hurt any brute of the system could inflict.

"Well, so long, brother," Philadelphia Red next called to me. "So long. Be good, an' love the Warden. An' if you see 'em, just tell 'em that you saw me but that you didn't see me saw."

The sergeant was red with rage, and, by the receipt of various kicks and blows, I paid for Red's pleasantry.

CHAPTER VIII

In solitary, in Cell One, Warden Atherton and Captain Jamie proceeded to put me to the inquisition. As Warden Atherton said to me:

"Standing, you're going to come across with that dynamite, or I'll kill you in the jacket. Harder cases than you have come across before I got done with them. You've got your choice—dynamite or curtains."

"Then I guess it is curtains," I answered, "because I don't know of any dynamite."

This irritated the Warden to immediate action. "Lie down," he commanded.

I obeyed, for I had learned the folly of fighting three or four strong men. They laced me tightly, and gave me a hundred hours. Once each twenty-four hours I was permitted a drink of water. I had no desire for food, nor was food offered me. Toward the end of the hundred hours Jackson, the prison doctor, examined my physical condition several times.

But I had grown too used to the jacket during my incorrigible days to let a single jacketing injure me. Naturally, it weakened me, took the life out of me; but I had learned muscular tricks for stealing a little space while they were lacing me. At the end of the first hundred hours' bout I was worn and tired, but that was all. Another bout of this duration they gave me, after a day and a night to recuperate. And then they gave one hundred and fifty hours. Much of this time I was physically numb and mentally delirious. Also, by an effort of will, I managed to sleep away long hours.

Next, Warden Atherton tried a variation. I was given irregular intervals of jacket and recuperation. I never knew when I was to go into the jacket. Thus I would have ten hours' recuperation, and do twenty in the jacket; or I would receive only four hours' rest. At the most unexpected hours of the night my door would clang open and the changing guards would lace me. Sometimes rhythms were instituted. Thus, for three days and nights I alternated eight hours in the jacket and eight hours out. And then, just as I was growing accustomed to this rhythm, it was suddenly altered and I was given two days and nights straight.

And ever the eternal question was propounded to me: Where was the dynamite? Sometimes Warden Atherton was furious with me. On occasion, when I had endured an extra severe jacketing, he almost pleaded with me to confess. Once he even promised me three months in the hospital of absolute rest and good food, and then the trusty job in the library.

Dr. Jackson, a weak stick of a creature with a smattering of medicine, grew sceptical. He insisted that jacketing, no matter how prolonged, could never kill me; and his insistence was a challenge to the Warden to continue the attempt.

"These lean college guys 'd fool the devil," he grumbled. "They're tougher 'n raw-hide. Just the same we'll wear him down. Standing, you hear me. What you've got ain't a caution to what you're going to get. You might as well come across now and save trouble. I'm a man of my word. You've heard me say dynamite or curtains. Well, that stands. Take your choice."

"Surely you don't think I'm holding out because I enjoy it?" I managed to gasp, for at the moment Pie-Face Jones was forcing his foot into my back in order to cinch me tighter, while I was trying with my muscle to steal slack. "There is nothing to confess. Why, I'd cut off my right hand right now to be able to lead you to any dynamite."

"Oh, I've seen your educated kind before," he sneered. "You get wheels in your head, some of you, that make you stick to any old idea. You get baulky, like horses. Tighter, Jones; that ain't half a cinch. Standing, if you don't come across it's curtains. I stick by that."

One compensation I learned. As one grows weaker one is less susceptible to suffering. There is less hurt because there is less to hurt. And the man already well weakened grows weaker more slowly. It is of common knowledge that unusually strong men suffer more severely from ordinary sicknesses than do women or invalids. As the reserves of strength are consumed there is less strength to lose. After all superfluous flesh is gone what is left is stringy and resistant. In fact, that was what I became—a sort of string-like organism that persisted in living.

Morrell and Oppenheimer were sorry for me, and rapped me sympathy and advice. Oppenheimer told me he had gone through it, and worse, and still lived.

"Don't let them beat you out," he spelled with his knuckles. "Don't let them kill you, for that would suit them. And don't squeal on the plant."

"But there isn't any plant," I rapped back with the edge of the sole of my shoe against the grating—I was in the jacket at the time and so could talk only with my feet. "I don't know anything about the damned dynamite."

"That's right," Oppenheimer praised. "He's the stuff, ain't he, Ed?"

Which goes to show what chance I had of convincing Warden Atherton of my ignorance of the dynamite. His very persistence in the quest convinced a man like Jake Oppenheimer, who could only admire me for the fortitude with which I kept a close mouth.

During this first period of the jacket-inquisition I managed to sleep a great deal. My dreams were remarkable. Of course they were vivid and real, as most dreams are. What made them remarkable was their coherence and continuity. Often I addressed bodies of scientists on abstruse subjects, reading aloud to them carefully prepared papers on my own researches or on my own deductions from the researches and experiments of others. When I awakened my voice would seem still ringing in my ears, while my eyes still could see typed on the white paper whole sentences and paragraphs that I could read again and marvel at ere the vision faded. In passing, I call attention to the fact that at the time I noted that the process of reasoning employed in these dream speeches was invariably deductive.

Then there was a great farming section, extending north and south for hundreds of miles in some part of the temperate regions, with a climate and flora and fauna largely resembling those of California. Not once, nor twice, but thousands of different times I journeyed through this dream-region. The point I desire to call attention to was that it was always the same region. No essential feature of it ever differed in the different dreams. Thus it was always an eight-hour drive behind mountain horses from the alfalfa meadows (where I kept many Jersey cows) to the straggly village beside the big dry creek, where I caught the little narrow-gauge train. Every land-mark in that eight-hour drive in the mountain buckboard, every tree, every mountain, every ford and bridge, every ridge and eroded hillside was ever the same.

In this coherent, rational farm-region of my strait-jacket dreams the minor details, according to season and to the labour of men, did change. Thus on the upland pastures behind my alfalfa meadows I developed a new farm with the aid of Angora goats. Here I marked the changes with every dream-visit, and the changes were in accordance with the time that elapsed between visits.

Oh, those brush-covered slopes! How I can see them now just as when the goats were first introduced. And how I remembered the consequent changes—the paths beginning to form as the goats literally ate their way through the dense thickets; the disappearance of the younger, smaller bushes that were not too tall for total browsing; the vistas that formed in all directions through the older, taller bushes, as the goats browsed as high as they could stand and reach on their hind legs; the driftage of the pasture grasses that followed in the wake of the clearing by the goats. Yes, the continuity of such dreaming was its charm. Came the day when the men with axes chopped down all the taller brush so as to give the goats access to the leaves and buds and bark. Came the day, in winter weather, when the dry denuded skeletons of all these bushes were gathered into heaps and burned. Came the day when I moved my goats on to other brush-impregnable hillsides, with following in their wake my cattle, pasturing knee-deep in the succulent grasses that grew where before had been only brush. And came the day when I moved my cattle on, and my plough-men went back and forth across the slopes' contour—ploughing the rich sod under to rot to live and crawling humous in which to bed my seeds of crops to be.

Yes, and in my dreams, often, I got off the little narrow-gauge train where the straggly village stood beside the big dry creek, and got into the

65

buckboard behind my mountain horses, and drove hour by hour past all the old familiar landmarks of my alfalfa meadows, and on to my upland pastures where my rotated crops of corn and barley and clover were ripe for harvesting and where I watched my men engaged in the harvest, while beyond, ever climbing, my goats browsed the higher slopes of brush into cleared, tilled fields.

But these were dreams, frank dreams, fancied adventures of my deductive subconscious mind. Quite unlike them, as you shall see, were my other adventures when I passed through the gates of the living death and relived the reality of the other lives that had been mine in other days.

In the long hours of waking in the jacket I found that I dwelt a great deal on Cecil Winwood, the poet-forger who had wantonly put all this torment on me, and who was even then at liberty out in the free world again. No; I did not hate him. The word is too weak. There is no word in the language strong enough to describe my feelings. I can say only that I knew the gnawing of a desire for vengeance on him that was a pain in itself and that exceeded all the bounds of language. I shall not tell you of the hours I devoted to plans of torture on him, nor of the diabolical means and devices of torture that I invented for him. Just one example. I was enamoured of the ancient trick whereby an iron basin, containing a rat, is fastened to a man's body. The only way out for the rat is through the man himself. As I say, I was enamoured of this until I realized that such a death was too quick, whereupon I dwelt long and favourably on the Moorish trick of—but no, I promised to relate no further of this matter. Let it suffice that many of my pain-maddening waking hours were devoted to dreams of vengeance on Cecil Winwood.

CHAPTER IX

One thing of great value I learned in the long, pain-weary hours of waking—namely, the mastery of the body by the mind. I learned to suffer passively, as, undoubtedly, all men have learned who have passed through the post-graduate courses of strait-jacketing. Oh, it is no easy trick to keep the brain in such serene repose that it is quite oblivious to the throbbing, exquisite complaint of some tortured nerve.

And it was this very mastery of the flesh by the spirit which I so acquired that enabled me easily to practise the secret Ed Morrell told to me.

"Think it is curtains?" Ed Morrell rapped to me one night.

I had just been released from one hundred hours, and I was weaker than I had ever been before. So weak was I that though my whole body was one mass of bruise and misery, nevertheless I scarcely was aware that I had a body.

"It looks like curtains," I rapped back. "They will get me if they keep it up much longer."

"Don't let them," he advised. "There is a way. I learned it myself, down in the dungeons, when Massie and I got ours good and plenty. I pulled through. But Massie croaked. If I hadn't learned the trick, I'd have croaked along with him. You've got to be pretty weak first, before you try it. If you try it when you are strong, you make a failure of it, and then that queers you for ever after. I made the mistake of telling Jake the trick when he was strong. Of course, he could not pull it off, and in the times since when he did need it, it was too late, for his first failure had queered it. He won't even believe it now. He thinks I am kidding him. Ain't that right, Jake?"

And from cell thirteen Jake rapped back, "Don't swallow it, Darrell. It's a sure fairy story."

"Go on and tell me," I rapped to Morrell.

"That is why I waited for you to get real weak," he continued. "Now you need it, and I am going to tell you. It's up to you. If you have got the will you can do it. I've done it three times, and I know."

"Well, what is it?" I rapped eagerly.

"The trick is to die in the jacket, to will yourself to die. I know you don't get me yet, but wait. You know how you get numb in the jacket—how your arm or your leg goes to sleep. Now you can't help that, but you can take it for the idea and improve on it. Don't wait for your legs or anything to go to sleep. You lie on your back as comfortable as you can get, and you begin to use your will.

"And this is the idea you must think to yourself, and that you must believe all the time you're thinking it. If you don't believe, then there's nothing to it. The thing you must think and believe is that your body is one thing and your spirit is another thing. You are you, and your body is something else that don't amount to shucks. Your body don't count. You're the boss. You don't need any body. And thinking and believing all this you proceed to prove it by using your will. You make your body die.

"You begin with the toes, one at a time. You make your toes die. You will them to die. And if you've got the belief and the will your toes will die. That is the big job—to start the dying. Once you've got the first toe dead, the rest is easy, for you don't have to do any more believing. You know. Then you put all your will into making the rest of the body die. I tell you, Darrell, I know. I've done it three times.

"Once you get the dying started, it goes right along. And the funny thing is that you are all there all the time. Because your toes are dead don't make you in the least bit dead. By-and-by your legs are dead to the knees, and then to the thighs, and you are just the same as you always were. It is your body that is dropping out of the game a chunk at a time. And you are just you, the same you were before you began."

"And then what happens?" I queried.

"Well, when your body is all dead, and you are all there yet, you just skin out and leave your body. And when you leave your body you leave the cell. Stone walls and iron doors are to hold bodies in. They can't hold the spirit in. You see, you have proved it. You are spirit outside of your body. You can look at your body from outside of it. I tell you I know because I have done it three times—looked at my body lying there with me outside of it."

"Ha! ha! ha!" Jake Oppenheimer rapped his laughter thirteen cells away.

"You see, that's Jake's trouble," Morrell went on. "He can't believe. That one time he tried it he was too strong and failed. And now he thinks I am kidding."

"When you die you are dead, and dead men stay dead," Oppenheimer retorted.

"I tell you I've been dead three times," Morrell argued.

"And lived to tell us about it," Oppenheimer jeered.

"But don't forget one thing, Darrell," Morrell rapped to me. "The thing is ticklish. You have a feeling all the time that you are taking liberties. I can't explain it, but I always had a feeling if I was away when they came and let my body out of the jacket that I couldn't get back into my body again. I mean that my body would be dead for keeps. And I didn't want it to be dead. I didn't want to give Captain Jamie and the rest that satisfaction. But I tell you, Darrell, if you can turn the trick you can laugh at the Warden. Once you make your body die that way it don't matter whether they keep you in the jacket a month on end. You don't suffer none, and your body don't suffer. You know there are cases of people who have slept a whole year at a time. That's the way it will be with your body. It just stays there in the jacket, not hurting or anything, just waiting for you to come back.

"You try it. I am giving you the straight steer."

"And if he don't come back?" Oppenheimer, asked.

"Then the laugh will be on him, I guess, Jake," Morrell answered. "Unless, maybe, it will be on us for sticking round this old dump when we could get away that easy."

And here the conversation ended, for Pie-Face Jones, waking crustily from stolen slumber, threatened Morrell and Oppenheimer with a report next morning that would mean the jacket for them. Me he did not threaten, for he knew I was doomed for the jacket anyway.

I lay long there in the silence, forgetting the misery of my body while I considered this proposition Morrell had advanced. Already, as I have explained, by mechanical self-hypnosis I had sought to penetrate back through time to my previous selves. That I had partly succeeded I knew; but all that I had experienced was a fluttering of apparitions that merged erratically and were without continuity.

But Morrell's method was so patently the reverse of my method of self-hypnosis that I was fascinated. By my method, my consciousness went first of all. By his method, consciousness persisted last of all, and, when the body was quite gone, passed into stages so sublimated that it left the body, left the prison of San Quentin, and journeyed afar, and was still consciousness.

It was worth a trial, anyway, I concluded. And, despite the sceptical attitude of the scientist that was mine, I believed. I had no doubt I could do what Morrell said he had done three times. Perhaps this faith that so easily possessed me was due to my extreme debility. Perhaps I was not strong enough to be sceptical. This was the hypothesis already suggested by Morrell. It was a conclusion of pure empiricism, and I, too, as you shall see, demonstrated it empirically.

CHAPTER X

And above all things, next morning Warden Atherton came into my cell on murder intent. With him were Captain Jamie, Doctor Jackson, Pie-Face Jones, and Al Hutchins. Al Hutchins was serving a forty-years' sentence, and was in hopes of being pardoned out. For four years he had been head trusty of San Quentin. That this was a position of great power you will realize when I tell you that the graft alone of the head trusty was estimated at three thousand dollars a year. Wherefore Al Hutchins, in possession of ten or twelve thousand dollars and of the promise of a pardon, could be depended upon to do the Warden's bidding blind.

I have just said that Warden Atherton came into my cell intent on murder. His face showed it. His actions proved it.

"Examine him," he ordered Doctor Jackson.

That wretched apology of a creature stripped from me my dirt-encrusted shirt that I had worn since my entrance to solitary, and exposed my poor wasted body, the skin ridged like brown parchment over the ribs and sore-infested from the many bouts with the jacket. The examination was shamelessly perfunctory.

"Will he stand it?" the Warden demanded.

"Yes," Doctor Jackson answered.

"How's the heart?"

"Splendid."

"You think he'll stand ten days of it, Doc.?"

"Sure."

"I don't believe it," the Warden announced savagely. "But we'll try it just the same.—Lie down, Standing."

I obeyed, stretching myself face-downward on the flat-spread jacket. The Warden seemed to debate with himself for a moment.

"Roll over," he commanded.

I made several efforts, but was too weak to succeed, and could only sprawl and squirm in my helplessness.

"Putting it on," was Jackson's comment.

"Well, he won't have to put it on when I'm done with him," said the Warden. "Lend him a hand. I can't waste any more time on him."

So they rolled me over on my back, where I stared up into Warden Atherton's face.

"Standing," he said slowly, "I've given you all the rope I am going to. I am sick and tired of your stubbornness. My patience is exhausted. Doctor Jackson says you are in condition to stand ten days in the jacket. You can figure your chances. But I am going to give you your last chance now. Come across with the dynamite. The moment it is in my hands I'll take you out of here. You can bathe and shave and get clean clothes. I'll let you loaf for six months on hospital grub, and then I'll put you trusty in the library. You can't ask me to be fairer with you than that. Besides, you're not squealing on anybody. You are the only person in San Quentin who knows where the dynamite is. You won't hurt anybody's feelings by giving in, and you'll be all to the good from the moment you do give in. And if you don't—"

He paused and shrugged his shoulders significantly.

"Well, if you don't, you start in the ten days right now."

The prospect was terrifying. So weak was I that I was as certain as the Warden was that it meant death in the jacket. And then I remembered Morrell's trick. Now, if ever, was the need of it; and now, if ever, was the time to practise the faith of it. I smiled up in the face of Warden Atherton. And I put faith in that smile, and faith in the proposition I made to him.

"Warden," I said, "do you see the way I am smiling? Well, if, at the end of the ten days, when you unlace me, I smile up at you in the same way, will you give a sack of Bull Durham and a package of brown papers to Morrell and Oppenheimer?"

"Ain't they the crazy ginks, these college guys," Captain Jamie snorted.

Warden Atherton was a choleric man, and he took my request for insulting braggadocio.

"Just for that you get an extra cinching," he informed me.

"I made you a sporting proposition, Warden," I said quietly. "You can cinch me as tight as you please, but if I smile ten days from now will you give the Bull Durham to Morrell and Oppenheimer?"

"You are mighty sure of yourself," he retorted.

"That's why I made the proposition," I replied.

"Getting religion, eh?" he sneered.

"No," was my answer. "It merely happens that I possess more life than you can ever reach the end of. Make it a hundred days if you want, and I'll smile at you when it's over."

"I guess ten days will more than do you, Standing."

"That's your opinion," I said. "Have you got faith in it? If you have you won't even lose the price of the two five-cents sacks of tobacco. Anyway, what have you got to be afraid of?"

"For two cents I'd kick the face off of you right now," he snarled.

"Don't let me stop you." I was impudently suave. "Kick as hard as you please, and I'll still have enough face left with which to smile. In the meantime, while you are hesitating, suppose you accept my original proposition."

A man must be terribly weak and profoundly desperate to be able, under such circumstances, to beard the Warden in solitary. Or he may be both, and, in addition, he may have faith. I know now that I had the faith and so acted on it. I believed what Morrell had told me. I believed in the lordship of the mind over the body. I believed that not even a hundred days in the jacket could kill me.

Captain Jamie must have sensed this faith that informed me, for he said:

"I remember a Swede that went crazy twenty years ago. That was before your time, Warden. He'd killed a man in a quarrel over twenty-five cents and got life for it. He was a cook. He got religion. He said that a golden chariot was coming to take him to heaven, and he sat down on top the red-hot range and sang hymns and hosannahs while he cooked. They dragged him off, but he croaked two days afterward in hospital. He was cooked to the bone. And to the end he swore he'd never felt the heat. Couldn't get a squeal out of him."

"We'll make Standing squeal," said the Warden.

"Since you are so sure of it, why don't you accept my proposition?" I challenged.

The Warden was so angry that it would have been ludicrous to me had I not been in so desperate plight. His face was convulsed. He clenched his hands, and, for a moment, it seemed that he was about to fall upon me and give me a beating. Then, with an effort, he controlled himself.

"All right, Standing," he snarled. "I'll go you. But you bet your sweet life you'll have to go some to smile ten days from now. Roll him over, boys, and cinch him till you hear his ribs crack. Hutchins, show him you know how to do it."

And they rolled me over and laced me as I had never been laced before. The head trusty certainly demonstrated his ability. I tried to steal what little space I could. Little it was, for I had long since shed my flesh, while my muscles were attenuated to mere strings. I had neither the strength nor bulk to steal more than a little, and the little I stole I swear I managed by sheer expansion at the joints of the bones of my frame. And of this little I was robbed by Hutchins, who, in the old days before he was made head trusty, had learned all the tricks of the jacket from the inside of the jacket.

You see, Hutchins was a cur at heart, or a creature who had once been a man, but who had been broken on the wheel. He possessed ten or twelve thousand dollars, and his freedom was in sight if he obeyed orders. Later,

I learned that there was a girl who had remained true to him, and who was even then waiting for him. The woman factor explains many things of men.

If ever a man deliberately committed murder, Al Hutchins did that morning in solitary at the Warden's bidding. He robbed me of the little space I stole. And, having robbed me of that, my body was defenceless, and, with his foot in my back while he drew the lacing light, he constricted me as no man had ever before succeeded in doing. So severe was this constriction of my frail frame upon my vital organs that I felt, there and then, immediately, that death was upon me. And still the miracle of faith was mine. I did not believe that I was going to die. I knew—I say I *knew*—that I was not going to die. My head was swimming, and my heart was pounding from my toenails to the hair-roots in my scalp.

"That's pretty tight," Captain Jamie urged reluctantly.

"The hell it is," said Doctor Jackson. "I tell you nothing can hurt him. He's a wooz. He ought to have been dead long ago."

Warden Atherton, after a hard struggle, managed to insert his forefinger between the lacing and my back. He brought his foot to bear upon me, with the weight of his body added to his foot, and pulled, but failed to get any fraction of an inch of slack.

"I take my hat off to you, Hutchins," he said. "You know your job. Now roll him over and let's look at him."

They rolled me over on my back. I stared up at them with bulging eyes. This I know: Had they laced me in such fashion the first time I went into the jacket, I would surely have died in the first ten minutes. But I was well trained. I had behind me the thousands of hours in the jacket, and, plus that, I had faith in what Morrell had told me.

"Now, laugh, damn you, laugh," said the Warden to me. "Start that smile you've been bragging about."

So, while my lungs panted for a little air, while my heart threatened to burst, while my mind reeled, nevertheless I was able to smile up into the Warden's face.

CHAPTER XI

The door clanged, shutting out all but a little light, and I was left alone on my back. By the tricks I had long since learned in the jacket, I managed to writhe myself across the floor an inch at a time until the edge of the sole of my right shoe touched the door. There was an immense cheer in this. I was not utterly alone. If the need arose, I could at least rap knuckle talk to Morrell.

But Warden Atherton must have left strict injunctions on the guards, for, though I managed to call Morrell and tell him I intended trying the experiment, he was prevented by the guards from replying. Me they could only curse, for, in so far as I was in the jacket for a ten days' bout, I was beyond all threat of punishment.

I remember remarking at the time my serenity of mind. The customary pain of the jacket was in my body, but my mind was so passive that I was no more aware of the pain than was I aware of the floor beneath me or the walls around me. Never was a man in better mental and spiritual condition for such an experiment. Of course, this was largely due to my extreme weakness. But there was more to it. I had long schooled myself to be oblivious to pain. I had neither doubts nor fears. All the content of my mind seemed to be an absolute faith in the over-lordship of the mind. This passivity was almost dream-like, and yet, in its way, it was positive almost to a pitch of exaltation.

I began my concentration of will. Even then my body was numbing and prickling through the loss of circulation. I directed my will to the little toe of my right foot, and I willed that toe to cease to be alive in my consciousness. I willed that toe to die—to die so far as I, its lord, and a different thing entirely from it, was concerned. There was the hard struggle. Morrell had warned me that it would be so. But there was no flicker of doubt to disturb my faith. I knew that that toe would die, and I knew when it was dead. Joint by joint it had died under the compulsion of my will.

The rest was easy, but slow, I will admit. Joint by joint, toe by toe, all the toes of both my feet ceased to be. And joint by joint, the process went on. Came the time when my flesh below the ankles had ceased. Came the time when all below my knees had ceased.

Such was the pitch of my perfect exaltation, that I knew not the slightest prod of rejoicing at my success. I knew nothing save that I was making my body die. All that was I was devoted to that sole task. I performed the work as thoroughly as any mason laying bricks, and I regarded the work as just about as commonplace as would a brick-mason regard his work.

At the end of an hour my body was dead to the hips, and from the hips up, joint by joint, I continued to will the ascending death.

It was when I reached the level of my heart that the first blurring and dizzying of my consciousness' occurred. For fear that I should lose consciousness, I willed to hold the death I had gained, and shifted my concentration to my fingers. My brain cleared again, and the death of my arms to the shoulders was most rapidly accomplished.

At this stage my body was all dead, so far as I was concerned, save my head and a little patch of my chest. No longer did the pound and smash of my compressed heart echo in my brain. My heart was beating steadily but feebly. The joy of it, had I dared joy at such a moment, would have been the cessation of sensations.

At this point my experience differs from Morrell's. Still willing automatically, I began to grow dreamy, as one does in that borderland between sleeping and waking. Also, it seemed as if a prodigious enlargement of my brain was taking place within the skull itself that did not enlarge. There were occasional glintings and flashings of light as if even I, the overlord, had ceased for a moment and the next moment was again myself, still the tenant of the fleshly tenement that I was making to die.

Most perplexing was the seeming enlargement of brain. Without having passed through the wall of skull, nevertheless it seemed to me that the periphery of my brain was already outside my skull and still expanding. Along with this was one of the most remarkable sensations or experiences that I have ever encountered. Time and space, in so far as they were the stuff of my consciousness, underwent an enormous extension. Thus, without opening my eyes to verify, I knew that the walls of my narrow cell had receded until it was like a vast audience-chamber. And while I contemplated the matter, I knew that they continued to recede. The whim struck me for a moment that if a similar expansion were taking place with the whole prison, then the outer walls of San Quentin must be far out in the Pacific Ocean on one side and on the other side must be encroaching on the Nevada desert. A companion whim was that since matter could permeate matter, then the walls of my cell might well permeate the prison walls, pass through the prison walls, and thus put my cell outside the prison and put me at liberty. Of course, this was pure fantastic whim, and I knew it at the time for what it was.

The extension of time was equally remarkable. Only at long intervals did my heart beat. Again a whim came to me, and I counted the seconds, slow and sure, between my heart-beats. At first, as I clearly noted, over a hundred seconds intervened between beats. But as I continued to count the intervals extended so that I was made weary of counting.

And while this illusion of the extension of time and space persisted and grew, I found myself dreamily considering a new and profound problem. Morrell had told me that he had won freedom from his body by killing his body—or by eliminating his body from his consciousness, which, of course, was in effect the same thing. Now, my body was so near to being entirely dead that I knew in all absoluteness that by a quick concentration of will on the yet-alive patch of my torso it, too, would cease to be. But—and here was the problem, and Morrell had not warned me: should I also will my head to be dead? If I did so, no matter what befell the spirit of Darrell Standing, would not the body of Darrell Standing be for ever dead?

I chanced the chest and the slow-beating heart. The quick compulsion of my will was rewarded. I no longer had chest nor heart. I was only a mind, a soul, a consciousness—call it what you will—incorporate in a nebulous brain that, while it still centred inside my skull, was expanded, and was continuing to expand, beyond my skull.

And then, with flashings of light, I was off and away. At a bound I had vaulted prison roof and California sky, and was among the stars. I say "stars" advisedly. I walked among the stars. I was a child. I was clad in frail, fleece-like, delicate-coloured robes that shimmered in the cool starlight. These robes, of course, were based upon my boyhood observance of circus actors and my boyhood conception of the garb of young angels.

Nevertheless, thus clad, I trod interstellar space, exalted by the knowledge that I was bound on vast adventure, where, at the end, I would find all the cosmic formulæ and have made clear to me the ultimate secret of the universe. In my hand I carried a long glass wand. It was borne in upon me that with the tip of this wand I must touch each star in passing. And I knew, in all absoluteness, that did I but miss one star I should be precipitated into some unplummeted abyss of unthinkable and eternal punishment and guilt.

Long I pursued my starry quest. When I say "long," you must bear in mind the enormous extension of time that had occurred in my brain. For centuries I trod space, with the tip of my wand and with unerring eye and hand tapping each star I passed. Ever the way grew brighter. Ever the ineffable goal of infinite wisdom grew nearer. And yet I made no mistake. This was no other self of mine. This was no experience that had once been mine. I was aware all the time that it was I, Darrell Standing, who walked among the stars and tapped them with a wand of glass. In short, I knew that here was nothing real, nothing that had ever been nor could ever be. I knew that it was nothing else than a ridiculous orgy of the imagination, such as men enjoy in drug dreams, in delirium, or in mere ordinary slumber.

And then, as all went merry and well with me on my celestial quest, the tip of my wand missed a star, and on the instant I knew I had been guilty of a great crime. And on the instant a knock, vast and compulsive, inexorable and mandatory as the stamp of the iron hoof of doom, smote me and reverberated across the universe. The whole sidereal system coruscated, reeled and fell in flame.

I was torn by an exquisite and disruptive agony. And on the instant I was Darrell Standing, the life-convict, lying in his strait-jacket in solitary. And I knew the immediate cause of that summons. It was a rap of the knuckle by Ed Morrell, in Cell Five, beginning the spelling of some message.

And now, to give some comprehension of the extension of time and space that I was experiencing. Many days afterwards I asked Morrell what he had tried to convey to me. It was a simple message, namely: "Standing, are you there?" He had tapped it rapidly, while the guard was at the far end of the corridor into which the solitary cells opened. As I say, he had tapped the message very rapidly. And now behold! Between the first tap and the second I was off and away among the stars, clad in fleecy garments, touching each star as I passed in my pursuit of the formulæ that would explain the last mystery of life. And, as before, I pursued the quest for centuries. Then came the summons, the stamp of the hoof of doom, the exquisite disruptive agony, and again I was back in my cell in San Quentin. It was the second tap of Ed Morrell's knuckle. The interval between it and the first tap could have been no more than a fifth of a second. And yet, so unthinkably enormous was the extension of time to me, that in the course of that fifth of a second I had been away star-roving for long ages.

Now I know, my reader, that the foregoing seems all a farrago. I agree with you. It is farrago. It was experience, however. It was just as real to me as is the snake beheld by a man in delirium tremens.

Possibly, by the most liberal estimate, it may have taken Ed Morrell two minutes to tap his question. Yet, to me, æons elapsed between the first tap of his knuckle and the last. No longer could I tread my starry path with that ineffable pristine joy, for my way was beset with dread of the inevitable summons that would rip and tear me as it jerked me back to my strait-jacket hell. Thus my æons of star-wandering were æons of dread.

And all the time I knew it was Ed Morrell's knuckle that thus cruelly held me earth-bound. I tried to speak to him, to ask him to cease. But so thoroughly had I eliminated my body from my consciousness that I was unable to resurrect it. My body lay dead in the jacket, though I still inhabited the skull. In vain I strove to will my foot to tap my message to Morrell. I reasoned I had a foot. And yet, so thoroughly had I carried out the experiment, I had no foot.

Next—and I know now that it was because Morrell had spelled his message quite out—I pursued my way among the stars and was not called back. After that, and in the course of it, I was aware, drowsily, that I was falling asleep, and that it was delicious sleep. From time to time, drowsily, I stirred—please, my reader, don't miss that verb—I STIRRED. I moved my legs, my arms. I was aware of clean, soft bed linen against my skin. I was aware of bodily well-being. Oh, it was delicious! As thirsting men on the desert dream of splashing fountains and flowing wells, so dreamed I of easement from the constriction of the jacket, of cleanliness in the place of filth, of smooth velvety skin of health in place of my poor parchment-crinkled hide. But I dreamed with a difference, as you shall see.

I awoke. Oh, broad and wide awake I was, although I did not open my eyes. And please know that in all that follows I knew no surprise whatever. Everything was the natural and the expected. I was I, be sure of that. *But I was not Darrell Standing.* Darrell Standing had no more to do with the being I was than did Darrell Standing's parchment-crinkled skin have aught to do with the cool, soft skin that was mine. Nor was I aware of any Darrell Standing—as I could not well be, considering that Darrell Standing was as yet unborn and would not be born for centuries. But you shall see.

I lay with closed eyes, lazily listening. From without came the clacking of many hoofs moving orderly on stone flags. From the accompanying jingle of metal bits of man-harness and steed-harness I knew some cavalcade was passing by on the street beneath my windows. Also, I wondered idly who it was. From somewhere—and I knew where, for I knew it was from the inn yard—came the ring and stamp of hoofs and an impatient neigh that I recognized as belonging to my waiting horse.

Came steps and movements—steps openly advertised as suppressed with the intent of silence and that yet were deliberately noisy with the secret intent of rousing me if I still slept. I smiled inwardly at the rascal's trick.

"Pons," I ordered, without opening my eyes, "water, cold water, quick, a deluge. I drank over long last night, and now my gullet scorches."

"And slept over long to-day," he scolded, as he passed me the water, ready in his hand.

I sat up, opened my eyes, and carried the tankard to my lips with both my hands. And as I drank I looked at Pons.

Now note two things. I spoke in French; I was not conscious that I spoke in French. Not until afterward, back in solitary, when I remembered what I am narrating, did I know that I had spoken in French—ay, and spoken well. As for me, Darrell Standing, at present writing these lines in Murderers' Row of Folsom Prison, why, I know only high school French sufficient to enable me to read the language. As for my speaking it—impossible. I can scarcely intelligibly pronounce my way through a menu.

But to return. Pons was a little withered old man. He was born in our house—I know, for it chanced that mention was made of it this very day I am describing. Pons was all of sixty years. He was mostly toothless, and, despite a pronounced limp that compelled him to go slippity-hop, he was very alert and spry in all his movements. Also, he was impudently familiar. This was because he had been in my house sixty years. He had been my father's servant before I could toddle, and after my father's death (Pons and I talked of it this day) he became my servant. The limp he had acquired on a stricken field in Italy, when the horsemen charged across. He had just dragged my father clear of the hoofs when he was lanced through the thigh, overthrown, and trampled. My father, conscious but helpless from his own wounds, witnessed it all. And so, as I say, Pons had earned such a right to impudent familiarity that at least there was no gainsaying him by my father's son.

Pons shook his head as I drained the huge draught.

"Did you hear it boil?" I laughed, as I handed back the empty tankard.

"Like your father," he said hopelessly. "But your father lived to learn better, which I doubt you will do."

"He got a stomach affliction," I devilled, "so that one mouthful of spirits turned it outside in. It were wisdom not to drink when one's tank will not hold the drink."

While we talked Pons was gathering to my bedside my clothes for the day.

"Drink on, my master," he answered. "It won't hurt you. You'll die with a sound stomach."

"You mean mine is an iron-lined stomach?" I wilfully misunderstood him.

"I mean—" he began with a quick peevishness, then broke off as he realized my teasing and with a pout of his withered lips draped my new sable cloak upon a chair-back. "Eight hundred ducats," he sneered. "A thousand goats and a hundred fat oxen in a coat to keep you warm. A score of farms on my gentleman's fine back."

"And in that a hundred fine farms, with a castle or two thrown in, to say nothing, perhaps, of a palace," I said, reaching out my hand and touching the rapier which he was just in the act of depositing on the chair.

"So your father won with his good right arm," Pons retorted. "But what your father won he held."

Here Pons paused to hold up to scorn my new scarlet satin doublet—a wondrous thing of which I had been extravagant.

"Sixty ducats for that," Pons indicted. "Your father'd have seen all the tailors and Jews of Christendom roasting in hell before he'd a-paid such a price."

And while we dressed—that is, while Pons helped me to dress—I continued to quip with him.

"It is quite clear, Pons, that you have not heard the news," I said slyly.

Whereat up pricked his ears like the old gossip he was.

"Late news?" he queried. "Mayhap from the English Court?"

"Nay," I shook my head. "But news perhaps to you, but old news for all of that. Have you not heard? The philosophers of Greece were whispering it nigh two thousand years ago. It is because of that news that I put twenty fat farms on my back, live at Court, and am become a dandy. You see, Pons, the world is a most evil place, life is most sad, all men die, and, being dead . . . well, are dead. Wherefore, to escape the evil and the sadness, men in these days, like me, seek amazement, insensibility, and the madnesses of dalliance."

"But the news, master? What did the philosophers whisper about so long ago?"

"That God was dead, Pons," I replied solemnly. "Didn't you know that? God is dead, and I soon shall be, and I wear twenty fat farms on my back."

"God lives," Pons asserted fervently. "God lives, and his kingdom is at hand. I tell you, master, it is at hand. It may be no later than to-morrow that the earth shall pass away."

"So said they in old Rome, Pons, when Nero made torches of them to light his sports."

Pons regarded me pityingly.

"Too much learning is a sickness," he complained. "I was always opposed to it. But you must have your will and drag my old body about with you—a-studying astronomy and numbers in Venice, poetry and all the Italian *fol-de-rols* in Florence, and astrology in Pisa, and God knows what in that madman country of Germany. Pish for the philosophers! I tell you, master, I, Pons, your servant, a poor old man who knows not a letter from a pike-staff—I tell you God lives, and the time you shall appear before him is short." He paused with sudden recollection, and added: "He is here, the priest you spoke of."

On the instant I remembered my engagement.

"Why did you not tell me before?" I demanded angrily.

"What did it matter?" Pons shrugged his shoulders. "Has he not been waiting two hours as it is?"

"Why didn't you call me?"

He regarded me with a thoughtful, censorious eye.

"And you rolling to bed and shouting like chanticleer, 'Sing cucu, sing cucu, cucu nu nu cucu, sing cucu, sing cucu, sing cucu, sing cucu.'"

He mocked me with the senseless refrain in an ear-jangling falsetto. Without doubt I had bawled the nonsense out on my way to bed.

"You have a good memory," I commented drily, as I essayed a moment to drape my shoulders with the new sable cloak ere I tossed it to Pons to put aside. He shook his head sourly.

"No need of memory when you roared it over and over for the thousandth time till half the inn was a-knock at the door to spit you for the sleep-killer you were. And when I had you decently in the bed, did you not call me to you and command, if the devil called, to tell him my lady slept? And did you not call me back again, and, with a grip on my arm that leaves it bruised and black this day, command me, as I loved life, fat meat, and the warm fire, to call you not of the morning save for one thing?"

"Which was?" I prompted, unable for the life of me to guess what I could have said.

"Which was the heart of one, a black buzzard, you said, by name Martinelli—whoever he may be—for the heart of Martinelli smoking on a gold platter. The platter must be gold, you said; and you said I must call you by singing, 'Sing cucu, sing cucu, sing cucu.' Whereat you began to teach me how to sing, 'Sing cucu, sing cucu, sing cucu.'"

And when Pons had said the name, I knew it at once for the priest, Martinelli, who had been knocking his heels two mortal hours in the room without.

When Martinelli was permitted to enter and as he saluted me by title and name, I knew at once my name and all of it. I was Count Guillaume de Sainte-Maure. (You see, only could I know then, and remember afterward, what was in my conscious mind.)

The priest was Italian, dark and small, lean as with fasting or with a wasting hunger not of this world, and his hands were as small and slender as a woman's. But his eyes! They were cunning and trustless, narrow-slitted and heavy-lidded, at one and the same time as sharp as a ferret's and as indolent as a basking lizard's.

"There has been much delay, Count de Sainte-Maure," he began promptly, when Pons had left the room at a glance from me. "He whom I serve grows impatient."

"Change your tune, priest," I broke in angrily. "Remember, you are not now in Rome."

"My august master—" he began.

"Rules augustly in Rome, mayhap," I again interrupted. "This is France."

Martinelli shrugged his shoulders meekly and patiently, but his eyes, gleaming like a basilisk's, gave his shoulders the lie.

"My august master has some concern with the doings of France," he said quietly. "The lady is not for you. My master has other plans. . ." He moistened his thin lips with his tongue. "Other plans for the lady . . . and for you."

Of course, by the lady I knew he referred to the great Duchess Philippa, widow of Geoffrey, last Duke of Aquitaine. But great duchess, widow, and all, Philippa was a woman, and young, and gay, and beautiful, and, by my faith, fashioned for me.

"What are his plans?" I demanded bluntly.

"They are deep and wide, Count Sainte-Maure—too deep and wide for me to presume to imagine, much less know or discuss with you or any man."

"Oh, I know big things are afoot and slimy worms squirming underground," I said.

"They told me you were stubborn-necked, but I have obeyed commands."

Martinelli arose to leave, and I arose with him.

"I said it was useless," he went on. "But the last chance to change your mind was accorded you. My august master deals more fairly than fair."

"Oh, well, I'll think the matter over," I said airily, as I bowed the priest to the door.

He stopped abruptly at the threshold.

"The time for thinking is past," he said. "It is decision I came for."

"I will think the matter over," I repeated, then added, as afterthought: "If the lady's plans do not accord with mine, then mayhap the plans of your master may fruit as he desires. For remember, priest, he is no master of mine."

"You do not know my master," he said solemnly.

"Nor do I wish to know him," I retorted.

And I listened to the lithe, light step of the little intriguing priest go down the creaking stairs.

Did I go into the minutiæ of detail of all that I saw this half a day and half a night that I was Count Guillaume de Sainte-Maure, not ten books the size of this I am writing could contain the totality of the matter. Much I shall skip; in fact, I shall skip almost all; for never yet have I heard of a condemned man being reprieved in order that he might complete his memoirs—at least, not in California.

When I rode out in Paris that day it was the Paris of centuries agone. The narrow streets were an unsanitary scandal of filth and slime. But I must skip. And skip I shall, all of the afternoon's events, all of the ride outside the walls, of the grand fête given by Hugh de Meung, of the feasting and the drinking in which I took little part. Only of the end of the adventure will I write, which begins with where I stood jesting with Philippa herself—ah, dear God, she was wondrous beautiful. A great lady—ay, but before that, and after that, and always, a woman.

We laughed and jested lightly enough, as about us jostled the merry throng; but under our jesting was the deep earnestness of man and woman well advanced across the threshold of love and yet not too sure each of the other. I shall not describe her. She was small, exquisitely slender—but there, I am describing her. In brief, she was the one woman in the world for me, and little I recked the long arm of that gray old man in Rome could reach out half across Europe between my woman and me.

And the Italian, Fortini, leaned to my shoulder and whispered:

"One who desires to speak."

"One who must wait my pleasure," I answered shortly.

"I wait no man's pleasure," was his equally short reply.

And, while my blood boiled, I remembered the priest, Martinelli, and the gray old man at Rome. The thing was clear. It was deliberate. It was the long arm. Fortini smiled lazily at me while I thus paused for the moment to debate, but in his smile was the essence of all insolence.

This, of all times, was the time I should have been cool. But the old red anger began to kindle in me. This was the work of the priest. This was the Fortini, poverished of all save lineage, reckoned the best sword come up out of Italy in half a score of years. To-night it was Fortini. If he failed the gray old man's command to-morrow it would be another sword, the next day another. And, perchance still failing, then might I expect the common bravo's steel in my back or the common poisoner's philter in my wine, my meat, or bread.

"I am busy," I said. "Begone."

"My business with you presses," was his reply.

Insensibly our voices had slightly risen, so that Philippa heard.

"Begone, you Italian hound," I said. "Take your howling from my door. I shall attend to you presently."

"The moon is up," he said. "The grass is dry and excellent. There is no dew. Beyond the fish-pond, an arrow's flight to the left, is an open space, quiet and private."

"Presently you shall have your desire," I muttered impatiently.

But still he persisted in waiting at my shoulder.

"Presently," I said. "Presently I shall attend to you."

Then spoke Philippa, in all the daring spirit and the iron of her.

"Satisfy the gentleman's desire, Sainte-Maure. Attend to him now. And good fortune go with you." She paused to beckon to her her uncle, Jean de

Joinville, who was passing—uncle on her mother's side, of the de Joinvilles of Anjou. "Good fortune go with you," she repeated, and then leaned to me so that she could whisper: "And my heart goes with you, Sainte-Maure. Do not be long. I shall await you in the big hall."

I was in the seventh heaven. I trod on air. It was the first frank admittance of her love. And with such benediction I was made so strong that I knew I could kill a score of Fortinis and snap my fingers at a score of gray old men in Rome.

Jean de Joinville bore Philippa away in the press, and Fortini and I settled our arrangements in a trice. We separated—he to find a friend or so, and I to find a friend or so, and all to meet at the appointed place beyond the fish-pond.

First I found Robert Lanfranc, and, next, Henry Bohemond. But before I found them I encountered a windlestraw which showed which way blew the wind and gave promise of a very gale. I knew the windlestraw, Guy de Villehardouin, a raw young provincial, come up the first time to Court, but a fiery little cockerel for all of that. He was red-haired. His blue eyes, small and pinched close to ether, were likewise red, at least in the whites of them; and his skin, of the sort that goes with such types, was red and freckled. He had quite a parboiled appearance.

As I passed him by a sudden movement he jostled me. Oh, of course, the thing was deliberate. And he flamed at me while his hand dropped to his rapier.

"Faith," thought I, "the gray old man has many and strange tools," while to the cockerel I bowed and murmured, "Your pardon for my clumsiness. The fault was mine. Your pardon, Villehardouin."

But he was not to be appeased thus easily. And while he fumed and strutted I glimpsed Robert Lanfranc, beckoned him to us, and explained the happening.

"Sainte-Maure has accorded you satisfaction," was his judgment. "He has prayed your pardon."

"In truth, yes," I interrupted in my suavest tones. "And I pray your pardon again, Villehardouin, for my very great clumsiness. I pray your pardon a thousand times. The fault was mine, though unintentional. In my haste to an engagement I was clumsy, most woful clumsy, but without intention."

What could the dolt do but grudgingly accept the amends I so freely proffered him? Yet I knew, as Lanfranc and I hastened on, that ere many days, or hours, the flame-headed youth would see to it that we measured steel together on the grass.

I explained no more to Lanfranc than my need of him, and he was little interested to pry deeper into the matter. He was himself a lively youngster of no more than twenty, but he had been trained to arms, had fought in Spain, and had an honourable record on the grass. Merely his black eyes flashed when he learned what was toward, and such was his eagerness that it was he who gathered Henry Bohemond in to our number.

When the three of us arrived in the open space beyond the fish-pond Fortini and two friends were already waiting us. One was Felix Pasquini, nephew to the Cardinal of that name, and as close in his uncle's confidence as was his uncle close in the confidence of the gray old man. The other was Raoul de Goncourt, whose presence surprised me, he being too good and noble a man for the company he kept.

We saluted properly, and properly went about the business. It was nothing new to any of us. The footing was good, as promised. There was no dew. The moon shone fair, and Fortini's blade and mine were out and at earnest play.

This I knew: good swordsman as they reckoned me in France, Fortini was a better. This, too, I knew: that I carried my lady's heart with me this night, and that this night, because of me, there would be one Italian less in the world. I say I knew it. In my mind the issue could not be in doubt. And as our rapiers played I pondered the manner I should kill him. I was not minded for a long contest. Quick and brilliant had always been my way. And further, what of my past gay months of carousal and of singing "Sing cucu, sing cucu, sing cucu," at ungodly hours, I knew I was not conditioned for a long contest. Quick and brilliant was my decision.

But quick and brilliant was a difficult matter with so consummate a swordsman as Fortini opposed to me. Besides, as luck would have it, Fortini, always the cold one, always the tireless-wristed, always sure and long, as report had it, in going about such business, on this night elected, too, the quick and brilliant.

It was nervous, tingling work, for as surely as I sensed his intention of briefness, just as surely had he sensed mine. I doubt that I could have done the trick had it been broad day instead of moonlight. The dim light aided me. Also was I aided by divining, the moment in advance, what he had in mind. It was the time attack, a common but perilous trick that every novice knows, that has laid on his back many a good man who attempted it, and that is so fraught with danger to the perpetrator that swordsmen are not enamoured of it.

We had been at work barely a minute, when I knew under all his darting, flashing show of offence that Fortini meditated this very time attack. He desired of me a thrust and lunge, not that he might parry it but that he might time it and deflect it by the customary slight turn of the wrist, his rapier point directed to meet me as my body followed in the lunge. A ticklish thing—ay, a ticklish thing in the best of light. Did he deflect a fraction of a second too early, I should be warned and saved. Did he deflect a fraction of a second too late, my thrust would go home to him.

"Quick and brilliant is it?" was my thought. "Very well, my Italian friend, quick and brilliant shall it be, and especially shall it be quick."

In a way, it was time attack against time attack, but I would fool him on the time by being over-quick. And I was quick. As I said, we had been at work scarcely a minute when it happened. Quick? That thrust and lunge of mine were one. A snap of action it was, an explosion, an instantaneousness. I swear my thrust and lunge were a fraction of a second quicker than any man is supposed to thrust and lunge. I won the fraction of a second. By that fraction of a second too late Fortini attempted to deflect my blade and impale me on his. But it was his blade that was deflected. It flashed past my breast, and I was in—inside his weapon, which extended full length in the empty air behind me—and my blade was inside of him, and through him, heart-high, from right side of him to left side of him and outside of him beyond.

91

It is a strange thing to do, to spit a live man on a length of steel. I sit here in my cell, and cease from writing a space, while I consider the matter. And I have considered it often, that moonlight night in France of long ago, when I taught the Italian hound quick and brilliant. It was so easy a thing, that perforation of a torso. One would have expected more resistance. There would have been resistance had my rapier point touched bone. As it was, it encountered only the softness of flesh. Still it perforated so easily. I have the sensation of it now, in my hand, my brain, as I write. A woman's hatpin could go through a plum pudding not more easily than did my blade go through the Italian. Oh, there was nothing amazing about it at the time to Guillaume de Sainte-Maure, but amazing it is to me, Darrell Standing, as I recollect and ponder it across the centuries. It is easy, most easy, to kill a strong, live, breathing man with so crude a weapon as a piece of steel. Why, men are like soft-shell crabs, so tender, frail, and vulnerable are they.

But to return to the moonlight on the grass. My thrust made home, there was a perceptible pause. Not at once did Fortini fall. Not at once did I withdraw the blade. For a full second we stood in pause—I, with legs spread, and arched and tense, body thrown forward, right arm horizontal and straight out; Fortini, his blade beyond me so far that hilt and hand just rested lightly against my left breast, his body rigid, his eyes open and shining.

So statuesque were we for that second that I swear those about us were not immediately aware of what had happened. Then Fortini gasped and coughed slightly. The rigidity of his pose slackened. The hilt and hand against my breast wavered, then the arm drooped to his side till the rapier point rested on the lawn. By this time Pasquini and de Goncourt had sprung to him and he was sinking into their arms. In faith, it was harder for me to withdraw the steel than to drive it in. His flesh clung about it as if jealous to let it depart. Oh, believe me, it required a distinct physical effort to get clear of what I had done.

But the pang of the withdrawal must have stung him back to life and purpose, for he shook off his friends, straightened himself, and lifted his rapier into position. I, too, took position, marvelling that it was possible I had spitted him heart-high and yet missed any vital spot. Then, and before his friends could catch him, his legs crumpled under him and he went heavily to grass. They laid him on his back, but he was already dead, his face ghastly still under the moon, his right hand still a-clutch of the rapier.

Yes; it is indeed a marvellous easy thing to kill a man.

We saluted his friends and were about to depart, when Felix Pasquini detained me.

"Pardon me," I said. "Let it be to-morrow."

"We have but to move a step aside," he urged, "where the grass is still dry."

"Let me then wet it for you, Sainte-Maure," Lanfranc asked of me, eager himself to do for an Italian.

I shook my head.

"Pasquini is mine," I answered. "He shall be first to-morrow."

"Are there others?" Lanfranc demanded.

"Ask de Goncourt," I grinned. "I imagine he is already laying claim to the honour of being the third."

At this, de Goncourt showed distressed acquiescence. Lanfranc looked inquiry at him, and de Goncourt nodded.

"And after him I doubt not comes the cockerel," I went on.

And even as I spoke the red-haired Guy de Villehardouin, alone, strode to us across the moonlit grass.

"At least I shall have him," Lanfranc cried, his voice almost wheedling, so great was his desire.

"Ask him," I laughed, then turned to Pasquini. "To-morrow," I said. "Do you name time and place, and I shall be there."

"The grass is most excellent," he teased, "the place is most excellent, and I am minded that Fortini has you for company this night."

"'Twere better he were accompanied by a friend," I quipped. "And now your pardon, for I must go."

But he blocked my path.

"Whoever it be," he said, "let it be now."

For the first time, with him, my anger began to rise.

"You serve your master well," I sneered.

"I serve but my pleasure," was his answer. "Master I have none."

"Pardon me if I presume to tell you the truth," I said.

"Which is?" he queried softly.

"That you are a liar, Pasquini, a liar like all Italians."

He turned immediately to Lanfranc and Bohemond.

"You heard," he said. "And after that you cannot deny me him."

They hesitated and looked to me for counsel of my wishes. But Pasquini did not wait.

"And if you still have any scruples," he hurried on, "then allow me to remove them . . . thus."

And he spat in the grass at my feet. Then my anger seized me and was beyond me. The red wrath I call it—an overwhelming, all-mastering desire to kill and destroy. I forgot that Philippa waited for me in the great hall. All I knew was my wrongs—the unpardonable interference in my affairs by the gray old man, the errand of the priest, the insolence of Fortini, the impudence of Villehardouin, and here Pasquini standing in my way and spitting in the grass. I saw red. I thought red. I looked upon all these creatures as rank and noisome growths that must be hewn out of my path, out of the world. As a netted lion may rage against the meshes, so raged I against these creatures. They were all about me. In truth, I was in the trap. The one way out was to cut them down, to crush them into the earth and stamp upon them.

"Very well," I said, calmly enough, although my passion was such that my frame shook. "You first, Pasquini. And you next, de Goncourt? And at the end, de Villehardouin?"

Each nodded in turn and Pasquini and I prepared to step aside.

"Since you are in haste," Henry Bohemond proposed to me, "and since there are three of them and three of us, why not settle it at the one time?"

"Yes, yes," was Lanfranc's eager cry. "Do you take de Goncourt. De Villehardouin for mine."

But I waved my good friends back.

"They are here by command," I explained. "It is I they desire so strongly that by my faith I have caught the contagion of their desire, so that now I want them and will have them for myself."

I had observed that Pasquini fretted at my delay of speech-making, and I resolved to fret him further.

"You, Pasquini," I announced, "I shall settle with in short account. I would not that you tarried while Fortini waits your companionship. You, Raoul de Goncourt, I shall punish as you deserve for being in such bad company. You are getting fat and wheezy. I shall take my time with you until your fat melts and your lungs pant and wheeze like leaky bellows. You, de Villehardouin, I have not decided in what manner I shall kill."

And then I saluted Pasquini, and we were at it. Oh, I was minded to be rarely devilish this night. Quick and brilliant—that was the thing. Nor was I unmindful of that deceptive moonlight. As with Fortini would I settle with him if he dared the time attack. If he did not, and quickly, then I would dare it.

Despite the fret I had put him in, he was cautious. Nevertheless I compelled the play to be rapid, and in the dim light, depending less than usual on sight and more than usual on feel, our blades were in continual touch.

Barely was the first minute of play past when I did the trick. I feigned a slight slip of the foot, and, in the recovery, feigned loss of touch with Pasquini's blade. He thrust tentatively, and again I feigned, this time making a needlessly wide parry. The consequent exposure of myself was the bait I had purposely dangled to draw him on. And draw him on I did. Like a flash he took advantage of what he deemed an involuntary exposure. Straight and true was his thrust, and all his will and body were heartily in the weight of the lunge he made. And all had been feigned on my part and I was ready for him. Just lightly did my steel meet his as our blades slithered. And just firmly enough and no more did my wrist twist and deflect his blade on my basket hilt. Oh, such a slight deflection, a matter of inches, just barely sufficient to send his point past me so that it pierced a fold of my satin doublet in passing. Of course, his body followed his rapier in the lunge, while, heart-high, right side, my rapier point met his body. And my outstretched arm was stiff and straight as the steel into which it elongated, and behind the arm and the steel my body was braced and solid.

Heart-high, I say, my rapier entered Pasquini's side on the right, but it did not emerge, on the left, for, well-nigh through him, it met a rib (oh, man-killing is butcher's work!) with such a will that the forcing overbalanced him, so that he fell part backward and part sidewise to the ground. And even as he fell, and ere he struck, with jerk and wrench I cleared my weapon of him.

De Goncourt was to him, but he waved de Goncourt to attend on me. Not so swiftly as Fortini did Pasquini pass. He coughed and spat, and, helped by de Villehardouin, propped his elbow under him, rested his head on hand, and coughed and spat again.

"A pleasant journey, Pasquini," I laughed to him in my red anger. "Pray hasten, for the grass where you lie is become suddenly wet and if you linger you will catch your death of cold."

When I made immediately to begin with de Goncourt, Bohemond protested that I should rest a space.

"Nay," I said. "I have not properly warmed up." And to de Goncourt, "Now will we have you dance and wheeze—Salute!"

De Goncourt's heart was not in the work. It was patent that he fought under the compulsion of command. His play was old-fashioned, as any middle-aged man's is apt to be, but he was not an indifferent swordsman. He was cool, determined, dogged. But he was not brilliant, and he was oppressed with foreknowledge of defeat. A score of times, by quick and brilliant, he was mine. But I refrained. I have said that I was devilish-minded. Indeed I was. I wore him down. I backed him away from the moon so that he could see little of me because I fought in my own shadow. And while I wore him down until he began to wheeze as I had predicted, Pasquini, head on hand and watching, coughed and spat out his life.

"Now, de Goncourt," I announced finally. "You see I have you quite helpless. You are mine in any of a dozen ways. Be ready, brace yourself, for this is the way I will."

And, so saying, I merely went from carte to tierce, and as he recovered wildly and parried widely I returned to carte, took the opening, and drove home heart-high and through and through. And at sight of the conclusion Pasquini let go his hold on life, buried his face in the grass, quivered a moment, and lay still.

"Your master will be four servants short this night," I assured de Villehardouin, in the moment just ere we engaged.

And such an engagement! The boy was ridiculous. In what bucolic school of fence he had been taught was beyond imagining. He was downright clownish. "Short work and simple" was my judgment, while his red hair seemed a-bristle with very rage and while he pressed me like a madman.

Alas! It was his clownishness that undid me. When I had played with him and laughed at him for a handful of seconds for the clumsy boor he was, he became so angered that he forgot the worse than little fence he knew. With an arm-wide sweep of his rapier, as though it bore heft and a cutting edge, he whistled it through the air and rapped it down on my crown. I was in amaze. Never had so absurd a thing happened to me. He was wide open, and I could have run him through forthright. But, as I said, I was in amaze, and the next I knew was the pang of the entering steel as this clumsy provincial ran me through and charged forward, bull-like, till his hilt bruised my side and I was borne backward.

As I fell I could see the concern on the faces of Lanfranc and Bohemond and the glut of satisfaction in the face of de Villehardouin as he pressed me.

I was falling, but I never reached the grass. Came a blur of flashing lights, a thunder in my ears, a darkness, a glimmering of dim light slowly dawning, a wrenching, racking pain beyond all describing, and then I heard the voice of one who said:

"I can't feel anything."

I knew the voice. It was Warden Atherton's. And I knew myself for Darrell Standing, just returned across the centuries to the jacket hell of San Quentin. And I knew the touch of finger-tips on my neck was Warden Atherton's. And I knew the finger-tips that displaced his were Doctor Jackson's. And it was Doctor Jackson's voice that said:

"You don't know how to take a man's pulse from the neck. There—right there—put your fingers where mine are. D'ye get it? Ah, I thought so. Heart weak, but steady as a chronometer."

"It's only twenty-four hours," Captain Jamie said, "and he was never in like condition before."

"Putting it on, that's what he's doing, and you can stack on that," Al Hutchins, the head trusty, interjected.

"I don't know," Captain Jamie insisted. "When a man's pulse is that low it takes an expert to find it—"

"Aw, I served my apprenticeship in the jacket," Al Hutchins sneered. "And I've made you unlace me, Captain, when you thought I was croaking, and it was all I could do to keep from snickering in your face."

"What do you think, Doc?" Warden Atherton asked.

"I tell you the heart action is splendid," was the answer. "Of course it is weak. That is only to be expected. I tell you Hutchins is right. The man is feigning."

With his thumb he turned up one of my eyelids, whereat I opened my other eye and gazed up at the group bending over me.

"What did I tell you?" was Doctor Jackson's cry of triumph.

And then, although it seemed the effort must crack my face, I summoned all the will of me and smiled.

They held water to my lips, and I drank greedily. It must be remembered that all this while I lay helpless on my back, my arms pinioned along with my body inside the jacket. When they offered me food—dry prison bread—I shook my head. I closed my eyes in advertisement that I was tired of their presence. The pain of my partial resuscitation was unbearable. I could feel my body coming to life. Down the cords of my neck and into my patch of chest over the heart darting pains were making their way. And in my brain the memory was strong that Philippa waited me in the big hall, and I was desirous to escape away back to the half a day and half a night I had just lived in old France.

So it was, even as they stood about me, that I strove to eliminate the live portion of my body from my consciousness. I was in haste to depart, but Warden Atherton's voice held me back.

"Is there anything you want to complain about?" he asked.

Now I had but one fear, namely, that they would unlace me; so that it must be understood that my reply was not uttered in braggadocio but was meant to forestall any possible unlacing.

"You might make the jacket a little tighter," I whispered. "It's too loose for comfort. I get lost in it. Hutchins is stupid. He is also a fool. He doesn't know the first thing about lacing the jacket. Warden, you ought to put him in charge of the loom-room. He is a more profound master of inefficiency than the present incumbent, who is merely stupid without being a fool as well. Now get out, all of you, unless you can think of worse to do to me. In which case, by all means remain. I invite you heartily to remain, if you think in your feeble imaginings that you have devised fresh torture for me."

"He's a wooz, a true-blue, dyed-in-the-wool wooz," Doctor Jackson chanted, with the medico's delight in a novelty.

"Standing, you *are* a wonder," the Warden said. "You've got an iron will, but I'll break it as sure as God made little apples."

"And you've the heart of a rabbit," I retorted. "One-tenth the jacketing I have received in San Quentin would have squeezed your rabbit heart out of your long ears."

Oh, it was a touch, that, for the Warden did have unusual ears. They would have interested Lombroso, I am sure.

"As for me," I went on, "I laugh at you, and I wish no worse fate to the loom-room than that you should take charge of it yourself. Why, you've got me down and worked your wickedness on me, and still I live and laugh in your face. Inefficient? You can't even kill me. Inefficient? You couldn't kill a cornered rat with a stick of dynamite—*real* dynamite, and not the sort you are deluded into believing I have hidden away."

"Anything more?" he demanded, when I had ceased from my diatribe.

And into my mind flashed what I had told Fortini when he pressed his insolence on me.

"Begone, you prison cur," I said. "Take your yapping from my door."

It must have been a terrible thing for a man of Warden Atherton's stripe to be thus bearded by a helpless prisoner. His face whitened with rage and his voice shook as he threatened:

"By God, Standing, I'll do for you yet."

"There is only one thing you can do," I said. "You can tighten this distressingly loose jacket. If you won't, then get out. And I don't care if you fail to come back for a week or for the whole ten days."

And what can even the Warden of a great prison do in reprisal on a prisoner upon whom the ultimate reprisal has already been wreaked? It may be that Warden Atherton thought of some possible threat, for he began to speak. But my voice had strengthened with the exercise, and I began to sing, "Sing cucu, sing cucu, sing cucu." And sing I did until my door clanged and the bolts and locks squeaked and grated fast.

CHAPTER XII

Now that I had learned the trick the way was easy. And I knew the way was bound to become easier the more I travelled it. Once establish a line of least resistance, every succeeding journey along it will find still less resistance. And so, as you shall see, my journeys from San Quentin life into other lives were achieved almost automatically as time went by.

After Warden Atherton and his crew had left me it was a matter of minutes to will the resuscitated portion of my body back into the little death. Death in life it was, but it was only the little death, similar to the temporary death produced by an anæsthetic.

And so, from all that was sordid and vile, from brutal solitary and jacket hell, from acquainted flies and sweats of darkness and the knuckle-talk of the living dead, I was away at a bound into time and space.

Came the duration of darkness, and the slow-growing awareness of other things and of another self. First of all, in this awareness, was dust. It was in my nostrils, dry and acrid. It was on my lips. It coated my face, my hands, and especially was it noticeable on the finger-tips when touched by the ball of my thumb.

Next I was aware of ceaseless movement. All that was about me lurched and oscillated. There was jolt and jar, and I heard what I knew as a matter of course to be the grind of wheels on axles and the grate and clash of iron tyres against rock and sand. And there came to me the jaded voices of men, in curse and snarl of slow-plodding, jaded animals.

I opened my eyes, that were inflamed with dust, and immediately fresh dust bit into them. On the coarse blankets on which I lay the dust was half an inch thick. Above me, through sifting dust, I saw an arched roof of lurching, swaying canvas, and myriads of dust motes descended heavily in the shafts of sunshine that entered through holes in the canvas.

I was a child, a boy of eight or nine, and I was weary, as was the woman, dusty-visaged and haggard, who sat up beside me and soothed a crying babe in her arms. She was my mother; that I knew as a matter of course, just as I knew, when I glanced along the canvas tunnel of the wagon-top, that the shoulders of the man on the driver's seat were the shoulders of my father.

When I started to crawl along the packed gear with which the wagon was laden my mother said in a tired and querulous voice, "Can't you ever be still a minute, Jesse?"

That was my name, Jesse. I did not know my surname, though I heard my mother call my father John. I have a dim recollection of hearing, at one time or another, the other men address my father as Captain. I knew that he was the leader of this company, and that his orders were obeyed by all.

I crawled out through the opening in the canvas and sat down beside my father on the seat. The air was stifling with the dust that rose from the wagons and the many hoofs of the animals. So thick was the dust that it was like mist or fog in the air, and the low sun shone through it dimly and with a bloody light.

Not alone was the light of this setting sun ominous, but everything about me seemed ominous—the landscape, my father's face, the fret of the babe in my mother's arms that she could not still, the six horses my father drove that had continually to be urged and that were without any sign of colour, so heavily had the dust settled on them.

The landscape was an aching, eye-hurting desolation. Low hills stretched endlessly away on every hand. Here and there only on their slopes were occasional scrub growths of heat-parched brush. For the most part the surface of the hills was naked-dry and composed of sand and rock. Our way followed the sand-bottoms between the hills. And the sand-bottoms were bare, save for spots of scrub, with here and there short tufts of dry and withered grass. Water there was none, nor sign of water, except for washed gullies that told of ancient and torrential rains.

My father was the only one who had horses to his wagon. The wagons went in single file, and as the train wound and curved I saw that the other wagons were drawn by oxen. Three or four yoke of oxen strained and pulled weakly at each wagon, and beside them, in the deep sand, walked men with ox-goads, who prodded the unwilling beasts along. On a curve I counted the wagons ahead and behind. I knew that there were forty of them, including our own; for often I had counted them before. And as I counted them now, as a child will to while away tedium, they were all there, forty of them, all canvas-topped, big and massive, crudely fashioned, pitching and lurching, grinding and jarring over sand and sage-brush and rock.

To right and left of us, scattered along the train, rode a dozen or fifteen men and youths on horses. Across their pommels were long-barrelled rifles. Whenever any of them drew near to our wagon I could see that their faces, under the dust, were drawn and anxious like my father's. And my father, like them, had a long-barrelled rifle close to hand as he drove.

Also, to one side, limped a score or more of foot-sore, yoke-galled, skeleton oxen, that ever paused to nip at the occasional tufts of withered grass, and that ever were prodded on by the tired-faced youths who herded them. Sometimes one or another of these oxen would pause and low, and such lowing seemed as ominous as all else about me.

Far, far away I have a memory of having lived, a smaller lad, by the tree-lined banks of a stream. And as the wagon jolts along, and I sway on the seat with my father, I continually return and dwell upon that pleasant water flowing between the trees. I have a sense that for an interminable period I have lived in a wagon and travelled on, ever on, with this present company.

But strongest of all upon me is what is strong upon all the company, namely, a sense of drifting to doom. Our way was like a funeral march. Never did a laugh arise. Never did I hear a happy tone of voice. Neither peace nor ease marched with us. The faces of the men and youths who outrode the train were grim, set, hopeless. And as we toiled through the lurid dust of sunset often I scanned my father's face in vain quest of some message of cheer. I will not say that my father's face, in all its dusty haggardness, was hopeless. It was dogged, and oh! so grim and anxious, most anxious.

A thrill seemed to run along the train. My father's head went up. So did mine. And our horses raised their weary heads, scented the air with long-drawn snorts, and for the nonce pulled willingly. The horses of the outriders quickened their pace. And as for the herd of scarecrow oxen, it broke into a forthright gallop. It was almost ludicrous. The poor brutes were so clumsy in their weakness and haste. They were galloping skeletons draped in mangy hide, and they out-distanced the boys who herded them. But this was only for a time. Then they fell back to a walk, a quick, eager, shambling, sore-footed walk; and they no longer were lured aside by the dry bunch-grass.

"What is it?" my mother asked from within the wagon.

"Water," was my father's reply. "It must be Nephi."

And my mother: "Thank God! And perhaps they will sell us food."

And into Nephi, through blood-red dust, with grind and grate and jolt and jar, our great wagons rolled. A dozen scattered dwellings or shanties composed the place. The landscape was much the same as that through which we had passed. There were no trees, only scrub growths and sandy bareness. But here were signs of tilled fields, with here and there a fence. Also there was water. Down the stream ran no current. The bed, however, was damp, with now and again a water-hole into which the loose oxen and the saddle-horses stamped and plunged their muzzles to the eyes. Here, too, grew an occasional small willow.

"That must be Bill Black's mill they told us about," my father said, pointing out a building to my mother, whose anxiousness had drawn her to peer out over our shoulders.

An old man, with buckskin shirt and long, matted, sunburnt hair, rode back to our wagon and talked with father. The signal was given, and the head wagons of the train began to deploy in a circle. The ground favoured the evolution, and, from long practice, it was accomplished without a hitch, so that when the forty wagons were finally halted they formed a circle. All was bustle and orderly confusion. Many women, all tired-faced and dusty like my mother, emerged from the wagons. Also poured forth a very horde of children. There must have been at least fifty children, and it seemed I knew them all of long time; and there were at least two score of women. These went about the preparations for cooking supper.

104

While some of the men chopped sage-brush and we children carried it to the fires that were kindling, other men unyoked the oxen and let them stampede for water. Next the men, in big squads, moved the wagons snugly into place. The tongue of each wagon was on the inside of the circle, and, front and rear, each wagon was in solid contact with the next wagon before and behind. The great brakes were locked fast; but, not content with this, the wheels of all the wagons were connected with chains. This was nothing new to us children. It was the trouble sign of a camp in hostile country. One wagon only was left out of the circle, so as to form a gate to the corral. Later on, as we knew, ere the camp slept, the animals would be driven inside, and the gate-wagon would be chained like the others in place. In the meanwhile, and for hours, the animals would be herded by men and boys to what scant grass they could find.

While the camp-making went on my father, with several others of the men, including the old man with the long, sunburnt hair, went away on foot in the direction of the mill. I remember that all of us, men, women, and even the children, paused to watch them depart; and it seemed their errand was of grave import.

While they were away other men, strangers, inhabitants of desert Nephi, came into camp and stalked about. They were white men, like us, but they were hard-faced, stern-faced, sombre, and they seemed angry with all our company. Bad feeling was in the air, and they said things calculated to rouse the tempers of our men. But the warning went out from the women, and was passed on everywhere to our men and youths, that there must be no words.

One of the strangers came to our fire, where my mother was alone, cooking. I had just come up with an armful of sage-brush, and I stopped to listen and to stare at the intruder, whom I hated, because it was in the air to hate, because I knew that every last person in our company hated these strangers who were white-skinned like us and because of whom we had been compelled to make our camp in a circle.

This stranger at our fire had blue eyes, hard and cold and piercing. His hair was sandy. His face was shaven to the chin, and from under the chin, covering the neck and extending to the ears, sprouted a sandy fringe of whiskers well-streaked with gray. Mother did not greet him, nor did he greet her. He stood and glowered at her for some time, he cleared his throat and said with a sneer:

"Wisht you was back in Missouri right now I bet."

I saw mother tighten her lips in self-control ere she answered:

"We are from Arkansas."

"I guess you got good reasons to deny where you come from," he next said, "you that drove the Lord's people from Missouri."

Mother made no reply.

". . . Seein'," he went on, after the pause accorded her, "as you're now comin' a-whinin' an' a-beggin' bread at our hands that you persecuted."

Whereupon, and instantly, child that I was, I knew anger, the old, red, intolerant wrath, ever unrestrainable and unsubduable.

"You lie!" I piped up. "We ain't Missourians. We ain't whinin'. An' we ain't beggars. We got the money to buy."

"Shut up, Jesse!" my mother cried, landing the back of her hand stingingly on my mouth. And then, to the stranger, "Go away and let the boy alone."

"I'll shoot you full of lead, you damned Mormon!" I screamed and sobbed at him, too quick for my mother this time, and dancing away around the fire from the back-sweep of her hand.

As for the man himself, my conduct had not disturbed him in the slightest. I was prepared for I knew not what violent visitation from this terrible stranger, and I watched him warily while he considered me with the utmost gravity.

At last he spoke, and he spoke solemnly, with solemn shaking of the head, as if delivering a judgment.

106

"Like fathers like sons," he said. "The young generation is as bad as the elder. The whole breed is unregenerate and damned. There is no saving it, the young or the old. There is no atonement. Not even the blood of Christ can wipe out its iniquities."

"Damned Mormon!" was all I could sob at him. "Damned Mormon! Damned Mormon! Damned Mormon!"

And I continued to damn him and to dance around the fire before my mother's avenging hand, until he strode away.

When my father, and the men who had accompanied him, returned, camp-work ceased, while all crowded anxiously about him. He shook his head.

"They will not sell?" some woman demanded.

Again he shook his head.

A man spoke up, a blue-eyed, blond-whiskered giant of thirty, who abruptly pressed his way into the centre of the crowd.

"They say they have flour and provisions for three years, Captain," he said. "They have always sold to the immigration before. And now they won't sell. And it ain't our quarrel. Their quarrel's with the government, an' they're takin' it out on us. It ain't right, Captain. It ain't right, I say, us with our women an' children, an' California months away, winter comin' on, an' nothin' but desert in between. We ain't got the grub to face the desert."

He broke off for a moment to address the whole crowd.

"Why, you-all don't know what desert is. This around here ain't desert. I tell you it's paradise, and heavenly pasture, an' flowin' with milk an' honey alongside what we're goin' to face."

"I tell you, Captain, we got to get flour first. If they won't sell it, then we must just up an' take it."

Many of the men and women began crying out in approval, but my father hushed them by holding up his hand.

107

"I agree with everything you say, Hamilton," he began.

But the cries now drowned his voice, and he again held up his hand.

"Except one thing you forgot to take into account, Hamilton—a thing that you and all of us must take into account. Brigham Young has declared martial law, and Brigham Young has an army. We could wipe out Nephi in the shake of a lamb's tail and take all the provisions we can carry. But we wouldn't carry them very far. Brigham's Saints would be down upon us and we would be wiped out in another shake of a lamb's tail. You know it. I know it. We all know it."

His words carried conviction to listeners already convinced. What he had told them was old news. They had merely forgotten it in a flurry of excitement and desperate need.

"Nobody will fight quicker for what is right than I will," father continued. "But it just happens we can't afford to fight now. If ever a ruction starts we haven't a chance. And we've all got our women and children to recollect. We've got to be peaceable at any price, and put up with whatever dirt is heaped on us."

"But what will we do with the desert coming?" cried a woman who nursed a babe at her breast.

"There's several settlements before we come to the desert," father answered. "Fillmore's sixty miles south. Then comes Corn Creek. And Beaver's another fifty miles. Next is Parowan. Then it's twenty miles to Cedar City. The farther we get away from Salt Lake the more likely they'll sell us provisions."

"And if they won't?" the same woman persisted.

"Then we're quit of them," said my father. "Cedar City is the last settlement. We'll have to go on, that's all, and thank our stars we are quit of them. Two days' journey beyond is good pasture, and water. They call it Mountain Meadows. Nobody lives there, and that's the place we'll rest our cattle and feed them up before we tackle the desert. Maybe we can shoot some meat. And if the worst comes to the worst, we'll keep going as long as we can, then abandon the wagons, pack what we can on our animals, and make the last stages on foot. We can eat our cattle as we go along. It would be better to arrive in California without a rag to our backs than to leave our bones here; and leave them we will if we start a ruction."

With final reiterated warnings against violence of speech or act, the impromptu meeting broke up. I was slow in falling asleep that night. My rage against the Mormon had left my brain in such a tingle that I was still awake when my father crawled into the wagon after a last round of the night-watch. They thought I slept, but I heard mother ask him if he thought that the Mormons would let us depart peacefully from their land. His face was turned aside from her as he busied himself with pulling off a boot, while he answered her with hearty confidence that he was sure the Mormons would let us go if none of our own company started trouble.

But I saw his face at that moment in the light of a small tallow dip, and in it was none of the confidence that was in his voice. So it was that I fell asleep, oppressed by the dire fate that seemed to overhang us, and pondering upon Brigham Young who bulked in my child imagination as a fearful, malignant being, a very devil with horns and tail and all.

* * * * *

And I awoke to the old pain of the jacket in solitary. About me were the customary four: Warden Atherton, Captain Jamie, Doctor Jackson, and Al Hutchins. I cracked my face with my willed smile, and struggled not to lose control under the exquisite torment of returning circulation. I drank the water they held to me, waved aside the proffered bread, and refused to speak. I closed my eyes and strove to win back to the chain-locked wagon-circle at Nephi. But so long as my visitors stood about me and talked I could not escape.

One snatch of conversation I could not tear myself away from hearing.

"Just as yesterday," Doctor Jackson said. "No change one way or the other."

"Then he can go on standing it?" Warden Atherton queried.

"Without a quiver. The next twenty-four hours as easy as the last. He's a wooz, I tell you, a perfect wooz. If I didn't know it was impossible, I'd say he was doped."

"I know his dope," said the Warden. "It's that cursed will of his. I'd bet, if he made up his mind, that he could walk barefoot across red-hot stones, like those Kanaka priests from the South Seas."

Now perhaps it was the word "priests" that I carried away with me through the darkness of another flight in time. Perhaps it was the cue. More probably it was a mere coincidence. At any rate I awoke, lying upon a rough rocky floor, and found myself on my back, my arms crossed in such fashion that each elbow rested in the palm of the opposite hand. As I lay there, eyes closed, half awake, I rubbed my elbows with my palms and found that I was rubbing prodigious calluses. There was no surprise in this. I accepted the calluses as of long time and a matter of course.

I opened my eyes. My shelter was a small cave, no more than three feet in height and a dozen in length. It was very hot in the cave. Perspiration noduled the entire surface of my body. Now and again several nodules coalesced and formed tiny rivulets. I wore no clothing save a filthy rag about the middle. My skin was burned to a mahogany brown. I was very thin, and I contemplated my thinness with a strange sort of pride, as if it were an achievement to be so thin. Especially was I enamoured of my painfully prominent ribs. The very sight of the hollows between them gave me a sense of solemn elation, or, rather, to use a better word, of sanctification.

My knees were callused like my elbows. I was very dirty. My beard, evidently once blond, but now a dirt-stained and streaky brown, swept my midriff in a tangled mass. My long hair, similarly stained and tangled, was all about my shoulders, while wisps of it continually strayed in the way of my vision so that sometimes I was compelled to brush it aside with my hands. For the most part, however, I contented myself with peering through it like a wild animal from a thicket.

Just at the tunnel-like mouth of my dim cave the day reared itself in a wall of blinding sunshine. After a time I crawled to the entrance, and, for the sake of greater discomfort, lay down in the burning sunshine on a narrow ledge of rock. It positively baked me, that terrible sun, and the more it hurt me the more I delighted in it, or in myself rather, in that I was thus the master of my flesh and superior to its claims and remonstrances. When I found under me a particularly sharp, but not too sharp, rock-projection, I ground my body upon the point of it, rowelled my flesh in a very ecstasy of mastery and of purification.

It was a stagnant day of heat. Not a breath of air moved over the river valley on which I sometimes gazed. Hundreds of feet beneath me the wide river ran sluggishly. The farther shore was flat and sandy and stretched away to the horizon. Above the water were scattered clumps of palm-trees.

On my side, eaten into a curve by the river, were lofty, crumbling cliffs. Farther along the curve, in plain view from my eyrie, carved out of the living rock, were four colossal figures. It was the stature of a man to their ankle joints. The four colossi sat, with hands resting on knees, with arms crumbled quite away, and gazed out upon the river. At least three of them so gazed. Of the fourth all that remained were the lower limbs to the knees and the huge hands resting on the knees. At the feet of this one, ridiculously small, crouched a sphinx; yet this sphinx was taller than I.

I looked upon these carven images with contempt, and spat as I looked. I knew not what they were, whether forgotten gods or unremembered kings. But to me they were representative of the vanity of earth-men and earth-aspirations.

And over all this curve of river and sweep of water and wide sands beyond arched a sky of aching brass unflecked by the tiniest cloud.

The hours passed while I roasted in the sun. Often, for quite decent intervals, I forgot my heat and pain in dreams and visions and in memories. All this I knew—crumbling colossi and river and sand and sun and brazen sky—was to pass away in the twinkling of an eye. At any moment the trumps of the archangels might sound, the stars fall out of the sky, the heavens roll up as a scroll, and the Lord God of all come with his hosts for the final judgment.

Ah, I knew it so profoundly that I was ready for such sublime event. That was why I was here in rags and filth and wretchedness. I was meek and lowly, and I despised the frail needs and passions of the flesh. And I thought with contempt, and with a certain satisfaction, of the far cities of the plain I had known, all unheeding, in their pomp and lust, of the last day so near at hand. Well, they would see soon enough, but too late for them. And I should see. But I was ready. And to their cries and lamentations would I arise, reborn and glorious, and take my well-earned and rightful place in the City of God.

At times, between dreams and visions in which I was verily and before my time in the City of God, I conned over in my mind old discussions and controversies. Yes, Novatus was right in his contention that penitent apostates should never again be received into the churches. Also, there was no doubt that Sabellianism was conceived of the devil. So was Constantine, the arch-fiend, the devil's right hand.

Continually I returned to contemplation of the nature of the unity of God, and went over and over the contentions of Noetus, the Syrian. Better, however, did I like the contentions of my beloved teacher, Arius. Truly, if human reason could determine anything at all, there must have been a time, in the very nature of sonship, when the Son did not exist. In the nature of sonship there must have been a time when the Son commenced to exist. A father must be older than his son. To hold otherwise were a blasphemy and a belittlement of God.

And I remembered back to my young days when I had sat at the feet of Arius, who had been a presbyter of the city of Alexandria, and who had been robbed of the *bishop*ric by the blasphemous and heretical Alexander. Alexander the Sabellianite, that is what he was, and his feet had fast hold of hell.

Yes, I had been to the Council of Nicea, and seen it avoid the issue. And I remembered when the Emperor Constantine had banished Arius for his uprightness. And I remembered when Constantine repented for reasons of state and policy and commanded Alexander—the other Alexander, thrice cursed, *Bishop* of Constantinople—to receive Arius into communion on the morrow. And that very night did not Arius die in the street? They said it was a violent sickness visited upon him in answer to Alexander's prayer to God. But I said, and so said all we Arians, that the violent sickness was due to a poison, and that the poison was due to Alexander himself, *Bishop* of Constantinople and devil's poisoner.

And here I ground my body back and forth on the sharp stones, and muttered aloud, drunk with conviction:

"Let the Jews and Pagans mock. Let them triumph, for their time is short. And for them there will be no time after time."

I talked to myself aloud a great deal on that rocky shelf overlooking the river. I was feverish, and on occasion I drank sparingly of water from a stinking goatskin. This goatskin I kept hanging in the sun that the stench of the skin might increase and that there might be no refreshment of coolness in the water. Food there was, lying in the dirt on my cave-floor—a few roots and a chunk of mouldy barley-cake; and hungry I was, although I did not eat.

All I did that blessed, livelong day was to sweat and swelter in the sun, mortify my lean flesh upon the rock, gaze out of the desolation, resurrect old memories, dream dreams, and mutter my convictions aloud.

And when the sun set, in the swift twilight I took a last look at the world so soon to pass. About the feet of the colossi I could make out the creeping forms of beasts that laired in the once proud works of men. And to the snarls of the beasts I crawled into my hole, and, muttering and dozing, visioning fevered fancies and praying that the last day come quickly, I ebbed down into the darkness of sleep.

* * * * *

Consciousness came back to me in solitary, with the quartet of torturers about me.

"Blasphemous and heretical Warden of San Quentin whose feet have fast hold of hell," I gibed, after I had drunk deep of the water they held to my lips. "Let the jailers and the trusties triumph. Their time is short, and for them there is no time after time."

"He's out of his head," Warden Atherton affirmed.

"He's putting it over on you," was Doctor Jackson's surer judgment.

"But he refuses food," Captain Jamie protested.

"Huh, he could fast forty days and not hurt himself," the doctor answered.

"And I have," I said, "and forty nights as well. Do me the favour to tighten the jacket and then get out of here."

The head trusty tried to insert his forefinger inside the lacing.

"You couldn't get a quarter of an inch of slack with block and tackle," he assured them.

"Have you any complaint to make, Standing?" the Warden asked.

"Yes," was my reply. "On two counts."

"What are they?"

"First," I said, "the jacket is abominably loose. Hutchins is an ass. He could get a foot of slack if he wanted."

"What is the other count?" Warden Atherton asked.

"That you are conceived of the devil, Warden."

Captain Jamie and Doctor Jackson tittered, and the Warden, with a snort, led the way out of my cell.

* * * * *

Left alone, I strove to go into the dark and gain back to the wagon circle at Nephi. I was interested to know the outcome of that doomed drifting of our forty great wagons across a desolate and hostile land, and I was not at all interested in what came of the mangy hermit with his rock-roweled ribs and stinking water-skin. And I gained back, neither to Nephi nor the Nile, but to—

114

But here I must pause in the narrative, my reader, in order to explain a few things and make the whole matter easier to your comprehension. This is necessary, because my time is short in which to complete my jacket-memoirs. In a little while, in a very little while, they are going to take me out and hang me. Did I have the full time of a thousand lifetimes, I could not complete the last details of my jacket experiences. Wherefore I must briefen the narrative.

First of all, Bergson is right. Life cannot be explained in intellectual terms. As Confucius said long ago: "When we are so ignorant of life, can we know death?" And ignorant of life we truly are when we cannot explain it in terms of the understanding. We know life only phenomenally, as a savage may know a dynamo; but we know nothing of life noumenonally, nothing of the nature of the intrinsic stuff of life.

Secondly, Marinetti is wrong when he claims that matter is the only mystery and the only reality. I say and as you, my reader, realize, I speak with authority—I say that matter is the only illusion. Comte called the world, which is tantamount to matter, the great fetich, and I agree with Comte.

It is life that is the reality and the mystery. Life is vastly different from mere chemic matter fluxing in high modes of notion. Life persists. Life is the thread of fire that persists through all the modes of matter. I know. I am life. I have lived ten thousand generations. I have lived millions of years. I have possessed many bodies. I, the possessor of these many bodies, have persisted. I am life. I am the unquenched spark ever flashing and astonishing the face of time, ever working my will and wreaking my passion on the cloddy aggregates of matter, called bodies, which I have transiently inhabited.

For look you. This finger of mine, so quick with sensation, so subtle to feel, so delicate in its multifarious dexterities, so firm and strong to crook and bend or stiffen by means of cunning leverages—this finger is not I. Cut it off. I live. The body is mutilated. I am not mutilated. The spirit that is I is whole.

Very well. Cut off all my fingers. I am I. The spirit is entire. Cut off both hands. Cut off both arms at the shoulder-sockets. Cut off both legs at the hip-sockets. And I, the unconquerable and indestructible I, survive.

Am I any the less for these mutilations, for these subtractions of the flesh? Certainly not. Clip my hair. Shave from me with sharp razors my lips, my nose, my ears—ay, and tear out the eyes of me by the roots; and there, mewed in that featureless skull that is attached to a hacked and mangled torso, there in that cell of the chemic flesh, will still be I, unmutilated, undiminished.

Oh, the heart still beats. Very well. Cut out the heart, or, better, fling the flesh-remnant into a machine of a thousand blades and make mincemeat of it—and I, *I*, don't you understand, all the spirit and the mystery and the vital fire and life of me, am off and away. I have not perished. Only the body has perished, and the body is not I.

I believe Colonel de Rochas was correct when he asserted that under the compulsion of his will he sent the girl Josephine, while she was in hypnotic trance, back through the eighteen years she had lived, back through the silence and the dark ere she had been born, back to the light of a previous living when she was a bedridden old man, the ex-artilleryman, Jean-Claude Bourdon. And I believe that Colonel de Rochas did truly hypnotize this resurrected shade of the old man and, by compulsion of will, send him back through the seventy years of his life, back into the dark and through the dark into the light of day when he had been the wicked old woman, Philomène Carteron.

Already, have I not shown you, my reader, that in previous times, inhabiting various cloddy aggregates of matter, I have been Count Guillaume de Sainte-Maure, a mangy and nameless hermit of Egypt, and the boy Jesse, whose father was captain of forty wagons in the great westward emigration. And, also, am I not now, as I write these lines, Darrell Sanding, under sentence of death in Folsom Prison and one time professor of agronomy in the College of Agriculture of the University of California?

Matter is the great illusion. That is, matter manifests itself in form, and form is apparitional. Where, now, are the crumbling rock-cliffs of old Egypt where once I laired me like a wild beast while I dreamed of the City of God? Where, now, is the body of Guillaume de Sainte-Maure that was thrust through on the moonlit grass so long ago by the flame-headed Guy de

Villehardouin? Where, now, are the forty great wagons in the circle at Nephi, and all the men and women and children and lean cattle that sheltered inside that circle? All such things no longer are, for they were forms, manifestations of fluxing matter ere they melted into the flux again. They have passed and are not.

And now my argument becomes plain. The spirit is the reality that endures. I am spirit, and I endure. I, Darrell Standing, the tenant of many fleshly tenements, shall write a few more lines of these memoirs and then pass on my way. The form of me that is my body will fall apart when it has been sufficiently hanged by the neck, and of it naught will remain in all the world of matter. In the world of spirit the memory of it will remain. Matter has no memory, because its forms are evanescent, and what is engraved on its forms perishes with the forms.

One word more ere I return to my narrative. In all my journeys through the dark into other lives that have been mine I have never been able to guide any journey to a particular destination. Thus many new experiences of old lives were mine before ever I chanced to return to the boy Jesse at Nephi. Possibly, all told, I have lived over Jesse's experiences a score of times, sometimes taking up his career when he was quite small in the Arkansas settlements, and at least a dozen times carrying on past the point where I left him at Nephi. It were a waste of time to detail the whole of it; and so, without prejudice to the verity of my account, I shall skip much that is vague and tortuous and repetitional, and give the facts as I have assembled them out of the various times, in whole and part, as I relived them.

CHAPTER XIII

Long before daylight the camp at Nephi was astir. The cattle were driven out to water and pasture. While the men unchained the wheels and drew the wagons apart and clear for yoking in, the women cooked forty breakfasts over forty fires. The children, in the chill of dawn, clustered about the fires, sharing places, here and there, with the last relief of the night-watch waiting sleepily for coffee.

It requires time to get a large train such as ours under way, for its speed is the speed of the slowest. So the sun was an hour high and the day was already uncomfortably hot when we rolled out of Nephi and on into the sandy barrens. No inhabitant of the place saw us off. All chose to remain indoors, thus making our departure as ominous as they had made our arrival the night before.

Again it was long hours of parching heat and biting dust, sage-brush and sand, and a land accursed. No dwellings of men, neither cattle nor fences, nor any sign of human kind, did we encounter all that day; and at night we made our wagon-circle beside an empty stream, in the damp sand of which we dug many holes that filled slowly with water seepage.

Our subsequent journey is always a broken experience to me. We made camp so many times, always with the wagons drawn in circle, that to my child mind a weary long time passed after Nephi. But always, strong upon all of us, was that sense of drifting to an impending and certain doom.

We averaged about fifteen miles a day. I know, for my father had said it was sixty miles to Fillmore, the next Mormon settlement, and we made three camps on the way. This meant four days of travel. From Nephi to the last camp of which I have any memory we must have taken two weeks or a little less.

At Fillmore the inhabitants were hostile, as all had been since Salt Lake. They laughed at us when we tried to buy food, and were not above taunting us with being Missourians.

When we entered the place, hitched before the largest house of the dozen houses that composed the settlement were two saddle-horses, dusty, streaked with sweat, and drooping. The old man I have mentioned, the one with long, sunburnt hair and buckskin shirt and who seemed a sort of aide or lieutenant to father, rode close to our wagon and indicated the jaded saddle-animals with a cock of his head.

"Not sparin' horseflesh, Captain," he muttered in a low voice. "An' what in the name of Sam Hill are they hard-riding for if it ain't for us?"

But my father had already noted the condition of the two animals, and my eager eyes had seen him. And I had seen his eyes flash, his lips tighten, and haggard lines form for a moment on his dusty face. That was all. But I put two and two together, and knew that the two tired saddle-horses were just one more added touch of ominousness to the situation.

"I guess they're keeping an eye on us, Laban," was my father's sole comment.

It was at Fillmore that I saw a man that I was to see again. He was a tall, broad-shouldered man, well on in middle age, with all the evidence of good health and immense strength—strength not alone of body but of will. Unlike most men I was accustomed to about me, he was smooth-shaven. Several days' growth of beard showed that he was already well-grayed. His mouth was unusually wide, with thin lips tightly compressed as if he had lost many of his front teeth. His nose was large, square, and thick. So was his face square, wide between the cheekbones, underhung with massive jaws, and topped with a broad, intelligent forehead. And the eyes, rather small, a little more than the width of an eye apart, were the bluest blue I had ever seen.

It was at the flour-mill at Fillmore that I first saw this man. Father, with several of our company, had gone there to try to buy flour, and I, disobeying my mother in my curiosity to see more of our enemies, had tagged along unperceived. This man was one of four or five who stood in a group with the miller during the interview.

"You seen that smooth-faced old cuss?" Laban said to father, after we had got outside and were returning to camp.

Father nodded.

"Well, that's Lee," Laban continued. "I seen'm in Salt Lake. He's a regular son-of-a-gun. Got nineteen wives and fifty children, they all say. An' he's rank crazy on religion. Now, what's he followin' us up for through this God-forsaken country?"

Our weary, doomed drifting went on. The little settlements, wherever water and soil permitted, were from twenty to fifty miles apart. Between stretched the barrenness of sand and alkali and drought. And at every settlement our peaceful attempts to buy food were vain. They denied us harshly, and wanted to know who of us had sold them food when we drove them from Missouri. It was useless on our part to tell them we were from Arkansas. From Arkansas we truly were, but they insisted on our being Missourians.

At Beaver, five days' journey south from Fillmore, we saw Lee again. And again we saw hard-ridden horses tethered before the houses. But we did not see Lee at Parowan.

Cedar City was the last settlement. Laban, who had ridden on ahead, came back and reported to father. His first news was significant.

"I seen that Lee skedaddling out as I rid in, Captain. An' there's more men-folk an' horses in Cedar City than the size of the place 'd warrant."

But we had no trouble at the settlement. Beyond refusing to sell us food, they left us to ourselves. The women and children stayed in the houses, and though some of the men appeared in sight they did not, as on former occasions, enter our camp and taunt us.

It was at Cedar City that the Wainwright baby died. I remember Mrs. Wainwright weeping and pleading with Laban to try to get some cow's milk.

"It may save the baby's life," she said. "And they've got cow's milk. I saw fresh cows with my own eyes. Go on, please, Laban. It won't hurt you to try. They can only refuse. But they won't. Tell them it's for a baby, a wee little baby. Mormon women have mother's hearts. They couldn't refuse a cup of milk for a wee little baby."

And Laban tried. But, as he told father afterward, he did not get to see any Mormon women. He saw only the Mormon men, who turned him away.

This was the last Mormon outpost. Beyond lay the vast desert, with, on the other side of it, the dream land, ay, the myth land, of California. As our wagons rolled out of the place in the early morning I, sitting beside my father on the driver's seat, saw Laban give expression to his feelings. We had gone perhaps half a mile, and were topping a low rise that would sink Cedar City from view, when Laban turned his horse around, halted it, and stood up in the stirrups. Where he had halted was a new-made grave, and I knew it for the Wainwright baby's—not the first of our graves since we had crossed the Wasatch mountains.

He was a weird figure of a man. Aged and lean, long-faced, hollow-checked, with matted, sunburnt hair that fell below the shoulders of his buckskin shirt, his face was distorted with hatred and helpless rage. Holding his long rifle in his bridle-hand, he shook his free fist at Cedar City.

"God's curse on all of you!" he cried out. "On your children, and on your babes unborn. May drought destroy your crops. May you eat sand seasoned with the venom of rattlesnakes. May the sweet water of your springs turn to bitter alkali. May . . ."

Here his words became indistinct as our wagons rattled on; but his heaving shoulders and brandishing fist attested that he had only begun to lay the curse. That he expressed the general feeling in our train was evidenced by the many women who leaned from the wagons, thrusting out gaunt forearms and shaking bony, labour-malformed fists at the last of Mormondom. A man, who walked in the sand and goaded the oxen of the wagon behind ours, laughed and waved his goad. It was unusual, that laugh, for there had been no laughter in our train for many days.

"Give 'm hell, Laban," he encouraged. "Them's my sentiments."

And as our train rolled on I continued to look back at Laban, standing in his stirrups by the baby's grave. Truly he was a weird figure, with his long hair, his moccasins, and fringed leggings. So old and weather-beaten was his buckskin shirt that ragged filaments, here and there, showed where proud fringes once had been. He was a man of flying tatters. I remember, at his waist, dangled dirty tufts of hair that, far back in the journey, after a shower of rain, were wont to show glossy black. These I knew were Indian scalps, and the sight of them always thrilled me.

"It will do him good," father commended, more to himself than to me. "I've been looking for days for him to blow up."

"I wish he'd go back and take a couple of scalps," I volunteered.

My father regarded me quizzically.

"Don't like the Mormons, eh, son?"

I shook my head and felt myself swelling with the inarticulate hate that possessed me.

"When I grow up," I said, after a minute, "I'm goin' gunning for them."

"You, Jesse!" came my mother's voice from inside the wagon. "Shut your mouth instanter." And to my father: "You ought to be ashamed letting the boy talk on like that."

Two days' journey brought us to Mountain Meadows, and here, well beyond the last settlement, for the first time we did not form the wagon-circle. The wagons were roughly in a circle, but there were many gaps, and the wheels were not chained. Preparations were made to stop a week. The cattle must be rested for the real desert, though this was desert enough in all seeming. The same low hills of sand were about us, but sparsely covered with scrub brush. The flat was sandy, but there was some grass—more than we had encountered in many days. Not more than a hundred feet from camp was a weak spring that barely supplied human needs. But farther along the bottom various other weak springs emerged from the hillsides, and it was at these that the cattle watered.

We made camp early that day, and, because of the programme to stay a week, there was a general overhauling of soiled clothes by the women, who planned to start washing on the morrow. Everybody worked till nightfall.

While some of the men mended harness others repaired the frames and ironwork of the wagons. Them was much heating and hammering of iron and tightening of bolts and nuts. And I remember coming upon Laban, sitting cross-legged in the shade of a wagon and sewing away till nightfall on a new pair of moccasins. He was the only man in our train who wore moccasins and buckskin, and I have an impression that he had not belonged to our company when it left Arkansas. Also, he had neither wife, nor family, nor wagon of his own. All he possessed was his horse, his rifle, the clothes he stood up in, and a couple of blankets that were hauled in the Mason wagon.

Next morning it was that our doom fell. Two days' journey beyond the last Mormon outpost, knowing that no Indians were about and apprehending nothing from the Indians on any count, for the first time we had not chained our wagons in the solid circle, placed guards on the cattle, nor set a night-watch.

My awakening was like a nightmare. It came as a sudden blast of sound. I was only stupidly awake for the first moments and did nothing except to try to analyze and identify the various noises that went to compose the blast that continued without let up. I could hear near and distant explosions of rifles, shouts and curses of men, women screaming, and children bawling. Then I could make out the thuds and squeals of bullets that hit wood and iron in the wheels and under-construction of the wagon. Whoever it was that was shooting, the aim was too low. When I started to rise, my mother, evidently just in the act of dressing, pressed me down with her hand. Father, already up and about, at this stage erupted into the wagon.

"Out of it!" he shouted. "Quick! To the ground!"

He wasted no time. With a hook-like clutch that was almost a blow, so swift was it, he flung me bodily out of the rear end of the wagon. I had barely time to crawl out from under when father, mother, and the baby came down pell-mell where I had been.

"Here, Jesse!" father shouted to me, and I joined him in scooping out sand behind the shelter of a wagon-wheel. We worked bare-handed and wildly. Mother joined in.

"Go ahead and make it deeper, Jesse," father ordered,

He stood up and rushed away in the gray light, shouting commands as he ran. (I had learned by now my surname. I was Jesse Fancher. My father was Captain Fancher).

"Lie down!" I could hear him. "Get behind the wagon wheels and burrow in the sand! Family men, get the women and children out of the wagons! Hold your fire! No more shooting! Hold your fire and be ready for the rush when it comes! Single men, join Laban at the right, Cochrane at the left, and me in the centre! Don't stand up! Crawl for it!"

But no rush came. For a quarter of an hour the heavy and irregular firing continued. Our damage had come in the first moments of surprise when a number of the early-rising men were caught exposed in the light of the campfires they were building. The Indians—for Indians Laban declared them to be—had attacked us from the open, and were lying down and firing at us. In the growing light father made ready for them. His position was near to where I lay in the burrow with mother so that I heard him when he cried out:

"Now! all together!"

From left, right, and centre our rifles loosed in a volley. I had popped my head up to see, and I could make out more than one stricken Indian. Their fire immediately ceased, and I could see them scampering back on foot across the open, dragging their dead and wounded with them.

All was work with us on the instant. While the wagons were being dragged and chained into the circle with tongues inside—I saw women and little boys and girls flinging their strength on the wheel spokes to help—we took toll of our losses. First, and gravest of all, our last animal had been run off. Next, lying about the fires they had been building, were seven of our men. Four were dead, and three were dying. Other men, wounded, were being cared for by the women. Little Rish Hardacre had been struck in the arm by a heavy ball. He was no more than six, and I remember looking on with mouth agape while his mother held him on her lap and his father set about bandaging the wound. Little Rish had stopped crying. I could see the tears on his cheeks while he stared wonderingly at a sliver of broken bone sticking out of his forearm.

Granny White was found dead in the Foxwell wagon. She was a fat and helpless old woman who never did anything but sit down all the time and smoke a pipe. She was the mother of Abby Foxwell. And Mrs. Grant had been killed. Her husband sat beside her body. He was very quiet. There were no tears in his eyes. He just sat there, his rifle across his knees, and everybody left him alone.

Under father's directions the company was working like so many beavers. The men dug a big rifle pit in the centre of the corral, forming a breastwork out of the displaced sand. Into this pit the women dragged bedding, food, and all sorts of necessaries from the wagons. All the children helped. There was no whimpering, and little or no excitement. There was work to be done, and all of us were folks born to work.

The big rifle pit was for the women and children. Under the wagons, completely around the circle, a shallow trench was dug and an earthwork thrown up. This was for the fighting men.

Laban returned from a scout. He reported that the Indians had withdrawn the matter of half a mile, and were holding a powwow. Also he had seen them carry six of their number off the field, three of which, he said, were deaders.

From time to time, during the morning of that first day, we observed clouds of dust that advertised the movements of considerable bodies of mounted men. These clouds of dust came toward us, hemming us in on all sides. But we saw no living creature. One cloud of dirt only moved away from us. It was a large cloud, and everybody said it was our cattle being driven off. And our forty great wagons that had rolled over the Rockies and half across the continent stood in a helpless circle. Without cattle they could roll no farther.

125

At noon Laban came in from another scout. He had seen fresh Indians arriving from the south, showing that we were being closed in. It was at this time that we saw a dozen white men ride out on the crest of a low hill to the east and look down on us.

"That settles it," Laban said to father. "The Indians have been put up to it."

"They're white like us," I heard Abby Foxwell complain to mother. "Why don't they come in to us?"

"They ain't whites," I piped up, with a wary eye for the swoop of mother's hand. "They're Mormons."

That night, after dark, three of our young men stole out of camp. I saw them go. They were Will Aden, Abel Milliken, and Timothy Grant.

"They are heading for Cedar City to get help," father told mother while he was snatching a hasty bite of supper.

Mother shook her head.

"There's plenty of Mormons within calling distance of camp," she said. "If they won't help, and they haven't shown any signs, then the Cedar City ones won't either."

"But there are good Mormons and bad Mormons—" father began.

"We haven't found any good ones so far," she shut him off.

Not until morning did I hear of the return of Abel Milliken and Timothy Grant, but I was not long in learning. The whole camp was downcast by reason of their report. The three had gone only a few miles when they were challenged by white men. As soon as Will Aden spoke up, telling that they were from the Fancher Company, going to Cedar City for help, he was shot down. Milliken and Grant escaped back with the news, and the news settled the last hope in the hearts of our company. The whites were behind the Indians, and the doom so long apprehended was upon us.

This morning of the second day our men, going for water, were fired upon. The spring was only a hundred feet outside our circle, but the way to it was commanded by the Indians who now occupied the low hill to the east. It was close range, for the hill could not have been more than fifteen rods away. But the Indians were not good shots, evidently, for our men brought in the water without being hit.

Beyond an occasional shot into camp the morning passed quietly. We had settled down in the rifle pit, and, being used to rough living, were comfortable enough. Of course it was bad for the families of those who had been killed, and there was the taking care of the wounded. I was for ever stealing away from mother in my insatiable curiosity to see everything that was going on, and I managed to see pretty much of everything. Inside the corral, to the south of the big rifle pit, the men dug a hole and buried the seven men and two women all together. Only Mrs. Hastings, who had lost her husband and father, made much trouble. She cried and screamed out, and it took the other women a long time to quiet her.

On the low hill to the east the Indians kept up a tremendous powwowing and yelling. But beyond an occasional harmless shot they did nothing.

"What's the matter with the ornery cusses?" Laban impatiently wanted to know. "Can't they make up their minds what they're goin' to do, an' then do it?"

It was hot in the corral that afternoon. The sun blazed down out of a cloudless sky, and there was no wind. The men, lying with their rifles in the trench under the wagons, were partly shaded; but the big rifle pit, in which were over a hundred women and children, was exposed to the full power of the sun. Here, too, were the wounded men, over whom we erected awnings of blankets. It was crowded and stifling in the pit, and I was for ever stealing out of it to the firing-line, and making a great to-do at carrying messages for father.

Our grave mistake had been in not forming the wagon-circle so as to inclose the spring. This had been due to the excitement of the first attack, when we did not know how quickly it might be followed by a second one. And now it was too late. At fifteen rods' distance from the Indian position on the hill we did not dare unchain our wagons. Inside the corral, south of the graves, we constructed a latrine, and, north of the rifle pit in the centre, a couple of men were told off by father to dig a well for water.

In the mid-afternoon of that day, which was the second day, we saw Lee again. He was on foot, crossing diagonally over the meadow to the north-west just out of rifle-shot from us. Father hoisted one of mother's sheets on a couple of ox-goads lashed together. This was our white flag. But Lee took no notice of it, continuing on his way.

Laban was for trying a long shot at him, but father stopped him, saying that it was evident the whites had not made up their minds what they were going to do with us, and that a shot at Lee might hurry them into making up their minds the wrong way.

"Here, Jesse," father said to me, tearing a strip from the sheet and fastening it to an ox-goad. "Take this and go out and try to talk to that man. Don't tell him anything about what's happened to us. Just try to get him to come in and talk with us."

As I started to obey, my chest swelling with pride in my mission, Jed Dunham cried out that he wanted to go with me. Jed was about my own age.

"Dunham, can your boy go along with Jesse?" father asked Jed's father. "Two's better than one. They'll keep each other out of mischief."

So Jed and I, two youngsters of nine, went out under the white flag to talk with the leader of our enemies. But Lee would not talk. When he saw us coming he started to sneak away. We never got within calling distance of him, and after a while he must have hidden in the brush; for we never laid eyes on him again, and we knew he couldn't have got clear away.

Jed and I beat up the brush for hundreds of yards all around. They hadn't told us how long we were to be gone, and since the Indians did not fire on us we kept on going. We were away over two hours, though had either of us been alone he would have been back in a quarter of the time. But Jed was bound to outbrave me, and I was equally bound to outbrave him.

Our foolishness was not without profit. We walked, boldly about under our white flag, and learned how thoroughly our camp was beleaguered. To

128

the south of our train, not more than half a mile away, we made out a large Indian camp. Beyond, on the meadow, we could see Indian boys riding hard on their horses.

Then there was the Indian position on the hill to the east. We managed to climb a low hill so as to look into this position. Jed and I spent half an hour trying to count them, and concluded, with much guessing, that there must be at least a couple of hundred. Also, we saw white men with them and doing a great deal of talking.

North-east of our train, not more than four hundred yards from it, we discovered a large camp of whites behind a low rise of ground. And beyond we could see fifty or sixty saddle-horses grazing. And a mile or so away, to the north, we saw a tiny cloud of dust approaching. Jed and I waited until we saw a single man, riding fast, gallop into the camp of the whites.

When we got back into the corral the first thing that happened to me was a smack from mother for having stayed away so long; but father praised Jed and me when we gave our report.

"Watch for an attack now maybe, Captain," Aaron Cochrane said to father. "That man the boys seen has rid in for a purpose. The whites are holding the Indians till they get orders from higher up. Maybe that man brung the orders one way or the other. They ain't sparing horseflesh, that's one thing sure."

Half an hour after our return Laban attempted a scout under a white flag. But he had not gone twenty feet outside the circle when the Indians opened fire on him and sent him back on the run.

Just before sundown I was in the rifle pit holding the baby, while mother was spreading the blankets for a bed. There were so many of us that we were packed and jammed. So little room was there that many of the women the night before had sat up and slept with their heads bowed on their knees. Right alongside of me, so near that when he tossed his arms about he struck me on the shoulder, Silas Dunlap was dying. He had been shot in the head in the first attack, and all the second day was out of his head and raving and singing doggerel. One of his songs, that he sang over and over, until it made mother frantic nervous, was:

"Said the first little devil to the second little devil,

'Give me some tobaccy from your old tobaccy box.'

Said the second little devil to the first little devil,

'Stick close to your money and close to your rocks,

An' you'll always have tobaccy in your old tobaccy box.'"

I was sitting directly alongside of him, holding the baby, when the attack burst on us. It was sundown, and I was staring with all my eyes at Silas Dunlap who was just in the final act of dying. His wife, Sarah, had one hand resting on his forehead. Both she and her Aunt Martha were crying softly. And then it came—explosions and bullets from hundreds of rifles. Clear around from east to west, by way of the north, they had strung out in half a circle and were pumping lead in our position. Everybody in the rifle pit flattened down. Lots of the younger children set up a-squalling, and it kept the women busy hushing them. Some of the women screamed at first, but not many.

Thousands of shots must haven rained in on us in the next few minutes. How I wanted to crawl out to the trench under the wagons where our men were keeping up a steady but irregular fire! Each was shooting on his own whenever he saw a man to pull trigger on. But mother suspected me, for she made me crouch down and keep right on holding the baby.

I was just taking a look at Silas Dunlap—he was still quivering—when the little Castleton baby was killed. Dorothy Castleton, herself only about ten, was holding it, so that it was killed in her arms. She was not hurt at all. I heard them talking about it, and they conjectured that the bullet must have struck high on one of the wagons and been deflected down into the rifle pit. It was just an accident, they said, and that except for such accidents we were safe where we were.

When I looked again Silas Dunlap was dead, and I suffered distinct disappointment in being cheated out of witnessing that particular event. I had never been lucky enough to see a man actually die before my eyes.

Dorothy Castleton got hysterics over what had happened, and yelled and screamed for a long time and she set Mrs. Hastings going again. Altogether such a row was raised that father sent Watt Cummings crawling back to us to find out what was the matter.

Well along into twilight the heavy firing ceased, although there were scattering shots during the night. Two of our men were wounded in this second attack, and were brought into the rifle pit. Bill Tyler was killed instantly, and they buried him, Silas Dunlap, and the Castleton baby, in the dark alongside of the others.

All during the night men relieved one another at sinking the well deeper; but the only sign of water they got was damp sand. Some of the men fetched a few pails of water from the spring, but were fired upon, and they gave it up when Jeremy Hopkins had his left hand shot off at the wrist.

Next morning, the third day, it was hotter and dryer than ever. We awoke thirsty, and there was no cooking. So dry were our mouths that we could not eat. I tried a piece of stale bread mother gave me, but had to give it up. The firing rose and fell. Sometimes there were hundreds shooting into the camp. At other times came lulls in which not a shot was fired. Father was continually cautioning our men not to waste shots because we were running short of ammunition.

And all the time the men went on digging the well. It was so deep that they were hoisting the sand up in buckets. The men who hoisted were exposed, and one of them was wounded in the shoulder. He was Peter Bromley, who drove oxen for the Bloodgood wagon, and he was engaged to marry Jane Bloodgood. She jumped out of the rifle pit and ran right to him while the bullets were flying and led him back into shelter. About midday the well caved in, and there was lively work digging out the couple who were buried in the sand. Amos Wentworth did not come to for an hour. After that they timbered the well with bottom boards from the wagons and wagon

131

tongues, and the digging went on. But all they could get, and they were twenty feet down, was damp sand. The water would not seep.

By this time the conditions in the rifle pit were terrible. The children were complaining for water, and the babies, hoarse from much crying, went on crying. Robert Carr, another wounded man, lay about ten feet from mother and me. He was out of his head, and kept thrashing his arms about and calling for water. And some of the women were almost as bad, and kept raving against the Mormons and Indians. Some of the women prayed a great deal, and the three grown Demdike sisters, with their mother, sang gospel hymns. Other women got damp sand that was hoisted out of the bottom of the well, and packed it against the bare bodies of the babies to try to cool and soothe them.

The two Fairfax brothers couldn't stand it any longer, and, with pails in their hands, crawled out under a wagon and made a dash for the spring. Giles never got half way, when he went down. Roger made it there and back without being hit. He brought two pails part-full, for some splashed out when he ran. Giles crawled back, and when they helped him into the rifle pit he was bleeding at the mouth and coughing.

Two part-pails of water could not go far among over a hundred of us, not counting the, men. Only the babies, and the very little children, and the wounded men, got any. I did not get a sip, although mother dipped a bit of cloth into the several spoonfuls she got for the baby and wiped my mouth out. She did not even do that for herself, for she left me the bit of damp rag to chew.

The situation grew unspeakably worse in the afternoon. The quiet sun blazed down through the clear windless air and made a furnace of our hole in the sand. And all about us were the explosions of rifles and yells of the Indians. Only once in a while did father permit a single shot from the trench, and at that only by our best marksmen, such as Laban and Timothy Grant. But a steady stream of lead poured into our position all the time. There were no more disastrous ricochets, however; and our men in the trench, no longer firing, lay low and escaped damage. Only four were wounded, and only one of them very badly.

Father came in from the trench during a lull in the firing. He sat for a few minutes alongside mother and me without speaking. He seemed to be listening to all the moaning and crying for water that was going up. Once he climbed out of the rifle pit and went over to investigate the well. He brought back only damp sand, which he plastered thick on the chest and shoulders of Robert Carr. Then he went to where Jed Dunham and his mother were, and sent for Jed's father to come in from the trench. So closely packed were we that when anybody moved about inside the rifle pit he had to crawl carefully over the bodies of those lying down.

After a time father came crawling back to us.

"Jesse," he asked, "are you afraid of the Indians?"

I shook my head emphatically, guessing that I was to be seat on another proud mission.

"Are you afraid of the damned Mormons?"

"Not of any damned Mormon," I answered, taking advantage of the opportunity to curse our enemies without fear of the avenging back of mother's hand.

I noted the little smile that curled his tired lips for the moment when he heard my reply.

"Well, then, Jesse," he said, "will you go with Jed to the spring for water?"

I was all eagerness.

"We're going to dress the two of you up as girls," he continued, "so that maybe they won't fire on you."

I insisted on going as I was, as a male human that wore pants; but I surrendered quickly enough when father suggested that he would find some other boy to dress up and go along with Jed.

A chest was fetched in from the Chattox wagon. The Chattox girls were twins and of about a size with Jed and me. Several of the women got around to help. They were the Sunday dresses of the Chattox twins, and had come in the chest all the way from Arkansas.

In her anxiety mother left the baby with Sarah Dunlap, and came as far as the trench with me. There, under a wagon and behind the little breastwork of sand, Jed and I received our last instructions. Then we crawled out and stood up in the open. We were dressed precisely alike—white stockings, white dresses, with big blue sashes, and white sunbonnets. Jed's right and my left hand were clasped together. In each of our free hands we carried two small pails.

"Take it easy," father cautioned, as we began our advance. "Go slow. Walk like girls."

Not a shot was fired. We made the spring safely, filled our pails, and lay down and took a good drink ourselves. With a full pail in each hand we made the return trip. And still not a shot was fired.

I cannot remember how many journeys we made—fully fifteen or twenty. We walked slowly, always going out with hands clasped, always coming back slowly with four pails of water. It was astonishing how thirsty we were. We lay down several times and took long drinks.

But it was too much for our enemies. I cannot imagine that the Indians would have withheld their fire for so long, girls or no girls, had they not obeyed instructions from the whites who were with them. At any rate Jed and I were just starting on another trip when a rifle went off from the Indian hill, and then another.

"Come back!" mother cried out.

I looked at Jed, and found him looking at me. I knew he was stubborn and had made up his mind to be the last one in. So I started to advance, and at the same instant he started.

"You!—Jesse!" cried my mother. And there was more than a smacking in the way she said it.

134

Jed offered to clasp hands, but I shook my head.

"Run for it," I said.

And while we hotfooted it across the sand it seemed all the rifles on Indian hill were turned loose on us. I got to the spring a little ahead, so that Jed had to wait for me to fill my pails.

"Now run for it," he told me; and from the leisurely way he went about filling his own pails I knew he was determined to be in last.

So I crouched down, and, while I waited, watched the puffs of dust raised by the bullets. We began the return side by side and running.

"Not so fast," I cautioned him, "or you'll spill half the water."

That stung him, and he slacked back perceptibly. Midway I stumbled and fell headlong. A bullet, striking directly in front of me, filled my eyes with sand. For the moment I thought I was shot.

"Done it a-purpose," Jed sneered as I scrambled to my feet. He had stood and waited for me.

I caught his idea. He thought I had fallen deliberately in order to spill my water and go back for more. This rivalry between us was a serious matter—so serious, indeed, that I immediately took advantage of what he had imputed and raced back to the spring. And Jed Dunham, scornful of the bullets that were puffing dust all around him, stood there upright in the open and waited for me. We came in side by side, with honours even in our boys' foolhardiness. But when we delivered the water Jed had only one pailful. A bullet had gone through the other pail close to the bottom.

Mother took it out on me with a lecture on disobedience. She must have known, after what I had done, that father wouldn't let her smack me; for, while she was lecturing, father winked at me across her shoulder. It was the first time he had ever winked at me.

Back in the rifle pit Jed and I were heroes. The women wept and blessed us, and kissed us and mauled us. And I confess I was proud of the demonstration, although, like Jed, I let on that I did not like all such making-over. But Jeremy Hopkins, a great bandage about the stump of his left wrist, said we were the stuff white men were made out of—men like Daniel Boone, like Kit Carson, and Davy Crockett. I was prouder of that than all the rest.

The remainder of the day I seem to have been bothered principally with the pain of my right eye caused by the sand that had been kicked into it by the bullet. The eye was bloodshot, mother said; and to me it seemed to hurt just as much whether I kept it open or closed. I tried both ways.

Things were quieter in the rifle pit, because all had had water, though strong upon us was the problem of how the next water was to be procured. Coupled with this was the known fact that our ammunition was almost exhausted. A thorough overhauling of the wagons by father had resulted in finding five pounds of powder. A very little more was in the flasks of the men.

I remembered the sundown attack of the night before, and anticipated it this time by crawling to the trench before sunset. I crept into a place alongside of Laban. He was busy chewing tobacco, and did not notice me. For some time I watched him, fearing that when he discovered me he would order me back. He would take a long squint out between the wagon wheels, chew steadily a while, and then spit carefully into a little depression he had made in the sand.

"How's tricks?" I asked finally. It was the way he always addressed me.

"Fine," he answered. "Most remarkable fine, Jesse, now that I can chew again. My mouth was that dry that I couldn't chew from sun-up to when you brung the water."

Here a man showed head and shoulders over the top of the little hill to the north-east occupied by the whites. Laban sighted his rifle on him for a long minute. Then he shook his head.

"Four hundred yards. Nope, I don't risk it. I might get him, and then again I mightn't, an' your dad is mighty anxious about the powder."

"What do you think our chances are?" I asked, man-fashion, for, after my water exploit, I was feeling very much the man.

Laban seemed to consider carefully for a space ere he replied.

"Jesse, I don't mind tellin' you we're in a damned bad hole. But we'll get out, oh, we'll get out, you can bet your bottom dollar."

"Some of us ain't going to get out," I objected.

"Who, for instance?" he queried.

"Why, Bill Tyler, and Mrs. Grant, and Silas Dunlap, and all the rest."

"Aw, shucks, Jesse—they're in the ground already. Don't you know everybody has to bury their dead as they traipse along? They've ben doin' it for thousands of years I reckon, and there's just as many alive as ever they was. You see, Jesse, birth and death go hand-in-hand. And they're born as fast as they die—faster, I reckon, because they've increased and multiplied. Now you, you might a-got killed this afternoon packin' water. But you're here, ain't you, a-gassin' with me an' likely to grow up an' be the father of a fine large family in Californy. They say everything grows large in Californy."

This cheerful way of looking at the matter encouraged me to dare sudden expression of a long covetousness.

"Say, Laban, supposin' you got killed here—"

"Who?—me?" he cried.

"I'm just sayin' supposin'," I explained.

"Oh, all right then. Go on. Supposin' I am killed?"

"Will you give me your scalps?"

"Your ma'll smack you if she catches you a-wearin' them," he temporized.

"I don't have to wear them when she's around. Now if you got killed, Laban, somebody'd have to get them scalps. Why not me?"

"Why not?" he repeated. "That's correct, and why not you? All right, Jesse. I like you, and your pa. The minute I'm killed the scalps is yourn, and the scalpin' knife, too. And there's Timothy Grant for witness. Did you hear, Timothy?"

Timothy said he had heard, and I lay there speechless in the stifling trench, too overcome by my greatness of good fortune to be able to utter a word of gratitude.

I was rewarded for my foresight in going to the trench. Another general attack was made at sundown, and thousands of shots were fired into us. Nobody on our side was scratched. On the other hand, although we fired barely thirty shots, I saw Laban and Timothy Grant each get an Indian. Laban told me that from the first only the Indians had done the shooting. He was certain that no white had fired a shot. All of which sorely puzzled him. The whites neither offered us aid nor attacked us, and all the while were on visiting terms with the Indians who were attacking us.

Next morning found the thirst harsh upon us. I was out at the first hint of light. There had been a heavy dew, and men, women, and children were lapping it up with their tongues from off the wagon-tongues, brake-blocks, and wheel-tyres.

There was talk that Laban had returned from a scout just before daylight; that he had crept close to the position of the whites; that they were already up; and that in the light of their campfires he had seen them praying in a large circle. Also he reported from what few words he caught that they were praying about us and what was to be done with us.

"May God send them the light then," I heard one of the Demdike sisters say to Abby Foxwell.

"And soon," said Abby Foxwell, "for I don't know what we'll do a whole day without water, and our powder is about gone."

Nothing happened all morning. Not a shot was fired. Only the sun blazed down through the quiet air. Our thirst grew, and soon the babies were crying and the younger children whimpering and complaining. At noon Will Hamilton took two large pails and started for the spring. But before he could crawl under the wagon Ann Demdike ran and got her arms around him and tried to hold him back. But he talked to her, and kissed her, and went on. Not a shot was fired, nor was any fired all the time he continued to go out and bring back water.

"Praise God!" cried old Mrs. Demdike. "It is a sign. They have relented."

This was the opinion of many of the women.

About two o'clock, after we had eaten and felt better, a white man appeared, carrying a white flag. Will Hamilton went out and talked to him, came back and talked with father and the rest of our men, and then went out to the stranger again. Farther back we could see a man standing and looking on, whom we recognized as Lee.

With us all was excitement. The women were so relieved that they were crying and kissing one another, and old Mrs. Demdike and others were hallelujahing and blessing God. The proposal, which our men had accepted, was that we would put ourselves under the flag of truce and be protected from the Indians.

"We had to do it," I heard father tell mother.

He was sitting, droop-shouldered and dejected, on a wagon-tongue.

"But what if they intend treachery?" mother asked.

He shrugged his shoulders.

"We've got to take the chance that they don't," he said. "Our ammunition is gone."

Some of our men were unchaining one of our wagons and rolling it out of the way. I ran across to see what was happening. In came Lee himself, followed by two empty wagons, each driven by one man. Everybody crowded around Lee. He said that they had had a hard time with the Indians keeping them off of us, and that Major Higbee, with fifty of the Mormon militia, were ready to take us under their charge.

But what made father and Laban and some of the men suspicious was when Lee said that we must put all our rifles into one of the wagons so as not to arouse the animosity of the Indians. By so doing we would appear to be the prisoners of the Mormon militia.

Father straightened up and was about to refuse when he glanced to Laban, who replied in an undertone. "They ain't no more use in our hands than in the wagon, seein' as the powder's gone."

Two of our wounded men who could not walk were put into the wagons, and along with them were put all the little children. Lee seemed to be picking them out over eight and under eight. Jed and I were large for our age, and we were nine besides; so Lee put us with the older bunch and told us we were to march with the women on foot.

When he took our baby from mother and put it in a wagon she started to object. Then I saw her lips draw tightly together, and she gave in. She was a gray-eyed, strong-featured, middle-aged woman, large-boned and fairly stout. But the long journey and hardship had told on her, so that she was hollow-cheeked and gaunt, and like all the women in the company she wore an expression of brooding, never-ceasing anxiety.

It was when Lee described the order of march that Laban came to me. Lee said that the women and the children that walked should go first in the line, following behind the two wagons. Then the men, in single file, should follow the women. When Laban heard this he came to me, untied the scalps from his belt, and fastened them to my waist.

"But you ain't killed yet," I protested.

"You bet your life I ain't," he answered lightly.

"I've just reformed, that's all. This scalp-wearin' is a vain thing and heathen." He stopped a moment as if he had forgotten something, then, as he turned abruptly on his heel to regain the men of our company, he called over his shoulder, "Well, so long, Jesse."

I was wondering why he should say good-bye when a white man came riding into the corral. He said Major Higbee had sent him to tell us to hurry up, because the Indians might attack at any moment.

So the march began, the two wagons first. Lee kept along with the women and walking children. Behind us, after waiting until we were a couple of hundred feet in advance, came our men. As we emerged from the corral we could see the militia just a short distance away. They were leaning on their rifles and standing in a long line about six feet apart. As we passed them I could not help noticing how solemn-faced they were. They looked like men at a funeral. So did the women notice this, and some of them began to cry.

I walked right behind my mother. I had chosen this position so that she would not catch-sight of my scalps. Behind me came the three Demdike sisters, two of them helping the old mother. I could hear Lee calling all the time to the men who drove the wagons not to go so fast. A man that one of the Demdike girls said must be Major Higbee sat on a horse watching us go by. Not an Indian was in sight.

By the time our men were just abreast of the militia—I had just looked back to try to see where Jed Dunham was—the thing happened. I heard Major Higbee cry out in a loud voice, "Do your duty!" All the rifles of the militia seemed to go off at once, and our men were falling over and sinking down. All the Demdike women went down at one time. I turned quickly to see how mother was, and she was down. Right alongside of us, out of the bushes, came hundreds of Indians, all shooting. I saw the two Dunlap sisters start on the run across the sand, and took after them, for whites and Indians were all killing us. And as I ran I saw the driver of one of the wagons shooting the two wounded men. The horses of the other wagon were plunging and rearing and their driver was trying to hold them.

* * * * *

It was when the little boy that was I was running after the Dunlap girls that blackness came upon him. All memory there ceases, for Jesse Fancher there ceased, and, as Jesse Fancher, ceased for ever. The form that was Jesse Fancher, the body that was his, being matter and apparitional, like an apparition passed and was not. But the imperishable spirit did not cease. It continued to exist, and, in its next incarnation, became the residing spirit of that apparitional body known as Darrell Standing's which soon is to be taken out and hanged and sent into the nothingness whither all apparitions go.

There is a lifer here in Folsom, Matthew Davies, of old pioneer stock, who is trusty of the scaffold and execution chamber. He is an old man, and his folks crossed the plains in the early days. I have talked with him, and he has verified the massacre in which Jesse Fancher was killed. When this old lifer was a child there was much talk in his family of the Mountain Meadows Massacre. The children in the wagons, he said, were saved, because they were too young to tell tales.

All of which I submit. Never, in my life of Darrell Standing, have I read a line or heard a word spoken of the Fancher Company that perished at Mountain Meadows. Yet, in the jacket in San Quentin prison, all this knowledge came to me. I could not create this knowledge out of nothing, any more than could I create dynamite out of nothing. This knowledge and these facts I have related have but one explanation. They are out of the spirit content of me—the spirit that, unlike matter, does not perish.

In closing this chapter I must state that Matthew Davies also told me that some years after the massacre Lee was taken by United States Government officials to the Mountain Meadows and there executed on the site of our old corral.

CHAPTER XIV

When, at the conclusion of my first ten days' term in the jacket, I was brought back to consciousness by Doctor Jackson's thumb pressing open an eyelid, I opened both eyes and smiled up into the face of Warden Atherton.

"Too cussed to live and too mean to die," was his comment.

"The ten days are up, Warden," I whispered.

"Well, we're going to unlace you," he growled.

"It is not that," I said. "You observed my smile. You remember we had a little wager. Don't bother to unlace me first. Just give the Bull Durham and cigarette papers to Morrell and Oppenheimer. And for full measure here's another smile."

"Oh, I know your kind, Standing," the Warden lectured. "But it won't get you anything. If I don't break you, you'll break all strait-jacket records."

"He's broken them already," Doctor Jackson said. "Who ever heard of a man smiling after ten days of it?"

"Well and bluff," Warden Atherton answered. "Unlace him, Hutchins."

"Why such haste?" I queried, in a whisper, of course, for so low had life ebbed in me that it required all the little strength I possessed and all the will of me to be able to whisper even. "Why such haste? I don't have to catch a train, and I am so confounded comfortable as I am that I prefer not to be disturbed."

But unlace me they did, rolling me out of the fetid jacket and upon the floor, an inert, helpless thing.

"No wonder he was comfortable," said Captain Jamie. "He didn't feel anything. He's paralysed."

"Paralysed your grandmother," sneered the Warden. "Get him up on his feat and you'll see him stand."

Hutchins and the doctor dragged me to my feet.

"Now let go!" the Warden commanded.

Not all at once could life return into the body that had been practically dead for ten days, and as a result, with no power as yet over my flesh, I gave at the knees, crumpled, pitched sidewise, and gashed my forehead against the wall.

"You see," said Captain Jamie.

"Good acting," retorted the Warden. "That man's got nerve to do anything."

"You're right, Warden," I whispered from the floor. "I did it on purpose. It was a stage fall. Lift me up again, and I'll repeat it. I promise you lots of fun."

I shall not dwell upon the agony of returning circulation. It was to become an old story with me, and it bore its share in cutting the lines in my face that I shall carry to the scaffold.

When they finally left me I lay for the rest of the day stupid and half-comatose. There is such a thing as anæsthesia of pain, engendered by pain too exquisite to be borne. And I have known that anæsthesia.

By evening I was able to crawl about my cell, but not yet could I stand up. I drank much water, and cleansed myself as well as I could; but not until next day could I bring myself to eat, and then only by deliberate force of my will.

The program me, as given me by Warden Atherton, was that I was to rest up and recuperate for a few days, and then, if in the meantime I had not confessed to the hiding-place of the dynamite, I should be given another ten days in the jacket.

"Sorry to cause you so much trouble, Warden," I had said in reply. "It's a pity I don't die in the jacket and so put you out of your misery."

At this time I doubt that I weighed an ounce over ninety pounds. Yet, two years before, when the doors of San Quentin first closed on me, I had weighed one hundred and sixty-five pounds. It seems incredible that there was another ounce I could part with and still live. Yet in the months that followed, ounce by ounce I was reduced until I know I must have weighed nearer eighty than ninety pounds. I do know, after I managed my escape from solitary and struck the guard Thurston on the nose, that before they took me to San Rafael for trial, while I was being cleaned and shaved I weighed eighty-nine pounds.

There are those who wonder how men grow hard. Warden Atherton was a hard man. He made me hard, and my very hardness reacted on him and made him harder. And yet he never succeeded in killing me. It required the state law of California, a hanging judge, and an unpardoning governor to send me to the scaffold for striking a prison guard with my fist. I shall always contend that that guard had a nose most easily bleedable. I was a bat-eyed, tottery skeleton at the time. I sometimes wonder if his nose really did bleed. Of course he swore it did, on the witness stand. But I have known prison guards take oath to worse perjuries than that.

Ed Morrell was eager to know if I had succeeded with the experiment; but when he attempted to talk with me he was shut up by Smith, the guard who happened to be on duty in solitary.

"That's all right, Ed," I rapped to him. "You and Jake keep quiet, and I'll tell you about it. Smith can't prevent you from listening, and he can't prevent me from talking. They have done their worst, and I am still here."

"Cut that out, Standing!" Smith bellowed at me from the corridor on which all the cells opened.

Smith was a peculiarly saturnine individual, by far the most cruel and vindictive of our guards. We used to canvass whether his wife bullied him or whether he had chronic indigestion.

I continued rapping with my knuckles, and he came to the wicket to glare in at me.

"I told you to out that out," he snarled.

"Sorry," I said suavely. "But I have a sort of premonition that I shall go right on rapping. And—er—excuse me for asking a personal question—what are you going to do about it?"

"I'll—" he began explosively, proving, by his inability to conclude the remark, that he thought in henids.

"Yes?" I encouraged. "Just what, pray?"

"I'll have the Warden here," he said lamely.

"Do, please. A most charming gentleman, to be sure. A shining example of the refining influences that are creeping into our prisons. Bring him to me at once. I wish to report you to him."

"Me?"

"Yes, just precisely you," I continued. "You persist, in a rude and boorish manner, in interrupting my conversation with the other guests in this hostelry."

And Warden Atherton came. The door was unlocked, and he blustered into my cell. But oh, I was so safe! He had done his worst. I was beyond his power.

"I'll shut off your grub," he threatened.

"As you please," I answered. "I'm used to it. I haven't eaten for ten days, and, do you know, trying to begin to eat again is a confounded nuisance.

"Oh, ho, you're threatening me, are you? A hunger strike, eh?"

"Pardon me," I said, my voice sulky with politeness. "The proposition was yours, not mine. Do try and be logical on occasion. I trust you will believe me when I tell you that your illogic is far more painful for me to endure than all your tortures."

"Are you going to stop your knuckle-talking?" he demanded.

"No; forgive me for vexing you—for I feel so strong a compulsion to talk with my knuckles that—"

"For two cents I'll put you back in the jacket," he broke in.

"Do, please. I dote on the jacket. I am the jacket baby. I get fat in the jacket. Look at that arm." I pulled up my sleeve and showed a biceps so attenuated that when I flexed it it had the appearance of a string. "A real blacksmith's biceps, eh, Warden? Cast your eyes on my swelling chest. Sandow had better look out for his laurels. And my abdomen—why, man, I am growing so stout that my case will be a scandal of prison overfeeding. Watch out, Warden, or you'll have the taxpayers after you."

"Are you going to stop knuckle-talk?" he roared.

"No, thanking you for your kind solicitude. On mature deliberation I have decided that I shall keep on knuckle-talking."

He stared at me speechlessly for a moment, and then, out of sheer impotency, turned to go.

"One question, please."

"What is it?" he demanded over his shoulder.

"What are you going to do about it?"

From the choleric exhibition he gave there and then it has been an unceasing wonder with me to this day that he has not long since died of apoplexy.

Hour by hour, after the warden's discomfited departure, I rapped on and on the tale of my adventures. Not until that night, when Pie-Face Jones came on duty and proceeded to steal his customary naps, were Morrell and Oppenheimer able to do any talking.

"Pipe dreams," Oppenheimer rapped his verdict.

Yes, was my thought; our experiences *are* the stuff of our dreams.

147

"When I was a night messenger I hit the hop once," Oppenheimer continued. "And I want to tell you-you haven't anything on me when it came to seeing things. I guess that is what all the novel-writers do—hit the hop so as to throw their imagination into the high gear."

But Ed Morrell, who had travelled the same road as I, although with different results, believed my tale. He said that when his body died in the jacket, and he himself went forth from prison, he was never anybody but Ed Morrell. He never experienced previous existences. When his spirit wandered free, it wandered always in the present. As he told us, just as he was able to leave his body and gaze upon it lying in the jacket on the cell floor, so could he leave the prison, and, in the present, revisit San Francisco and see what was occurring. In this manner he had visited his mother twice, both times finding her asleep. In this spirit-roving he said he had no power over material things. He could not open or close a door, move any object, make a noise, nor manifest his presence. On the other hand, material things had no power over him. Walls and doors were not obstacles. The entity, or the real thing that was he, was thought, spirit.

"The grocery store on the corner, half a block from where mother lived, changed hands," he told us. "I knew it by the different sign over the place. I had to wait six months after that before I could write my first letter, but when I did I asked mother about it. And she said yes, it had changed."

"Did you read that grocery sign?" Jake Oppenheimer asked.

"Sure thing I did," was Morrell's response. "Or how could I have known it?"

"All right," rapped Oppenheimer the unbelieving. "You can prove it easy. Some time, when they shift some decent guards on us that will give us a peep at a newspaper, you get yourself thrown into the jacket, climb out of your body, and sashay down to little old 'Frisco. Slide up to Third and Market just about two or three a.m. when they are running the morning papers off the press. Read the latest news. Then make a swift sneak for San Quentin, get here before the newspaper tug crosses the bay, and tell me what you read. Then we'll wait and get a morning paper, when it comes in, from

148

a guard. Then, if what you told me is in that paper, I am with you to a fare-you-well."

It was a good test. I could not but agree with Oppenheimer that such a proof would be absolute. Morrell said he would take it up some time, but that he disliked to such an extent the process of leaving his body that he would not make the attempt until such time that his suffering in the jacket became too extreme to be borne.

"That is the way with all of them—won't come across with the goods," was Oppenheimer's criticism. "My mother believed in spirits. When I was a kid she was always seeing them and talking with them and getting advice from them. But she never come across with any goods from them. The spirits couldn't tell her where the old man could nail a job or find a gold-mine or mark an eight-spot in Chinese lottery. Not on your life. The bunk they told her was that the old man's uncle had had a goitre, or that the old man's grandfather had died of galloping consumption, or that we were going to move house inside four months, which last was dead easy, seeing as we moved on an average of six times a year."

I think, had Oppenheimer had the opportunity for thorough education, he would have made a Marinetti or a Haeckel. He was an earth-man in his devotion to the irrefragable fact, and his logic was admirable though frosty. "You've got to show me," was the ground rule by which he considered all things. He lacked the slightest iota of faith. This was what Morrell had pointed out. Lack of faith had prevented Oppenheimer from succeeding in achieving the little death in the jacket.

You will see, my reader, that it was not all hopelessly bad in solitary. Given three minds such as ours, there was much with which to while away the time. It might well be that we kept one another from insanity, although I must admit that Oppenheimer rotted five years in solitary entirely by himself, ere Morrell joined him, and yet had remained sane.

On the other hand, do not make the mistake of thinking that life in solitary was one wild orgy of blithe communion and exhilarating psychological research.

We had much and terrible pain. Our guards were brutes—your hang-dogs, citizen. Our surroundings were vile. Our food was filthy, monotonous, innutritious. Only men, by force of will, could live on so unbalanced a ration. I know that our prize cattle, pigs, and sheep on the University Demonstration Farm at Davis would have faded away and died had they received no more scientifically balanced a ration than what we received.

We had no books to read. Our very knuckle-talk was a violation of the rules. The world, so far as we were concerned, practically did not exist. It was more a ghost-world. Oppenheimer, for instance, had never seen an automobile or a motor-cycle. News did occasionally filter in—but such dim, long-after-the-event, unreal news. Oppenheimer told me he had not learned of the Russo-Japanese war until two years after it was over.

We were the buried alive, the living dead. Solitary was our tomb, in which, on occasion, we talked with our knuckles like spirits rapping at a séance.

News? Such little things were news to us. A change of bakers—we could tell it by our bread. What made Pie-face Jones lay off a week? Was it vacation or sickness? Why was Wilson, on the night shift for only ten days, transferred elsewhere? Where did Smith get that black eye? We would speculate for a week over so trivial a thing as the last.

Some convict given a month in solitary was an event. And yet we could learn nothing from such transient and ofttimes stupid Dantes who would remain in our inferno too short a time to learn knuckle-talk ere they went forth again into the bright wide world of the living.

Still, again, all was not so trivial in our abode of shadows. As example, I taught Oppenheimer to play chess. Consider how tremendous such an achievement is—to teach a man, thirteen cells away, by means of knuckle-raps; to teach him to visualize a chessboard, to visualize all the pieces, pawns and positions, to know the various manners of moving; and to teach him it all so thoroughly that he and I, by pure visualization, were in the end able to play entire games of chess in our minds. In the end, did I say? Another tribute to the magnificence of Oppenheimer's mind: in the end he became my master at the game—he who had never seen a chessman in his life.

What image of a *bishop*, for instance, could possibly form in his mind when I rapped our code-sign for *bishop*? In vain and often I asked him this very question. In vain he tried to describe in words that mental image of something he had never seen but which nevertheless he was able to handle in such masterly fashion as to bring confusion upon me countless times in the course of play.

I can only contemplate such exhibitions of will and spirit and conclude, as I so often conclude, that precisely there resides reality. The spirit only is real. The flesh is phantasmagoria and apparitional. I ask you how—I repeat, I ask you *how* matter or flesh in any form can play chess on an imaginary board with imaginary pieces, across a vacuum of thirteen cell spanned only with knuckle-taps?

CHAPTER XV

I was once Adam Strang, an Englishman. The period of my living, as near as I can guess it, was somewhere between 1550 and 1650, and I lived to a ripe old age, as you shall see. It has been a great regret to me, ever since Ed Morrell taught me the way of the little death, that I had not been a more thorough student of history. I should have been able to identity and place much that is obscure to me. As it is, I am compelled to grope and guess my way to times and places of my earlier existences.

A peculiar thing about my Adam Strang existence is that I recollect so little of the first thirty years of it. Many times, in the jacket, has Adam Strang recrudesced, but always he springs into being full-statured, heavy-thewed, a full thirty years of age.

I, Adam Strang, invariably assume my consciousness on a group of low, sandy islands somewhere under the equator in what must be the western Pacific Ocean. I am always at home there, and seem to have been there some time. There are thousands of people on these islands, although I am the only white man. The natives are a magnificent breed, big-muscled, broad-shouldered, tall. A six-foot man is a commonplace. The king, Raa Kook, is at least six inches above six feet, and though he would weigh fully three hundred pounds, is so equitably proportioned that one could not call him fat. Many of his chiefs are as large, while the women are not much smaller than the men.

There are numerous islands in the group, over all of which Raa Kook is king, although the cluster of islands to the south is restive and occasionally in revolt. These natives with whom I live are Polynesian, I know, because their hair is straight and black. Their skin is a sun-warm golden-brown. Their speech, which I speak uncommonly easy, is round and rich and musical, possessing a paucity of consonants, being composed principally of vowels. They love flowers, music, dancing, and games, and are childishly simple and happy in their amusements, though cruelly savage in their angers and wars.

I, Adam Strang, know my past, but do not seem to think much about it. I live in the present. I brood neither over past nor future. I am careless, improvident, uncautious, happy out of sheer well-being and overplus of physical energy. Fish, fruits, vegetables, and seaweed—a full stomach—and I am content. I am high in place with Raa Kook, than whom none is higher, not even Abba Taak, who is highest over the priest. No man dare lift hand or weapon to me. I am taboo—sacred as the sacred canoe-house under the floor of which repose the bones of heaven alone knows how many previous kings of Raa Kook's line.

I know all about how I happened to be wrecked and be there alone of all my ship's company—it was a great drowning and a great wind; but I do not moon over the catastrophe. When I think back at all, rather do I think far back to my childhood at the skirts of my milk-skinned, flaxen-haired, buxom English mother. It is a tiny village of a dozen straw-thatched cottages in which I lived. I hear again blackbirds and thrushes in the hedges, and see again bluebells spilling out from the oak woods and over the velvet turf like a creaming of blue water. And most of all I remember a great, hairy-fetlocked stallion, often led dancing, sidling, and nickering down the narrow street. I was frightened of the huge beast and always fled screaming to my mother, clutching her skirts and hiding in them wherever I might find her.

But enough. The childhood of Adam Strang is not what I set out to write.

I lived for several years on the islands which are nameless to me, and upon which I am confident I was the first white man. I was married to Lei-Lei, the king's sister, who was a fraction over six feet and only by that fraction topped me. I was a splendid figure of a man, broad-shouldered, deep-chested, well-set-up. Women of any race, as you shall see, looked on me with a favouring eye. Under my arms, sun-shielded, my skin was milk-white as my mother's. My eyes were blue. My moustache, beard and hair were that golden-yellow such as one sometimes sees in paintings of the northern sea-kings. Ay—I must have come of that old stock, long-settled in England, and, though born in a countryside cottage, the sea still ran so salt in my blood that I early found my way to ships to become a sea-cuny. That is what I was—neither officer nor gentleman, but sea-cuny, hard-worked, hard-bitten, hard-enduring.

I was of value to Raa Kook, hence his royal protection. I could work in iron, and our wrecked ship had brought the first iron to Raa Kook's land. On occasion, ten leagues to the north-west, we went in canoes to get iron from the wreck. The hull had slipped off the reef and lay in fifteen fathoms. And in fifteen fathoms we brought up the iron. Wonderful divers and workers under water were these natives. I learned to do my fifteen fathoms, but never could I equal them in their fishy exploits. On the land, by virtue of my English training and my strength, I could throw any of them. Also, I taught them quarter-staff, until the game became a very contagion and broken heads anything but novelties.

Brought up from the wreck was a journal, so torn and mushed and pulped by the sea-water, with ink so run about, that scarcely any of it was decipherable. However, in the hope that some antiquarian scholar may be able to place more definitely the date of the events I shall describe, I here give an extract. The peculiar spelling may give the clue. Note that while the letter *s* is used, it more commonly is replaced by the letter *f*.

The wind being favourable, gave us an opportunity of examining and drying some of our provifion, particularly, fome Chinefe hams and dry filh, which conftituted part of our victualling. Divine service alfo was performed on deck. In the afternoon the wind was foutherly, with frefh gales, but dry, fo that we were able the following morning to clean between decks, and alfo to fumigate the fhip with gunpowder.

But I must hasten, for my narrative is not of Adam Strang the shipwrecked sea-cuny on a coral isle, but of Adam Strang, later named Yi Yong-ik, the Mighty One, who was one time favourite of the powerful Yunsan, who was lover and husband of the Lady Om of the princely house of Min, and who was long time beggar and pariah in all the villages of all the coasts and roads of Cho-Sen. (Ah, ha, I have you there—Cho-Sen. It means the land of the morning calm. In modern speech it is called Korea.)

Remember, it was between three and four centuries back that I lived, the first white man, on the coral isles of Raa Kook. In those waters, at that time, the keels of ships were rare. I might well have lived out my days there, in peace and fatness, under the sun where frost was not, had it not been for the *Sparwehr*. The *Sparwehr* was a Dutch merchantman daring the uncharted seas for Indies beyond the Indies. And she found me instead, and I was all she found.

Have I not said that I was a gay-hearted, golden, bearded giant of an irresponsible boy that had never grown up? With scarce a pang, when the *Sparwehrs'* water-casks were filled, I left Raa Kook and his pleasant land, left Lei-Lei and all her flower-garlanded sisters, and with laughter on my lips and familiar ship-smells sweet in my nostrils, sailed away, sea-cuny once more, under Captain Johannes Maartens.

A marvellous wandering, that which followed on the old *Sparwehr*. We were in quest of new lands of silk and spices. In truth, we found fevers, violent deaths, pestilential paradises where death and beauty kept charnel-house together. That old Johannes Maartens, with no hint of romance in that stolid face and grizzly square head of his, sought the islands of Solomon, the mines of Golconda—ay, he sought old lost Atlantis which he hoped to find still afloat unscuppered. And he found head-hunting, tree-dwelling anthropophagi instead.

We landed on strange islands, sea-pounded on their shores and smoking at their summits, where kinky-haired little animal-men made monkey-wailings in the jungle, planted their forest run-ways with thorns and stake-pits, and blew poisoned splinters into us from out the twilight jungle bush. And whatsoever man of us was wasp-stung by such a splinter died horribly and howling. And we encountered other men, fiercer, bigger, who faced us on the beaches in open fight, showering us with spears and arrows, while the great tree drums and the little tom-toms rumbled and rattled war across the tree-filled hollows, and all the hills were pillared with signal-smokes.

Hendrik Hamel was supercargo and part owner of the *Sparwehr* adventure, and what he did not own was the property of Captain Johannes

Maartens. The latter spoke little English, Hendrik Hamel but little more. The sailors, with whom I gathered, spoke Dutch only. But trust a sea-cuny to learn Dutch—ay, and Korean, as you shall see.

Toward the end we came to the charted country of Japan. But the people would have no dealings with us, and two sworded officials, in sweeping robes of silk that made Captain Johannes Maartens' mouth water, came aboard of us and politely requested us to begone. Under their suave manners was the iron of a warlike race, and we knew, and went our way.

We crossed the Straits of Japan and were entering the Yellow Sea on our way to China, when we laid the *Sparwehr* on the rocks. She was a crazy tub the old *Sparwehr*, so clumsy and so dirty with whiskered marine-life on her bottom that she could not get out of her own way. Close-hauled, the closest she could come was to six points of the wind; and then she bobbed up and down, without way, like a derelict turnip. Galliots were clippers compared with her. To tack her about was undreamed of; to wear her required all hands and half a watch. So situated, we were caught on a lee shore in an eight-point shift of wind at the height of a hurricane that had beaten our souls sick for forty-eight hours.

We drifted in upon the land in the chill light of a stormy dawn across a heartless cross-sea mountain high. It was dead of winter, and between smoking snow-squalls we could glimpse the forbidding coast, if coast it might be called, so broken was it. There were grim rock isles and islets beyond counting, dim snow-covered ranges beyond, and everywhere upstanding cliffs too steep for snow, outjuts of headlands, and pinnacles and slivers of rock upthrust from the boiling sea.

There was no name to this country on which we drove, no record of it ever having been visited by navigators. Its coast-line was only hinted at in our chart. From all of which we could argue that the inhabitants were as inhospitable as the little of their land we could see.

The *Sparwehr* drove in bow-on upon a cliff. There was deep water to its sheer foot, so that our sky-aspiring bowsprit crumpled at the impact and snapped short off. The foremast went by the board, with a great snapping of rope-shrouds and stays, and fell forward against the cliff.

I have always admired old Johannes Maartens. Washed and rolled off the high poop by a burst of sea, we were left stranded in the waist of the ship, whence we fought our way for'ard to the steep-pitched forecastle-head. Others joined us. We lashed ourselves fast and counted noses. We were eighteen. The rest had perished.

Johannes Maartens touched me and pointed upward through cascading salt-water from the back-fling of the cliff. I saw what he desired. Twenty feet below the truck the foremast ground and crunched against a boss of the cliff. Above the boss was a cleft. He wanted to know if I would dare the leap from the mast-head into the cleft. Sometimes the distance was a scant six feet. At other times it was a score, for the mast reeled drunkenly to the rolling and pounding of the hull on which rested its splintered butt.

I began the climb. But they did not wait. One by one they unlashed themselves and followed me up the perilous mast. There was reason for haste, for at any moment the *Sparwehr* might slip off into deep water. I timed my leap, and made it, landing in the cleft in a scramble and ready to lend a hand to those who leaped after. It was slow work. We were wet and half freezing in the wind-drive. Besides, the leaps had to be timed to the roll of the hull and the sway of the mast.

The cook was the first to go. He was snapped off the mast-end, and his body performed cart-wheels in its fall. A fling of sea caught him and crushed him to a pulp against the cliff. The cabin boy, a bearded man of twenty-odd, lost hold, slipped, swung around the mast, and was pinched against the boss of rock. Pinched? The life squeezed from him on the instant. Two others followed the way of the cook. Captain Johannes Maartens was the last, completing the fourteen of us that clung on in the cleft. An hour afterward the *Sparwehr* slipped off and sank in deep water.

Two days and nights saw us near to perishing on that cliff, for there was way neither up nor down. The third morning a fishing-boat found us. The men were clad entirely in dirt white, with their long hair done up in a curious knot on their pates—the marriage knot, as I was afterward to learn, and also, as I was to learn, a handy thing to clutch hold of with one hand whilst you clouted with the other when an argument went beyond words.

The boat went back to the village for help, and most of the villagers, most of their gear, and most of the day were required to get us down. They were a poor and wretched folk, their food difficult even for the stomach of a sea-cuny to countenance. Their rice was brown as chocolate. Half the husks remained in it, along with bits of chaff, splinters, and unidentifiable dirt which made one pause often in the chewing in order to stick into his mouth thumb and forefinger and pluck out the offending stuff. Also, they ate a sort of millet, and pickles of astounding variety and ungodly hot.

Their houses were earthen-walled and straw-thatched. Under the floors ran flues through which the kitchen smoke escaped, warming the sleeping-room in its passage. Here we lay and rested for days, soothing ourselves with their mild and tasteless tobacco, which we smoked in tiny bowls at the end of yard-long pipes. Also, there was a warm, sourish, milky-looking drink, heady only when taken in enormous doses. After guzzling I swear gallons of it, I got singing drunk, which is the way of sea-cunies the world over. Encouraged by my success, the others persisted, and soon we were all a-roaring, little reeking of the fresh snow gale piping up outside, and little worrying that we were cast away in an uncharted, God-forgotten land. Old Johannes Maartens laughed and trumpeted and slapped his thighs with the best of us. Hendrik Hamel, a cold-blooded, chilly-poised dark brunette of a Dutchman with beady black eyes, was as rarely devilish as the rest of us, and shelled out silver like any drunken sailor for the purchase of more of the milky brew. Our carrying-on was a scandal; but the women fetched the drink while all the village that could crowd in jammed the room to witness our antics.

The white man has gone around the world in mastery, I do believe, because of his unwise uncaringness. That has been the manner of his going, although, of course, he was driven on by restiveness and lust for booty. So it was that Captain Johannes Maartens, Hendrik Hamel, and the twelve sea-cunies of us roystered and bawled in the fisher village while the winter gales whistled across the Yellow Sea.

From the little we had seen of the land and the people we were not impressed by Cho-Sen. If these miserable fishers were a fair sample of the natives, we could understand why the land was unvisited of navigators. But we were to learn different. The village was on an in-lying island, and its headmen must have sent word across to the mainland; for one morning three big two-masted junks with lateens of rice-matting dropped anchor off the beach.

When the sampans came ashore Captain Johannes Maartens was all interest, for here were silks again. One strapping Korean, all in pale-tinted silks of various colours, was surrounded by half a dozen obsequious attendants, also clad in silk. Kwan Yung-jin, as I came to know his name, was a *yang-ban*, or noble; also he was what might be called magistrate or governor of the district or province. This means that his office was appointive, and that he was a tithe-squeezer or tax-farmer.

Fully a hundred soldiers were also landed and marched into the village. They were armed with three-pronged spears, slicing spears, and chopping spears, with here and there a matchlock of so heroic mould that there were two soldiers to a matchlock, one to carry and set the tripod on which rested the muzzle, the other to carry and fire the gun. As I was to learn, sometimes the gun went off, sometimes it did not, all depending upon the adjustment of the fire-punk and the condition of the powder in the flash-pan.

So it was that Kwan-Yung-jin travelled. The headmen of the village were cringingly afraid of him, and for good reason, as we were not overlong in finding out. I stepped forward as interpreter, for already I had the hang of several score of Korean words. He scowled and waved me aside. But what did I reek? I was as tall as he, outweighed him by a full two stone, and my skin was white, my hair golden. He turned his back and addressed the head man of the village while his six silken satellites made a cordon between us. While he talked more soldiers from the ship carried up several shoulder-loads of inch-planking. These planks were about six feet long and two feet wide, and curiously split in half lengthwise. Nearer one end than the other was a round hole larger than a man's neck.

Kwan Yung-jin gave a command. Several of the soldiers approached Tromp, who was sitting on the ground nursing a felon. Now Tromp was a rather stupid, slow-thinking, slow-moving cuny, and before he knew what was doing one of the planks, with a scissors-like opening and closing, was about his neck and clamped. Discovering his predicament, he set up a bull-roaring and dancing, till all had to back away to give him clear space for the flying ends of his plank.

Then the trouble began, for it was plainly Kwan Yung-jin's intention to plank all of us. Oh, we fought, bare-fisted, with a hundred soldiers and as many villagers, while Kwan Yung-jin stood apart in his silks and lordly disdain. Here was where I earned my name Yi Yong-ik, the Mighty. Long after our company was subdued and planked I fought on. My fists were of the hardness of topping-mauls, and I had the muscles and will to drive them.

To my joy, I quickly learned that the Koreans did not understand a fist-blow and were without the slightest notion of guarding. They went down like tenpins, fell over each other in heaps. But Kwan Yung-jin was my man, and all that saved him when I made my rush was the intervention of his satellites. They were flabby creatures. I made a mess of them and a muss and muck of their silks ere the multitude could return upon me. There were so many of them. They clogged my blows by the sneer numbers of them, those behind shoving the front ones upon me. And how I dropped them! Toward the end they were squirming three-deep under my feet. But by the time the crews of the three junks and most of the village were on top of me I was fairly smothered. The planking was easy.

"God in heaven, what now!" asked Vandervoot, another cuny, when we had been bundled aboard a junk.

We sat on the open deck, like so many trussed fowls, when he asked the question, and the next moment, as the junk heeled to the breeze, we shot down the deck, planks and all, fetching up in the lee-scuppers with skinned necks. And from the high poop Kwan Yung-jin gazed down at us as if he did not see us. For many years to come Vandervoot was known amongst us as "What-Now Vandervoot." Poor devil! He froze to death one night on the streets of Keijo; with every door barred against him.

To the mainland we were taken and thrown into a stinking, vermin-infested prison. Such was our introduction to the officialdom of Cho-Sen. But I was to be revenged for all of us on Kwan Yung-jin, as you shall see, in the days when the Lady Om was kind and power was mine.

160

In prison we lay for many days. We learned afterward the reason. Kwan Yung-jin had sent a dispatch to Keijo, the capital, to find what royal disposition was to be made of us. In the meantime we were a menagerie. From dawn till dark our barred windows were besieged by the natives, for no member of our race had they ever seen before. Nor was our audience mere rabble. Ladies, borne in palanquins on the shoulders of coolies, came to see the strange devils cast up by the sea, and while their attendants drove back the common folk with whips, they would gaze long and timidly at us. Of them we saw little, for their faces were covered, according to the custom of the country. Only dancing girls, low women, and granddams ever were seen abroad with exposed faces.

I have often thought that Kwan Yung-jin suffered from indigestion, and that when the attacks were acute he took it out on us. At any rate, without rhyme or reason, whenever the whim came to him, we were all taken out on the street before the prison and well beaten with sticks to the gleeful shouts of the multitude. The Asiatic is a cruel beast, and delights in spectacles of human suffering.

At any rate we were pleased when an end to our beatings came. This was caused by the arrival of Kim. Kim? All I can say, and the best I can say, is that he was the whitest man I ever encountered in Cho-Sen. He was a captain of fifty men when I met him. He was in command of the palace guards before I was done doing my best by him. And in the end he died for the Lady Om's sake and for mine. Kim—well, Kim was Kim.

Immediately he arrived the planks were taken from our necks and we were lodged in the beet inn the place boasted. We were still prisoners, but honourable prisoners, with a guard of fifty mounted soldiers. The next day we were under way on the royal highroad, fourteen sailormen astride the dwarf horses that obtain in Cho-Sen, and bound for Keijo itself. The Emperor, so Kim told me, had expressed a desire to gaze upon the strangeness of the sea devils.

It was a journey of many days, half the length of Cho-Sen, north and south as it lies. It chanced, at the first off-saddling, that I strolled around

161

to witness the feeding of the dwarf horses. And what I witnessed set me bawling, "What now, Vandervoot?" till all our crew came running. As I am a living man what the horses were feeding on was bean soup, hot bean soup at that, and naught else did they have on all the journey but hot bean soup. It was the custom of the country.

They were truly dwarf horses. On a wager with Kim I lifted one, despite his squeals and struggles, squarely across my shoulders, so that Kim's men, who had already heard my new name, called me Yi Yong-ik, the Mighty One. Kim was a large man as Koreans go, and Koreans are a tall muscular race, and Kim fancied himself a bit. But, elbow to elbow and palm to palm, I put his arm down at will. And his soldiers and the gaping villagers would look on and murmur "Yi Yong-ik."

In a way we were a travelling menagerie. The word went on ahead, so that all the country folk flocked to the roadside to see us pass. It was an unending circus procession. In the towns at night our inns were besieged by multitudes, so that we got no peace until the soldiers drove them off with lance-pricks and blows. But first Kim would call for the village strong men and wrestlers for the fun of seeing me crumple them and put them in the dirt.

Bread there was none, but we ate white rice (the strength of which resides in one's muscles not long), a meat which we found to be dog (which animal is regularly butchered for food in Cho-Sen), and the pickles ungodly hot but which one learns to like exceeding well. And there was drink, real drink, not milky slush, but white, biting stuff distilled from rice, a pint of which would kill a weakling and make a strong man mad and merry. At the walled city of Chong-ho I put Kim and the city notables under the table with the stuff—or on the table, rather, for the table was the floor where we squatted to cramp-knots in my hams for the thousandth time. And again all muttered "Yi Yong-ik," and the word of my prowess passed on before even to Keijo and the Emperor's Court.

I was more an honoured guest than a prisoner, and invariably I rode by Kim's side, my long legs near reaching the ground, and, where the going was deep, my feet scraping the muck. Kim was young. Kim was human. Kim

162

was universal. He was a man anywhere in any country. He and I talked and laughed and joked the day long and half the night. And I verify ate up the language. I had a gift that way anyway. Even Kim marvelled at the way I mastered the idiom. And I learned the Korean points of view, the Korean humour, the Korean soft places, weak places, touchy places. Kim taught me flower songs, love songs, drinking songs. One of the latter was his own, of the end of which I shall give you a crude attempt at translation. Kim and Pak, in their youth, swore a pact to abstain from drinking, which pact was speedily broken. In old age Kim and Pak sing:

"No, no, begone! The merry bowl

Again shall bolster up my soul

Against itself. What, good man, hold!

Canst tell me where red wine is sold?

Nay, just beyond yon peach-tree? There?

Good luck be thine; I'll thither fare."

Hendrik Hamel, scheming and crafty, ever encouraged and urged me in my antic course that brought Kim's favour, not alone to me, but through me to Hendrik Hamel and all our company. I here mention Hendrik Hamel as my adviser, for it has a bearing on much that followed at Keijo in the winning of Yunsan's favour, the Lady Om's heart, and the Emperor's tolerance. I had the will and the fearlessness for the game I played, and some of the wit; but most of the wit I freely admit was supplied me by Hendrik Hamel.

And so we journeyed up to Keijo, from walled city to walled city across a snowy mountain land that was hollowed with innumerable fat farming valleys. And every evening, at fall of day, beacon fires sprang from peak to peak and ran along the land. Always Kim watched for this nightly display. From all the coasts of Cho-Sen, Kim told me, these chains of fire-speech ran

163

to Keijo to carry their message to the Emperor. One beacon meant the land was in peace. Two beacons meant revolt or invasion. We never saw but one beacon. And ever, as we rode, Vandervoot brought up the rear, wondering, "God in heaven, what now?"

Keijo we found a vast city where all the population, with the exception of the nobles or *yang-bans*, dressed in the eternal white. This, Kim explained, was an automatic determination and advertisement of caste. Thus, at a glance, could one tell, the status of an individual by the degrees of cleanness or of filthiness of his garments. It stood to reason that a coolie, possessing but the clothes he stood up in, must be extremely dirty. And to reason it stood that the individual in immaculate white must possess many changes and command the labour of laundresses to keep his changes immaculate. As for the *yang-ban*s who wore the pale, vari-coloured silks, they were beyond such common yardstick of place.

After resting in an inn for several days, during which time we washed our garments and repaired the ravages of shipwreck and travel, we were summoned before the Emperor. In the great open space before the palace wall were colossal stone dogs that looked more like tortoises. They crouched on massive stone pedestals of twice the height of a tall man. The walls of the palace were huge and of dressed stone. So thick were these walls that they could defy a breach from the mightiest of cannon in a year-long siege. The mere gateway was of the size of a palace in itself, rising pagoda-like, in many retreating stories, each story fringed with tile-roofing. A smart guard of soldiers turned out at the gateway. These, Kim told me, were the Tiger Hunters of Pyeng-yang, the fiercest and most terrible fighting men of which Cho-Sen could boast.

But enough. On mere description of the Emperor's palace a thousand pages of my narrative could be worthily expended. Let it suffice that here we knew power in all its material expression. Only a civilization deep and wide and old and strong could produce this far-walled, many-gabled roof of kings.

To no audience-hall were we sea-cunies led, but, as we took it, to a feasting-hall. The feasting was at its end, and all the throng was in a merry

164

mood. And such a throng! High dignitaries, princes of the blood, sworded nobles, pale priests, weather-tanned officers of high command, court ladies with faces exposed, painted *ki-sang* or dancing girls who rested from entertaining, and duennas, waiting women, eunuchs, lackeys, and palace slaves a myriad of them.

All fell away from us, however, when the Emperor, with a following of intimates, advanced to look us over. He was a merry monarch, especially so for an Asiatic. Not more than forty, with a clear, pallid skin that had never known the sun, he was paunched and weak-legged. Yet he had once been a fine man. The noble forehead attested that. But the eyes were bleared and weak-lidded, the lips twitching and trembling from the various excesses in which he indulged, which excesses, as I was to learn, were largely devised and pandered by Yunsan, the Buddhist priest, of whom more anon.

In our sea-garments we mariners were a motley crew, and motley was the cue of our reception. Exclamations of wonder at our strangeness gave way to laughter. The *ki-sang* invaded us, dragging us about, making prisoners of us, two or three of them to one of us, leading us about like go many dancing boars and putting us through our antics. It was offensive, true, but what could poor sea-cunies do? What could old Johannes Maartens do, with a bevy of laughing girls about him, tweaking his nose, pinching his arms, tickling his ribs till he pranced? To escape such torment Hans Amden cleared a space and gave a clumsy-footed Hollandish breakdown till all the Court roared its laughter.

It was offensive to me who had been equal and boon companion of Kim for many days. I resisted the laughing *ki-sang*. I braced my legs and stood upright with folded arms; nor could pinch or tickle bring a quiver from me. Thus they abandoned me for easier prey.

"For God's sake, man, make an impression," Hendrik Hamel, who had struggled to me with three *ki-sang* dragging behind, mumbled.

Well might he mumble, for whenever he opened his mouth to speak they crammed it with sweets.

"Save us from this folly," he persisted, ducking his head about to avoid their sweet-filled palms. "We must have dignity, understand, dignity. This will ruin us. They are making tame animals of us, playthings. When they grow tired of us they will throw us out. You're doing the right thing. Stick to it. Stand them off. Command respect, respect for all of us—"

The last was barely audible, for by this time the *ki-sang* had stuffed his mouth to speechlessness.

As I have said, I had the will and the fearlessness, and I racked my sea-cuny brains for the wit. A palace eunuch, tickling my neck with a feather from behind, gave me my start. I had already drawn attention by my aloofness and imperviousness to the attacks of the *ki-sang*, so that many were looking on at the eunuch's baiting of me. I gave no sign, made no move, until I had located him and distanced him. Then, like a shot, without turning head or body, merely by my arm I fetched him an open, back-handed slap. My knuckles landed flat on his cheek and jaw. There was a crack like a spar parting in a gale. He was bowled clean over, landing in a heap on the floor a dozen feet away.

There was no laughter, only cries of surprise and murmurings and whisperings of "Yi Yong-ik." Again I folded my arms and stood with a fine assumption of haughtiness. I do believe that I, Adam Strang, had among other things the soul of an actor in me. For see what follows. I was now the most significant of our company. Proud-eyed, disdainful, I met unwavering the eyes upon me and made them drop, or turn away—all eyes but one. These were the eyes of a young woman, whom I judged, by richness of dress and by the half-dozen women fluttering at her back, to be a court lady of distinction. In truth, she was the Lady Om, princess of the house of Min. Did I say young? She was fully my own age, thirty, and for all that and her ripeness and beauty a princess still unmarried, as I was to learn.

She alone looked me in the eyes without wavering until it was I who turned away. She did not look me down, for there was neither challenge nor antagonism in her eyes—only fascination. I was loth to admit this defeat by one small woman, and my eyes, turning aside, lighted on the disgraceful rout of my comrades and the trailing *ki-sang* and gave me the pretext. I clapped my hands in the Asiatic fashion when one gives command.

"Let be!" I thundered in their own language, and in the form one addressee underlings.

Oh, I had a chest and a throat, and could bull-roar to the hurt of eardrums. I warrant so loud a command had never before cracked the sacred air of the Emperor's palace.

The great room was aghast. The women were startled, and pressed toward one another as for safety. The *ki-sang* released the cunies and shrank away giggling apprehensively. Only the Lady Om made no sign nor motion but continued to gaze wide-eyed into my eyes which had returned to hers.

Then fell a great silence, as if all waited some word of doom. A multitude of eyes timidly stole back and forth from the Emperor to me and from me to the Emperor. And I had wit to keep the silence and to stand there, arms folded, haughty and remote.

"He speaks our language," quoth the Emperor at the last; and I swear there was such a relinquishment of held breaths that the whole room was one vast sigh.

"I was born with this language," I replied, my cuny wits running rashly to the first madness that prompted. "I spoke it at my mother's breast. I was the marvel of my land. Wise men journeyed far to see me and to hear. But no man knew the words I spoke. In the many years since I have forgotten much, but now, in Cho-Sen, the words come back like long-lost friends."

An impression I certainly made. The Emperor swallowed and his lips twitched ere he asked:

"How explain you this?"

"I am an accident," I answered, following the wayward lead my wit had opened. "The gods of birth were careless, and I was mislaid in a far land and nursed by an alien people. I am Korean, and now, at last, I have come to my home."

What an excited whispering and conferring took place. The Emperor himself interrogated Kim.

"He was always thus, our speech in his mouth, from the time he came out of the sea," Kim lied like the good fellow he was.

"Bring me *yang-ban*'s garments as befits me," I interrupted, "and you shall see." As I was led away in compliance, I turned on the *ki-sang*. "And leave my slaves alone. They have journeyed far and are weary. They are my faithful slaves."

In another room Kim helped me change, sending the lackeys away; and quick and to the point was the dress-rehearsal he gave me. He knew no more toward what I drove than did I, but he was a good fellow.

The funny thing, once back in the crowd and spouting Korean which I claimed was rusty from long disuse, was that Hendrik Hamel and the rest, too stubborn-tongued to learn new speech, did not know a word I uttered.

"I am of the blood of the house of Koryu," I told the Emperor, "that ruled at Songdo many a long year agone when my house arose on the ruins of Silla."

Ancient history, all, told me by Kim on the long ride, and he struggled with his face to hear me parrot his teaching.

"These," I said, when the Emperor had asked me about my company, "these are my slaves, all except that old churl there"—I indicated Johannes Maartens—"who is the son of a freed man." I told Hendrik Hamel to approach. "This one," I wantoned on, "was born in my father's house of a seed slave who was born there before him. He is very close to me. We are of an age, born on the same day, and on that day my father gave him me."

Afterwards, when Hendrik Hamel was eager to know all that I had said, and when I told him, he reproached me and was in a pretty rage.

"The fat's in the fire, Hendrik," quoth I. "What I have done has been out of witlessness and the need to be saying something. But done it is. Nor you nor I can pluck forth the fat. We must act our parts and make the best of it."

Taiwun, the Emperor's brother, was a sot of sots, and as the night wore on he challenged me to a drinking. The Emperor was delighted, and commanded a dozen of the noblest sots to join in the bout. The women were dismissed, and we went to it, drink for drink, measure for measure. Kim I kept by me, and midway along, despite Hendrik Hamel's warning scowls, dismissed him and the company, first requesting, and obtaining, palace lodgment instead of the inn.

Next day the palace was a-buzz with my feast, for I had put Taiwun and all his champions snoring on the mats and walked unaided to my bed. Never, in the days of vicissitude that came later, did Taiwun doubt my claim of Korean birth. Only a Korean, he averred, could possess so strong a head.

The palace was a city in itself, and we were lodged in a sort of summer-house that stood apart. The princely quarters were mine, of course, and Hamel and Maartens, with the rest of the grumbling cunies, had to content themselves with what remained.

I was summoned before Yunsan, the Buddhist priest I have mentioned. It was his first glimpse of me and my first of him. Even Kim he dismissed from me, and we sat alone on deep mats in a twilight room. Lord, Lord, what a man and a mind was Yunsan! He made to probe my soul. He knew things of other lands and places that no one in Cho-Sen dreamed to know. Did he believe my fabled birth? I could not guess, for his face was less changeful than a bowl of bronze.

What Yunsan's thoughts were only Yunsan knew. But in him, this poor-clad, lean-bellied priest, I sensed the power behind power in all the palace and in all Cho-Sen. I sensed also, through the drift of speech, that he had use of me. Now was this use suggested by the Lady Om?—a nut I gave Hendrik Hamel to crack. I little knew, and less I cared, for I lived always in the moment and let others forecast, forfend, and travail their anxiety.

I answered, too, the summons of the Lady Om, following a sleek-faced, cat-footed eunuch through quiet palace byways to her apartments. She lodged as a princess of the blood should lodge. She, too, had a palace to herself, among lotus ponds where grow forests of trees centuries old but so dwarfed that they reached no higher than my middle. Bronze bridges, so delicate and rare that they looked as if fashioned by jewel-smiths, spanned her lily ponds, and a bamboo grove screened her palace apart from all the palace.

My head was awhirl. Sea-cuny that I was, I was no dolt with women, and I sensed more than idle curiosity in her sending for me. I had heard love-tales of common men and queens, and was a-wondering if now it was my fortune to prove such tales true.

The Lady Om wasted little time. There were women about her, but she regarded their presence no more than a carter his horses. I sat beside her on deep mats that made the room half a couch, and wine was given me and sweets to nibble, served on tiny, foot-high tables inlaid with pearl.

Lord, Lord, I had but to look into her eyes—But wait. Make no mistake. The Lady Om was no fool. I have said she was of my own age. All of thirty she was, with the poise of her years. She knew what she wanted. She knew what she did not want. It was because of this she had never married, although all pressure that an Asiatic court could put upon a woman had been vainly put upon her to compel her to marry Chong Mong-ju. He was a lesser cousin of the great Min family, himself no fool, and grasping so greedily for power as to perturb Yunsan, who strove to retain all power himself and keep the palace and Cho-Sen in ordered balance. Thus Yunsan it was who in secret allied himself with the Lady Om, saved her from her cousin, used her to trim her cousin's wings. But enough of intrigue. It was long before I guessed a tithe of it, and then largely through the Lady Om's confidences and Hendrik Hamel's conclusions.

The Lady Om was a very flower of woman. Women such as she are born rarely, scarce twice a century the whole world over. She was unhampered by rule or convention. Religion, with her, was a series of abstractions, partly learned from Yunsan, partly worked out for herself. Vulgar religion, the public religion, she held, was a device to keep the toiling millions to their toil. She had a will of her own, and she had a heart all womanly. She was a beauty—yes, a beauty by any set rule of the world. Her large black eyes were neither slitted nor slanted in the Asiatic way. They were long, true, but set squarely, and with just the slightest hint of obliqueness that was all for piquancy.

I have said she was no fool. Behold! As I palpitated to the situation, princess and sea-cuny and love not a little that threatened big, I racked my cuny's brains for wit to carry the thing off with manhood credit. It chanced, early in this first meeting, that I mentioned what I had told all the Court, that I was in truth a Korean of the blood of the ancient house of Koryu.

"Let be," she said, tapping my lips with her peacock fan. "No child's tales here. Know that with me you are better and greater than of any house of Koryu. You are . . ."

She paused, and I waited, watching the daring grow in her eyes.

"You are a man," she completed. "Not even in my sleep have I ever dreamed there was such a man as you on his two legs upstanding in the world."

Lord, Lord! and what could a poor sea-cuny do? This particular sea-cuny, I admit, blushed through his sea tan till the Lady Om's eyes were twin pools of roguishness in their teasing deliciousness and my arms were all but about her. And she laughed tantalizingly and alluringly, and clapped her hands for her women, and I knew that the audience, for this once, was over. I knew, also, there would be other audiences, there must be other audiences.

Back to Hamel, my head awhirl.

"The woman," said he, after deep cogitation. He looked at me and sighed an envy I could not mistake. "It is your brawn, Adam Strang, that bull throat of yours, your yellow hair. Well, it's the game, man. Play her, and all will be well with us. Play her, and I shall teach you how."

I bristled. Sea-cuny I was, but I was man, and to no man would I be beholden in my way with women. Hendrik Hamel might be one time part-owner of the old *Sparwehr*, with a navigator's knowledge of the stars and deep versed in books, but with women, no, there I would not give him better.

He smiled that thin-lipped smile of his, and queried:

171

"How like you the Lady Om?"

"In such matters a cuny is naught particular," I temporized.

"How like you her?" he repeated, his beady eyes boring into me.

"Passing well, ay, and more than passing well, if you will have it."

"Then win to her," he commanded, "and some day we will get ship and escape from this cursed land. I'd give half the silks of the Indies for a meal of Christian food again."

He regarded me intently.

"Do you think you can win to her?" he questioned.

I was half in the air at the challenge. He smiled his satisfaction.

"But not too quickly," he advised. "Quick things are cheap things. Put a prize upon yourself. Be chary of your kindnesses. Make a value of your bull throat and yellow hair, and thank God you have them, for they are of more worth in a woman's eyes than are the brains of a dozen philosophers."

Strange whirling days were those that followed, what of my audiences with the Emperor, my drinking bouts with Taiwun, my conferences with Yunsan, and my hours with the Lady Om. Besides, I sat up half the nights, by Hamel's command, learning from Kim all the minutiæ of court etiquette and manners, the history of Korea and of gods old and new, and the forms of polite speech, noble speech, and coolie speech. Never was sea-cuny worked so hard. I was a puppet—puppet to Yunsan, who had need of me; puppet to Hamel, who schemed the wit of the affair that was so deep that alone I should have drowned. Only with the Lady Om was I man, not puppet . . . and yet, and yet, as I look back and ponder across time, I have my doubts. I think the Lady Om, too, had her will with me, wanting me for her heart's desire. Yet in this she was well met, for it was not long ere she was my heart's desire, and such was the immediacy of my will that not her will, nor Hendrik Hamel's, nor Yunsan's, could hold back my arms from about her.

In the meantime, however, I was caught up in a palace intrigue I could not fathom. I could catch the drift of it, no more, against Chong Mong-ju, the princely cousin of the Lady Om. Beyond my guessing there were cliques and cliques within cliques that made a labyrinth of the palace and extended to all the Seven Coasts. But I did not worry. I left that to Hendrik Hamel. To him I reported every detail that occurred when he was not with me; and he, with furrowed brows, sitting darkling by the hour, like a patient spider unravelled the tangle and spun the web afresh. As my body slave he insisted upon attending me everywhere; being only barred on occasion by Yunsan. Of course I barred him from my moments with the Lady Om, but told him in general what passed, with exception of tenderer incidents that were not his business.

I think Hamel was content to sit back and play the secret part. He was too cold-blooded not to calculate that the risk was mine. If I prospered, he prospered. If I crashed to ruin, he might creep out like a ferret. I am convinced that he so reasoned, and yet it did not save him in the end, as you shall see.

"Stand by me," I told Kim, "and whatsoever you wish shall be yours. Have you a wish?"

"I would command the Tiger Hunters of Pyeng-Yang, and so command the palace guards," he answered.

"Wait," said I, "and that will you do. I have said it."

The how of the matter was beyond me. But he who has naught can dispense the world in largess; and I, who had naught, gave Kim captaincy of the palace guards. The best of it is that I did fulfil my promise. Kim did come to command the Tiger Hunters, although it brought him to a sad end.

Scheming and intriguing I left to Hamel and Yunsan, who were the politicians. I was mere man and lover, and merrier than theirs was the time I had. Picture it to yourself—a hard-bitten, joy-loving sea-cuny, irresponsible, unaware ever of past or future, wining and dining with kings, the accepted lover of a princess, and with brains like Hamel's and Yunsan's to do all planning and executing for me.

More than once Yunsan almost divined the mind behind my mind; but when he probed Hamel, Hamel proved a stupid slave, a thousand times less interested in affairs of state and policy than was he interested in my health and comfort and garrulously anxious about my drinking contests with Taiwun. I think the Lady Om guessed the truth and kept it to herself; wit was not her desire, but, as Hamel had said, a bull throat and a man's yellow hair.

Much that pawed between us I shall not relate, though the Lady Om is dear dust these centuries. But she was not to be denied, nor was I; and when a man and woman will their hearts together heads may fall and kingdoms crash and yet they will not forgo.

Came the time when our marriage was mooted—oh, quietly, at first, most quietly, as mere palace gossip in dark corners between eunuchs and waiting-women. But in a palace the gossip of the kitchen scullions will creep to the throne. Soon there was a pretty to-do. The palace was the pulse of Cho-Sen, and when the palace rocked, Cho-Sen trembled. And there was reason for the rocking. Our marriage would be a blow straight between the eyes of Chong Mong-ju. He fought, with a show of strength for which Yunsan was ready. Chong Mong-ju disaffected half the provincial priesthood, until they pilgrimaged in processions a mile long to the palace gates and frightened the Emperor into a panic.

But Yunsan held like a rock. The other half of the provincial priesthood was his, with, in addition, all the priesthood of the great cities such as Keijo, Fusan, Songdo, Pyen-Yang, Chenampo, and Chemulpo. Yunsan and the Lady Om, between them, twisted the Emperor right about. As she confessed to me afterward, she bullied him with tears and hysteria and threats of a scandal that would shake the throne. And to cap it all, at the psychological moment, Yunsan pandered the Emperor to novelties of excess that had been long preparing.

"You must grow your hair for the marriage knot," Yunsan warned me one day, with the ghost of a twinkle in his austere eyes, more nearly facetious and human than I had ever beheld him.

Now it is not meet that a princess espouse a sea-cuny, or even a claimant of the ancient blood of Koryu, who is without power, or place, or visible symbols of rank. So it was promulgated by imperial decree that I was a prince of Koryu. Next, after breaking the bones and decapitating the then governor of the five provinces, himself an adherent of Chong Mong-ju, I was made governor of the seven home provinces of ancient Koryu. In Cho-Sen seven is the magic number. To complete this number two of the provinces were taken over from the hands of two more of Chong Mong-ju's adherents.

Lord, Lord, a sea-cuny . . . and dispatched north over the Mandarin Road with five hundred soldiers and a retinue at my back! I was a governor of seven provinces, where fifty thousand troops awaited me. Life, death, and torture, I carried at my disposal. I had a treasury and a treasurer, to say nothing of a regiment of scribes. Awaiting me also was a full thousand of tax-farmers; who squeezed the last coppers from the toiling people.

The seven provinces constituted the northern march. Beyond lay what is now Manchuria, but which was known by us as the country of the Hong-du, or "Red Heads." They were wild raiders, on occasion crossing the Yalu in great masses and over-running northern Cho-Sen like locusts. It was said they were given to cannibal practices. I know of experience that they were terrible fighters, most difficult to convince of a beating.

A whirlwind year it was. While Yunsan and the Lady Om at Keijo completed the disgrace of Chong Mong-ju, I proceeded to make a reputation for myself. Of course it was really Hendrik Hamel at my back, but I was the fine figure-head that carried it off. Through me Hamel taught our soldiers drill and tactics and taught the Red Heads strategy. The fighting was grand, and though it took a year, the year's end saw peace on the northern border and no Red Heads but dead Red Heads on our side the Yalu.

I do not know if this invasion of the Red Heads is recorded in Western history, but if so it will give a clue to the date of the times of which I write. Another clue: when was Hideyoshi the Shogun of Japan? In my time I heard the echoes of the two invasions, a generation before, driven by Hideyoshi through the heart of Cho-Sen from Fusan in the south to as far north as

Pyeng-Yang. It was this Hideyoshi who sent back to Japan a myriad tubs of pickled ears and noses of Koreans slain in battle. I talked with many old men and women who had seen the fighting and escaped the pickling.

Back to Keijo and the Lady Om. Lord, Lord, she was a woman. For forty years she was my woman. I know. No dissenting voice was raised against the marriage. Chong Mong-ju, clipped of power, in disgrace, had retired to sulk somewhere on the far north-east coast. Yunsan was absolute. Nightly the single beacons flared their message of peace across the land. The Emperor grew more weak-legged and blear-eyed what of the ingenious deviltries devised for him by Yunsan. The Lady Om and I had won to our hearts' desires. Kim was in command of the palace guards. Kwan Yung-jin, the provincial governor who had planked and beaten us when we were first cast away, I had shorn of power and banished for ever from appearing within the walls of Keijo.

Oh, and Johannes Maartens. Discipline is well hammered into a sea-cuny, and, despite my new greatness, I could never forget that he had been my captain in the days we sought new Indies in the *Sparwehr*. According to my tale first told in Court, he was the only free man in my following. The rest of the cunies, being considered my slaves, could not aspire to office of any sort under the crown. But Johannes could, and did. The sly old fox! I little guessed his intent when he asked me to make him governor of the paltry little province of Kyong-ju. Kyong-ju had no wealth of farms or fisheries. The taxes scarce paid the collecting, and the governorship was little more than an empty honour. The place was in truth a graveyard—a sacred graveyard, for on Tabong Mountain were shrined and sepultured the bones of the ancient kings of Silla. Better governor of Kyong-ju than retainer of Adam Strang, was what I thought was in his mind; nor did I dream that it was except for fear of loneliness that caused him to take four of the cunies with him.

Gorgeous were the two years that followed. My seven provinces I governed mainly though needy *yang-ban*s selected for me by Yunsan. An occasional inspection, done in state and accompanied by the Lady Om, was all that was required of me. She possessed a summer palace on the south coast, which we frequented much. Then there were man's diversions. I became patron of the sport of wrestling, and revived archery among the *yang-bans*. Also, there was tiger-hunting in the northern mountains.

A remarkable thing was the tides of Cho-Sen. On our north-east coast there was scarce a rise and fall of a foot. On our west coast the neap tides ran as high as sixty feet. Cho-Sen had no commerce, no foreign traders. There was no voyaging beyond her coasts, and no voyaging of other peoples to her coasts. This was due to her immemorial policy of isolation. Once in a decade or a score of years Chinese ambassadors arrived, but they came overland, around the Yellow Sea, across the country of the Hong-du, and down the Mandarin Road to Keijo. The round trip was a year-long journey. Their mission was to exact from our Emperor the empty ceremonial of acknowledgment of China's ancient suzerainty.

But Hamel, from long brooding, was ripening for action. His plans grew apace. Cho-Sen was Indies enough for him could he but work it right. Little he confided, but when he began to play to have me made admiral of the Cho-Sen navy of junks, and to inquire more than casually of the details of the store-places of the imperial treasury, I could put two and two together.

Now I did not care to depart from Cho-Sen except with the Lady Om. When I broached the possibility of it she told me, warm in my arms, that I was her king and that wherever I led she would follow. As you shall see it was truth, full truth, that she uttered.

It was Yunsan's fault for letting Chong Mong-ju live. And yet it was not Yunsan's fault. He had not dared otherwise. Disgraced at Court, nevertheless Chong Mong-ju had been too popular with the provincial priesthood. Yunsan had been compelled to hold his hand, and Chong Mong-ju, apparently sulking on the north-east coast, had been anything but idle. His emissaries, chiefly Buddhist priests, were everywhere, went everywhere, gathering in even the least of the provincial magistrates to allegiance to him. It takes the cold patience of the Asiatic to conceive and execute huge and complicated conspiracies. The strength of Chong Mong-ju's palace clique grew beyond Yunsan's wildest dreaming. Chong Mong-ju corrupted the very palace guards, the Tiger Hunters of Pyeng-Yang whom Kim commanded.

And while Yunsan nodded, while I devoted myself to sport and to the Lady Om, while Hendrik Hamel perfected plans for the looting of the Imperial treasury, and while Johannes Maartens schemed his own scheme among the tombs of Tabong Mountain, the volcano of Chong Mong-ju's devising gave no warning beneath us.

Lord, Lord, when the storm broke! It was stand out from under, all hands, and save your necks. And there were necks that were not saved. The springing of the conspiracy was premature. Johannes Maartens really precipitated the catastrophe, and what he did was too favourable for Chong Mong-ju not to advantage by.

For, see. The people of Cho-Sen are fanatical ancestor-worshippers, and that old pirate of a booty-lusting Dutchman, with his four cunies, in far Kyong-ju, did no less a thing than raid the tombs of the gold-coffined, long-buried kings of ancient Silla. The work was done in the night, and for the rest of the night they travelled for the sea-coast. But the following day a dense fog lay over the land and they lost their way to the waiting junk which Johannes Maartens had privily outfitted. He and the cunies were rounded in by Yi Sun-sin, the local magistrate, one of Chong Mong-ju's adherents. Only Herman Tromp escaped in the fog, and was able, long after, to tell me of the adventure.

That night, although news of the sacrilege was spreading through Cho-Sen and half the northern provinces had risen on their officials, Keijo and the Court slept in ignorance. By Chong Mong-ju's orders the beacons flared their nightly message of peace. And night by night the peace-beacons flared, while day and night Chong Mong-ju's messengers killed horses on all the roads of Cho-Sen. It was my luck to see his messenger arrive at Keijo. At twilight, as I rode out through the great gate of the capital, I saw the jaded horse fall and the exhausted rider stagger in on foot; and I little dreamed that that man carried my destiny with him into Keijo.

His message sprang the palace revolution. I was not due to return until midnight, and by midnight all was over. At nine in the evening the conspirators secured possession of the Emperor in his own apartments. They compelled him to order the immediate attendance of the heads of all departments, and as they presented themselves, one by one, before his eyes, they were cut down. Meantime the Tiger Hunters were up and out of hand. Yunsan and Hendrik Hamel were badly beaten with the flats of swords and made prisoners. The seven other cunies escaped from the palace along with the Lady Om. They were enabled to do this by Kim, who held the way, sword in hand, against his own Tiger Hunters. They cut him down and trod over him. Unfortunately he did not die of his wounds.

Like a flaw of wind on a summer night the revolution, a palace revolution of course, blew and was past. Chong Mong-ju was in the saddle. The Emperor ratified whatever Chong Mong-ju willed. Beyond gasping at the sacrilege of the king's tombs and applauding Chong Mong-ju, Cho-Sen was unperturbed. Heads of officials fell everywhere, being replaced by Chong Mong-ju's appointees; but there were no risings against the dynasty.

And now to what befell us. Johannes Maartens and his three cunies, after being exhibited to be spat upon by the rabble of half the villages and walled cities of Cho-Sen, were buried to their necks in the ground of the open space before the palace gate. Water was given them that they might live longer to yearn for the food, steaming hot and savoury and changed hourly, that was place temptingly before them. They say old Johannes Maartens lived longest, not giving up the ghost for a full fifteen days.

Kim was slowly crushed to death, bone by bone and joint by joint, by the torturers, and was a long time in dying. Hamel, whom Chong Mong-ju divined as my brains, was executed by the paddle—in short, was promptly and expeditiously beaten to death to the delighted shouts of the Keijo populace. Yunsan was given a brave death. He was playing a game of chess with the jailer, when the Emperor's, or, rather, Chong Mong-ju's, messenger arrived with the poison-cup. "Wait a moment," said Yunsan. "You should be better-mannered than to disturb a man in the midst of a game of chess. I shall drink directly the game is over." And while the messenger waited Yunsan finished the game, winning it, then drained the cup.

It takes an Asiatic to temper his spleen to steady, persistent, life-long revenge. This Chong Mong-ju did with the Lady Om and me. He did not destroy us. We were not even imprisoned. The Lady Om was degraded of all rank and divested of all possessions. An imperial decree was promulgated and posted in the last least village of Cho-Sen to the effect that I was of the house of Koryu and that no man might kill me. It was further declared that the eight sea-cunies who survived must not be killed. Neither were they to be favoured. They were to be outcasts, beggars on the highways. And that is what the Lady Om and I became, beggars on the highways.

Forty long years of persecution followed, for Chong Mong-ju's hatred of the Lady Om and me was deathless. Worse luck, he was favoured with long life as well as were we cursed with it. I have said the Lady Om was a wonder of a woman. Beyond endlessly repeating that statement, words fail me, with which to give her just appreciation. Somewhere I have heard that a great lady once said to her lover: "A tent and a crust of bread with you." In effect that is what the Lady Om said to me. More than to say it, she lived the last letter of it, when more often than not crusts were not plentiful and the sky itself was our tent.

Every effort I made to escape beggary was in the end frustrated by Chong Mong-ju. In Songdo I became a fuel-carrier, and the Lady Om and I shared a hut that was vastly more comfortable than the open road in bitter winter weather. But Chong Mong-ju found me out, and I was beaten and planked and put out upon the road. That was a terrible winter, the winter poor "What-Now" Vandervoot froze to death on the streets of Keijo.

In Pyeng-yang I became a water-carrier, for know that that old city, whose walls were ancient even in the time of David, was considered by the people to be a canoe, and that, therefore, to sink a well inside the walls would be to scupper the city. So all day long thousands of coolies, water-jars yoked to their shoulders, tramp out the river gate and back. I became one of these, until Chong Mong-ju sought me out, and I was beaten and planked and set upon the highway.

Ever it was the same. In far Wiju I became a dog-butcher, killing the brutes publicly before my open stall, cutting and hanging the caresses for sale, tanning the hides under the filth of the feet of the passers-by by spreading

180

the hides, raw-side up, in the muck of the street. But Chong Mong-ju found me out. I was a dyer's helper in Pyonhan, a gold-miner in the placers of Kang-wun, a rope-maker and twine-twister in Chiksan. I plaited straw hats in Padok, gathered grass in Whang-hai, and in Masenpo sold myself to a rice farmer to toil bent double in the flooded paddies for less than a coolie's pay. But there was never a time or place that the long arm of Chong Mong-ju did not reach out and punish and thrust me upon the beggar's way.

The Lady Om and I searched two seasons and found a single root of the wild mountain ginseng, which is esteemed so rare and precious a thing by the doctors that the Lady Om and I could have lived a year in comfort from the sale of our one root. But in the selling of it I was apprehended, the root confiscated, and I was better beaten and longer planked than ordinarily.

Everywhere the wandering members of the great Peddlers' Guild carried word of me, of my comings and goings and doings, to Chong Mong-ju at Keijo. Only twice, in all the days after my downfall, did I meet Chong Mong-ju face to face. The first time was a wild winter night of storm in the high mountains of Kang-wun. A few hoarded coppers had bought for the Lady Om and me sleeping space in the dirtiest and coldest corner of the one large room of the inn. We were just about to begin on our meagre supper of horse-beans and wild garlic cooked into a stew with a scrap of bullock that must have died of old age, when there was a tinkling of bronze pony bells and the stamp of hoofs without. The doors opened, and entered Chong Mong-ju, the personification of well-being, prosperity and power, shaking the snow from his priceless Mongolian furs. Place was made for him and his dozen retainers, and there was room for all without crowding, when his eyes chanced to light on the Lady Om and me.

"The vermin there in the corner—clear it out," he commanded.

And his horse-boys lashed us with their whips and drove us out into the storm. But there was to be another meeting, after long years, as you shall see.

There was no escape. Never was I permitted to cross the northern frontier. Never was I permitted to put foot to a sampan on the sea. The Peddlers' Guild carried these commands of Chong Mong-ju to every village and every soul in all Cho-Sen. I was a marked man.

181

Lord, Lord, Cho-Sen, I know your every highway and mountain path, all your walled cities and the least of your villages. For two-score years I wandered and starved over you, and the Lady Om ever wandered and starved with me. What we in extremity have eaten!—Leavings of dog's flesh, putrid and unsaleable, flung to us by the mocking butchers; *minari*, a water-cress gathered from stagnant pools of slime; spoiled *kimchi* that would revolt the stomachs of peasants and that could be smelled a mile. Ay—I have stolen bones from curs, gleaned the public road for stray grains of rice, robbed ponies of their steaming bean-soup on frosty nights.

It is not strange that I did not die. I knew and was upheld by two things: the first, the Lady Om by my side; the second, the certain faith that the time would come when my thumbs and fingers would fast-lock in the gullet of Chong Mong-ju.

Turned always away at the city gates of Keijo, where I sought Chong Mong-ju, we wandered on, through seasons and decades of seasons, across Cho-Sen, whose every inch of road was an old story to our sandals. Our history and identity were wide-scattered as the land was wide. No person breathed who did not know us and our punishment. There were coolies and peddlers who shouted insults at the Lady Om and who felt the wrath of my clutch in their topknots, the wrath of my knuckles in their faces. There were old women in far mountain villages who looked on the beggar woman by my side, the lost Lady Om, and sighed and shook their heads while their eyes dimmed with tears. And there were young women whose faces warmed with compassion as they gazed on the bulk of my shoulders, the blue of my eyes, and my long yellow hair—I who had once been a prince of Koryu and the ruler of provinces. And there were rabbles of children that tagged at our heels, jeering and screeching, pelting us with filth of speech and of the common road.

Beyond the Yalu, forty miles wide, was the strip of waste that constituted the northern frontier and that ran from sea to sea. It was not really waste land, but land that had been deliberately made waste in carrying out Cho-Sen's policy of isolation. On this forty-mile strip all farms, villages and cities had been destroyed. It was no man's land, infested with wild animals and traversed by companies of mounted Tiger Hunters whose business was to kill any human being they found. That way there was no escape for us, nor was there any escape for us by sea.

As the years passed my seven fellow-cunies came more to frequent Fusan. It was on the south-east coast where the climate was milder. But more than climate, it lay nearest of all Cho-Sen to Japan. Across the narrow straits, just farther than the eye can see, was the one hope of escape Japan, where doubtless occasional ships of Europe came. Strong upon me is the vision of those seven ageing men on the cliffs of Fusan yearning with all their souls across the sea they would never sail again.

At times junks of Japan were sighted, but never lifted a familiar topsail of old Europe above the sea-rim. Years came and went, and the seven cunies and myself and the Lady Om, passing through middle life into old age, more and more directed our footsteps to Fusan. And as the years came and went, now one, now another failed to gather at the usual place. Hans Amden was the first to die. Jacob Brinker, who was his road-mate, brought the news. Jacob Brinker was the last of the seven, and he was nearly ninety when he died, outliving Tromp a scant two years. I well remember the pair of them, toward the last, worn and feeble, in beggars' rags, with beggars' bowls, sunning themselves side by side on the cliffs, telling old stories and cackling shrill-voiced like children. And Tromp would maunder over and over of how Johannes Maartens and the cunies robbed the kings on Tabong Mountain, each embalmed in his golden coffin with an embalmed maid on either side; and of how these ancient proud ones crumbled to dust within the hour while the cunies cursed and sweated at junking the coffins.

As sure as loot is loot, old Johannes Maartens would have got away and across the Yellow Sea with his booty had it not been for the fog next day that lost him. That cursed fog! A song was made of it, that I heard and hated through all Cho-Sen to my dying day. Here run two lines of it:

> "*Yanggukeni chajin anga*
> *Wheanpong tora deunda,*
> The thick fog of the Westerners
> Broods over Whean peak."

For forty years I was a beggar of Cho-Sen. Of the fourteen of us that were cast away only I survived. The Lady Om was of the same indomitable stuff, and we aged together. She was a little, weazened, toothless old woman toward the last; but ever she was the wonder woman, and she carried my heart in hers to the end. For an old man, three score and ten, I still retained great strength. My face was withered, my yellow hair turned white, my broad shoulders shrunken, and yet much of the strength of my sea-cuny days resided in the muscles left me.

Thus it was that I was able to do what I shall now relate. It was a spring morning on the cliffs of Fusan, hard by the highway, that the Lady Om and I sat warming in the sun. We were in the rags of beggary, prideless in the dust, and yet I was laughing heartily at some mumbled merry quip of the Lady Om when a shadow fell upon us. It was the great litter of Chong Mong-ju, borne by eight coolies, with outriders before and behind and fluttering attendants on either side.

Two emperors, civil war, famine, and a dozen palace revolutions had come and gone; and Chong Mong-ju remained, even then the great power at Keijo. He must have been nearly eighty that spring morning on the cliffs when he signalled with palsied hand for his litter to be rested down that he might gaze upon us whom he had punished for so long.

"Now, O my king," the Lady Om mumbled low to me, then turned to whine an alms of Chong Mong-ju, whom she affected not to recognize.

And I knew what was her thought. Had we not shared it for forty years? And the moment of its consummation had come at last. So I, too, affected not to recognize my enemy, and, putting on an idiotic senility, I, too, crawled in the dust toward the litter whining for mercy and charity.

The attendants would have driven me back, but with age-quavering cackles Chong Mong-ju restrained them. He lifted himself on a shaking elbow, and with the other shaking hand drew wider apart the silken curtains. His withered old face was transfigured with delight as he gloated on us.

"O my king," the Lady Om whined to me in her beggar's chant; and I knew all her long-tried love and faith in my emprise were in that chant.

And the red wrath was up in me, ripping and tearing at my will to be free. Small wonder that I shook with the effort to control. The shaking, happily, they took for the weakness of age. I held up my brass begging bowl, and whined more dolefully, and bleared my eyes to hide the blue fire I knew was in them, and calculated the distance and my strength for the leap.

Then I was swept away in a blaze of red. There was a crashing of curtains and curtain-poles and a squawking and squalling of attendants as my hands closed on Chong Mong-ju's throat. The litter overturned, and I scarce knew whether I was heads or heels, but my clutch never relaxed.

In the confusion of cushions and quilts and curtains, at first few of the attendants' blows found me. But soon the horsemen were in, and their heavy whip-butts began to fall on my head, while a multitude of hands clawed and tore at me. I was dizzy, but not unconscious, and very blissful with my old fingers buried in that lean and scraggly old neck I had sought for so long. The blows continued to rain on my head, and I had whirling thoughts in which I likened myself to a bulldog with jaws fast-locked. Chong Mong-ju could not escape me, and I know he was well dead ere darkness, like that of an anæsthetic, descended upon me there on the cliffs of Fusan by the Yellow Sea.

CHAPTER XVI

Warden Atherton, when he thinks of me, must feel anything but pride. I have taught him what spirit is, humbled him with my own spirit that rose invulnerable, triumphant, above all his tortures. I sit here in Folsom, in Murderers' Row, awaiting my execution; Warden Atherton still holds his political job and is king over San Quentin and all the damned within its walls; and yet, in his heart of hearts, he knows that I am greater than he.

In vain Warden Atherton tried to break my spirit. And there were times, beyond any shadow of doubt, when he would have been glad had I died in the jacket. So the long inquisition went on. As he had told me, and as he told me repeatedly, it was dynamite or curtains.

Captain Jamie was a veteran in dungeon horrors, yet the time came when he broke down under the strain I put on him and on the rest of my torturers. So desperate did he become that he dared words with the Warden and washed his hands of the affair. From that day until the end of my torturing he never set foot in solitary.

Yes, and the time came when Warden Atherton grew afraid, although he still persisted in trying to wring from me the hiding-place of the non-existent dynamite. Toward the last he was badly shaken by Jake Oppenheimer. Oppenheimer was fearless and outspoken. He had passed unbroken through all their prison hells, and out of superior will could beard them to their teeth. Morrell rapped me a full account of the incident. I was unconscious in the jacket at the time.

"Warden," Oppenheimer had said, "you've bitten off more than you can chew. It ain't a case of killing Standing. It's a case of killing three men, for as sure as you kill him, sooner or later Morrell and I will get the word out and what you have done will be known from one end of California to the other. You've got your choice. You've either got to let up on Standing or kill all three of us. Standing's got your goat. So have I. So has Morrell. You are a stinking coward, and you haven't got the backbone and guts to carry out the dirty butcher's work you'd like to do."

Oppenheimer got a hundred hours in the jacket for it, and, when he was unlaced, spat in the Warden's face and received a second hundred hours on end. When he was unlaced this time, the Warden was careful not to be in solitary. That he was shaken by Oppenheimer's words there is no doubt.

But it was Doctor Jackson who was the arch-fiend. To him I was a novelty, and he was ever eager to see how much more I could stand before I broke.

"He can stand twenty days off the bat," he bragged to the Warden in my presence.

"You are conservative," I broke in. "I can stand forty days. Pshaw! I can stand a hundred when such as you administer it." And, remembering my sea-cuny's patience of forty years' waiting ere I got my hands on Chong Mong-ju's gullet, I added: "You prison curs, you don't know what a man is. You think a man is made in your own cowardly images. Behold, I am a man. You are feeblings. I am your master. You can't bring a squeal out of me. You think it remarkable, for you know how easily you would squeal."

Oh, I abused them, called them sons of toads, hell's scullions, slime of the pit. For I was above them, beyond them. They were slaves. I was free spirit. My flesh only lay pent there in solitary. I was not pent. I had mastered the flesh, and the spaciousness of time was mine to wander in, while my poor flesh, not even suffering, lay in the little death in the jacket.

Much of my adventures I rapped to my two comrades. Morrell believed, for he had himself tasted the little death. But Oppenheimer, enraptured with my tales, remained a sceptic to the end. His regret was naïve, and at times really pathetic, in that I had devoted my life to the science of agriculture instead of to fiction writing.

"But, man," I reasoned with him, "what do I know of myself about this Cho-Sen? I am able to identify it with what is to-day called Korea, and that is about all. That is as far as my reading goes. For instance, how possibly, out of my present life's experience, could I know anything about *kimchi*? Yet I know *kimchi*. It is a sort of sauerkraut. When it is spoiled it stinks to heaven.

187

I tell you, when I was Adam Strang, I ate *kimchi* thousands of times. I know good *kimchi*, bad *kimchi*, rotten *kimchi*. I know the best *kimchi* is made by the women of Wosan. Now how do I know that? It is not in the content of my mind, Darrell Standing's mind. It is in the content of Adam Strang's mind, who, through various births and deaths, bequeathed his experiences to me, Darrell Standing, along with the rest of the experiences of those various other lives that intervened. Don't you see, Jake? That is how men come to be, to grow, how spirit develops."

"Aw, come off," he rapped back with the quick imperative knuckles I knew so well. "Listen to your uncle talk now. I am Jake Oppenheimer. I always have been Jake Oppenheimer. No other guy is in my makings. What I know I know as Jake Oppenheimer. Now what do I know? I'll tell you one thing. I know *kimchi*. *Kimchi* is a sort of sauerkraut made in a country that used to be called Cho-Sen. The women of Wosan make the best *kimchi*, and when *kimchi* is spoiled it stinks to heaven. You keep out of this, Ed. Wait till I tie the professor up.

"Now, professor, how do I know all this stuff about *kimchi*? It is not in the content of my mind."

"But it is," I exulted. "I put it there."

"All right, old boss. Then who put it into your mind?"

"Adam Strang."

"Not on your tintype. Adam Strang is a pipe-dream. You read it somewhere."

"Never," I averred. "The little I read of Korea was the war correspondence at the time of the Japanese-Russian War."

"Do you remember all you read?" Oppenheimer queried.

"No."

"Some you forget?"

"Yes, but—"

"That's all, thank you," he interrupted, in the manner of a lawyer abruptly concluding a cross-examination after having extracted a fatal admission from a witness.

It was impossible to convince Oppenheimer of my sincerity. He insisted that I was making it up as I went along, although he applauded what he called my "to-be-continued-in-our-next," and, at the times they were resting me up from the jacket, was continually begging and urging me to run off a few more chapters.

"Now, professor, cut out that high-brow stuff," he would interrupt Ed Morrell's and my metaphysical discussions, "and tell us more about the *ki-sang* and the cunies. And, say, while you're about it, tell us what happened to the Lady Om when that rough-neck husband of hers choked the old geezer and croaked."

How often have I said that form perishes. Let me repeat. Form perishes. Matter has no memory. Spirit only remembers, as here, in prison cells, after the centuries, knowledge of the Lady Om and Chong Mong-ju persisted in my mind, was conveyed by me into Jake Oppenheimer's mind, and by him was reconveyed into my mind in the argot and jargon of the West. And now I have conveyed it into your mind, my reader. Try to eliminate it from your mind. You cannot. As long as you live what I have told will tenant your mind. Mind? There is nothing permanent but mind. Matter fluxes, crystallizes, and fluxes again, and forms are never repeated. Forms disintegrate into the eternal nothingness from which there is no return. Form is apparitional and passes, as passed the physical forms of the Lady Om and Chong Mong-ju. But the memory of them remains, shall always remain as long as spirit endures, and spirit is indestructible.

"One thing sticks out as big as a house," was Oppenheimer's final criticism of my Adam Strang adventure. "And that is that you've done more hanging around Chinatown dumps and hop-joints than was good for a respectable college professor. Evil communications, you know. I guess that's what brought you here."

Before I return to my adventures I am compelled to tell one remarkable incident that occurred in solitary. It is remarkable in two ways. It shows the astounding mental power of that child of the gutters, Jake Oppenheimer; and it is in itself convincing proof of the verity of my experiences when in the jacket coma.

"Say, professor," Oppenheimer tapped to me one day. "When you was spieling that Adam Strang yarn, I remember you mentioned playing chess with that royal souse of an emperor's brother. Now is that chess like our kind of chess?"

Of course I had to reply that I did not know, that I did not remember the details after I returned to my normal state. And of course he laughed good-naturedly at what he called my foolery. Yet I could distinctly remember that in my Adam Strang adventure I had frequently played chess. The trouble was that whenever I came back to consciousness in solitary, unessential and intricate details faded from my memory.

It must be remembered that for convenience I have assembled my intermittent and repetitional jacket experiences into coherent and consecutive narratives. I never knew in advance where my journeys in time would take me. For instance, I have a score of different times returned to Jesse Fancher in the wagon-circle at Mountain Meadows. In a single ten-days' bout in the jacket I have gone back and back, from life to life, and often skipping whole series of lives that at other times I have covered, back to prehistoric time, and back of that to days ere civilization began.

So I resolved, on my next return from Adam Strang's experiences, whenever it might be, that I should, immediately, I on resuming consciousness, concentrate upon what visions and memories. I had brought back of chess playing. As luck would have it, I had to endure Oppenheimer's chaffing for a full month ere it happened. And then, no sooner out of jacket and circulation restored, than I started knuckle-rapping the information.

Further, I taught Oppenheimer the chess Adam Strang had played in Cho-Sen centuries agone. It was different from Western chess, and yet could not but be fundamentally the same, tracing back to a common origin, probably India. In place of our sixty-four squares there are eighty-one squares.

We have eight pawns on a side; they have nine; and though limited similarly, the principle of moving is different.

Also, in the Cho-Sen game, there are twenty pieces and pawns against our sixteen, and they are arrayed in three rows instead of two. Thus, the nine pawns are in the front row; in the middle row are two pieces resembling our castles; and in the back row, midway, stands the king, flanked in order on either side by "gold money," "silver money," "knight," and "spear." It will be observed that in the Cho-Sen game there is no queen. A further radical variation is that a captured piece or pawn is not removed from the board. It becomes the property of the captor and is thereafter played by him.

Well, I taught Oppenheimer this game—a far more difficult achievement than our own game, as will be admitted, when the capturing and recapturing and continued playing of pawns and pieces is considered. Solitary is not heated. It would be a wickedness to ease a convict from any spite of the elements. And many a dreary day of biting cold did Oppenheimer and I forget that and the following winter in the absorption of Cho-Sen chess.

But there was no convincing him that I had in truth brought this game back to San Quentin across the centuries. He insisted that I had read about it somewhere, and, though I had forgotten the reading, the stuff of the reading was nevertheless in the content of my mind, ripe to be brought out in any pipe-dream. Thus he turned the tenets and jargon of psychology back on me.

"What's to prevent your inventing it right here in solitary?" was his next hypothesis. "Didn't Ed invent the knuckle-talk? And ain't you and me improving on it right along? I got you, bo. You invented it. Say, get it patented. I remember when I was night-messenger some guy invented a fool thing called Pigs in Clover and made millions out of it."

"There's no patenting this," I replied. "Doubtlessly the Asiatics have been playing it for thousands of years. Won't you believe me when I tell you I didn't invent it?"

"Then you must have read about it, or seen the Chinks playing it in some of those hop-joints you was always hanging around," was his last word.

But I have a last word. There is a Japanese murderer here in Folsom—or was, for he was executed last week. I talked the matter over with him; and the game Adam Strang played, and which I taught Oppenheimer, proved quite similar to the Japanese game. They are far more alike than is either of them like the Western game.

CHAPTER XVII

You, my reader, will remember, far back at the beginning of this narrative, how, when a little lad on the Minnesota farm, I looked at the photographs of the Holy Land and recognized places and pointed out changes in places. Also you will remember, as I described the scene I had witnessed of the healing of the lepers, I told the missionary that I was a big man with a big sword, astride a horse and looking on.

That childhood incident was merely a trailing cloud of glory, as Wordsworth puts it. Not in entire forgetfulness had I, little Darrell Standing, come into the world. But those memories of other times and places that glimmered up to the surface of my child consciousness soon failed and faded. In truth, as is the way with all children, the shades of the prison-house closed about me, and I remembered my mighty past no more. Every man born of woman has a past mighty as mine. Very few men born of women have been fortunate enough to suffer years of solitary and strait-jacketing. That was my good fortune. I was enabled to remember once again, and to remember, among other things, the time when I sat astride a horse and beheld the lepers healed.

My name was Ragnar Lodbrog. I was in truth a large man. I stood half a head above the Romans of my legion. But that was later, after the time of my journey from Alexandria to Jerusalem, that I came to command a legion. It was a crowded life, that. Books and books, and years of writing could not record it all. So I shall briefen and no more than hint at the beginnings of it.

Now all is clear and sharp save the very beginning. I never knew my mother. I was told that I was tempest-born, on a beaked ship in the Northern Sea, of a captured woman, after a sea fight and a sack of a coastal stronghold. I never heard the name of my mother. She died at the height of the tempest. She was of the North Danes, so old Lingaard told me. He told me much that I was too young to remember, yet little could he tell. A sea fight and a sack, battle and plunder and torch, a flight seaward in the long ships to escape destruction upon the rocks, and a killing strain and struggle against the frosty, foundering seas—who, then, should know aught or mark a stranger woman in her hour with her feet fast set on the way of death? Many died. Men marked the living women, not the dead.

Sharp-bitten into my child imagination are the incidents immediately after my birth, as told me by old Lingaard. Lingaard, too old to labour at the sweeps, had been surgeon, undertaker, and midwife of the huddled captives in the open midships. So I was delivered in storm, with the spume of the cresting seas salt upon me.

Not many hours old was I when Tostig Lodbrog first laid eyes on me. His was the lean ship, and his the seven other lean ships that had made the foray, fled the rapine, and won through the storm. Tostig Lodbrog was also called Muspell, meaning "The Burning"; for he was ever aflame with wrath. Brave he was, and cruel he was, with no heart of mercy in that great chest of his. Ere the sweat of battle had dried on him, leaning on his axe, he ate the heart of Ngrun after the fight at Hasfarth. Because of mad anger he sold his son, Garulf, into slavery to the Juts. I remember, under the smoky rafters of Brunanbuhr, how he used to call for the skull of Guthlaf for a drinking beaker. Spiced wine he would have from no other cup than the skull of Guthlaf.

And to him, on the reeling deck after the storm was past, old Lingaard brought me. I was only hours old, wrapped naked in a salt-crusted wolfskin. Now it happens, being prematurely born, that I was very small.

"Ho! ho!—a dwarf!" cried Tostig, lowering a pot of mead half-drained from his lips to stare at me.

The day was bitter, but they say he swept me naked from the wolfskin, and by my foot, between thumb and forefinger, dangled me to the bite of the wind.

"A roach!" he ho-ho'd. "A shrimp! A sea-louse!" And he made to squash me between huge forefinger and thumb, either of which, Lingaard avers, was thicker than my leg or thigh.

But another whim was upon him.

"The youngling is a-thirst. Let him drink."

And therewith, head-downward, into the half-pot of mead he thrust me. And might well have drowned in this drink of men—I who had never known a mother's breast in the briefness of time I had lived—had it not been for Lingaard. But when he plucked me forth from the brew, Tostig Lodbrog struck him down in a rage. We rolled on the deck, and the great bear hounds, captured in the fight with the North Danes just past, sprang upon us.

"Ho! ho!" roared Tostig Lodbrog, as the old man and I and the wolfskin were mauled and worried by the dogs.

But Lingaard gained his feet, saving me but losing the wolfskin to the hounds.

Tostig Lodbrog finished the mead and regarded me, while Lingaard knew better than to beg for mercy where was no mercy.

"Hop o' my thumb," quoth Tostig. "By Odin, the women of the North Danes are a scurvy breed. They birth dwarfs, not men. Of what use is this thing? He will never make a man. Listen you, Lingaard, grow him to be a drink-boy at Brunanbuhr. And have an eye on the dogs lest they slobber him down by mistake as a meat-crumb from the table."

I knew no woman. Old Lingaard was midwife and nurse, and for nursery were reeling decks and the stamp and trample of men in battle or storm. How I survived puling infancy, God knows. I must have been born iron in a day of iron, for survive I did, to give the lie to Tostig's promise of dwarf-hood. I outgrew all beakers and tankards, and not for long could he half-drown me in his mead pot. This last was a favourite feat of his. It was his raw humour, a sally esteemed by him delicious wit.

My first memories are of Tostig Lodbrog's beaked ships and fighting men, and of the feast hall at Brunanbuhr when our boats lay beached beside the frozen fjord. For I was made drink-boy, and amongst my earliest recollections are toddling with the wine-filled skull of Guthlaf to the head of the table where Tostig bellowed to the rafters. They were madmen, all of madness, but it seemed the common way of life to me who knew naught else. They were men of quick rages and quick battling. Their thoughts were ferocious; so was their eating ferocious, and their drinking. And I grew like them. How else could I grow, when I served the drink to the bellowings of drunkards and to the skalds singing of Hialli, and the bold Hogni, and of the Niflung's gold, and of Gudrun's revenge on Atli when she gave him the hearts of his children and hers to eat while battle swept the benches, tore down the hangings raped from southern coasts, and, littered the feasting board with swift corpses.

Oh, I, too, had a rage, well tutored in such school. I was but eight when I showed my teeth at a drinking between the men of Brunanbuhr and the Juts who came as friends with the jarl Agard in his three long ships. I stood at Tostig Lodbrog's shoulder, holding the skull of Guthlaf that steamed and stank with the hot, spiced wine. And I waited while Tostig should complete his ravings against the North Dane men. But still he raved and still I waited, till he caught breath of fury to assail the North Dane woman. Whereat I remembered my North Dane mother, and saw my rage red in my eyes, and smote him with the skull of Guthlaf, so that he was wine-drenched, and wine-blinded, and fire-burnt. And as he reeled unseeing, smashing his great groping clutches through the air at me, I was in and short-dirked him thrice in belly, thigh and buttock, than which I could reach no higher up the mighty frame of him.

And the jarl Agard's steel was out, and his Juts joining him as he shouted:

"A bear cub! A bear cub! By Odin, let the cub fight!"

And there, under that roaring roof of Brunanbuhr, the babbling drink-boy of the North Danes fought with mighty Lodbrog. And when, with one stroke, I was flung, dazed and breathless, half the length of that great board, my flying body mowing down pots and tankards, Lodbrog cried out command:

"Out with him! Fling him to the hounds!"

But the jarl would have it no, and clapped Lodbrog on the shoulder, and asked me as a gift of friendship.

And south I went, when the ice passed out of the fjord, in Jarl Agard's ships. I was made drink-boy and sword-bearer to him, and in lieu of other name was called Ragnar Lodbrog. Agard's country was neighbour to the Frisians, and a sad, flat country of fog and fen it was. I was with him for three years, to his death, always at his back, whether hunting swamp wolves or drinking in the great hall where Elgiva, his young wife, often sat among her women. I was with Agard in south foray with his ships along what would be now the coast of France, and there I learned that still south were warmer seasons and softer climes and women.

But we brought back Agard wounded to death and slow-dying. And we burned his body on a great pyre, with Elgiva, in her golden corselet, beside him singing. And there were household slaves in golden collars that burned of a plenty there with her, and nine female thralls, and eight male slaves of the Angles that were of gentle birth and battle-captured. And there were live hawks so burned, and the two hawk-boys with their birds.

But I, the drink-boy, Ragnar Lodbrog, did not burn. I was eleven, and unafraid, and had never worn woven cloth on my body. And as the flames sprang up, and Elgiva sang her death-song, and the thralls and slaves screeched their unwillingness to die, I tore away my fastenings, leaped, and gained the fens, the gold collar of my slavehood still on my neck, footing it with the hounds loosed to tear me down.

In the fens were wild men, masterless men, fled slaves, and outlaws, who were hunted in sport as the wolves were hunted.

For three years I knew never roof nor fire, and I grew hard as the frost, and would have stolen a woman from the Juts but that the Frisians by mischance, in a two days' hunt, ran me down. By them I was looted of my gold collar and traded for two wolf-hounds to Edwy, of the Saxons, who put an iron collar on me, and later made of me and five other slaves a present to Athel of the East Angles. I was thrall and fighting man, until, lost in an unlucky raid far to the east beyond our marches, I was sold among the Huns, and was a swineherd until I escaped south into the great forests and was taken in as a freeman by the Teutons, who were many, but who lived in small tribes and drifted southward before the Hun advance.

And up from the south into the great forests came the Romans, fighting men all, who pressed us back upon the Huns. It was a crushage of the peoples for lack of room; and we taught the Romans what fighting was, although in truth we were no less well taught by them.

But always I remembered the sun of the south-land that I had glimpsed in the ships of Agard, and it was my fate, caught in this south drift of the Teutons, to be captured by the Romans and be brought back to the sea which I had not seen since I was lost away from the East Angles. I was made a sweep-slave in the galleys, and it was as a sweep-slave that at last I came to Rome.

All the story is too long of how I became a freeman, a citizen, and a soldier, and of how, when I was thirty, I journeyed to Alexandria, and from Alexandria to Jerusalem. Yet what I have told from the time when I was baptized in the mead-pot of Tostig Lodbrog I have been compelled to tell in order that you may understand what manner of man rode in through the Jaffa Gate and drew all eyes upon him.

Well might they look. They were small breeds, lighter-boned and lighter-thewed, these Romans and Jews, and a blonde like me they had never gazed upon. All along the narrow streets they gave before me but stood to stare wide-eyed at this yellow man from the north, or from God knew where so far as they knew aught of the matter.

Practically all Pilate's troops were auxiliaries, save for a handful of Romans about the palace and the twenty Romans who rode with me. Often enough have I found the auxiliaries good soldiers, but never so steadily dependable as the Romans. In truth they were better fighting men the year round than were we men of the North, who fought in great moods and sulked in great moods. The Roman was invariably steady and dependable.

There was a woman from the court of Antipas, who was a friend of Pilate's wife and whom I met at Pilate's the night of my arrival. I shall call her Miriam, for Miriam was the name I loved her by. If it were merely difficult to describe the charm of women, I would describe Miriam. But how describe emotion in words? The charm of woman is wordless. It is different from perception that culminates in reason, for it arises in sensation and culminates in emotion, which, be it admitted, is nothing else than super-sensation.

In general, any woman has fundamental charm for any man. When this charm becomes particular, then we call it love. Miriam had this particular charm for me. Verily I was co-partner in her charm. Half of it was my own man's life in me that leapt and met her wide-armed and made in me all that she was desirable plus all my desire of her.

Miriam was a grand woman. I use the term advisedly. She was fine-bodied, commanding, over and above the average Jewish woman in stature and in line. She was an aristocrat in social caste; she was an aristocrat by nature. All her ways were large ways, generous ways. She had brain, she had wit, and, above all, she had womanliness. As you shall see, it was her womanliness that betrayed her and me in they end. Brunette, olive-skinned, oval-faced, her hair was blue-black with its blackness and her eyes were twin wells of black. Never were more pronounced types of blonde and brunette in man and woman met than in us.

And we met on the instant. There was no self-discussion, no waiting, wavering, to make certain. She was mine the moment I looked upon her. And by the same token she knew that I belonged to her above all men. I strode to her. She half-lifted from her couch as if drawn upward to me. And then we looked with all our eyes, blue eyes and black, until Pilate's wife, a thin, tense, overwrought woman, laughed nervously. And while I bowed to the wife and gave greeting, I thought I saw Pilate give Miriam a significant glance, as if to say, "Is he not all I promised?" For he had had word of my coming from Sulpicius Quirinius, the legate of Syria. As well had Pilate and I been known to each other before ever he journeyed out to be procurator over the Semitic volcano of Jerusalem.

Much talk we had that night, especially Pilate, who spoke in detail of the local situation, and who seemed lonely and desirous to share his anxieties with some one and even to bid for counsel. Pilate was of the solid type of Roman, with sufficient imagination intelligently to enforce the iron policy of Rome, and not unduly excitable under stress.

But on this night it was plain that he was worried. The Jews had got on his nerves. They were too volcanic, spasmodic, eruptive. And further,

199

they were subtle. The Romans had a straight, forthright way of going about anything. The Jews never approached anything directly, save backwards, when they were driven by compulsion. Left to themselves, they always approached by indirection. Pilate's irritation was due, as he explained, to the fact that the Jews were ever intriguing to make him, and through him Rome, the catspaw in the matter of their religious dissensions. As was well known to me, Rome did not interfere with the religious notions of its conquered peoples; but the Jews were for ever confusing the issues and giving a political cast to purely unpolitical events.

Pilate waxed eloquent over the diverse sects and the fanatic uprisings and riotings that were continually occurring.

"Lodbrog," he said, "one can never tell what little summer cloud of their hatching may turn into a thunderstorm roaring and rattling about one's ears. I am here to keep order and quiet. Despite me they make the place a hornets' nest. Far rather would I govern Scythians or savage Britons than these people who are never at peace about God. Right now there is a man up to the north, a fisherman turned preacher, and miracle-worker, who as well as not may soon have all the country by the ears and my recall on its way from Rome."

This was the first I had heard of the man called Jesus, and I little remarked it at the time. Not until afterward did I remember him, when the little summer cloud had become a full-fledged thunderstorm.

"I have had report of him," Pilate went on. "He is not political. There is no doubt of that. But trust Caiaphas, and Hanan behind Caiaphas, to make of this fisherman a political thorn with which to prick Rome and ruin me."

"This Caiaphas, I have heard of him as high priest, then who is this Hanan?" I asked.

"The real high priest, a cunning fox," Pilate explained. "Caiaphas was appointed by Gratus, but Caiaphas is the shadow and the mouthpiece of Hanan."

"They have never forgiven you that little matter of the votive shields," Miriam teased.

200

Whereupon, as a man will when his sore place is touched, Pilate launched upon the episode, which had been an episode, no more, at the beginning, but which had nearly destroyed him. In all innocence before his palace he had affixed two shields with votive inscriptions. Ere the consequent storm that burst on his head had passed the Jews had written their complaints to Tiberius, who approved them and reprimanded Pilate.

I was glad, a little later, when I could have talk with Miriam. Pilate's wife had found opportunity to tell me about her. She was of old royal stock. Her sister was wife of Philip, tetrarch of Gaulonitis and Batanæa. Now this Philip was brother to Antipas, tetrarch of Galilee and Peræa, and both were sons of Herod, called by the Jews the "Great." Miriam, as I understood, was at home in the courts of both tetrarchs, being herself of the blood. Also, when a girl, she had been betrothed to Archelaus at the time he was ethnarch of Jerusalem. She had a goodly fortune in her own right, so that marriage had not been compulsory. To boot, she had a will of her own, and was doubtless hard to please in so important a matter as husbands.

It must have been in the very air we breathed, for in no time Miriam and I were at it on the subject of religion. Truly, the Jews of that day battened on religion as did we on fighting and feasting. For all my stay in that country there was never a moment when my wits were not buzzing with the endless discussions of life and death, law, and God. Now Pilate believed neither in gods, nor devils, nor anything. Death, to him, was the blackness of unbroken sleep; and yet, during his years in Jerusalem, he was ever vexed with the inescapable fuss and fury of things religious. Why, I had a horse-boy on my trip into Idumæa, a wretched creature that could never learn to saddle and who yet could talk, and most learnedly, without breath, from nightfall to sunrise, on the hair-splitting differences in the teachings of all the rabbis from Shemaiah to Gamaliel.

But to return to Miriam.

"You believe you are immortal," she was soon challenging me. "Then why do you fear to talk about it?"

"Why burden my mind with thoughts about certainties?" I countered.

"But are you certain?" she insisted. "Tell me about it. What is it like—your immortality?"

And when I had told her of Niflheim and Muspell, of the birth of the giant Ymir from the snowflakes, of the cow Andhumbla, and of Fenrir and Loki and the frozen Jötuns—as I say, when I had told her of all this, and of Thor and Odin and our own Valhalla, she clapped her hands and cried out, with sparkling eyes:

"Oh, you barbarian! You great child! You yellow giant-thing of the frost! You believer of old nurse tales and stomach satisfactions! But the spirit of you, that which cannot die, where will it go when your body is dead?"

"As I have said, Valhalla," I answered. "And my body shall be there, too."

"Eating?—drinking?—fighting?"

"And loving," I added. "We must have our women in heaven, else what is heaven for?"

"I do not like your heaven," she said. "It is a mad place, a beast place, a place of frost and storm and fury."

"And your heaven?" I questioned.

"Is always unending summer, with the year at the ripe for the fruits and flowers and growing things."

I shook my head and growled:

"I do not like your heaven. It is a sad place, a soft place, a place for weaklings and eunuchs and fat, sobbing shadows of men."

My remarks must have glamoured her mind, for her eyes continued to sparkle, and mine was half a guess that she was leading me on.

"My heaven," she said, "is the abode of the blest."

"Valhalla is the abode of the blest," I asserted. "For look you, who cares for flowers where flowers always are? in my country, after the iron winter breaks and the sun drives away the long night, the first blossoms twinkling on the melting ice-edge are things of joy, and we look, and look again.

"And fire!" I cried out. "Great glorious fire! A fine heaven yours where a man cannot properly esteem a roaring fire under a tight roof with wind and snow a-drive outside."

"A simple folk, you," she was back at me. "You build a roof and a fire in a snowbank and call it heaven. In my heaven we do not have to escape the wind and snow."

"No," I objected. "We build roof and fire to go forth from into the frost and storm and to return to from the frost and storm. Man's life is fashioned for battle with frost and storm. His very fire and roof he makes by his battling. I know. For three years, once, I knew never roof nor fire. I was sixteen, and a man, ere ever I wore woven cloth on my body. I was birthed in storm, after battle, and my swaddling cloth was a wolfskin. Look at me and see what manner of man lives in Valhalla."

And look she did, all a-glamour, and cried out:

"You great, yellow giant-thing of a man!" Then she added pensively, "Almost it saddens me that there may not be such men in my heaven."

"It is a good world," I consoled her. "Good is the plan and wide. There is room for many heavens. It would seem that to each is given the heaven that is his heart's desire. A good country, truly, there beyond the grave. I doubt not I shall leave our feast halls and raid your coasts of sun and flowers, and steal you away. My mother was so stolen."

And in the pause I looked at her, and she looked at me, and dared to look. And my blood ran fire. By Odin, this was a woman!

What might have happened I know not, for Pilate, who had ceased from his talk with Ambivius and for some time had sat grinning, broke the pause.

"A rabbi, a Teutoberg rabbi!" he gibed. "A new preacher and a new doctrine come to Jerusalem. Now will there be more dissensions, and riotings, and stonings of prophets. The gods save us, it is a mad-house. Lodbrog, I little thought it of you. Yet here you are, spouting and fuming as wildly as any madman from the desert about what shall happen to you when you are dead. One life at a time, Lodbrog. It saves trouble. It saves trouble."

"Go on, Miriam, go on," his wife cried.

She had sat entranced during the discussion, with hands tightly clasped, and the thought flickered up in my mind that she had already been corrupted by the religious folly of Jerusalem. At any rate, as I was to learn in the days that followed, she was unduly bent upon such matters. She was a thin woman, as if wasted by fever. Her skin was tight-stretched. Almost it seemed I could look through her hands did she hold them between me and the light. She was a good woman, but highly nervous, and, at times, fancy-flighted about shades and signs and omens. Nor was she above seeing visions and hearing voices. As for me, I had no patience with such weaknesses. Yet was she a good woman with no heart of evil.

* * * * *

I was on a mission for Tiberius, and it was my ill luck to see little of Miriam. On my return from the court of Antipas she had gone into Batanæa to Philip's court, where was her sister. Once again I was back in Jerusalem, and, though it was no necessity of my business to see Philip, who, though weak, was faithful to Roman will, I journeyed into Batanæa in the hope of meeting with Miriam.

Then there was my trip into Idumæa. Also, I travelled into Syria in obedience to the command of Sulpicius Quirinius, who, as imperial legate, was curious of my first-hand report of affairs in Jerusalem. Thus, travelling wide and much, I had opportunity to observe the strangeness of the Jews who were so madly interested in God. It was their peculiarity. Not content with leaving such matters to their priests, they were themselves for ever turning priests and preaching wherever they could find a listener. And listeners they found a-plenty.

They gave up their occupations to wander about the country like beggars, disputing and bickering with the rabbis and Talmudists in the synagogues and temple porches. It was in Galilee, a district of little repute, the inhabitants of which were looked upon as witless, that I crossed the track of the man Jesus. It seems that he had been a carpenter, and after that a fisherman, and that his fellow-fishermen had ceased dragging their nets and followed him in his wandering life. Some few looked upon him as a prophet, but the most contended that he was a madman. My wretched horse-boy, himself claiming Talmudic knowledge second to none, sneered at Jesus, calling him the king of the beggars, calling his doctrine Ebionism, which, as he explained to me, was to the effect that only the poor should win to heaven, while the rich and powerful were to burn for ever in some lake of fire.

It was my observation that it was the custom of the country for every man to call every other man a madman. In truth, in my judgment, they were all mad. There was a plague of them. They cast out devils by magic charms, cured diseases by the laying on of hands, drank deadly poisons unharmed, and unharmed played with deadly snakes—or so they claimed. They ran away to starve in the deserts. They emerged howling new doctrine, gathering crowds about them, forming new sects that split on doctrine and formed more sects.

"By Odin," I told Pilate, "a trifle of our northern frost and snow would cool their wits. This climate is too soft. In place of building roofs and hunting meat, they are ever building doctrine."

"And altering the nature of God," Pilate corroborated sourly. "A curse on doctrine."

"So say I," I agreed. "If ever I get away with unaddled wits from this mad land, I'll cleave through whatever man dares mention to me what may happen after I am dead."

Never were such trouble makers. Everything under the sun was pious or impious to them. They, who were so clever in hair-splitting argument, seemed incapable of grasping the Roman idea of the State. Everything political was religious; everything religious was political. Thus every procurator's hands were full. The Roman eagles, the Roman statues, even the votive shields of Pilate, were deliberate insults to their religion.

The Roman taking of the census was an abomination. Yet it had to be done, for it was the basis of taxation. But there it was again. Taxation by the State was a crime against their law and God. Oh, that Law! It was not the Roman law. It was their law, what they called God's law. There were the zealots, who murdered anybody who broke this law. And for a procurator to punish a zealot caught red-handed was to raise a riot or an insurrection.

Everything, with these strange people, was done in the name of God. There were what we Romans called the *thaumaturgi*. They worked miracles to prove doctrine. Ever has it seemed to me a witless thing to prove the multiplication table by turning a staff into a serpent, or even into two serpents. Yet these things the *thaumaturgi* did, and always to the excitement of the common people.

Heavens, what sects and sects! Pharisees, Essenes, Sadducees—a legion of them! No sooner did they start with a new quirk when it turned political. Coponius, procurator fourth before Pilate, had a pretty time crushing the Gaulonite sedition which arose in this fashion and spread down from Gamala.

In Jerusalem, that last time I rode in, it was easy to note the increasing excitement of the Jews. They ran about in crowds, chattering and spouting. Some were proclaiming the end of the world. Others satisfied themselves with the imminent destruction of the Temple. And there were rank revolutionises who announced that Roman rule was over and the new Jewish kingdom about to begin.

Pilate, too, I noted, showed heavy anxiety. That they were giving him a hard time of it was patent. But I will say, as you shall see, that he matched their subtlety with equal subtlety; and from what I saw of him I have little doubt but what he would have confounded many a disputant in the synagogues.

"But half a legion of Romans," he regretted to me, "and I would take Jerusalem by the throat . . . and then be recalled for my pains, I suppose."

Like me, he had not too much faith in the auxiliaries; and of Roman soldiers we had but a scant handful.

Back again, I lodged in the palace, and to my great joy found Miriam there. But little satisfaction was mine, for the talk ran long on the situation. There was reason for this, for the city buzzed like the angry hornets' nest it was. The fast called the Passover—a religious affair, of course—was near, and thousands were pouring in from the country, according to custom, to celebrate the feast in Jerusalem. These newcomers, naturally, were all excitable folk, else they would not be bent on such pilgrimage. The city was packed with them, so that many camped outside the walls. As for me, I could not distinguish how much of the ferment was due to the teachings of the wandering fisherman, and how much of it was due to Jewish hatred for Rome.

"A tithe, no more, and maybe not so much, is due to this Jesus," Pilate answered my query. "Look to Caiaphas and Hanan for the main cause of the excitement. They know what they are about. They are stirring it up, to what end who can tell, except to cause me trouble."

"Yes, it is certain that Caiaphas and Hanan are responsible," Miriam said, "but you, Pontius Pilate, are only a Roman and do not understand. Were you a Jew, you would realize that there is a greater seriousness at the bottom of it than mere dissension of the sectaries or trouble-making for you and Rome. The high priests and Pharisees, every Jew of place or wealth, Philip, Antipas, myself—we are all fighting for very life.

"This fisherman may be a madman. If so, there is a cunning in his madness. He preaches the doctrine of the poor. He threatens our law, and our law is our life, as you have learned ere this. We are jealous of our law, as you would be jealous of the air denied your body by a throttling hand on your throat. It is Caiaphas and Hanan and all they stand for, or it is the fisherman. They must destroy him, else he will destroy them."

"Is it not strange, so simple a man, a fisherman?" Pilate's wife breathed forth. "What manner of man can he be to possess such power? I would that I could see him. I would that with my own eyes I could see so remarkable a man."

Pilate's brows corrugated at her words, and it was clear that to the burden on his nerves was added the overwrought state of his wife's nerves.

"If you would see him, beat up the dens of the town," Miriam laughed spitefully. "You will find him wine-bibbing or in the company of nameless women. Never so strange a prophet came up to Jerusalem."

"And what harm in that?" I demanded, driven against my will to take the part of the fisherman. "Have I not wine-guzzled a-plenty and passed strange nights in all the provinces? The man is a man, and his ways are men's ways, else am I a madman, which I here deny."

Miriam shook her head as she spoke.

"He is not mad. Worse, he is dangerous. All Ebionism is dangerous. He would destroy all things that are fixed. He is a revolutionist. He would destroy what little is left to us of the Jewish state and Temple."

Here Pilate shook his head.

"He is not political. I have had report of him. He is a visionary. There is no sedition in him. He affirms the Roman tax even."

"Still you do not understand," Miriam persisted. "It is not what he plans; it is the effect, if his plans are achieved, that makes him a revolutionist. I doubt that he foresees the effect. Yet is the man a plague, and, like any plague, should be stamped out."

"From all that I have heard, he is a good-hearted, simple man with no evil in him," I stated.

And thereat I told of the healing of the ten lepers I had witnessed in Samaria on my way through Jericho.

Pilate's wife sat entranced at what I told. Came to our ears distant shoutings and cries of some street crowd, and we knew the soldiers were keeping the streets cleared.

"And you believe this wonder, Lodbrog?" Pilate demanded. "You believe that in the flash of an eye the festering sores departed from the lepers?"

"I saw them healed," I replied. "I followed them to make certain. There was no leprosy in them."

"But did you see them sore?—before the healing?" Pilate insisted.

I shook my head.

"I was only told so," I admitted. "When I saw them afterward, they had all the seeming of men who had once been lepers. They were in a daze. There was one who sat in the sun and ever searched his body and stared and stared at the smooth flesh as if unable to believe his eyes. He would not speak, nor look at aught else than his flesh, when I questioned him. He was in a maze. He sat there in the sun and stared and stared."

Pilate smiled contemptuously, and I noted the quiet smile on Miriam's face was equally contemptuous. And Pilate's wife sat as if a corpse, scarce breathing, her eyes wide and unseeing.

Spoke Ambivius: "Caiaphas holds—he told me but yesterday—that the fisherman claims that he will bring God down on earth and make here a new kingdom over which God will rule—"

"Which would mean the end of Roman rule," I broke in.

"That is where Caiaphas and Hanan plot to embroil Rome," Miriam explained. "It is not true. It is a lie they have made."

Pilate nodded and asked:

"Is there not somewhere in your ancient books a prophecy that the priests here twist into the intent of this fisherman's mind?"

To this she agreed, and gave him the citation. I relate the incident to evidence the depth of Pilate's study of this people he strove so hard to keep in order.

"What I have heard," Miriam continued, "is that this Jesus preaches the end of the world and the beginning of God's kingdom, not here, but in heaven."

"I have had report of that," Pilate raid. "It is true. This Jesus holds the justness of the Roman tax. He holds that Rome shall rule until all rule passes away with the passing of the world. I see more clearly the trick Hanan is playing me."

"It is even claimed by some of his followers," Ambivius volunteered, "that he is God Himself."

209

"I have no report that he has so said," Pilate replied.

"Why not?" his wife breathed. "Why not? Gods have descended to earth before."

"Look you," Pilate said. "I have it by creditable report, that after this Jesus had worked some wonder whereby a multitude was fed on several loaves and fishes, the foolish Galileans were for making him a king. Against his will they would make him a king. To escape them he fled into the mountains. No madness there. He was too wise to accept the fate they would have forced upon him."

"Yet that is the very trick Hanan would force upon you," Miriam reiterated. "They claim for him that he would be king of the Jews—an offence against Roman law, wherefore Rome must deal with him."

Pilate shrugged his shoulders.

"A king of the beggars, rather; or a king of the dreamers. He is no fool. He is visionary, but not visionary of this world's power. All luck go with him in the next world, for that is beyond Rome's jurisdiction."

"He holds that property is sin—that is what hits the Pharisees," Ambivius spoke up.

Pilate laughed heartily.

"This king of the beggars and his fellow-beggars still do respect property," he explained. "For, look you, not long ago they had even a treasurer for their wealth. Judas his name was, and there were words in that he stole from their common purse which he carried."

"Jesus did not steal?" Pilate's wife asked.

"No," Pilate answered; "it was Judas, the treasurer."

"Who was this John?" I questioned. "He was in trouble up Tiberias way and Antipas executed him."

"Another one," Miriam answered. "He was born near Hebron. He was an enthusiast and a desert-dweller. Either he or his followers claimed that he was Elijah raised from the dead. Elijah, you see, was one of our old prophets."

210

"Was he seditious?" I asked.

Pilate grinned and shook his head, then said:

"He fell out with Antipas over the matter of Herodias. John was a moralist. It is too long a story, but he paid for it with his head. No, there was nothing political in that affair."

"It is also claimed by some that Jesus is the Son of David," Miriam said. "But it is absurd. Nobody at Nazareth believes it. You see, his whole family, including his married sisters, lives there and is known to all of them. They are a simple folk, mere common people."

"I wish it were as simple, the report of all this complexity that I must send to Tiberius," Pilate grumbled. "And now this fisherman is come to Jerusalem, the place is packed with pilgrims ripe for any trouble, and Hanan stirs and stirs the broth."

"And before he is done he will have his way," Miriam forecast. "He has laid the task for you, and you will perform it."

"Which is?" Pilate queried.

"The execution of this fisherman."

Pilate shook his head stubbornly, but his wife cried out:

"No! No! It would be a shameful wrong. The man has done no evil. He has not offended against Rome."

She looked beseechingly to Pilate, who continued to shake his head.

"Let them do their own beheading, as Antipas did," he growled. "The fisherman counts for nothing; but I shall be no catspaw to their schemes. If they must destroy him, they must destroy him. That is their affair."

"But you will not permit it," cried Pilate's wife.

"A pretty time would I have explaining to Tiberius if I interfered," was his reply.

211

"No matter what happens," said Miriam, "I can see you writing explanations, and soon; for Jesus is already come up to Jerusalem and a number of his fishermen with him."

Pilate showed the irritation this information caused him.

"I have no interest in his movements," he pronounced. "I hope never to see him."

"Trust Hanan to find him for you," Miriam replied, "and to bring him to your gate."

Pilate shrugged his shoulders, and there the talk ended. Pilate's wife, nervous and overwrought, must claim Miriam to her apartments, so that nothing remained for me but to go to bed and doze off to the buzz and murmur of the city of madmen.

* * * * *

Events moved rapidly. Over night the white heat of the city had scorched upon itself. By midday, when I rode forth with half a dozen of my men, the streets were packed, and more reluctant than ever were the folk to give way before me. If looks could kill I should have been a dead man that day. Openly they spat at sight of me, and, everywhere arose snarls and cries.

Less was I a thing of wonder, and more was I the thing hated in that I wore the hated harness of Rome. Had it been any other city, I should have given command to my men to lay the flats of their swords on those snarling fanatics. But this was Jerusalem, at fever heat, and these were a people unable in thought to divorce the idea of State from the idea of God.

Hanan the Sadducee had done his work well. No matter what he and the Sanhedrim believed of the true inwardness of the situation, it was clear this rabble had been well tutored to believe that Rome was at the bottom of it.

I encountered Miriam in the press. She was on foot, attended only by a woman. It was no time in such turbulence for her to be abroad garbed as became her station. Through her sister she was indeed sister-in-law to Antipas for whom few bore love. So she was dressed discreetly, her face covered, so that she might pass as any Jewish woman of the lower orders. But not to my eye could she hide that fine stature of her, that carriage and walk, so different from other women's, of which I had already dreamed more than once.

Few and quick were the words we were able to exchange, for the way jammed on the moment, and soon my men and horses were being pressed and jostled. Miriam was sheltered in an angle of house-wall.

"Have they got the fisherman yet?" I asked.

"No; but he is just outside the wall. He has ridden up to Jerusalem on an ass, with a multitude before and behind; and some, poor dupes, have hailed him as he passed as King of Israel. That finally is the pretext with which Hanan will compel Pilate. Truly, though not yet taken, the sentence is already written. This fisherman is a dead man."

"But Pilate will not arrest him," I defended. Miriam shook her head.

"Hanan will attend to that. They will bring him before the Sanhedrim. The sentence will be death. They may stone him."

"But the Sanhedrim has not the right to execute," I contended.

"Jesus is not a Roman," she replied. "He is a Jew. By the law of the Talmud he is guilty of death, for he has blasphemed against the law."

Still I shook my head.

"The Sanhedrim has not the right."

"Pilate is willing that it should take that right."

"But it is a fine question of legality," I insisted. "You know what the Romans are in such matters."

"Then will Hanan avoid the question," she smiled, "by compelling Pilate to crucify him. In either event it will be well."

A surging of the mob was sweeping our horses along and grinding our knees together. Some fanatic had fallen, and I could feel my horse recoil and half rear as it tramped on him, and I could hear the man screaming and the snarling menace from all about rising to a roar. But my head was over my shoulder as I called back to Miriam:

"You are hard on a man you have said yourself is without evil."

"I am hard upon the evil that will come of him if he lives," she replied.

Scarcely did I catch her words, for a man sprang in, seizing my bridle-rein and leg and struggling to unhorse me. With my open palm, leaning forward, I smote him full upon cheek and jaw. My hand covered the face of him, and a hearty will of weight was in the blow. The dwellers in Jerusalem are not used to man's buffets. I have often wondered since if I broke the fellow's neck.

* * * * *

Next I saw Miriam was the following day. I met her in the court of Pilate's palace. She seemed in a dream. Scarce her eyes saw me. Scarce her wits embraced my identity. So strange was she, so in daze and amaze and far-seeing were her eyes, that I was reminded of the lepers I had seen healed in Samaria.

She became herself by an effort, but only her outward self. In her eyes was a message unreadable. Never before had I seen woman's eyes so.

She would have passed me ungreeted had I not confronted her way. She paused and murmured words mechanically, but all the while her eyes dreamed through me and beyond me with the largeness of the vision that filled them.

"I have seen Him, Lodbrog," she whispered. "I have seen Him."

"The gods grant that he is not so ill-affected by the sight of you, whoever he may be," I laughed.

She took no notice of my poor-timed jest, and her eyes remained full with vision, and she would have passed on had I not again blocked her way.

"Who is this he?" I demanded. "Some man raised from the dead to put such strange light in your eyes?"

"One who has raised others from the dead," she replied. "Truly I believe that He, this Jesus, has raised the dead. He is the Prince of Light, the Son of God. I have seen Him. Truly I believe that He is the Son of God."

Little could I glean from her words, save that she had met this wandering fisherman and been swept away by his folly. For surely this Miriam was not the Miriam who had branded him a plague and demanded that he be stamped out as any plague.

"He has charmed you," I cried angrily.

Her eyes seemed to moisten and grow deeper as she gave confirmation.

"Oh, Lodbrog, His is charm beyond all thinking, beyond all describing. But to look upon Him is to know that here is the all-soul of goodness and of compassion. I have seen Him. I have heard Him. I shall give all I have to the poor, and I shall follow Him."

Such was her certitude that I accepted it fully, as I had accepted the amazement of the lepers of Samaria staring at their smooth flesh; and I was bitter that so great a woman should be so easily wit-addled by a vagrant wonder-worker.

"Follow him," I sneered. "Doubtless you will wear a crown when he wins to his kingdom."

She nodded affirmation, and I could have struck her in the face for her folly. I drew aside, and as she moved slowly on she murmured:

"His kingdom is not here. He is the Son of David. He is the Son of God. He is whatever He has said, or whatever has been said of Him that is good and great."

* * * * *

"A wise man of the East," I found Pilate chuckling. "He is a thinker, this unlettered fisherman. I have sought more deeply into him. I have fresh report. He has no need of wonder-workings. He out-sophisticates the most sophistical of them. They have laid traps, and He has laughed at their traps. Look you. Listen to this."

Whereupon he told me how Jesus had confounded his confounders when they brought to him for judgment a woman taken in adultery.

"And the tax," Pilate exulted on. "'To Cæsar what is Cæsar's, to God what is God's,' was his answer to them. That was Hanan's trick, and Hanan is confounded. At last has there appeared one Jew who understands our Roman conception of the State."

* * * * *

Next I saw Pilate's wife. Looking into her eyes I knew, on the instant, after having seen Miriam's eyes, that this tense, distraught woman had likewise seen the fisherman.

"The Divine is within Him," she murmured to me. "There is within Him a personal awareness of the indwelling of God."

"Is he God?" I queried, gently, for say something I must.

She shook her head.

"I do not know. He has not said. But this I know: of such stuff gods are made."

* * * * *

"A charmer of women," was my privy judgment, as I left Pilate's wife walking in dreams and visions.

The last days are known to all of you who read these lines, and it was in those last days that I learned that this Jesus was equally a charmer of men. He charmed Pilate. He charmed me.

After Hanan had sent Jesus to Caiaphas, and the Sanhedrim, assembled in Caiaphas's house, had condemned Jesus to death, Jesus, escorted by a howling mob, was sent to Pilate for execution.

Now, for his own sake and for Rome's sake, Pilate did not want to execute him. Pilate was little interested in the fisherman and greatly interested in peace and order. What cared Pilate for a man's life?—for many men's lives? The school of Rome was iron, and the governors sent out by Rome to rule conquered peoples were likewise iron. Pilate thought and acted in governmental abstractions. Yet, look: when Pilate went out scowling to meet the mob that had fetched the fisherman, he fell immediately under the charm of the man.

I was present. I know. It was the first time Pilate had ever seen him. Pilate went out angry. Our soldiers were in readiness to clear the court of its noisy vermin. And immediately Pilate laid eyes on the fisherman Pilate was subdued—nay, was solicitous. He disclaimed jurisdiction, demanded that they should judge the fisherman by their law and deal with him by their law, since the fisherman was a Jew and not a Roman. Never were there Jews so obedient to Roman rule. They cried out that it was unlawful, under Rome, for them to put any man to death. Yet Antipas had beheaded John and come to no grief of it.

And Pilate left them in the court, open under the sky, and took Jesus alone into the judgment hall. What happened therein I know not, save that when Pilate emerged he was changed. Whereas before he had been disinclined to execute because he would not be made a catspaw to Hanan, he was now disinclined to execute because of regard for the fisherman. His effort now was to save the fisherman. And all the while the mob cried: "Crucify him! Crucify him!"

You, my reader, know the sincerity of Pilate's effort. You know how he tried to befool the mob, first by mocking Jesus as a harmless fool; and second by offering to release him according to the custom of releasing one prisoner at time of the Passover. And you know how the priests' quick whisperings led the mob to cry out for the release of the murderer Bar-Abba.

In vain Pilate struggled against the fate being thrust upon him by the priests. By sneer and jibe he hoped to make a farce of the transaction. He laughingly called Jesus the King of the Jews and ordered him to be scourged. His hope was that all would end in laughter and in laugher be forgotten.

I am glad to say that no Roman soldiers took part in what followed. It was the soldiers of the auxiliaries who crowned and cloaked Jesus, put the reed of sovereignty in his hand, and, kneeling, hailed him King of the Jews. Although it failed, it was a play to placate. And I, looking on, learned the charm of Jesus. Despite the cruel mockery of situation, he was regal. And I was quiet as I gazed. It was his own quiet that went into me. I was soothed and satisfied, and was without bewilderment. This thing had to be. All was well. The serenity of Jesus in the heart of the tumult and pain became my serenity. I was scarce moved by any thought to save him.

On the other hand, I had gazed on too many wonders of the human in my wild and varied years to be affected to foolish acts by this particular wonder. I was all serenity. I had no word to say. I had no judgment to pass. I knew that things were occurring beyond my comprehension, and that they must occur.

Still Pilate struggled. The tumult increased. The cry for blood rang through the court, and all were clamouring for crucifixion. Again Pilate went back into the judgment hall. His effort at a farce having failed, he attempted to disclaim jurisdiction. Jesus was not of Jerusalem. He was a born subject of Antipas, and to Antipas Pilate was for sending Jesus.

But the uproar was by now communicating itself to the city. Our troops outside the palace were being swept away in the vast street mob. Rioting had begun that in the flash of an eye could turn into civil war and revolution. My own twenty legionaries were close to hand and in readiness. They loved the fanatic Jews no more than did I, and would have welcomed my command to clear the court with naked steel.

When Pilate came out again his words for Antipas' jurisdiction could not be heard, for all the mob was shouting that Pilate was a traitor, that if he let the fisherman go he was no friend of Tiberius. Close before me, as I leaned against the wall, a mangy, bearded, long-haired fanatic sprang up and down unceasingly, and unceasingly chanted: "Tiberius is emperor; there is no king! Tiberius is emperor; there is no king!" I lost patience. The man's near noise was an offence. Lurching sidewise, as if by accident, I ground my foot on his to a terrible crushing. The fool seemed not to notice. He was too mad to be aware of the pain, and he continued to chant: "Tiberius is emperor; there is no king!"

218

I saw Pilate hesitate. Pilate, the Roman governor, for the moment was Pilate the man, with a man's anger against the miserable creatures clamouring for the blood of so sweet and simple, brave and good a spirit as this Jesus.

I saw Pilate hesitate. His gaze roved to me, as if he were about to signal to me to let loose; and I half-started forward, releasing the mangled foot under my foot. I was for leaping to complete that half-formed wish of Pilate and to sweep away in blood and cleanse the court of the wretched scum that howled in it.

It was not Pilate's indecision that decided me. It was this Jesus that decided Pilate and me. This Jesus looked at me. He commanded me. I tell you this vagrant fisherman, this wandering preacher, this piece of driftage from Galilee, commanded me. No word he uttered. Yet his command was there, unmistakable as a trumpet call. And I stayed my foot, and held my hand, for who was I to thwart the will and way of so greatly serene and sweetly sure a man as this? And as I stayed I knew all the charm of him—all that in him had charmed Miriam and Pilate's wife, that had charmed Pilate himself.

You know the rest. Pilate washed his hands of Jesus' blood, and the rioters took his blood upon their own heads. Pilate gave orders for the crucifixion. The mob was content, and content, behind the mob, were Caiaphas, Hanan, and the Sanhedrim. Not Pilate, not Tiberius, not Roman soldiers crucified Jesus. It was the priestly rulers and priestly politicians of Jerusalem. I saw. I know. And against his own best interests Pilate would have saved Jesus, as I would have, had it not been that no other than Jesus himself willed that he was not to be saved.

Yes, and Pilate had his last sneer at this people he detested. In Hebrew, Greek, and Latin he had a writing affixed to Jesus' cross which read, "The King of the Jews." In vain the priests complained. It was on this very pretext that they had forced Pilate's hand; and by this pretext, a scorn and insult to the Jewish race, Pilate abided. Pilate executed an abstraction that had never existed in the real. The abstraction was a cheat and a lie manufactured in the priestly mind. Neither the priests nor Pilate believed it. Jesus denied it. That abstraction was "The King of the Jews."

* * * * *

The storm was over in the courtyard. The excitement had simmered down. Revolution had been averted. The priests were content, the mob was satisfied, and Pilate and I were well disgusted and weary with the whole affair. And yet for him and me was more and most immediate storm. Before Jesus was taken away one of Miriam's women called me to her. And I saw Pilate, summoned by one of his wife's women, likewise obey.

"Oh, Lodbrog, I have heard," Miriam met me. We were alone, and she was close to me, seeking shelter and strength within my arms. "Pilate has weakened. He is going to crucify Him. But there is time. Your own men are ready. Ride with them. Only a centurion and a handful of soldiers are with Him. They have not yet started. As soon as they do start, follow. They must not reach Golgotha. But wait until they are outside the city wall. Then countermand the order. Take an extra horse for Him to ride. The rest is easy. Ride away into Syria with Him, or into Idumæa, or anywhere so long as He be saved."

She concluded with her arms around my neck, her face upturned to mine and temptingly close, her eyes greatly solemn and greatly promising.

Small wonder I was slow of speech. For the moment there was but one thought in my brain. After all the strange play I had seen played out, to have this come upon me! I did not misunderstand. The thing was clear. A great woman was mine if . . . if I betrayed Rome. For Pilate was governor, his order had gone forth; and his voice was the voice of Rome.

As I have said, it was the woman of her, her sheer womanliness, that betrayed Miriam and me in the end. Always she had been so clear, so reasonable, so certain of herself and me, so that I had forgotten, or, rather, I there learned once again the eternal lesson learned in all lives, that woman is ever woman . . . that in great decisive moments woman does not reason but feels; that the last sanctuary and innermost pulse to conduct is in woman's heart and not in woman's head.

Miriam misunderstood my silence, for her body moved softly within my arms as she added, as if in afterthought:

220

"Take two spare horses, Lodbrog. I shall ride the other . . . with you . . . with you, away over the world, wherever you may ride."

It was a bribe of kings; it was an act, paltry and contemptible, that was demanded of me in return. Still I did not speak. It was not that I was in confusion or in any doubt. I was merely sad—greatly and suddenly sad, in that I knew I held in my arms what I would never hold again.

"There is but one man in Jerusalem this day who can save Him," she urged, "and that man is you, Lodbrog."

Because I did not immediately reply she shook me, as if in impulse to clarify wits she considered addled. She shook me till my harness rattled.

"Speak, Lodbrog, speak!" she commanded. "You are strong and unafraid. You are all man. I know you despise the vermin who would destroy Him. You, you alone can save Him. You have but to say the word and the thing is done; and I will well love you and always love you for the thing you have done."

"I am a Roman," I said slowly, knowing full well that with the words I gave up all hope of her.

"You are a man-slave of Tiberius, a hound of Rome," she flamed, "but you owe Rome nothing, for you are not a Roman. You yellow giants of the north are not Romans."

"The Romans are the elder brothers of us younglings of the north," I answered. "Also, I wear the harness and I eat the bread of Rome." Gently I added: "But why all this fuss and fury for a mere man's life? All men must die. Simple and easy it is to die. To-day, or a hundred years, it little matters. Sure we are, all of us, of the same event in the end."

Quick she was, and alive with passion to save as she thrilled within my arms.

"You do not understand, Lodbrog. This is no mere man. I tell you this is a man beyond men—a living God, not of men, but over men."

I held her closely and knew that I was renouncing all the sweet woman of her as I said:

"We are man and woman, you and I. Our life is of this world. Of these other worlds is all a madness. Let these mad dreamers go the way of their dreaming. Deny them not what they desire above all things, above meat and wine, above song and battle, even above love of woman. Deny them not their hearts' desires that draw them across the dark of the grave to their dreams of lives beyond this world. Let them pass. But you and I abide here in all the sweet we have discovered of each other. Quickly enough will come the dark, and you depart for your coasts of sun and flowers, and I for the roaring table of Valhalla."

"No! no!" she cried, half-tearing herself away. "You do not understand. All of greatness, all of goodness, all of God are in this man who is more than man; and it is a shameful death to die. Only slaves and thieves so die. He is neither slave nor thief. He is an immortal. He is God. Truly I tell you He is God."

"He is immortal you say," I contended. "Then to die to-day on Golgotha will not shorten his immortality by a hair's breadth in the span of time. He is a god you say. Gods cannot die. From all I have been told of them, it is certain that gods cannot die."

"Oh!" she cried. "You will not understand. You are only a great giant thing of flesh."

"Is it not said that this event was prophesied of old time?" I queried, for I had been learning from the Jews what I deemed their subtleties of thinking.

"Yes, yes," she agreed, "the Messianic prophecies. This is the Messiah."

"Then who am I," I asked, "to make liars of the prophets? to make of the Messiah a false Messiah? Is the prophecy of your people so feeble a thing that I, a stupid stranger, a yellow northling in the Roman harness, can give the lie to prophecy and compel to be unfulfilled—the very thing willed by the gods and foretold by the wise men?"

"You do not understand," she repeated.

"I understand too well," I replied. "Am I greater than the gods that I may thwart the will of the gods? Then are gods vain things and the playthings of men. I am a man. I, too, bow to the gods, to all gods, for I do believe in all gods, else how came all gods to be?"

She flung herself so that my hungry arms were empty of her, and we stood apart and listened to the uproar of the street as Jesus and the soldiers emerged and started on their way. And my heart was sore in that so great a woman could be so foolish. She would save God. She would make herself greater than God.

"You do not love me," she said slowly, and slowly grew in her eyes a promise of herself too deep and wide for any words.

"I love you beyond your understanding, it seems," was my reply. "I am proud to love you, for I know I am worthy to love you and am worth all love you may give me. But Rome is my foster-mother, and were I untrue to her, of little pride, of little worth would be my love for you."

The uproar that followed about Jesus and the soldiers died away along the street. And when there was no further sound of it Miriam turned to go, with neither word nor look for me.

I knew one last rush of mad hunger for her. I sprang and seized her. I would horse her and ride away with her and my men into Syria away from this cursed city of folly. She struggled. I crushed her. She struck me on the face, and I continued to hold and crush her, for the blows were sweet. And there she ceased to struggle. She became cold and motionless, so that I knew there was no woman's love that my arms girdled. For me she was dead. Slowly I let go of her. Slowly she stepped back. As if she did not see me she turned and went away across the quiet room, and without looking back passed through the hangings and was gone.

* * * * *

I, Ragnar Lodbrog, never came to read nor write. But in my days I have listened to great talk. As I see it now, I never learned great talk, such as that of the Jews, learned in their law, nor such as that of the Romans, learned in their philosophy and in the philosophy of the Greeks. Yet have I talked in simplicity and straightness, as a man may well talk who has lived life from the ships of Tostig Lodbrog and the roof of Brunanbuhr across the world to Jerusalem and back again. And straight talk and simple I gave Sulpicius Quirinius, when I went away into Syria to report to him of the various matters that had been at issue in Jerusalem.

CHAPTER XVIII

Suspended animation is nothing new, not alone in the vegetable world and in the lower forms of animal life, but in the highly evolved, complex organism of man himself. A cataleptic trance is a cataleptic trance, no matter how induced. From time immemorial the fakir of India has been able voluntarily to induce such states in himself. It is an old trick of the fakirs to have themselves buried alive. Other men, in similar trances, have misled the physicians, who pronounced them dead and gave the orders that put them alive under the ground.

As my jacket experiences in San Quentin continued I dwelt not a little on this problem of suspended animation. I remembered having read that the far northern Siberian peasants made a practice of hibernating through the long winters just as bears and other wild animals do. Some scientist studied these peasants and found that during these periods of the "long sleep" respiration and digestion practically ceased, and that the heart was at so low tension as to defy detection by ordinary layman's examination.

In such a trance the bodily processes are so near to absolute suspension that the air and food consumed are practically negligible. On this reasoning, partly, was based my defiance of Warden Atherton and Doctor Jackson. It was thus that I dared challenge them to give me a hundred days in the jacket. And they did not dare accept my challenge.

Nevertheless I did manage to do without water, as well as food, during my ten-days' bouts. I found it an intolerable nuisance, in the deeps of dream across space and time, to be haled back to the sordid present by a despicable prison doctor pressing water to my lips. So I warned Doctor Jackson, first, that I intended doing without water while in the jacket; and next, that I would resist any efforts to compel me to drink.

Of course we had our little struggle; but after several attempts Doctor Jackson gave it up. Thereafter the space occupied in Darrell Standing's life by a jacket-bout was scarcely more than a few ticks of the clock. Immediately I was laced I devoted myself to inducing the little death. From practice it became simple and easy. I suspended animation and consciousness so quickly that I escaped the really terrible suffering consequent upon suspending circulation. Most quickly came the dark. And the next I, Darrell Standing, knew was the light again, the faces bending over me as I was unlaced, and the knowledge that ten days had passed in the twinkling of an eye.

But oh, the wonder and the glory of those ten days spent by me elsewhere! The journeys through the long chain of existences! The long darks, the growings of nebulous lights, and the fluttering apparitional selves that dawned through the growing light!

Much have I pondered upon the relation of these other selves to me, and of the relation of the total experience to the modern doctrine of evolution. I can truly say that my experience is in complete accord with our conclusions of evolution.

I, like any man, am a growth. I did not begin when I was born nor when I was conceived. I have been growing, developing, through incalculable myriads of millenniums. All these experiences of all these lives, and of countless other lives, have gone to the making of the soul-stuff or the spirit-stuff that is I. Don't you see? They are the stuff of me. Matter does not remember, for spirit is memory. I am this spirit compounded of the memories of my endless incarnations.

Whence came in me, Darrell Standing, the red pulse of wrath that has wrecked my life and put me in the condemned cells? Surely it did not come into being, was not created, when the babe that was to be Darrell Standing was conceived. That old red wrath is far older than my mother, far older than the oldest and first mother of men. My mother, at my inception, did not create that passionate lack of fear that is mine. Not all the mothers of the whole evolution of men manufactured fear or fearlessness in men. Far back beyond the first men were fear and fearlessness, love, hatred, anger, all the emotions, growing, developing, becoming the stuff that was to become men.

I am all of my past, as every protagonist of the Mendelian law must agree. All my previous selves have their voices, echoes, promptings in me. My every mode of action, heat of passion, flicker of thought is shaded, toned, infinitesimally shaded and toned, by that vast array of other selves that preceded me and went into the making of me.

The stuff of life is plastic. At the same time this stuff never forgets. Mould it as you will, the old memories persist. All manner of horses, from ton Shires to dwarf Shetlands, have been bred up and down from those first wild ponies domesticated by primitive man. Yet to this day man has not bred out the kick of the horse. And I, who am composed of those first horse-tamers, have not had their red anger bred out of me.

I am man born of woman. My days are few, but the stuff of me is indestructible. I have been woman born of woman. I have been a woman and borne my children. And I shall be born again. Oh, incalculable times again shall I be born; and yet the stupid dolts about me think that by stretching my neck with a rope they will make me cease.

Yes, I shall be hanged . . . soon. This is the end of June. In a little while they will try to befool me. They will take me from this cell to the bath, according to the prison custom of the weekly bath. But I shall not be brought back to this cell. I shall be dressed outright in fresh clothes and be taken to the death-cell. There they will place the death-watch on me. Night or day, waking or sleeping, I shall be watched. I shall not be permitted to put my head under the blankets for fear I may anticipate the State by choking myself.

Always bright light will blaze upon me. And then, when they have well wearied me, they will lead me out one morning in a shirt without a collar and drop me through the trap. Oh, I know. The rope they will do it with is well-stretched. For many a month now the hangman of Folsom has been stretching it with heavy weights so as to take the spring out of it.

Yes, I shall drop far. They have cunning tables of calculations, like interest tables, that show the distance of the drop in relation to the victim's weight. I am so emaciated that they will have to drop me far in order to break my neck. And then the onlookers will take their hats off, and as I swing the doctors will press their ears to my chest to count my fading heart-beats, and at last they will say that I am dead.

It is grotesque. It is the ridiculous effrontery of men-maggots who think they can kill me. I cannot die. I am immortal, as they are immortal; the difference is that I know it and they do not know it.

Pah! I was once a hangman, or an executioner, rather. Well I remember it! I used the sword, not the rope. The sword is the braver way, although all ways are equally inefficacious. Forsooth, as if spirit could be thrust through with steel or throttled by a rope!

CHAPTER XIX

Next to Oppenheimer and Morrell, who rotted with me through the years of darkness, I was considered the most dangerous prisoner in San Quentin. On the other hand I was considered the toughest—tougher even than Oppenheimer and Morrell. Of course by toughness I mean enduringness. Terrible as were the attempts to break them in body and in spirit, more terrible were the attempts to break me. And I endured. Dynamite or curtains had been Warden Atherton's ultimatum. And in the end it was neither. I could not produce the dynamite, and Warden Atherton could not induce the curtains.

It was not because my body was enduring, but because my spirit was enduring. And it was because, in earlier existences, my spirit had been wrought to steel-hardness by steel-hard experiences. There was one experience that for long was a sort of nightmare to me. It had neither beginning nor end. Always I found myself on a rocky, surge-battered islet so low that in storms the salt spray swept over its highest point. It rained much. I lived in a lair and suffered greatly, for I was without fire and lived on uncooked meat.

Always I suffered. It was the middle of some experience to which I could get no clue. And since, when I went into the little death I had no power of directing my journeys, I often found myself reliving this particularly detestable experience. My only happy moments were when the sun shone, at which times I basked on the rocks and thawed out the almost perpetual chill I suffered.

My one diversion was an oar and a jackknife. Upon this oar I spent much time, carving minute letters and cutting a notch for each week that passed. There were many notches. I sharpened the knife on a flat piece of rock, and no barber was ever more careful of his favourite razor than was I of that knife. Nor did ever a miser prize his treasure as did I prize the knife. It was as precious as my life. In truth, it was my life.

By many repetitions, I managed to bring back out of the jacket the legend that was carved on the oar. At first I could bring but little. Later, it grew easier, a matter of piecing portions together. And at last I had the thing complete. Here it is:

This is to acquaint the person into whose hands this Oar may fall, that Daniel Foss, a native of Elkton, in Maryland, one of the United States of America, and who sailed from the port of Philadelphia, in 1809, on board the brig Negociator, bound to the Friendly Islands, was cast upon this desolate island the February following, where he erected a hut and lived a number of years, subsisting on seals—he being the last who survived of the crew of said brig, which ran foul of an island of ice, and foundered on the 25th Nov. 1809.

There it was, quite clear. By this means I learned a lot about myself. One vexed point, however, I never did succeed in clearing up. Was this island situated in the far South Pacific or the far South Atlantic? I do not know enough of sailing-ship tracks to be certain whether the brig *Negociator* would sail for the Friendly Islands via Cape Horn or via the Cape of Good Hope. To confess my own ignorance, not until after I was transferred to Folsom did I learn in which ocean were the Friendly Islands. The Japanese murderer, whom I have mentioned before, had been a sailmaker on board the Arthur Sewall ships, and he told me that the probable sailing course would be by way of the Cape of Good Hope. If this were so, then the dates of sailing from Philadelphia and of being wrecked would easily determine which ocean. Unfortunately, the sailing date is merely 1809. The wreck might as likely have occurred in one ocean as the other.

Only once did I, in my trances, get a hint of the period preceding the time spent on the island. This begins at the moment of the brig's collision with the iceberg, and I shall narrate it, if for no other reason, at least to give an account of my curiously cool and deliberate conduct. This conduct at this time, as you shall see, was what enabled me in the end to survive alone of all the ship's company.

I was awakened, in my bunk in the forecastle, by a terrific crash. In fact, as was true of the other six sleeping men of the watch below, awaking and leaping from bunk to floor were simultaneous. We knew what had happened. The others waited for nothing, rushing only partly clad upon deck. But I knew what to expect, and I did wait. I knew that if we escaped at all, it would be by the longboat. No man could swim in so freezing a sea. And no man, thinly clad, could live long in the open boat. Also, I knew just about how long it would take to launch the boat.

So, by the light of the wildly swinging slush-lamp, to the tumult on deck and to cries of "She's sinking!" I proceeded to ransack my sea-chest for suitable garments. Also, since they would never use them again, I ransacked the sea chests of my shipmates. Working quickly but collectedly, I took nothing but the warmest and stoutest of clothes. I put on the four best woollen shirts the forecastle boasted, three pairs of pants, and three pairs of thick woollen socks. So large were my feet thus incased that I could not put on my own good boots. Instead, I thrust on Nicholas Wilton's new boots, which were larger and even stouter than mine. Also, I put on Jeremy Nalor's pea jacket over my own, and, outside of both, put on Seth Richard's thick canvas coat which I remembered he had fresh-oiled only a short while previous.

Two pairs of heavy mittens, John Robert's muffler which his mother had knitted for him, and Joseph Dawes' beaver cap atop my own, both bearing ear-and neck-flaps, completed my outfitting. The shouts that the brig was sinking redoubled, but I took a minute longer to fill my pockets with all the plug tobacco I could lay hands on. Then I climbed out on deck, and not a moment too soon.

The moon, bursting through a crack of cloud, showed a bleak and savage picture. Everywhere was wrecked gear, and everywhere was ice. The sails, ropes, and spars of the mainmast, which was still standing, were fringed with icicles; and there came over me a feeling almost of relief in that never again should I have to pull and haul on the stiff tackles and hammer ice so that the frozen ropes could run through the frozen shivs. The wind, blowing half a gale, cut with the sharpness that is a sign of the proximity of icebergs; and the big seas were bitter cold to look upon in the moonlight.

The longboat was lowering away to larboard, and I saw men, struggling on the ice-sheeted deck with barrels of provisions, abandon the food in their haste to get away. In vain Captain Nicholl strove with them. A sea, breaching across from windward, settled the matter and sent them leaping over the rail in heaps. I gained the captain's shoulder, and, holding on to him, I shouted in his ear that if he would board the boat and prevent the men from casting off, I would attend to the provisioning.

Little time was given me, however. Scarcely had I managed, helped by the second mate, Aaron Northrup, to lower away half-a-dozen barrels and kegs, when all cried from the boat that they were casting off. Good reason they had. Down upon us from windward was drifting a towering ice-mountain, while to leeward, close aboard, was another ice-mountain upon which we were driving.

Quicker in his leap was Aaron Northrup. I delayed a moment, even as the boat was shoving away, in order to select a spot amidships where the men were thickest, so that their bodies might break my fall. I was not minded to embark with a broken member on so hazardous a voyage in the longboat. That the men might have room at the oars, I worked my way quickly aft into the sternsheets. Certainly, I had other and sufficient reasons. It would be more comfortable in the sternsheets than in the narrow bow. And further, it would be well to be near the afterguard in whatever troubles that were sure to arise under such circumstances in the days to come.

In the sternsheets were the mate, Walter Drake, the surgeon, Arnold Bentham, Aaron Northrup, and Captain Nicholl, who was steering. The surgeon was bending over Northrup, who lay in the bottom groaning. Not so fortunate had he been in his ill-considered leap, for he had broken his right leg at the hip joint.

There was little time for him then, however, for we were labouring in a heavy sea directly between the two ice islands that were rushing together. Nicholas Wilton, at the stroke oar, was cramped for room; so I better stowed the barrels, and, kneeling and facing him, was able to add my weight to the oar. For'ard, I could see John Roberts straining at the bow oar. Pulling on his shoulders from behind, Arthur Haskins and the boy, Benny Hardwater, added their weight to his. In fact, so eager were all hands to help that more than one was thus in the way and cluttered the movements of the rowers.

It was close work, but we went clear by a matter of a hundred yards, so that I was able to turn my head and see the untimely end of the *Negociator*. She was caught squarely in the pinch and she was squeezed between the ice as a sugar plum might be squeezed between thumb and forefinger of a boy. In the shouting of the wind and the roar of water we heard nothing, although the crack of the brig's stout ribs and deckbeams must have been enough to waken a hamlet on a peaceful night.

Silently, easily, the brig's sides squeezed together, the deck bulged up, and the crushed remnant dropped down and was gone, while where she had been was occupied by the grinding conflict of the ice-islands. I felt regret at the destruction of this haven against the elements, but at the same time was well pleased at thought of my snugness inside my four shirts and three coats.

Yet it proved a bitter night, even for me. I was the warmest clad in the boat. What the others must have suffered I did not care to dwell upon over much. For fear that we might meet up with more ice in the darkness, we bailed and held the boat bow-on to the seas. And continually, now with one mitten, now with the other, I rubbed my nose that it might not freeze. Also, with memories lively in me of the home circle in Elkton, I prayed to God.

In the morning we took stock. To commence with, all but two or three had suffered frost-bite. Aaron Northrup, unable to move because of his broken hip, was very bad. It was the surgeon's opinion that both of Northrup's feet were hopelessly frozen.

The longboat was deep and heavy in the water, for it was burdened by the entire ship's company of twenty-one. Two of these were boys. Benny Hardwater was a bare thirteen, and Lish Dickery, whose family was near neighbour to mine in Elkton, was just turned sixteen. Our provisions consisted of three hundred-weight of beef and two hundred-weight of pork. The half-dozen loaves of brine-pulped bread, which the cook had brought, did not count. Then there were three small barrels of water and one small keg of beer.

Captain Nicholl frankly admitted that in this uncharted ocean he had no knowledge of any near land. The one thing to do was to run for more clement climate, which we accordingly did, setting our small sail and steering quartering before the fresh wind to the north-east.

The food problem was simple arithmetic. We did not count Aaron Northrup, for we knew he would soon be gone. At a pound per day, our five hundred pounds would last us twenty-five days; at half a pound, it would last fifty. So half a pound had it. I divided and issued the meat under the captain's eyes, and managed it fairly enough, God knows, although some of the men grumbled from the first. Also, from time to time I made fair division among the men of the plug tobacco I had stowed in my many pockets—a thing which I could not but regret, especially when I knew it was being wasted on this man and that who I was certain could not live a day more, or, at best, two days or three.

For we began to die soon in the open boat. Not to starvation but to the killing cold and exposure were those earlier deaths due. It was a matter of the survival of the toughest and the luckiest. I was tough by constitution, and lucky inasmuch as I was warmly clad and had not broken my leg like Aaron Northrup. Even so, so strong was he that, despite being the first to be severely frozen, he was days in passing. Vance Hathaway was the first. We found him in the gray of dawn crouched doubled in the bow and frozen stiff. The boy, Lish Dickery, was the second to go. The other boy, Benny Hardwater, lasted ten or a dozen days.

So bitter was it in the boat that our water and beer froze solid, and it was a difficult task justly to apportion the pieces I broke off with Northrup's claspknife. These pieces we put in our mouths and sucked till they melted. Also, on occasion of snow-squalls, we had all the snow we desired. All of which was not good for us, causing a fever of inflammation to attack our mouths so that the membranes were continually dry and burning. And there was no allaying a thirst so generated. To suck more ice or snow was merely to aggravate the inflammation. More than anything else, I think it was this that caused the death of Lish Dickery. He was out of his head and raving for twenty-four hours before he died. He died babbling for water, and yet he did not die for need of water. I resisted as much as possible the temptation to suck ice, contenting myself with a shred of tobacco in my cheek, and made out with fair comfort.

We stripped all clothing from our dead. Stark they came into the world, and stark they passed out over the side of the longboat and down into the dark freezing ocean. Lots were cast for the clothes. This was by Captain Nicholl's command, in order to prevent quarrelling.

It was no time for the follies of sentiment. There was not one of us who did not know secret satisfaction at the occurrence of each death. Luckiest of all was Israel Stickney in casting lots, so that in the end, when he passed, he was a veritable treasure trove of clothing. It gave a new lease of life to the survivors.

We continued to run to the north-east before the fresh westerlies, but our quest for warmer weather seemed vain. Ever the spray froze in the bottom of the boat, and I still chipped beer and drinking water with Northrup's knife. My own knife I reserved. It was of good steel, with a keen edge and stoutly fashioned, and I did not care to peril it in such manner.

By the time half our company was overboard, the boat had a reasonably high freeboard and was less ticklish to handle in the gusts. Likewise there was more room for a man to stretch out comfortably.

A source of continual grumbling was the food. The captain, the mate, the surgeon, and myself, talking it over, resolved not to increase the daily whack of half a pound of meat. The six sailors, for whom Tobias Snow made himself spokesman, contended that the death of half of us was equivalent to a doubling of our provisioning, and that therefore the ration should be increased to a pound. In reply, we of the afterguard pointed out that it was our chance for life that was doubled did we but bear with the half-pound ration.

It is true that eight ounces of salt meat did not go far in enabling us to live and to resist the severe cold. We were quite weak, and, because of our weakness, we frosted easily. Noses and cheeks were all black with frost-bite. It was impossible to be warm, although we now had double the garments we had started with.

Five weeks after the loss of the *Negociator* the trouble over the food came to a head. I was asleep at the time—it was night—when Captain Nicholl caught Jud Hetchkins stealing from the pork barrel. That he was abetted by the other five men was proved by their actions. Immediately Jud Hetchkins was discovered, the whole six threw themselves upon us with their knives. It was close, sharp work in the dim light of the stars, and it was a mercy the boat was not overturned. I had reason to be thankful for my many shirts and coats which served me as an armour. The knife-thrusts scarcely more than drew blood through the so great thickness of cloth, although I was scratched to bleeding in a round dozen of places.

The others were similarly protected, and the fight would have ended in no more than a mauling all around, had not the mate, Walter Dakon, a very powerful man, hit upon the idea of ending the matter by tossing the mutineers overboard. This was joined in by Captain Nicholl, the surgeon, and myself, and in a trice five of the six were in the water and clinging to the gunwale. Captain Nicholl and the surgeon were busy amidships with the sixth, Jeremy Nalor, and were in the act of throwing him overboard, while the mate was occupied with rapping the fingers along the gunwale with a boat-stretcher. For the moment I had nothing to do, and so was able to observe the tragic end of the mate. As he lifted the stretcher to rap Seth Richards' fingers, the latter, sinking down low in the water and then jerking himself up by both hands, sprang half into the boat, locked his arms about the mate and, falling backward and outboard, dragged the mate with him. Doubtlessly he never relaxed his grip, and both drowned together.

Thus left alive of the entire ship's company were three of us: Captain Nicholl, Arnold Bentham (the surgeon), and myself. Seven had gone in the twinkling of an eye, consequent on Jud Hetchkins' attempt to steal provisions. And to me it seemed a pity that so much good warm clothing had been wasted there in the sea. There was not one of us who could not have managed gratefully with more.

Captain Nicholl and the surgeon were good men and honest. Often enough, when two of us slept, the one awake and steering could have stolen from the meat. But this never happened. We trusted one another fully, and we would have died rather than betray that trust.

236

We continued to content ourselves with half a pound of meat each per day, and we took advantage of every favouring breeze to work to the north'ard. Not until January fourteenth, seven weeks since the wreck, did we come up with a warmer latitude. Even then it was not really warm. It was merely not so bitterly cold.

Here the fresh westerlies forsook us and we bobbed and blobbed about in doldrummy weather for many days. Mostly it was calm, or light contrary winds, though sometimes a burst of breeze, as like as not from dead ahead, would last for a few hours. In our weakened condition, with so large a boat, it was out of the question to row. We could merely hoard our food and wait for God to show a more kindly face. The three of us were faithful Christians, and we made a practice of prayer each day before the apportionment of food. Yes, and each of us prayed privately, often and long.

By the end of January our food was near its end. The pork was entirely gone, and we used the barrel for catching and storing rainwater. Not many pounds of beef remained. And in all the nine weeks in the open boat we had raised no sail and glimpsed no land. Captain Nicholl frankly admitted that after sixty-three days of dead reckoning he did not know where we were.

The twentieth of February saw the last morsel of food eaten. I prefer to skip the details of much that happened in the next eight days. I shall touch only on the incidents that serve to show what manner of men were my companions. We had starved so long, that we had no reserves of strength on which to draw when the food utterly ceased, and we grew weaker with great rapidity.

On February twenty-fourth we calmly talked the situation over. We were three stout-spirited men, full of life and toughness, and we did not want to die. No one of us would volunteer to sacrifice himself for the other two. But we agreed on three things: we must have food; we must decide the matter by casting lots; and we would cast the lots next morning if there were no wind.

Next morning there was wind, not much of it, but fair, so that we were able to log a sluggish two knots on our northerly course. The mornings of the twenty-sixth and twenty-seventh found us with a similar breeze. We were fearfully weak, but we abided by our decision and continued to sail.

But with the morning of the twenty-eighth we knew the time was come. The longboat rolled drearily on an empty, windless sea, and the stagnant, overcast sky gave no promise of any breeze. I cut three pieces of cloth, all of a size, from my jacket. In the ravel of one of these pieces was a bit of brown thread. Whoever drew this lost. I then put the three lots into my hat, covering it with Captain Nicholl's hat.

All was ready, but we delayed for a time while each prayed silently and long, for we knew that we were leaving the decision to God. I was not unaware of my own honesty and worth; but I was equally aware of the honesty and worth of my companions, so that it perplexed me how God could decide so fine-balanced and delicate a matter.

The captain, as was his right and due, drew first. After his hand was in the hat he delayed for sometime with closed eyes, his lips moving a last prayer. And he drew a blank. This was right—a true decision I could not but admit to myself; for Captain Nicholl's life was largely known to me and I knew him to be honest, upright, and God-fearing.

Remained the surgeon and me. It was one or the other, and, according to ship's rating, it was his due to draw next. Again we prayed. As I prayed I strove to quest back in my life and cast a hurried tally-sheet of my own worth and unworth.

I held the hat on my knees with Captain Nicholl's hat over it. The surgeon thrust in his hand and fumbled about for some time, while I wondered whether the feel of that one brown thread could be detected from the rest of the ravel.

At last he withdrew his hand. The brown thread was in his piece of cloth. I was instantly very humble and very grateful for God's blessing thus extended to me; and I resolved to keep more faithfully than ever all of His commandments. The next moment I could not help but feel that the surgeon and the captain were pledged to each other by closer ties of position and intercourse than with me, and that they were in a measure disappointed with the outcome. And close with that thought ran the conviction that they were such true men that the outcome would not interfere with the plan arranged.

I was right. The surgeon bared arm and knife and prepared to open a great vein. First, however, he spoke a few words.

"I am a native of Norfolk in the Virginias," he said, "where I expect I have now a wife and three children living. The only favour that I have to request of you is, that should it please God to deliver either of you from your perilous situation, and should you be so fortunate as to reach once more your native country, that you would acquaint my unfortunate family with my wretched fate."

Next he requested courteously of us a few minutes in which to arrange his affairs with God. Neither Captain Nicholl nor I could utter a word, but with streaming eyes we nodded our consent.

Without doubt Arnold Bentham was the best collected of the three of us. My own anguish was prodigious, and I am confident that Captain Nicholl suffered equally. But what was one to do? The thing was fair and proper and had been decided by God.

But when Arnold Bentham had completed his last arrangements and made ready to do the act, I could contain myself no longer, and cried out:

"Wait! We who have endured so much surely can endure a little more. It is now mid-morning. Let us wait until twilight. Then, if no event has appeared to change our dreadful destiny, do you Arnold Bentham, do as we have agreed."

He looked to Captain Nicholl for confirmation of my suggestion, and Captain Nicholl could only nod. He could utter no word, but in his moist and frosty blue eyes was a wealth of acknowledgment I could not misread.

I did not, I could not, deem it a crime, having so determined by fair drawing of lots, that Captain Nicholl and myself should profit by the death of Arnold Bentham. I could not believe that the love of life that actuated us had been implanted in our breasts by aught other than God. It was God's will, and we His poor creatures could only obey and fulfil His will. And yet, God was kind. In His all-kindness He saved us from so terrible, though so righteous, an act.

Scarce had a quarter of an hour passed, when a fan of air from the west, with a hint of frost and damp in it, crisped on our cheeks. In another five minutes we had steerage from the filled sail, and Arnold Bentham was at the steering sweep.

"Save what little strength you have," he had said. "Let me consume the little strength left in me in order that it may increase your chance to survive."

And so he steered to a freshening breeze, while Captain Nicholl and I lay sprawled in the boat's bottom and in our weakness dreamed dreams and glimpsed visions of the dear things of life far across the world from us.

It was an ever-freshening breeze of wind that soon began to puff and gust. The cloud stuff flying across the sky foretold us of a gale. By midday Arnold Bentham fainted at the steering, and, ere the boat could broach in the tidy sea already running, Captain Nicholl and I were at the steering sweep with all the four of our weak hands upon it. We came to an agreement, and, just as Captain Nicholl had drawn the first lot by virtue of his office, so now he took the first spell at steering. Thereafter the three of us spelled one another every fifteen minutes. We were very weak and we could not spell longer at a time.

By mid-afternoon a dangerous sea was running. We should have rounded the boat to, had our situation not been so desperate, and let her drift bow-on to a sea-anchor extemporized of our mast and sail. Had we broached in those great, over-topping seas, the boat would have been rolled over and over.

Time and again, that afternoon, Arnold Bentham, for our sakes, begged that we come to a sea-anchor. He knew that we continued to run only in the hope that the decree of the lots might not have to be carried out. He was a noble man. So was Captain Nicholl noble, whose frosty eyes had wizened to points of steel. And in such noble company how could I be less noble? I thanked God repeatedly, through that long afternoon of peril, for the privilege of having known two such men. God and the right dwelt in them and no matter what my poor fate might be, I could but feel well recompensed by such companionship. Like them I did not want to die, yet was unafraid to die. The quick, early doubt I had had of these two men was long since dissipated. Hard the school, and hard the men, but they were noble men, God's own men.

I saw it first. Arnold Bentham, his own death accepted, and Captain Nicholl, well nigh accepting death, lay rolling like loose-bodied dead men in the boat's bottom, and I was steering when I saw it. The boat, foaming and surging with the swiftness of wind in its sail, was uplifted on a crest, when, close before me, I saw the sea-battered islet of rock. It was not half a mile off. I cried out, so that the other two, kneeling and reeling and clutching for support, were peering and staring at what I saw.

"Straight for it, Daniel," Captain Nicholl mumbled command. "There may be a cove. There may be a cove. It is our only chance."

Once again he spoke, when we were atop that dreadful lee shore with no cove existent.

"Straight for it, Daniel. If we go clear we are too weak ever to win back against sea and wind."

He was right. I obeyed. He drew his watch and looked, and I asked the time. It was five o'clock. He stretched out his hand to Arnold Bentham, who met and shook it weakly; and both gazed at me, in their eyes extending that same hand-clasp. It was farewell, I knew; for what chance had creatures so feeble as we to win alive over those surf-battered rocks to the higher rocks beyond?

Twenty feet from shore the boat was snatched out of my control. In a trice it was overturned and I was strangling in the salt. I never saw my companions again. By good fortune I was buoyed by the steering-oar I still grasped, and by great good fortune a fling of sea, at the right instant, at the right spot, threw me far up the gentle slope of the one shelving rock on all that terrible shore. I was not hurt. I was not bruised. And with brain reeling from weakness I was able to crawl and scramble farther up beyond the clutching backwash of the sea.

I stood upright, knowing myself saved, and thanking God, and staggering as I stood. Already the boat was pounded to a thousand fragments. And though I saw them not, I could guess how grievously had been pounded the bodies of Captain Nicholl and Arnold Bentham. I saw an oar on the edge of the foam, and at certain risk I drew it clear. Then I fell to my knees, knowing myself fainting. And yet, ere I fainted, with a sailor's instinct I dragged my body on and up among the cruel hurting rocks to faint finally beyond the reach of the sea.

I was near a dead man myself, that night, mostly in stupor, only dimly aware at times of the extremity of cold and wet that I endured. Morning brought me astonishment and terror. No plant, not a blade of grass, grew on that wretched projection of rock from the ocean's bottom. A quarter of a mile in width and a half mile in length, it was no more than a heap of rocks. Naught could I discover to gratify the cravings of exhausted nature. I was consumed with thirst, yet was there no fresh water. In vain I tasted to my mouth's undoing every cavity and depression in the rocks. The spray of the gale so completely had enveloped every portion of the island that every depression was filled with water salt as the sea.

Of the boat remained nothing—not even a splinter to show that a boat had been. I stood possessed of my garments, a stout knife, and the one oar I had saved. The gale had abated, and all that day, staggering and falling, crawling till hands and knees bled, I vainly sought water.

That night, nearer death than ever, I sheltered behind a rock from the wind. A heavy shower of rain made me miserable. I removed my various coats and spread them to soak up the rain; but, when I came to wring the moisture from them into my mouth, I was disappointed, because the cloth had been thoroughly impregnated with the salt of the ocean in which I had been immersed. I lay on my back, my mouth open to catch the few rain-drops that fell directly into it. It was tantalizing, but it kept my membranes moist and me from madness.

The second day I was a very sick man. I, who had not eaten for so long, began to swell to a monstrous fatness—my legs, my arms, my whole body.

With the slightest of pressures my fingers would sink in a full inch into my skin, and the depressions so made were long in going away. Yet did I labour sore in order to fulfil God's will that I should live. Carefully, with my hands, I cleaned out the salt water from every slight hole, in the hope that succeeding showers of rain might fill them with water that I could drink.

My sad lot and the memories of the loved ones at Elkton threw me into a melancholy, so that I often lost my recollection for hours at a time. This was a mercy, for it veiled me from my sufferings that else would have killed me.

In the night I was roused by the beat of rain, and I crawled from hole to hole, lapping up the rain or licking it from the rocks. Brackish it was, but drinkable. It was what saved me, for, toward morning, I awoke to find myself in a profuse perspiration and quite free of all delirium.

Then came the sun, the first time since my stay on the island, and I spread most of my garments to dry. Of water I drank my careful fill, and I calculated there was ten days' supply if carefully husbanded. It was amazing how rich I felt with this vast wealth of brackish water. And no great merchant, with all his ships returned from prosperous voyages, his warehouses filled to the rafters, his strong-boxes overflowing, could have felt as wealthy as did I when I discovered, cast up on the rocks, the body of a seal that had been dead for many days. Nor did I fail, first, to thank God on my knees for this manifestation of His ever-unfailing kindness. The thing was clear to me: God had not intended I should die. From the very first He had not so intended.

I knew the debilitated state of my stomach, and I ate sparingly in the knowledge that my natural voracity would surely kill me did I yield myself to it. Never had sweeter morsels passed my lips, and I make free to confess that I shed tears of joy, again and again, at contemplation of that putrefied carcass.

My heart of hope beat strong in me once more. Carefully I preserved the portions of the carcass remaining. Carefully I covered my rock cisterns with flat stones so that the sun's rays might not evaporate the precious fluid and in precaution against some upspringing of wind in the night and the sudden flying of spray. Also I gathered me tiny fragments of seaweed and dried them in the sun for an easement between my poor body and the rough rocks whereon I made my lodging. And my garments were dry—the first time in days; so that I slept the heavy sleep of exhaustion and of returning health.

When I awoke to a new day I was another man. The absence of the sun did not depress me, and I was swiftly to learn that God, not forgetting me while I slumbered, had prepared other and wonderful blessings for me. I would have fain rubbed my eyes and looked again, for, as far as I could see, the rocks bordering upon the ocean were covered with seals. There were thousands of them, and in the water other thousands disported themselves, while the sound that went up from all their throats was prodigious and deafening. I knew it when: I saw it—meat lay there for the taking, meat sufficient for a score of ships' companies.

I directly seized my oar—than which there was no other stick of wood on the island—and cautiously advanced upon all that immensity of provender. It was quickly guessed by me that these creatures of the sea were unacquainted with man. They betrayed no signals of timidity at my approach, and I found it a boy's task to rap them on the head with the oar.

And when I had so killed my third and my fourth, I went immediately and strangely mad. Indeed quite bereft was I of all judgment as I slew and slew and continued to slay. For the space of two hours I toiled unceasingly with the oar till I was ready to drop. What excess of slaughter I might have been guilty of I know not, for at the end of that time, as if by a signal, all the seals that still lived threw themselves into the water and swiftly disappeared.

I found the number of slain seals to exceed two hundred, and I was shocked and frightened because of the madness of slaughter that had possessed me. I had sinned by wanton wastefulness, and after I had duly refreshed myself with this good wholesome food, I set about as well as I could to make amends. But first, ere the great task began, I returned thanks to that Being through whose mercy I had been so miraculously preserved. Thereupon I laboured until dark, and after dark, skinning the seals, cutting the meat into strips, and placing it upon the tops of rocks to dry in the sun. Also, I found small deposits of salt in the nooks and crannies of the rocks on the weather side of the island. This I rubbed into the meat as a preservative.

Four days I so toiled, and in the end was foolishly proud before God in that no scrap of all that supply of meat had been wasted. The unremitting labour was good for my body, which built up rapidly by means of this wholesome diet in which I did not stint myself. Another evidence of God's mercy; never, in the eight years I spent on that barren islet, was there so long a spell of clear weather and steady sunshine as in the period immediately following the slaughter of the seals.

Months were to pass ore ever the seals revisited my island. But in the meantime I was anything but idle. I built me a hut of stone, and, adjoining it, a storehouse for my cured meat. The hut I roofed with many sealskins, so that it was fairly water-proof. But I could never cease to marvel, when the rain beat on that roof, that no less than a king's ransom in the London fur market protected a castaway sailor from the elements.

I was quickly aware of the importance of keeping some kind of reckoning of time, without which I was sensible that I should soon lose all knowledge of the day of the week, and be unable to distinguish one from the other, and not know which was the Lord's day.

I remembered back carefully to the reckoning of time kept in the longboat by Captain Nicholl; and carefully, again and again, to make sure beyond any shadow of uncertainty, I went over the tale of the days and nights I had spent on the island. Then, by seven stones outside my hut, I kept my weekly calendar. In one place on the oar I cut a small notch for each week, and in another place on the oar I notched the months, being duly careful indeed, to reckon in the additional days to each month over and beyond the four weeks.

Thus I was enabled to pay due regard to the Sabbath. As the only mode of worship I could adopt, I carved a short hymn, appropriate to my situation, on the oar, which I never failed to chant on the Sabbath. God, in His all-mercy, had not forgotten me; nor did I, in those eight years, fail at all proper times to remember God.

It was astonishing the work required, under such circumstances, to supply one's simple needs of food and shelter. Indeed, I was rarely idle, that

245

first year. The hut, itself a mere lair of rocks, nevertheless took six weeks of my time. The tardy curing and the endless scraping of the sealskins, so as to make them soft and pliable for garments, occupied my spare moments for months and months.

Then there was the matter of my water supply. After any heavy gale, the flying spray salted my saved rainwater, so that at times I was grievously put to live through till fresh rains fell unaccompanied by high winds. Aware that a continual dropping will wear a stone, I selected a large stone, fine and tight of texture and, by means of smaller stones, I proceeded to pound it hollow. In five weeks of most arduous toil I managed thus to make a jar which I estimated to hold a gallon and a half. Later, I similarly made a four-gallon jar. It took me nine weeks. Other small ones I also made from time to time. One, that would have contained eight gallons, developed a flaw when I had worked seven weeks on it.

But it was not until my fourth year on the island, when I had become reconciled to the possibility that I might continue to live there for the term of my natural life, that I created my masterpiece. It took me eight months, but it was tight, and it held upwards of thirty gallons. These stone vessels were a great gratification to me—so much so, that at times I forgot my humility and was unduly vain of them. Truly, they were more elegant to me than was ever the costliest piece of furniture to any queen. Also, I made me a small rock vessel, containing no more than a quart, with which to convey water from the catching-places to my large receptacles. When I say that this one-quart vessel weighed all of two stone, the reader will realize that the mere gathering of the rainwater was no light task.

Thus, I rendered my lonely situation as comfortable as could be expected. I had completed me a snug and secure shelter; and, as to provision, I had always on hand a six months' supply, preserved by salting and drying. For these things, so essential to preserve life, and which one could scarcely have expected to obtain upon a desert island, I was sensible that I could not be too thankful.

Although denied the privilege of enjoying the society of any human creature, not even of a dog or a cat, I was far more reconciled to my lot than thousands probably would have been. Upon the desolate spot, where fate had placed me, I conceived myself far more happy than many, who, for ignominious crimes, were doomed to drag out their lives in solitary confinement with conscience ever biting as a corrosive canker.

However dreary my prospects, I was not without hope that that Providence, which, at the very moment when hunger threatened me with dissolution, and when I might easily have been engulfed in the maw of the sea, had cast me upon those barren rocks, would finally direct some one to my relief.

If deprived of the society of my fellow creatures, and of the conveniences of life, I could not but reflect that my forlorn situation was yet attended with some advantages. Of the whole island, though small, I had peaceable possession. No one, it was probable, would ever appear to dispute my claim, unless it were the amphibious animals of the ocean. Since the island was almost inaccessible, at night my repose was not disturbed by continual apprehension of the approach of cannibals or of beasts of prey. Again and again I thanked God on my knees for these various and many benefactions.

Yet is man ever a strange and unaccountable creature. I, who had asked of God's mercy no more than putrid meat to eat and a sufficiency of water not too brackish, was no sooner blessed with an abundance of cured meat and sweet water than I began to know discontent with my lot. I began to want fire, and the savour of cooked meat in my mouth. And continually I would discover myself longing for certain delicacies of the palate such as were part of the common daily fare on the home table at Elkton. Strive as I would, ever my fancy eluded my will and wantoned in day-dreaming of the good things I had eaten and of the good things I would eat if ever I were rescued from my lonely situation.

It was the old Adam in me, I suppose—the taint of that first father who was the first rebel against God's commandments. Most strange is man, ever insatiable, ever unsatisfied, never at peace with God or himself, his days filled

247

with restlessness and useless endeavour, his nights a glut of vain dreams of desires wilful and wrong. Yes, and also I was much annoyed by my craving for tobacco. My sleep was often a torment to me, for it was then that my desires took licence to rove, so that a thousand times I dreamed myself possessed of hogsheads of tobacco—ay, and of warehouses of tobacco, and of shiploads and of entire plantations of tobacco.

But I revenged myself upon myself. I prayed God unceasingly for a humble heart, and chastised my flesh with unremitting toil. Unable to improve my mind, I determined to improve my barren island. I laboured four months at constructing a stone wall thirty feet long, including its wings, and a dozen feet high. This was as a protection to the hut in the periods of the great gales when all the island was as a tiny petrel in the maw of the hurricane. Nor did I conceive the time misspent. Thereafter I lay snug in the heart of calm while all the air for a hundred feet above my head was one stream of gust-driven water.

In the third year I began me a pillar of rock. Rather was it a pyramid, four-square, broad at the base, sloping upward not steeply to the apex. In this fashion I was compelled to build, for gear and timber there was none in all the island for the construction of scaffolding. Not until the close of the fifth year was my pyramid complete. It stood on the summit of the island. Now, when I state that the summit was but forty feet above the sea, and that the peak of my pyramid was forty feet above the summit, it will be conceived that I, without tools, had doubled the stature of the island. It might be urged by some unthinking ones that I interfered with God's plan in the creation of the world. Not so, I hold. For was not I equally a part of God's plan, along with this heap of rocks upjutting in the solitude of ocean? My arms with which to work, my back with which to bend and lift, my hands cunning to clutch and hold—were not these parts too in God's plan? Much I pondered the matter. I know that I was right.

In the sixth year I increased the base of my pyramid, so that in eighteen months thereafter the height of my monument was fifty feet above the height of the island. This was no tower of Babel. It served two right purposes. It gave me a lookout from which to scan the ocean for ships, and increased the likelihood of my island being sighted by the careless roving eye of any seaman. And it kept my body and mind in health. With hands never idle, there was small opportunity for Satan on that island. Only in my dreams did he torment me, principally with visions of varied foods and with imagined indulgence in the foul weed called tobacco.

On the eighteenth day of the month of June, in the sixth year of my sojourn on the island, I descried a sail. But it passed far to leeward at too great a distance to discover me. Rather than suffering disappointment, the very appearance of this sail afforded me the liveliest satisfaction. It convinced me of a fact that I had before in a degree doubted, to wit: that these seas were sometimes visited by navigators.

Among other things, where the seals hauled up out of the sea, I built wide-spreading wings of low rock walls that narrowed to a *cul de sac*, where I might conveniently kill such seals as entered without exciting their fellows outside and without permitting any wounded or frightening seal to escape and spread a contagion of alarm. Seven months to this structure alone were devoted.

As the time passed, I grew more contented with my lot, and the devil came less and less in my sleep to torment the old Adam in me with lawless visions of tobacco and savoury foods. And I continued to eat my seal meat and call it good, and to drink the sweet rainwater of which always I had plenty, and to be grateful to God. And God heard me, I know, for during all my term on that island I knew never a moment of sickness, save two, both of which were due to my gluttony, as I shall later relate.

In the fifth year, ere I had convinced myself that the keels of ships did on occasion plough these seas, I began carving on my oar minutes of the more remarkable incidents that had attended me since I quitted the peaceful shores of America. This I rendered as intelligible and permanent as possible, the letters being of the smallest size. Six, and even five, letters were often a day's work for me, so painstaking was I.

And, lest it should prove my hard fortune never to meet with the long-wished opportunity to return to my friends and to my family at Elkton, I engraved, or nitched, on the broad end of the oar, the legend of my ill fate which I have already quoted near the beginning of this narrative.

This oar, which had proved so serviceable to me in my destitute situation, and which now contained a record of my own fate and that of my shipmates, I spared no pains to preserve. No longer did I risk it in knocking seals on the head. Instead, I equipped myself with a stone club, some three feet in length and of suitable diameter, which occupied an even month in the fashioning. Also, to secure the oar from the weather (for I used it in mild breezes as a flagstaff on top of my pyramid from which to fly a flag I made me from one of my precious shirts) I contrived for it a covering of well-cured sealskins.

In the month of March of the sixth year of my confinement I experienced one of the most tremendous storms that was perhaps ever witnessed by man. It commenced at about nine in the evening, with the approach of black clouds and a freshening wind from the south-west, which, by eleven, had become a hurricane, attended with incessant peals of thunder and the sharpest lightning I had ever witnessed.

I was not without apprehension for the safety of the island. Over every part the seas made a clean breach, except of the summit of my pyramid. There the life was nigh beaten and suffocated out of my body by the drive of the wind and spray. I could not but be sensible that my existence was spared solely because of my diligence in erecting the pyramid and so doubling the stature of the island.

Yet, in the morning, I had great reason for thankfulness. All my saved rainwater was turned brackish, save that in my largest vessel which was sheltered in the lee of the pyramid. By careful economy I knew I had drink sufficient until the next rain, no matter how delayed, should fall. My hut was quite washed out by the seas, and of my great store of seal meat only a wretched, pulpy modicum remained. Nevertheless I was agreeably surprised to find the rocks plentifully distributed with a sort of fish more nearly like the mullet than any I had ever observed. Of these I picked up no less than twelve hundred and nineteen, which I split and cured in the sun after the manner of cod. This welcome change of diet was not without its consequence. I was guilty of gluttony, and for all of the succeeding night I was near to death's door.

In the seventh year of my stay on the island, in the very same month of March, occurred a similar storm of great violence. Following upon it, to my astonishment, I found an enormous dead whale, quite fresh, which had been cast up high and dry by the waves. Conceive my gratification when in the bowels of the great fish I found deeply imbedded a harpoon of the common sort with a few fathoms of new line attached thereto.

Thus were my hopes again revived that I should finally meet with an opportunity to quit the desolate island. Beyond doubt these seas were frequented by whalemen, and, so long as I kept up a stout heart, sooner or later I should be saved. For seven years I had lived on seal meat, so that at sight of the enormous plentitude of different and succulent food I fell a victim to my weakness and ate of such quantities that once again I was well nigh to dying. And yet, after all, this, and the affair of the small fish, were mere indispositions due to the foreignness of the food to my stomach, which had learned to prosper on seal meat and on nothing but seal meat.

Of that one whale I preserved a full year's supply of provision. Also, under the sun's rays, in the rock hollows, I tried out much of the oil, which, with the addition of salt, was a welcome thing in which to dip my strips of seal-meat whilst dining. Out of my precious rags of shirts I could even have contrived a wick, so that, with the harpoon for steel and rock for flint, I might have had a light at night. But it was a vain thing, and I speedily forwent the thought of it. I had no need for light when God's darkness descended, for I had schooled myself to sleep from sundown to sunrise, winter and summer.

I, Darrell Standing, cannot refrain from breaking in on this recital of an earlier existence in order to note a conclusion of my own. Since human personality is a growth, a sum of all previous existences added together, what possibility was there for Warden Atherton to break down my spirit in the inquisition of solitary? I am life that survived, a structure builded up through the ages of the past—and such a past! What were ten days and nights in the jacket to me?—to me, who had once been Daniel Foss, and for eight years learned patience in that school of rocks in the far South Ocean?

* * * * *

At the end of my eighth year on the island in the month of September, when I had just sketched most ambitious plans to raise my pyramid to sixty feet above the summit of the island, I awoke one morning to stare out upon a ship with topsails aback and nearly within hail. That I might be discovered, I swung my oar in the air, jumped from rock to rock, and was guilty of all manner of livelinesses of action, until I could see the officers on the quarter-deck looking at me through their spyglasses. They answered by pointing to the extreme westerly end of the island, whither I hastened and discovered their boat manned by half a dozen men. It seems, as I was to learn afterward, the ship had been attracted by my pyramid and had altered its course to make closer examination of so strange a structure that was greater of height than the wild island on which it stood.

But the surf proved to be too great to permit the boat to land on my inhospitable shore. After divers unsuccessful attempts they signalled me that they must return to the ship. Conceive my despair at thus being unable to quit the desolate island. I seized my oar (which I had long since determined to present to the Philadelphia Museum if ever I were preserved) and with it plunged headlong into the foaming surf. Such was my good fortune, and my strength and agility, that I gained the boat.

I cannot refrain from telling here a curious incident. The ship had by this time drifted so far away, that we were all of an hour in getting aboard. During this time I yielded to my propensities that had been baffled for eight long years, and begged of the second mate, who steered, a piece of tobacco to chew. This granted, the second mate also proffered me his pipe, filled with prime Virginia leaf. Scarce had ten minutes passed when I was taken violently sick. The reason for this was clear. My system was entirely purged of tobacco, and what I now suffered was tobacco poisoning such as afflicts any boy at the time of his first smoke. Again I had reason to be grateful to God, and from that day to the day of my death, I neither used nor desired the foul weed.

* * * * *

I, Darrell Standing, must now complete the amazingness of the details of this existence which I relived while unconscious in the strait-jacket in San Quentin prison. I often wondered if Daniel Foss had been true in his resolve and deposited the carved oar in the Philadelphia Museum.

It is a difficult matter for a prisoner in solitary to communicate with the outside world. Once, with a guard, and once with a short-timer in solitary, I entrusted, by memorization, a letter of inquiry addressed to the curator of the Museum. Although under the most solemn pledges, both these men failed me. It was not until after Ed Morrell, by a strange whirl of fate, was released from solitary and appointed head trusty of the entire prison, that I was able to have the letter sent. I now give the reply, sent me by the curator of the Philadelphia Museum, and smuggled to me by Ed Morrell:

* * * * *

"It is true there is such an oar here as you have described. But few persons can know of it, for it is not on exhibition in the public rooms. In fact, and I have held this position for eighteen years, I was unaware of its existence myself.

"But upon consulting our old records I found that such an oar had been presented by one Daniel Foss, of Elkton, Maryland, in the year 1821. Not until after a long search did we find the oar in a disused attic lumber-room of odds and ends. The notches and the legend are carved on the oar just as you have described.

"We have also on file a pamphlet presented at the same time, written by the said Daniel Foss, and published in Boston by the firm of N. Coverly, Jr., in the year 1834. This pamphlet describes eight years of a castaway's life on a desert island. It is evident that this mariner, in his old age and in want, hawked this pamphlet about among the charitable.

"I am very curious to learn how you became aware of this oar, of the existence of which we of the museum were ignorant. Am I correct in assuming that you have read an account in some diary published later by this Daniel Foss? I shall be glad for any information on the subject, and am proceeding at once to have the oar and the pamphlet put back on exhibition.

"Very truly yours,

"HOSEA SALSBURTY." {1}

CHAPTER XX

The time came when I humbled Warden Atherton to unconditional surrender, making a vain and empty mouthing of his ultimatum, "Dynamite or curtains." He gave me up as one who could not be killed in a strait-jacket. He had had men die after several hours in the jacket. He had had men die after several days in the jacket, although, invariably, they were unlaced and carted into hospital ere they breathed their last . . . and received a death certificate from the doctor of pneumonia, or Bright's disease, or valvular disease of the heart.

But me Warden Atherton could never kill. Never did the urgency arise of carting my maltreated and perishing carcass to the hospital. Yet I will say that Warden Atherton tried his best and dared his worst. There was the time when he double-jacketed me. It is so rich an incident that I must tell it.

It happened that one of the San Francisco newspapers (seeking, as every newspaper and as every commercial enterprise seeks, a market that will enable it to realize a profit) tried to interest the radical portion of the working class in prison reform. As a result, union labour possessing an important political significance at the time, the time-serving politicians at Sacramento appointed a senatorial committee of investigation of the state prisons.

This State Senate committee *investigated* (pardon my italicized sneer) San Quentin. Never was there so model an institution of detention. The convicts themselves so testified. Nor can one blame them. They had experienced similar investigations in the past. They knew on which side their bread was buttered. They knew that all their sides and most of their ribs would ache very quickly after the taking of their testimony . . . if said testimony were adverse to the prison administration. Oh, believe me, my reader, it is a very ancient story. It was ancient in old Babylon, many a thousand years ago, as I well remember of that old time when I rotted in prison while palace intrigues shook the court.

As I have said, every convict testified to the humaneness of Warden Atherton's administration. In fact, so touching were their testimonials to the kindness of the Warden, to the good and varied quality of the food and the cooking, to the gentleness of the guards, and to the general decency and ease and comfort of the prison domicile, that the opposition newspapers of San Francisco raised an indignant cry for more rigour in the management of our prisons, in that, otherwise, honest but lazy citizens would be seduced into seeking enrolment as prison guests.

The Senate Committee even invaded solitary, where the three of us had little to lose and nothing to gain. Jake Oppenheimer spat in its faces and told its members, all and sundry, to go to hell. Ed Morrell told them what a noisome stews the place was, insulted the Warden to his face, and was recommended by the committee to be given a taste of the antiquated and obsolete punishments that, after all, must have been devised by previous Wardens out of necessity for the right handling of hard characters like him.

I was careful not to insult the Warden. I testified craftily, and as a scientist, beginning with small beginnings, making an art of my exposition, step by step, by tiny steps, inveigling my senatorial auditors on into willingness and eagerness to listen to the next exposure, the whole fabric so woven that there was no natural halting place at which to drop a period or interpolate a query . . . in this fashion, thus, I got my tale across.

Alas! no whisper of what I divulged ever went outside the prison walls. The Senate Committee gave a beautiful whitewash to Warden Atherton and San Quentin. The crusading San Francisco newspaper assured its working-class readers that San Quentin was whiter than snow, and further, that while it was true that the strait-jacket was still a recognized legal method of punishment for the refractory, that, nevertheless, at the present time, under the present humane and spiritually right-minded Warden, the strait-jacket was never, under any circumstance, used.

And while the poor asses of labourers read and believed, while the Senate Committee dined and wined with the Warden at the expense of the state and the tax payer, Ed Morrell, Jake Oppenheimer, and I were lying in our jackets, laced just a trifle more tightly and more vindictively than we had ever been laced before.

"It is to laugh," Ed Morrell tapped to me, with the edge of the sole of his shoe.

"I should worry," tapped Jake.

And as for me, I too capped my bitter scorn and laughter, remembered the prison houses of old Babylon, smiled to myself a huge cosmic smile, and drifted off and away into the largeness of the little death that made me heir of all the ages and the rider full-panoplied and astride of time.

Yea, dear brother of the outside world, while the whitewash was running off the press, while the august senators were wining and dining, we three of the living dead, buried alive in solidarity, were sweating our pain in the canvas torture.

And after the dinner, warm with wine, Warden Atherton himself came to see how fared it with us. Me, as usual, they found in coma. Doctor Jackson for the first time must have been alarmed. I was brought back across the dark to consciousness with the bite of ammonia in my nostrils. I smiled into the faces bent over me.

"Shamming," snorted the Warden, and I knew by the flush on his face and the thickness in his tongue that he had been drinking.

I licked my lips as a sign for water, for I desired to speak.

"You are an ass," I at last managed to say with cold distinctness. "You are an ass, a coward, a cur, a pitiful thing so low that spittle would be wasted on your face. In such matter Jake Oppenheimer is over-generous with you. As for me, without shame I tell you the only reason I do not spit upon you is that I cannot demean myself nor so degrade my spittle."

"I've reached the limit of my patience!" he bellowed. "I will kill you, Standing!"

"You've been drinking," I retorted. "And I would advise you, if you must say such things, not to take so many of your prison curs into your confidence. They will snitch on you some day, and you will lose your job."

But the wine was up and master of him.

"Put another jacket on him," he commanded. "You are a dead man, Standing. But you'll not die in the jacket. We'll bury you from the hospital."

This time, over the previous jacket, the second jacket was put on from behind and laced up in front.

"Lord, Lord, Warden, it is bitter weather," I sneered. "The frost is sharp. Wherefore I am indeed grateful for your giving me two jackets. I shall be almost comfortable."

"Tighter!" he urged to Al Hutchins, who was drawing the lacing. "Throw your feet into the skunk. Break his ribs."

I must admit that Hutchins did his best.

"You *will* lie about me," the Warden raved, the flush of wine and wrath flooding ruddier into his face. "Now see what you get for it. Your number is taken at last, Standing. This is your finish. Do you hear? This is your finish."

"A favour, Warden," I whispered faintly. Faint I was. Perforce I was nearly unconscious from the fearful constriction. "Make it a triple jacketing," I managed to continue, while the cell walls swayed and reeled about me and while I fought with all my will to hold to my consciousness that was being squeezed out of me by the jackets. "Another jacket . . . Warden . . . It . . . will . . . be . . . so . . . much . . . er . . . warmer."

And my whisper faded away as I ebbed down into the little death.

I was never the same man after that double-jacketing. Never again, to this day, no matter what my food, was I properly nurtured. I suffered internal injuries to an extent I never cared to investigate. The old pain in my ribs and stomach is with me now as I write these lines. But the poor, maltreated machinery has served its purpose. It has enabled me to live thus far, and it will enable me to live the little longer to the day they take me out in the shirt without a collar and stretch my neck with the well-stretched rope.

But the double-jacketing was the last straw. It broke down Warden Atherton. He surrendered to the demonstration that I was unkillable. As I told him once:

"The only way you can get me, Warden, is to sneak in here some night with a hatchet."

Jake Oppenheimer was responsible for a good one on the Warden which I must relate:

"I say, Warden, it must be straight hell for you to have to wake up every morning with yourself on your pillow."

And Ed Morrell to the Warden:

"Your mother must have been damn fond of children to have raised you."

It was really an offence to me when the jacketing ceased. I sadly missed that dream world of mine. But not for long. I found that I could suspend animation by the exercise of my will, aided mechanically by constricting my chest and abdomen with the blanket. Thus I induced physiological and psychological states similar to those caused by the jacket. So, at will, and without the old torment, I was free to roam through time.

Ed Morrell believed all my adventures, but Jake Oppenheimer remained sceptical to the last. It was during my third year in solitary that I paid Oppenheimer a visit. I was never able to do it but that once, and that one time was wholly unplanned and unexpected.

It was merely after unconsciousness had come to me that I found myself in his cell. My body, I knew, lay in the jacket back in my own cell. Although never before had I seen him, I knew that this man was Jake Oppenheimer. It was summer weather, and he lay without clothes on top his blanket. I was shocked by his cadaverous face and skeleton-like body. He was not even the shell of a man. He was merely the structure of a man, the bones of a man, still cohering, stripped practically of all flesh and covered with a parchment-like skin.

Not until back in my own cell and consciousness was I able to mull the thing over and realize that just as was Jake Oppenheimer, so was Ed Morrell, so was I. And I could not but thrill as I glimpsed the vastitude of spirit that inhabited these frail, perishing carcasses of us—the three incorrigibles of solitary. Flesh is a cheap, vain thing. Grass is flesh, and flesh becomes grass; but the spirit is the thing that abides and survives. I have no patience with these flesh-worshippers. A taste of solitary in San Quentin would swiftly convert them to a due appreciation and worship of the spirit.

But to return to my experience in Oppenheimer's cell. His body was that of a man long dead and shrivelled by desert heat. The skin that covered it was of the colour of dry mud. His sharp, yellow-gray eyes seemed the only part of him that was alive. They were never at rest. He lay on his back, and the eyes darted hither and thither, following the flight of the several flies that disported in the gloomy air above him. I noted, too, a scar, just above his right elbow, and another scar on his right ankle.

After a time he yawned, rolled over on his side, and inspected an angry-looking sore just above his hip. This he proceeded to cleanse and dress by the crude methods men in solitary must employ. I recognized the sore as one of the sort caused by the strait-jacket. On my body, at this moment of writing, are hundreds of scars of the jacket.

Next, Oppenheimer rolled on his back, gingerly took one of his front upper tooth—an eye teeth—between thumb and forefinger, and consideratively moved it back and forth. Again he yawned, stretched his arms, rolled over, and knocked the call to Ed Morrell.

I read the code as a matter of course.

"Thought you might be awake," Oppenheimer tapped. "How goes it with the Professor?"

Then, dim and far, I could hear Morrell's taps enunciating that they had put me in the jacket an hour before, and that, as usual, I was already deaf to all knuckle talk.

260

"He is a good guy," Oppenheimer rapped on. "I always was suspicious of educated mugs, but he ain't been hurt none by his education. He is sure square. Got all the spunk in the world, and you could not get him to squeal or double cross in a million years."

To all of which, and with amplification, Ed Morrell agreed. And I must, right here, ere I go a word further, say that I have lived many years and many lives, and that in those many lives I have known proud moments; but that the proudest moment I have ever known was the moment when my two comrades in solitary passed this appraisal of me. Ed Morrell and Jake Oppenheimer were great spirits, and in all time no greater honour was ever accorded me than this admission of me to their comradeship. Kings have knighted me, emperors have ennobled me, and, as king myself, I have known stately moments. Yet of it all nothing do I adjudge so splendid as this accolade delivered by two lifers in solitary deemed by the world as the very bottom-most of the human cesspool.

Afterwards, recuperating from this particular bout with the jacket, I brought up my visit to Jake's cell as a proof that my spirit did leave my body. But Jake was unshakable.

"It is guessing that is more than guessing," was his reply, when I had described to him his successive particular actions at the time my spirit had been in his cell. "It is figuring. You have been close to three years in solitary yourself, Professor, and you can come pretty near to figuring what any guy will do to be killing time. There ain't a thing you told me that you and Ed ain't done thousands of times, from lying with your clothes off in hot weather to watching flies, tending sores, and rapping."

Morrell sided with me, but it was no use.

"Now don't take it hard, Professor," Jake tapped. "I ain't saying you lied. I just say you get to dreaming and figuring in the jacket without knowing you're doing it. I know you believe what you say, and that you think it happened; but it don't buy nothing with me. You figure it, but you don't know you figure it—that is something you know all the time, though you don't know you know it until you get into them dreamy, woozy states."

"Hold on, Jake," I tapped. "You know I have never seen you with my own eyes. Is that right?"

"I got to take your word for it, Professor. You might have seen me and not known it was me."

"The point is," I continued, "not having seen you with your clothes off, nevertheless I am able to tell you about that scar above your right elbow, and that scar on your right ankle."

"Oh, shucks," was his reply. "You'll find all that in my prison description and along with my mug in the rogues' gallery. They is thousands of chiefs of police and detectives know all that stuff."

"I never heard of it," I assured him.

"You don't remember that you ever heard of it," he corrected. "But you must have just the same. Though you have forgotten about it, the information is in your brain all right, stored away for reference, only you've forgot where it is stored. You've got to get woozy in order to remember."

"Did you ever forget a man's name you used to know as well as your own brother's? I have. There was a little juror that convicted me in Oakland the time I got handed my fifty-years. And one day I found I'd forgotten his name. Why, bo, I lay here for weeks puzzling for it. Now, just because I could not dig it out of my memory box was no sign it was not there. It was mislaid, that was all. And to prove it, one day, when I was not even thinking about it, it popped right out of my brain to the tip of my tongue. 'Stacy,' I said right out loud. 'Joseph Stacy.' That was it. Get my drive?

"You only tell me about them scars what thousands of men know. I don't know how you got the information, I guess you don't know yourself. That ain't my lookout. But there she is. Telling me what many knows buys nothing with me. You got to deliver a whole lot more than that to make me swallow the rest of your whoppers."

Hamilton's Law of Parsimony in the weighing of evidence! So intrinsically was this slum-bred convict a scientist, that he had worked out Hamilton's law and rigidly applied it.

And yet—and the incident is delicious—Jake Oppenheimer was intellectually honest. That night, as I was dozing off, he called me with the customary signal.

"Say, Professor, you said you saw me wiggling my loose tooth. That has got my goat. That is the one thing I can't figure out any way you could know. It only went loose three days ago, and I ain't whispered it to a soul."

CHAPTER XXI

Pascal somewhere says: "In viewing the march of human evolution, the philosophic mind should look upon humanity as one man, and not as a conglomeration of individuals."

I sit here in Murderers' Row in Folsom, the drowsy hum of flies in my ears as I ponder that thought of Pascal. It is true. Just as the human embryo, in its brief ten lunar months, with bewildering swiftness, in myriad forms and semblances a myriad times multiplied, rehearses the entire history of organic life from vegetable to man; just as the human boy, in his brief years of boyhood, rehearses the history of primitive man in acts of cruelty and savagery, from wantonness of inflicting pain on lesser creatures to tribal consciousness expressed by the desire to run in gangs; just so, I, Darrell Standing, have rehearsed and relived all that primitive man was, and did, and became until he became even you and me and the rest of our kind in a twentieth century civilization.

Truly do we carry in us, each human of us alive on the planet to-day, the incorruptible history of life from life's beginning. This history is written in our tissues and our bones, in our functions and our organs, in our brain cells and in our spirits, and in all sorts of physical and psychic atavistic urgencies and compulsions. Once we were fish-like, you and I, my reader, and crawled up out of the sea to pioneer in the great, dry-land adventure in the thick of which we are now. The marks of the sea are still on us, as the marks of the serpent are still on us, ere the serpent became serpent and we became we, when pre-serpent and pre-we were one. Once we flew in the air, and once we dwelt arboreally and were afraid of the dark. The vestiges remain, graven on you and me, and graven on our seed to come after us to the end of our time on earth.

What Pascal glimpsed with the vision of a seer, I have lived. I have seen myself that one man contemplated by Pascal's philosophic eye. Oh, I have a tale, most true, most wonderful, most real to me, although I doubt that I have wit to tell it, and that you, my reader, have wit to perceive it when told. I say that I have seen myself that one man hinted at by Pascal. I have lain in the long trances of the jacket and glimpsed myself a thousand living men living the thousand lives that are themselves the history of the human man climbing upward through the ages.

Ah, what royal memories are mine, as I flutter through the æons of the long ago. In single jacket trances I have lived the many lives involved in the thousand-years-long Odysseys of the early drifts of men. Heavens, before I was of the flaxen-haired Aesir, who dwelt in Asgard, and before I was of the red-haired Vanir, who dwelt in Vanaheim, long before those times I have memories (living memories) of earlier drifts, when, like thistledown before the breeze, we drifted south before the face of the descending polar ice-cap.

I have died of frost and famine, fight and flood. I have picked berries on the bleak backbone of the world, and I have dug roots to eat from the fat-soiled fens and meadows. I have scratched the reindeer's semblance and the semblance of the hairy mammoth on ivory tusks gotten of the chase and on the rock walls of cave shelters when the winter storms moaned outside. I have cracked marrow-bones on the sites of kingly cities that had perished centuries before my time or that were destined to be builded centuries after my passing. And I have left the bones of my transient carcasses in pond bottoms, and glacial gravels, and asphaltum lakes.

I have lived through the ages known to-day among the scientists as the Paleolithic, the Neolithic, and the Bronze. I remember when with our domesticated wolves we herded our reindeer to pasture on the north shore of the Mediterranean where now are France and Italy and Spain. This was before the ice-sheet melted backward toward the pole. Many processions of the equinoxes have I lived through and died in, my reader . . . only that I remember and that you do not.

I have been a Son of the Plough, a Son of the Fish, a Son of the Tree. All religions from the beginnings of man's religious time abide in me. And when the Dominie, in the chapel, here in Folsom of a Sunday, worships God in his own good modern way, I know that in him, the Dominie, still abide the worships of the Plough, the Fish, the Tree—ay, and also all worships of Astarte and the Night.

I have been an Aryan master in old Egypt, when my soldiers scrawled obscenities on the carven tombs of kings dead and gone and forgotten aforetime. And I, the Aryan master in old Egypt, have myself builded my two burial places—the one a false and mighty pyramid to which a generation of slaves could attest; the other humble, meagre, secret, rock-hewn in a desert valley by slaves who died immediately their work was done. . . . And I wonder me here in Folsom, while democracy dreams its enchantments o'er the twentieth century world, whether there, in the rock-hewn crypt of that secret, desert valley, the bones still abide that once were mine and that stiffened my animated body when I was an Aryan master high-stomached to command.

And on the great drift, southward and eastward under the burning sun that perished all descendants of the houses of Asgard and Vanaheim, I have been a king in Ceylon, a builder of Aryan monuments under Aryan kings in old Java and old Sumatra. And I have died a hundred deaths on the great South Sea drift ere ever the rebirth of me came to plant monuments, that only Aryans plant, on volcanic tropic islands that I, Darrell Standing, cannot name, being too little versed to-day in that far sea geography.

If only I were articulate to paint in the frail medium of words what I see and know and possess incorporated in my consciousness of the mighty driftage of the races in the times before our present written history began! Yes, we had our history even then. Our old men, our priests, our wise ones, told our history into tales and wrote those tales in the stars so that our seed after us should not forget. From the sky came the life-giving rain and the sunlight. And we studied the sky, learned from the stars to calculate time and apportion the seasons; and we named the stars after our heroes and our foods and our devices for getting food; and after our wanderings, and drifts, and adventures; and after our functions and our furies of impulse and desire.

And, alas! we thought the heavens unchanging on which we wrote all our humble yearnings and all the humble things we did or dreamed of doing. When I was a Son of the Bull, I remember me a lifetime I spent at star-gazing. And, later and earlier, there were other lives in which I sang with the priests and bards the taboo-songs of the stars wherein we believed was written our imperishable record. And here, at the end of it all, I pore over

266

books of astronomy from the prison library, such as they allow condemned men to read, and learn that even the heavens are passing fluxes, vexed with star-driftage as the earth is by the drifts of men.

Equipped with this modern knowledge, I have, returning through the little death from my earlier lives, been able to compare the heavens then and now. And the stars do change. I have seen pole stars and pole stars and dynasties of pole stars. The pole star to-day is in Ursa Minor. Yet, in those far days I have seen the pole star in Draco, in Hercules, in Vega, in Cygnus, and in Cepheus. No; not even the stars abide, and yet the memory and the knowledge of them abides in me, in the spirit of me that is memory and that is eternal. Only spirit abides. All else, being mere matter, passes, and must pass.

Oh, I do see myself to-day that one man who appeared in the elder world, blonde, ferocious, a killer and a lover, a meat-eater and a root-digger, a gypsy and a robber, who, club in hand, through millenniums of years wandered the world around seeking meat to devour and sheltered nests for his younglings and sucklings.

I am that man, the sum of him, the all of him, the hairless biped who struggled upward from the slime and created love and law out of the anarchy of fecund life that screamed and squalled in the jungle. I am all that that man was and did become. I see myself, through the painful generations, snaring and killing the game and the fish, clearing the first fields from the forest, making rude tools of stone and bone, building houses of wood, thatching the roofs with leaves and straw, domesticating the wild grasses and meadow-roots, fathering them to become the progenitors of rice and millet and wheat and barley and all manner of succulent edibles, learning to scratch the soil, to sow, to reap, to store, beating out the fibres of plants to spin into thread and to weave into cloth, devising systems of irrigation, working in metals, making markets and trade-routes, building boats, and founding navigation—ay, and organizing village life, welding villages to villages till they became tribes, welding tribes together till they became nations, ever seeking the laws of things, ever making the laws of humans so that humans might live together in amity and by united effort beat down and destroy all manner of creeping, crawling, squalling things that might else destroy them.

I was that man in all his births and endeavours. I am that man to-day, waiting my due death by the law that I helped to devise many a thousand years ago, and by which I have died many times before this, many times. And as I contemplate this vast past history of me, I find several great and splendid influences, and, chiefest of these, the love of woman, man's love for the woman of his kind. I see myself, the one man, the lover, always the lover. Yes, also was I the great fighter, but somehow it seems to me as I sit here and evenly balance it all, that I was, more than aught else, the great lover. It was because I loved greatly that I was the great fighter.

Sometimes I think that the story of man is the story of the love of woman. This memory of all my past that I write now is the memory of my love of woman. Ever, in the ten thousand lives and guises, I loved her. I love her now. My sleep is fraught with her; my waking fancies, no matter whence they start, lead me always to her. There is no escaping her, that eternal, splendid, ever-resplendent figure of woman.

Oh, make no mistake. I am no callow, ardent youth. I am an elderly man, broken in health and body, and soon to die. I am a scientist and a philosopher. I, as all the generations of philosophers before me, know woman for what she is—her weaknesses, and meannesses, and immodesties, and ignobilities, her earth-bound feet, and her eyes that have never seen the stars. But—and the everlasting, irrefragable fact remains: *Her feet are beautiful, her eyes are beautiful, her arms and breasts are paradise, her charm is potent beyond all charm that has ever dazzled men; and, as the pole willy-nilly draws the needle, just so, willy-nilly, does she draw men.*

Woman has made me laugh at death and distance, scorn fatigue and sleep. I have slain men, many men, for love of woman, or in warm blood have baptized our nuptials or washed away the stain of her favour to another. I have gone down to death and dishonour, my betrayal of my comrades and of the stars black upon me, for woman's sake—for my sake, rather, I desired her so. And I have lain in the barley, sick with yearning for her, just to see her pass and glut my eyes with the swaying wonder of her and of her hair, black with the night, or brown or flaxen, or all golden-dusty with the sun.

For woman *is* beautiful . . . to man. She is sweet to his tongue, and fragrance in his nostrils. She is fire in his blood, and a thunder of trumpets; her voice is beyond all music in his ears; and she can shake his soul that else stands steadfast in the draughty presence of the Titans of the Light and of the Dark. And beyond his star-gazing, in his far-imagined heavens, Valkyrie or houri, man has fain made place for her, for he could see no heaven without her. And the sword, in battle, singing, sings not so sweet a song as the woman sings to man merely by her laugh in the moonlight, or her love-sob in the dark, or by her swaying on her way under the sun while he lies dizzy with longing in the grass.

I have died of love. I have died for love, as you shall see. In a little while they will take me out, me, Darrell Standing, and make me die. And that death shall be for love. Oh, not lightly was I stirred when I slew Professor Haskell in the laboratory at the University of California. He was a man. I was a man. And there was a woman beautiful. Do you understand? She was a woman and I was a man and a lover, and all the heredity of love was mine up from the black and squalling jungle ere love was love and man was man.

Oh, ay, it is nothing new. Often, often, in that long past have I given life and honour, place and power for love. Man is different from woman. She is close to the immediate and knows only the need of instant things. We know honour above her honour, and pride beyond her wildest guess of pride. Our eyes are far-visioned for star-gazing, while her eyes see no farther than the solid earth beneath her feet, the lover's breast upon her breast, the infant lusty in the hollow of her arm. And yet, such is our alchemy compounded of the ages, woman works magic in our dreams and in our veins, so that more than dreams and far visions and the blood of life itself is woman to us, who, as lovers truly say, is more than all the world. Yet is this just, else would man not be man, the fighter and the conqueror, treading his red way on the face of all other and lesser life—for, had man not been the lover, the royal lover, he could never have become the kingly fighter. We fight best, and die best, and live best, for what we love.

I am that one man. I see myself the many selves that have gone into the constituting of me. And ever I see the woman, the many women, who have made me and undone me, who have loved me and whom I have loved.

269

I remember, oh, long ago when human kind was very young, that I made me a snare and a pit with a pointed stake upthrust in the middle thereof, for the taking of Sabre-Tooth. Sabre-Tooth, long-fanged and long-haired, was the chiefest peril to us of the squatting place, who crouched through the nights over our fires and by day increased the growing shell-bank beneath us by the clams we dug and devoured from the salt mud-flats beside us.

And when the roar and the squall of Sabre-Tooth roused us where we squatted by our dying embers, and I was wild with far vision of the proof of the pit and the stake, it was the woman, arms about me, leg-twining, who fought with me and restrained me not to go out through the dark to my desire. She was part-clad, for warmth only, in skins of animals, mangy and fire-burnt, that I had slain; she was swart and dirty with camp smoke, unwashed since the spring rains, with nails gnarled and broken, and hands that were calloused like footpads and were more like claws than like hands; but her eyes were blue as the summer sky is, as the deep sea is, and there was that in her eyes, and in her clasped arms about me, and in her heart beating against mine, that withheld me . . . though through the dark until dawn, while Sabre-Tooth squalled his wrath and his agony, I could hear my comrades snickering and sniggling to their women in that I had not the faith in my emprise and invention to venture through the night to the pit and the stake I had devised for the undoing of Sabre-Tooth. But my woman, my savage mate held me, savage that I was, and her eyes drew me, and her arms chained me, and her twining legs and heart beating to mine seduced me from my far dream of things, my man's achievement, the goal beyond goals, the taking and the slaying of Sabre-Tooth on the stake in the pit.

Once I wan Ushu, the archer. I remember it well. For I was lost from my own people, through the great forest, till I emerged on the flat lands and grass lands, and was taken in by a strange people, kin in that their skin was white, their hair yellow, their speech not too remote from mine. And she was Igar, and I drew her as I sang in the twilight, for she was destined a race-mother, and she was broad-built and full-dugged, and she could not but draw to the man heavy-muscled, deep-chested, who sang of his prowess in man-slaying and in meat-getting, and so, promised food and protection to her in her weakness whilst she mothered the seed that was to hunt the meat and live after her.

And these people knew not the wisdom of my people, in that they snared and pitted their meat and in battle used clubs and stone throwing-sticks and were unaware of the virtues of arrows swift-flying, notched on the end to fit the thong of deer-sinew, well-twisted, that sprang into straightness when released to the spring of the ask-stick bent in the middle.

And while I sang, the stranger men laughed in the twilight. And only she, Igar, believed and had faith in me. I took her alone to the hunting, where the deer sought the water-hole. And my bow twanged and sang in the covert, and the deer fell fast-stricken, and the warm meat was sweet to us, and she was mine there by the water-hole.

And because of Igar I remained with the strange men. And I taught them the making of bows from the red and sweet-smelling wood like unto cedar. And I taught them to keep both eyes open, and to aim with the left eye, and to make blunt shafts for small game, and pronged shafts of bone for the fish in the clear water, and to flake arrow-heads from obsidian for the deer and the wild horse, the elk and old Sabre-Tooth. But the flaking of stone they laughed at, till I shot an elk through and through, the flaked stone standing out and beyond, the feathered shaft sunk in its vitals, the whole tribe applauding.

I was Ushu, the archer, and Igar was my woman and mate. We laughed under the sun in the morning, when our man-child and woman-child, yellowed like honey-bees, sprawled and rolled in the mustard, and at night she lay close in my arms, and loved me, and urged me, because of my skill at the seasoning of woods and the flaking of arrow-heads, that I should stay close by the camp and let the other men bring to me the meat from the perils of hunting. And I listened, and grew fat and short-breathed, and in the long nights, unsleeping, worried that the men of the stranger tribe brought me meat for my wisdom and honour, but laughed at my fatness and undesire for the hunting and fighting.

And in my old age, when our sons were man-grown and our daughters were mothers, when up from the southland the dark men, flat-browed, kinky-headed, surged like waves of the sea upon us and we fled back before them to the hill-slopes, Igar, like my mates far before and long after, leg-twining, arm-clasping, unseeing far visions, strove to hold me aloof from the battle.

271

And I tore myself from her, fat and short-breathed, while she wept that no longer I loved her, and I went out to the night-fighting and dawn-fighting, where, to the singing of bowstrings and the shrilling of arrows, feathered, sharp-pointed, we showed them, the kinky-heads, the skill of the killing and taught them the wit and the willing of slaughter.

And as I died them at the end of the fighting, there were death songs and singing about me, and the songs seemed to sing as these the words I have written when I was Ushu, the archer, and Igar, my mate-woman, leg-twining, arm-clasping, would have held me back from the battle.

Once, and heaven alone knows when, save that it was in the long ago when man was young, we lived beside great swamps, where the hills drew down close to the wide, sluggish river, and where our women gathered berries and roots, and there were herds of deer, of wild horses, of antelope, and of elk, that we men slew with arrows or trapped in the pits or hill-pockets. From the river we caught fish in nets twisted by the women of the bark of young trees.

I was a man, eager and curious as the antelope when we lured it by waving grass clumps where we lay hidden in the thick of the grass. The wild rice grew in the swamp, rising sheer from the water on the edges of the channels. Each morning the blackbirds awoke us with their chatter as they left their roosts to fly to the swamp. And through the long twilight the air was filled with their noise as they went back to their roosts. It was the time that the rice ripened. And there were ducks also, and ducks and blackbirds feasted to fatness on the ripe rice half unhusked by the sun.

Being a man, ever restless, ever questing, wondering always what lay beyond the hills and beyond the swamps and in the mud at the river's bottom, I watched the wild ducks and blackbirds and pondered till my pondering gave me vision and I saw. And this is what I saw, the reasoning of it:

Meat was good to eat. In the end, tracing it back, or at the first, rather, all meat came from grass. The meat of the duck and of the blackbird came from the seed of the swamp rice. To kill a duck with an arrow scarce paid for the labour of stalking and the long hours in hiding. The blackbirds were too small for arrow-killing save by the boys who were learning and preparing for the taking of larger game. And yet, in rice season, blackbirds and ducks were succulently fat. Their fatness came from the rice. Why should I and mine not be fat from the rice in the same way?

And I thought it out in camp, silent, morose, while the children squabbled about me unnoticed, and while Arunga, my mate-woman, vainly scolded me and urged me to go hunting for more meat for the many of us.

Arunga was the woman I had stolen from the hill-tribes. She and I had been a dozen moons in learning common speech after I captured her. Ah, that day when I leaped upon her, down from the over-hanging tree-branch as she padded the runway! Fairly upon her shoulders with the weight of my body I smote her, my fingers wide-spreading to clutch her. She squalled like a cat there in the runway. She fought me and bit me. The nails of her hands were like the claws of a tree-cat as they tore at me. But I held her and mastered her, and for two days beat her and forced her to travel with me down out of the canyons of the Hill-Men to the grass lands where the river flowed through the rice-swamps and the ducks and the blackbirds fed fat.

I saw my vision when the rice was ripe. I put Arunga in the bow of the fire-hollowed log that was most rudely a canoe. I bade her paddle. In the stern I spread a deerskin she had tanned. With two stout sticks I bent the stalks over the deerskin and threshed out the grain that else the blackbirds would have eaten. And when I had worked out the way of it, I gave the two stout sticks to Arunga, and sat in the bow paddling and directing.

In the past we had eaten the raw rice in passing and not been pleased with it. But now we parched it over our fire so that the grains puffed and exploded in whiteness and all the tribe came running to taste.

After that we became known among men as the Rice-Eaters and as the Sons of the Rice. And long, long after, when we were driven by the Sons of the River from the swamps into the uplands, we took the seed of the rice with us and planted it. We learned to select the largest grains for the seed, so that all the rice we thereafter ate was larger-grained and puffier in the parching and the boiling.

But Arunga. I have said she squalled and scratched like a cat when I stole her. Yet I remember the time when her own kin of the Hill-Men caught me and carried me away into the hills. They were her father, his brother, and her two own blood-brothers. But she was mine, who had lived with me. And at night, where I lay bound like a wild pig for the slaying, and they slept weary by the fire, she crept upon them and brained them with the war-club that with my hands I had fashioned. And she wept over me, and loosed me, and fled with me, back to the wide sluggish river where the blackbirds and wild ducks fed in the rice swamps—for this was before the time of the coming of the Sons of the River.

For she was Arunga, the one woman, the eternal woman. She has lived in all times and places. She will always live. She is immortal. Once, in a far land, her name was Ruth. Also has her name been Iseult, and Helen, Pocahontas, and Unga. And no stranger man, from stranger tribes, but has found her and will find her in the tribes of all the earth.

I remember so many women who have gone into the becoming of the one woman. There was the time that Har, my brother, and I, sleeping and pursuing in turn, ever hounding the wild stallion through the daytime and night, and in a wide circle that met where the sleeping one lay, drove the stallion unresting through hunger and thirst to the meekness of weakness, so that in the end he could but stand and tremble while we bound him with ropes twisted of deer-hide. On our legs alone, without hardship, aided merely by wit—the plan was mine—my brother and I walked that fleet-footed creature into possession.

And when all was ready for me to get on his back—for that had been my vision from the first—Selpa, my woman, put her arms about me, and raised her voice and persisted that Har, and not I, should ride, for Har had neither wife nor young ones and could die without hurt. Also, in the end she wept, so that I was raped of my vision, and it was Har, naked and clinging, that bestrode the stallion when he vaulted away.

It was sunset, and a time of great wailing, when they carried Har in from the far rocks where they found him. His head was quite broken, and like

274

honey from a fallen bee-tree his brains dripped on the ground. His mother strewed wood-ashes on her head and blackened her face. His father cut off half the fingers of one hand in token of sorrow. And all the women, especially the young and unwedded, screamed evil names at me; and the elders shook their wise heads and muttered and mumbled that not their fathers nor their fathers' fathers had betrayed such a madness. Horse meat was good to eat; young colts were tender to old teeth; and only a fool would come to close grapples with any wild horse save when an arrow had pierced it, or when it struggled on the stake in the midst of the pit.

And Selpa scolded me to sleep, and in the morning woke me with her chatter, ever declaiming against my madness, ever pronouncing her claim upon me and the claims of our children, till in the end I grew weary, and forsook my far vision, and said never again would I dream of bestriding the wild horse to fly swift as its feet and the wind across the sands and the grass lands.

And through the years the tale of my madness never ceased from being told over the camp-fire. Yet was the very telling the source of my vengeance; for the dream did not die, and the young ones, listening to the laugh and the sneer, redreamed it, so that in the end it was Othar, my eldest-born, himself a sheer stripling, that walked down a wild stallion, leapt on its back, and flew before all of us with the speed of the wind. Thereafter, that they might keep up with him, all men were trapping and breaking wild horses. Many horses were broken, and some men, but I lived at the last to the day when, at the changing of camp-sites in the pursuit of the meat in its seasons, our very babes, in baskets of willow-withes, were slung side and side on the backs of our horses that carried our camp-trappage and dunnage.

I, a young man, had seen my vision, dreamed my dream; Selpa, the woman, had held me from that far desire; but Othar, the seed of us to live after, glimpsed my vision and won to it, so that our tribe became wealthy in the gains of the chase.

There was a woman—on the great drift down out of Europe, a weary drift of many generations, when we brought into India the shorthorn cattle and the planting of barley. But this woman was long before we reached India. We were still in the mid-most of that centuries-long drift, and no shrewdness of geography can now place for me that ancient valley.

275

The woman was Nuhila. The valley was narrow, not long, and the swift slope of its floor and the steep walls of its rim were terraced for the growing of rice and of millet—the first rice and millet we Sons of the Mountain had known. They were a meek people in that valley. They had become soft with the farming of fat land made fatter by water. Theirs was the first irrigation we had seen, although we had little time to mark their ditches and channels by which all the hill waters flowed to the fields they had builded. We had little time to mark, for we Sons of the Mountain, who were few, were in flight before the Sons of the Snub-Nose, who were many. We called them the Noseless, and they called themselves the Sons of the Eagle. But they were many, and we fled before them with our shorthorn cattle, our goats, and our barleyseed, our women and children.

While the Snub-Noses slew our youths at the rear, we slew at our fore the folk of the valley who opposed us and were weak. The village was mud-built and grass-thatched; the encircling wall was of mud, but quite tall. And when we had slain the people who had built the wall, and sheltered within it our herds and our women and children, we stood on the wall and shouted insult to the Snub-Noses. For we had found the mud granaries filled with rice and millet. Our cattle could eat the thatches. And the time of the rains was at hand, so that we should not want for water.

It was a long siege. Near to the beginning, we gathered together the women, and elders, and children we had not slain, and forced them out through the wall they had builded. But the Snub-Noses slew them to the last one, so that there was more food in the village for us, more food in the valley for the Snub-Noses.

It was a weary long siege. Sickness smote us, and we died of the plague that arose from our buried ones. We emptied the mud-granaries of their rice and millet. Our goats and shorthorns ate the thatch of the houses, and we, ere the end, ate the goats and the shorthorns.

Where there had been five men of us on the wall, there came a time when there was one; where there had been half a thousand babes and younglings of ours, there were none. It was Nuhila, my woman, who cut off her hair and twisted it that I might have a strong string for my bow. The other women did likewise, and when the wall was attacked, stood shoulder to shoulder with us, in the midst of our spears and arrows raining down potsherds and cobblestones on the heads of the Snub-Noses.

Even the patient Snub-Noses we well-nigh out-patienced. Came a time when of ten men of us, but one was alive on the wall, and of our women remained very few, and the Snub-Noses held parley. They told us we were a strong breed, and that our women were men-mothers, and that if we would let them have our women they would leave us alone in the valley to possess for ourselves and that we could get women from the valleys to the south.

And Nuhila said no. And the other women said no. And we sneered at the Snub-Noses and asked if they were weary of fighting. And we were as dead men then, as we sneered at our enemies, and there was little fight left in us we were so weak. One more attack on the wall would end us. We knew it. Our women knew it. And Nuhila said that we could end it first and outwit the Snub-Noses. And all our women agreed. And while the Snub-Noses prepared for the attack that would be final, there, on the wall, we slew our women. Nuhila loved me, and leaned to meet the thrust of my sword, there on the wall. And we men, in the love of tribehood and tribesmen, slew one another till remained only Horda and I alive in the red of the slaughter. And Horda was my elder, and I leaned to his thrust. But not at once did I die. I was the last of the Sons of the Mountain, for I saw Horda, himself fall on his blade and pass quickly. And dying with the shouts of the oncoming Snub-Noses growing dim in my ears, I was glad that the Snub-Noses would have no sons of us to bring up by our women.

I do not know when this time was when I was a Son of the Mountain and when we died in the narrow valley where we had slain the Sons of the Rice and the Millet. I do not know, save that it was centuries before the wide-spreading drift of all us Sons of the Mountain fetched into India, and that it was long before ever I was an Aryan master in Old Egypt building my two burial places and defacing the tombs of kings before me.

I should like to tell more of those far days, but time in the present is short. Soon I shall pass. Yet am I sorry that I cannot tell more of those early drifts, when there was crushage of peoples, or descending ice-sheets, or migrations of meat.

Also, I should like to tell of Mystery. For always were we curious to solve the secrets of life, death, and decay. Unlike the other animals, man was for ever gazing at the stars. Many gods he created in his own image and in the images of his fancy. In those old times I have worshipped the sun and the dark. I have worshipped the husked grain as the parent of life. I have worshipped Sar, the Corn Goddess. And I have worshipped sea gods, and river gods, and fish gods.

Yes, and I remember Ishtar ere she was stolen from us by the Babylonians, and Ea, too, was ours, supreme in the Under World, who enabled Ishtar to conquer death. Mitra, likewise, was a good old Aryan god, ere he was filched from us or we discarded him. And I remember, on a time, long after the drift when we brought the barley into India, that I came down into India, a horse-trader, with many servants and a long caravan at my back, and that at that time they were worshipping Bodhisatwa.

Truly, the worships of the Mystery wandered as did men, and between filchings and borrowings the gods had as vagabond a time of it as did we. As the Sumerians took the loan of Shamashnapishtin from us, so did the Sons of Shem take him from the Sumerians and call him Noah.

Why, I smile me to-day, Darrell Standing, in Murderers' Row, in that I was found guilty and awarded death by twelve jurymen staunch and true. Twelve has ever been a magic number of the Mystery. Nor did it originate with the twelve tribes of Israel. Star-gazers before them had placed the twelve signs of the Zodiac in the sky. And I remember me, when I was of the Assir, and of the Vanir, that Odin sat in judgment over men in the court of the twelve gods, and that their names were Thor, Baldur, Niord, Frey, Tyr, Bregi, Heimdal, Hoder, Vidar, Ull, Forseti, and Loki.

Even our Valkyries were stolen from us and made into angels, and the wings of the Valkyries' horses became attached to the shoulders of the angels. And our Helheim of that day of ice and frost has become the hell of to-day, which is so hot an abode that the blood boils in one's veins, while with us, in our Helheim, the place was so cold as to freeze the marrow inside the bones. And the very sky, that we dreamed enduring, eternal, has drifted and veered, so that we find to-day the scorpion in the place where of old we knew the goat, and the archer in the place of the crab.

Worships and worships! Ever the pursuit of the Mystery! I remember the lame god of the Greeks, the master-smith. But their vulcan was the Germanic Wieland, the master-smith captured and hamstrung lame of a leg by Nidung, the kind of the Nids. But before that he was our master-smith, our forger and hammerer, whom we named Il-marinen. And him we begat of our fancy, giving him the bearded sun-god for father, and nursing him by the stars of the bear. For, he, Vulcan, or Wieland, or Il-marinen, was born under the pine tree, from the hair of the wolf, and was called also the bear-father ere ever the Germans and Greeks purloined and worshipped him. In that day we called ourselves the Sons of the Bear and the Sons of the Wolf, and the bear and the wolf were our totems. That was before our drift south on which we joined with the Sons of the Tree-Grove and taught them our totems and tales.

Yes, and who was Kashyapa, who was Pururavas, but our lame master-smith, our iron-worker, carried by us in our drifts and re-named and worshipped by the south-dwellers and the east-dwellers, the Sons of the Pole and of the Fire Drill and Fire Socket.

But the tale is too long, though I should like to tell of the three-leaved Herb of Life by which Sigmund made Sinfioti alive again. For this is the very soma-plant of India, the holy grail of King Arthur, the—but enough! enough!

And yet, as I calmly consider it all, I conclude that the greatest thing in life, in all lives, to me and to all men, has been woman, is woman, and will be woman so long as the stars drift in the sky and the heavens flux eternal change. Greater than our toil and endeavour, the play of invention and fancy, battle and star-gazing and mystery—greatest of all has been woman.

Even though she has sung false music to me, and kept my feet solid on the ground, and drawn my star-roving eyes ever back to gaze upon her, she, the conserver of life, the earth-mother, has given me my great days and nights and fulness of years. Even mystery have I imaged in the form of her, and in my star-charting have I placed her figure in the sky.

All my toils and devices led to her; all my far visions saw her at the end. When I made the fire-drill and fire-socket, it was for her. It was for her, although I did not know it, that I put the stake in the pit for old Sabre-

Tooth, tamed the horse, slew the mammoth, and herded my reindeer south in advance of the ice-sheet. For her I harvested the wild rice, tamed the barley, the wheat, and the corn.

For her, and the seed to come after whose image she bore, I have died in tree-tops and stood long sieges in cave-mouths and on mud-walls. For her I put the twelve signs in the sky. It was she I worshipped when I bowed before the ten stones of jade and adored them as the moons of gestation.

Always has woman crouched close to earth like a partridge hen mothering her young; always has my wantonness of roving led me out on the shining ways; and always have my star-paths returned me to her, the figure everlasting, the woman, the one woman, for whose arms I had such need that clasped in them I have forgotten the stars.

For her I accomplished Odysseys, scaled mountains, crossed deserts; for her I led the hunt and was forward in battle; and for her and to her I sang my songs of the things I had done. All ecstasies of life and rhapsodies of delight have been mine because of her. And here, at the end, I can say that I have known no sweeter, deeper madness of being than to drown in the fragrant glory and forgetfulness of her hair.

One word more. I remember me Dorothy, just the other day, when I still lectured on agronomy to farmer-boy students. She was eleven years old. Her father was dean of the college. She was a woman-child, and a woman, and she conceived that she loved me. And I smiled to myself, for my heart was untouched and lay elsewhere.

Yet was the smile tender, for in the child's eyes I saw the woman eternal, the woman of all times and appearances. In her eyes I saw the eyes of my mate of the jungle and tree-top, of the cave and the squatting-place. In her eyes I saw the eyes of Igar when I was Ushu the archer, the eyes of Arunga when I was the rice-harvester, the eyes of Selpa when I dreamed of bestriding the stallion, the eyes of Nuhila who leaned to the thrust of my sword. Yes, there was that in her eyes that made them the eyes of Lei-Lei whom I left with a laugh on my lips, the eyes of the Lady Om for forty years my beggar-mate on highway and byway, the eyes of Philippa for whom I was slain on the grass in old France, the eyes of my mother when I was the lad Jesse at the Mountain Meadows in the circle of our forty great wagons.

280

She was a woman-child, but she was daughter of all women, as her mother before her, and she was the mother of all women to come after her. She was Sar, the corn-goddess. She was Isthar who conquered death. She was Sheba and Cleopatra; she was Esther and Herodias. She was Mary the Madonna, and Mary the Magdalene, and Mary the sister of Martha, also she was Martha. And she was Brünnhilde and Guinevere, Iseult and Juliet, Héloïse and Nicolette. Yes, and she was Eve, she was Lilith, she was Astarte. She was eleven years old, and she was all women that had been, all women to be.

I sit in my cell now, while the flies hum in the drowsy summer afternoon, and I know that my time is short. Soon they will apparel me in the shirt without a collar. . . . But hush, my heart. The spirit is immortal. After the dark I shall live again, and there will be women. The future holds the little women for me in the lives I am yet to live. And though the stars drift, and the heavens lie, ever remains woman, resplendent, eternal, the one woman, as I, under all my masquerades and misadventures, am the one man, her mate.

CHAPTER XXII

My time grows very short. All the manuscript I have written is safely smuggled out of the prison. There is a man I can trust who will see that it is published. No longer am I in Murderers Row. I am writing these lines in the death cell, and the death-watch is set on me. Night and day is this death-watch on me, and its paradoxical function is to see that I do not die. I must be kept alive for the hanging, or else will the public be cheated, the law blackened, and a mark of demerit placed against the time-serving warden who runs this prison and one of whose duties is to see that his condemned ones are duly and properly hanged. Often I marvel at the strange way some men make their livings.

This shall be my last writing. To-morrow morning the hour is set. The governor has declined to pardon or reprieve, despite the fact that the Anti-Capital-Punishment League has raised quite a stir in California. The reporters are gathered like so many buzzards. I have seen them all. They are queer young fellows, most of them, and most queer is it that they will thus earn bread and butter, cocktails and tobacco, room-rent, and, if they are married, shoes and schoolbooks for their children, by witnessing the execution of Professor Darrell Standing, and by describing for the public how Professor Darrell Standing died at the end of a rope. Ah, well, they will be sicker than I at the end of the affair.

As I sit here and muse on it all, the footfalls of the death-watch going up and down outside my cage, the man's suspicious eyes ever peering in on me, almost I weary of eternal recurrence. I have lived so many lives. I weary of the endless struggle and pain and catastrophe that come to those who sit in the high places, tread the shining ways, and wander among the stars.

Almost I hope, when next I reinhabit form, that it shall be that of a peaceful farmer. There is my dream-farm. I should like to engage just for one whole life in that. Oh, my dream-farm! My alfalfa meadows, my efficient Jersey cattle, my upland pastures, my brush-covered slopes melting into tilled fields, while ever higher up the slopes my angora goats eat away brush to tillage!

There is a basin there, a natural basin high up the slopes, with a generous watershed on three sides. I should like to throw a dam across the fourth side, which is surprisingly narrow. At a paltry price of labour I could impound twenty million gallons of water. For, see: one great drawback to farming in California is our long dry summer. This prevents the growing of cover crops, and the sensitive soil, naked, a mere surface dust-mulch, has its humus burned out of it by the sun. Now with that dam I could grow three crops a year, observing due rotation, and be able to turn under a wealth of green manure. . . .

* * * * *

I have just endured a visit from the Warden. I say "endured" advisedly. He is quite different from the Warden of San Quentin. He was very nervous, and perforce I had to entertain him. This is his first hanging. He told me so. And I, with a clumsy attempt at wit, did not reassure him when I explained that it was also my first hanging. He was unable to laugh. He has a girl in high school, and his boy is a freshman at Stanford. He has no income outside his salary, his wife is an invalid, and he is worried in that he has been rejected by the life insurance doctors as an undesirable risk. Really, the man told me almost all his troubles. Had I not diplomatically terminated the interview he would still be here telling me the remainder of them.

My last two years in San Quentin were very gloomy and depressing. Ed Morrell, by one of the wildest freaks of chance, was taken out of solitary and made head trusty of the whole prison. This was Al Hutchins' old job, and it carried a graft of three thousand dollars a year. To my misfortune, Jake Oppenheimer, who had rotted in solitary for so many years, turned sour on the world, on everything. For eight months he refused to talk even to me.

In prison, news will travel. Give it time and it will reach dungeon and solitary cell. It reached me, at last, that Cecil Winwood, the poet-forger, the snitcher, the coward, and the stool, was returned for a fresh forgery. It will be remembered that it was this Cecil Winwood who concocted the fairy story that I had changed the plant of the non-existent dynamite and who was responsible for the five years I had then spent in solitary.

I decided to kill Cecil Winwood. You see, Morrell was gone, and Oppenheimer, until the outbreak that finished him, had remained in the silence. Solitary had grown monotonous for me. I had to do something. So I remembered back to the time when I was Adam Strang and patiently nursed revenge for forty years. What he had done I could do if once I locked my hands on Cecil Winwood's throat.

It cannot be expected of me to divulge how I came into possession of the four needles. They were small cambric needles. Emaciated as my body was, I had to saw four bars, each in two places, in order to make an aperture through which I could squirm. I did it. I used up one needle to each bar. This meant two cuts to a bar, and it took a month to a cut. Thus I should have been eight months in cutting my way out. Unfortunately, I broke my last needle on the last bar, and I had to wait three months before I could get another needle. But I got it, and I got out.

I regret greatly that I did not get Cecil Winwood. I had calculated well on everything save one thing. The certain chance to find Winwood would be in the dining-room at dinner hour. So I waited until Pie-Face Jones, the sleepy guard, should be on shift at the noon hour. At that time I was the only inmate of solitary, so that Pie-Face Jones was quickly snoring. I removed my bars, squeezed out, stole past him along the ward, opened the door and was free . . . to a portion of the inside of the prison.

And here was the one thing I had not calculated on—myself. I had been five years in solitary. I was hideously weak. I weighed eighty-seven pounds. I was half blind. And I was immediately stricken with agoraphobia. I was affrighted by spaciousness. Five years in narrow walls had unfitted me for the enormous declivity of the stairway, for the vastitude of the prison yard.

The descent of that stairway I consider the most heroic exploit I ever accomplished. The yard was deserted. The blinding sun blazed down on it. Thrice I essayed to cross it. But my senses reeled and I shrank back to the wall for protection. Again, summoning all my courage, I attempted it. But my poor blear eyes, like a bat's, startled me at my shadow on the flagstones. I attempted to avoid my own shadow, tripped, fell over it, and like a drowning man struggling for shore crawled back on hands and knees to the wall.

I leaned against the wall and cried. It was the first time in many years that I had cried. I remember noting, even in my extremity, the warmth of the tears on my cheeks and the salt taste when they reached my lips. Then I had a chill, and for a time shook as with an ague. Abandoning the openness of the yard as too impossible a feat for one in my condition, still shaking with the chill, crouching close to the protecting wall, my hands touching it, I started to skirt the yard.

Then it was, somewhere along, that the guard Thurston espied me. I saw him, distorted by my bleared eyes, a huge, well-fed monster, rushing upon me with incredible speed out of the remote distance. Possibly, at that moment, he was twenty feet away. He weighed one hundred and seventy pounds. The struggle between us can be easily imagined, but somewhere in that brief struggle it was claimed that I struck him on the nose with my fist to such purpose as to make that organ bleed.

At any rate, being a lifer, and the penalty in California for battery by a lifer being death, I was so found guilty by a jury which could not ignore the asseverations of the guard Thurston and the rest of the prison hang-dogs that testified, and I was so sentenced by a judge who could not ignore the law as spread plainly on the statute book.

I was well pummelled by Thurston, and all the way back up that prodigious stairway I was roundly kicked, punched, and cuffed by the horde of trusties and guards who got in one another's way in their zeal to assist him. Heavens, if his nose did bleed, the probability is that some of his own kind were guilty of causing it in the confusion of the scuffle. I shouldn't care if I were responsible for it myself, save that it is so pitiful a thing for which to hang a man. . . .

* * * *

I have just had a talk with the man on shift of my death-watch. A little less than a year ago, Jake Oppenheimer occupied this same death-cell on the road to the gallows which I will tread to-morrow. This man was one of the death-watch on Jake. He is an old soldier. He chews tobacco constantly, and untidily, for his gray beard and moustache are stained yellow. He is a widower, with fourteen living children, all married, and is the grandfather of thirty-one living grandchildren, and the great-grandfather of four younglings, all girls. It was like pulling teeth to extract such information. He is a queer old codger, of a low order of intelligence. That is why, I fancy, he has lived so long and fathered so numerous a progeny. His mind must have crystallized thirty years ago. His ideas are none of them later than that vintage. He rarely says more than yes and no to me. It is not because he is surly. He has no ideas to utter. I don't know, when I live again, but what one incarnation such as his would be a nice vegetative existence in which to rest up ere I go star-roving again. . . .

But to go back. I must take a line in which to tell, after I was hustled and bustled, kicked and punched, up that terrible stairway by Thurston and the rest of the prison-dogs, of the infinite relief of my narrow cell when I found myself back in solitary. It was all so safe, so secure. I felt like a lost child returned home again. I loved those very walls that I had so hated for five years. All that kept the vastness of space, like a monster, from pouncing upon me were those good stout walls of mine, close to hand on every side. Agoraphobia is a terrible affliction. I have had little opportunity to experience it, but from that little I can only conclude that hanging is a far easier matter. . . .

I have just had a hearty laugh. The prison doctor, a likable chap, has just been in to have a yarn with me, incidentally to proffer me his good offices in the matter of dope. Of course I declined his proposition to "shoot me" so full of morphine through the night that to-morrow I would not know, when I marched to the gallows, whether I was "coming or going."

But the laugh. It was just like Jake Oppenheimer. I can see the lean keenness of the man as he strung the reporters with his deliberate bull which they thought involuntary. It seems, his last morning, breakfast finished, incased in the shirt without a collar, that the reporters, assembled for his last word in his cell, asked him for his views on capital punishment.

—Who says we have more than the slightest veneer of civilization coated over our raw savagery when a group of living men can ask such a question of a man about to die and whom they are to see die?

But Jake was ever game. "Gentlemen," he said, "I hope to live to see the day when capital punishment is abolished."

I have lived many lives through the long ages. Man, the individual, has made no moral progress in the past ten thousand years. I affirm this absolutely. The difference between an unbroken colt and the patient draught-horse is purely a difference of training. Training is the only moral difference between the man of to-day and the man of ten thousand years ago. Under his thin skin of morality which he has had polished onto him, he is the same savage that he was ten thousand years ago. Morality is a social fund, an accretion through the painful ages. The new-born child will become a savage unless it is trained, polished, by the abstract morality that has been so long accumulating.

"Thou shalt not kill"—piffle! They are going to kill me to-morrow morning. "Thou shalt not kill"—piffle! In the shipyards of all civilized countries they are laying to-day the keels of Dreadnoughts and of Superdreadnoughts. Dear friends, I who am about to die, salute you with—"Piffle!"

I ask you, what finer morality is preached to-day than was preached by Christ, by Buddha, by Socrates and Plato, by Confucius and whoever was the author of the "Mahabharata"? Good Lord, fifty thousand years ago, in our totem-families, our women were cleaner, our family and group relations more rigidly right.

I must say that the morality we practised in those old days was a finer morality than is practised to-day. Don't dismiss this thought hastily. Think of our child labour, of our police graft and our political corruption, of our food adulteration and of our slavery of the daughters of the poor. When I was a Son of the Mountain and a Son of the Bull, prostitution had no meaning. We were clean, I tell you. We did not dream such depths of depravity. Yea, so are all the lesser animals of to-day clean. It required man, with his imagination, aided by his mastery of matter, to invent the deadly sins. The lesser animals, the other animals, are incapable of sin.

I read hastily back through the many lives of many times and many places. I have never known cruelty more terrible, nor so terrible, as the cruelty of our prison system of to-day. I have told you what I have endured in the jacket and in solitary in the first decade of this twentieth century after Christ. In the old days we punished drastically and killed quickly. We did it because we so desired, because of whim, if you so please. But we were not hypocrites. We did not call upon press, and pulpit, and university to sanction us in our wilfulness of savagery. What we wanted to do we went and did, on our legs upstanding, and we faced all reproof and censure on our legs upstanding, and did not hide behind the skirts of classical economists and bourgeois philosophers, nor behind the skirts of subsidized preachers, professors, and editors.

Why, goodness me, a hundred years ago, fifty years ago, five years ago, in these United States, assault and battery was not a civil capital crime. But this year, the year of Our Lord 1913, in the State of California, they hanged Jake Oppenheimer for such an offence, and to-morrow, for the civil capital crime of punching a man on the nose, they are going to take me out and hang me. Query: Doesn't it require a long time for the ape and the tiger to die when such statutes are spread on the statute book of California in the nineteen-hundred-and-thirteenth year after Christ? Lord, Lord, they only crucified Christ. They have done far worse to Jake Oppenheimer and me. . . .

* * * * *

As Ed Morrell once rapped to me with his knuckles: "The worst possible use you can put a man to is to hang him." No, I have little respect for capital punishment. Not only is it a dirty game, degrading to the hang-dogs who personally perpetrate it for a wage, but it is degrading to the commonwealth that tolerates it, votes for it, and pays the taxes for its maintenance. Capital punishment is so *silly*, so stupid, so horribly unscientific. "To be hanged by the neck until dead" is society's quaint phraseology . . .

* * * * *

Morning is come—my last morning. I slept like a babe throughout the night. I slept so peacefully that once the death-watch got a fright. He thought I had suffocated myself in my blankets. The poor man's alarm was pitiful. His bread and butter was at stake. Had it truly been so, it would

288

have meant a black mark against him, perhaps discharge and the outlook for an unemployed man is bitter just at present. They tell me that Europe began liquidating two years ago, and that now the United States has begun. That means either a business crisis or a quiet panic and that the armies of the unemployed will be large next winter, the bread-lines long. . . .

I have had my breakfast. It seemed a silly thing to do, but I ate it heartily. The Warden came with a quart of whiskey. I presented it to Murderers Row with my compliments. The Warden, poor man, is afraid, if I be not drunk, that I shall make a mess of the function and cast reflection on his management . . .

They have put on me the shirt without a collar. . .

It seems I am a very important man this day. Quite a lot of people are suddenly interested in me. . . .

The doctor has just gone. He has taken my pulse. I asked him to. It is normal. . . .

I write these random thoughts, and, a sheet at a time, they start on their secret way out beyond the walls. . . .

I am the calmest man in the prison. I am like a child about to start on a journey. I am eager to be gone, curious for the new places I shall see. This fear of the lesser death is ridiculous to one who has gone into the dark so often and lived again. . . .

The Warden with a quart of champagne. I have dispatched it down Murderers Row. Queer, isn't it, that I am so considered this last day. It must be that these men who are to kill me are themselves afraid of death. To quote Jake Oppenheimer: I, who am about to die, must seem to them something God-awful. . . .

Ed Morrell has just sent word in to me. They tell me he has paced up and down all night outside the prison wall. Being an ex-convict, they have red-taped him out of seeing me to say good-bye. Savages? I don't know. Possibly just children. I'll wager most of them will be afraid to be alone in the dark to-night after stretching my neck.

But Ed Morrell's message: "My hand is in yours, old pal. I know you'll swing off game." . . .

* * * * *

The reporters have just left. I'll see them next, and last time, from the scaffold, ere the hangman hides my face in the black cap. They will be looking curiously sick. Queer young fellows. Some show that they have been drinking. Two or three look sick with foreknowledge of what they have to witness. It seems easier to be hanged than to look on. . . .

* * * * *

My last lines. It seems I am delaying the procession. My cell is quite crowded with officials and dignitaries. They are all nervous. They want it over. Without a doubt, some of them have dinner engagements. I am really offending them by writing these few words. The priest has again preferred his request to be with me to the end. The poor man—why should I deny him that solace? I have consented, and he now appears quite cheerful. Such small things make some men happy! I could stop and laugh for a hearty five minutes, if they were not in such a hurry.

Here I close. I can only repeat myself. There is no death. Life is spirit, and spirit cannot die. Only the flesh dies and passes, ever a-crawl with the chemic ferment that informs it, ever plastic, ever crystallizing, only to melt into the flux and to crystallize into fresh and diverse forms that are ephemeral and that melt back into the flux. Spirit alone endures and continues to build upon itself through successive and endless incarnations as it works upward toward the light. What shall I be when I live again? I wonder. I wonder. . . .

FOOTNOTES

{1} Since the execution of Professor Darrell Standing, at which time the manuscript of his memoirs came into our hands, we have written to Mr. Hosea Salsburty, Curator of the Philadelphia Museum, and, in reply, have received confirmation of the existence of the oar and the pamphlet.—THE EDITOR.

THE KEMPTON-WACE
LETTERS

I. FROM DANE KEMPTON TO HERBERT WACE

London,

3 a Queen's Road, Chelsea, S.W.

August 14, 19—.

Yesterday I wrote formally, rising to the occasion like the conventional happy father rather than the man who believes in the miracle and lives for it. Yesterday I stinted myself. I took you in my arms, glad of what is and stately with respect for the fulness of your manhood. It is to-day that I let myself leap into yours in a passion of joy. I dwell on what has come to pass and inflate myself with pride in your fulfilment, more as a mother would, I think, and she your mother.

But why did you not write before? After all, the great event was not when you found your offer of marriage accepted, but when you found you had fallen in love. Then was your hour. Then was the time for congratulation, when the call was first sounded and the reveille of Time and About fell upon your soul and the march to another's destiny was begun. It is always more important to love than to be loved. I wish it had been vouchsafed me to be by when your spirit of a sudden grew willing to bestow itself without question or let or hope of return, when the self broke up and you grew fain to beat out your strength in praise and service for the woman who was soaring high in the blue wastes. You have known her long, and you must have been hers long, yet no word of her and of your love reached me. It was not kind to be silent.

Barbara spoke yesterday of your fastidiousness, and we told each other that you had gained a triumph of happiness in your love, for you are not of those who cheat themselves. You choose rigorously, straining for the heart of the end as do all rigorists who are also hedonists. Because we are in possession of this bit of data as to your temperamental cosmos we can congratulate you with the more abandon. Oh, Herbert, do you know that this is a rampant spring, and that on leaving Barbara I tramped out of the confines into the green, happier, it almost seems, than I have ever been? Do you know that because you love a woman and she loves you, and that because you are swept along by certain forces, that I am happy and feel myself in sight of my portion of immortality on earth, far more than because of my books, dear lad, far more?

I wish I could fly England and get to you. Should I have a shade less of you than formerly, if we were together now? From your too much green of wealth, a barrenness of friendship? It does not matter; what is her gain cannot be my loss. One power is mine,—without hindrance, in freedom and in right, to say to Ellen's son, "Godspeed!" to place Hester Stebbins's hand in his, and bid them forth to the sunrise, into the glory of day!

Ever your devoted father,

Dane Kempton.

II. FROM HERBERT WACE TO DANE KEMPTON

The Ridge,

Berkeley, California.

September 3, 19—.

Here I am, back in the old quarters once more, with the old afternoon climb across the campus and up into the sky, up to the old rooms, the old books, and the old view. You poor fog-begirt Dane Kempton, could you but have lounged with me on the window couch, an hour past, and watched the light pass out of the day through the Golden Gate and the night creep over the Berkeley Hills and down out of the east! Why should you linger on there in London town! We grow away from each other, it seems—you with your wonder-singing, I with my joyful science.

Poesy and economics! Alack! alack! How did I escape you, Dane, when mind and mood you mastered me? The auguries were fair. I, too, should have been a singer, and lo, I strive for science. All my boyhood was singing, what of you; and my father was a singer, too, in his own fine way. Dear to me is your likening of him to Waring.—"What's become of Waring?" He *was* Waring. I can think of him only as one who went away, "chose land travel or seafaring."

Gwynne says I am sometimes almost a poet—Gwynne, you know, Arthur Gwynne, who has come to live with me at The Ridge. "If it were not for your dismal science," he is sure to add; and to fire him I lay it to the defects of early training. I know he thinks that I never half appreciated you, and that I do not appreciate you now. If you will recollect, you praised his verses once. He cherishes that praise amongst his sweetest treasures. Poor dear good old Gwynne, tender, sensitive, shrinking, with the face of a seraph and the heart of a maid. Never were two men more incongruously companioned. I love him for himself. He tolerates me, I do secretly believe, because of you. He longs to meet you,—he knew you well through my father,—and we often talk you over. Be sure at every opportunity I tear off your halo and trundle it about. Trust me, you receive scant courtesy.

How I wander on. My pen is unruly after the long vacation; my thought yet wayward, what of the fever of successful wooing. And besides, ... how shall I say?... such was the gracious warmth of your letter, of both your letters, that I am at a loss. I feel weak, inadequate. It almost seems as though you had made a demand upon something that is not in me. Ah, you poets! It would seem your delight in my marriage were greater than mine. In my present mood, it is you who are young, you who love; I who have lived and am old.

Yes, I am going to be married. At this present moment, I doubt not, a million men and women are saying the same thing. Hewers of wood and drawers of water, princes and potentates, shy-shrinking maidens and brazen-faced hussies, all saying, "I am going to be married." And all looking forward to it as a crisis in their lives? No. After all, marriage is the way of the world. Considered biologically, it is an institution necessary for the perpetuation of the species. Why should it be a crisis? These million men and women will marry, and the work of the world go on just as it did before. Shuffle them about, and the work of the world would yet go on.

True, a month ago it did seem a crisis. I wrote you as much. It did seem a disturbing element in my life-work. One cannot view with equanimity that which appears to be totally disruptive of one's dear little system of living. But it only appeared so; I lacked perspective, that was all. As I look upon it now, everything fits well and all will run smoothly I am sure.

You know I had two years yet to work for my Doctorate. I still have them. As you see, I am back to the old quarters, settled down in the old groove, hammering away at the old grind. Nothing is changed. And besides my own studies, I have taken up an assistant instructorship in the Department of Economics. It is an ambitious course, and an important one. I don't know how they ever came to confide it to me, or how I found the temerity to attempt it,—which is neither here nor there. It is all agreed. Hester is a sensible girl.

The engagement is to be long. I shall continue my career as charted. Two years from now, when I shall have become a Doctor of Social Sciences (and candidate for numerous other things), I shall also become a benedict. My marriage and the presumably necessary honeymoon chime in with the summer vacation. There is no disturbing element even there. Oh, we are very practical, Hester and I. And we are both strong enough to lead each our own lives.

Which reminds me that you have not asked about her. First, let me shock you—she, too, is a scientist. It was in my undergraduate days that we met, and ere the half-hour struck we were quarrelling felicitously over Weismann and the neo-Darwinians. I was at Berkeley at the time, a cocksure junior; and she, far maturer as a freshman, was at Stanford, carrying more culture with her into her university than is given the average student to carry out.

Next, and here your arms open to her, she is a poet. Pre-eminently she is a poet—this must be always understood. She is the greater poet, I take it, in this dawning twentieth century, because she is a scientist; not in spite of being a scientist as some would hold. How shall I describe her? Perhaps as a George Eliot, fused with an Elizabeth Barrett, with a hint of Huxley and a trace of Keats. I may say she is something like all this, but I must say she is something other and different. There is about her a certain lightsomeness, a glow or flash almost Latin or oriental, or perhaps Celtic. Yes, that must be it—Celtic. But the high-stomached Norman is there and the stubborn Saxon. Her quickness and fine audacity are checked and poised, as it were, by that certain conservatism which gives stability to purpose and power to achievement. She is unafraid, and wide-looking and far-looking, but she is not over-looking. The Saxon grapples with the Celt, and the Norman forces the twain to do what the one would not dream of doing and what the other would dream beyond and never do. Do you catch me? Her most salient charm, is I think, her perfect poise, her exquisite adjustment.

Altogether she is a most wonderful woman, take my word for it. And after all she is described vicariously. Though she has published nothing and is exceeding shy, I shall send you some of her work. There will you find and know her. She is waiting for stronger voice and sings softly as yet. But hers will be no minor note, no middle flight. She is—well, she is Hester. In two years we shall be married. Two years, Dane. Surely you will be with us.

One thing more; in your letter a certain undertone which I could not fail to detect. *A shade less* of me than formerly?—I turn and look into your face—Waring's handiwork you remember—his painter's fancy of you in those golden days when I stood on the brink of the world, and you showed me the delights of the world and the way of my feet therein. So I turn and look, and look and wonder. A shade less of me, of you? Poesy and economics! Where lies the blame?

Herbert.

III. FROM DANE KEMPTON TO HERBERT WACE

London,

September 30, 19—.

It is because you know not what you do that I cannot forgive you. Could you know that your letter with its catalogue of advantages and arrangements must offend me as much as it belies (let us hope) you and the woman of your love, I would pardon the affront of it upon us all, and ascribe the unseemly want of warmth to reserve or to the sadness which grips the heart when joy is too palpitant. But something warns me that you are unaware of the chill your words breathe, and that is a lapse which it is impossible to meet with indulgence.

"He does not love her," was Barbara's quick decision, and she laid the open letter down with a definiteness which said that you, too, are laid out and laid low. Your sister's very wrists can be articulate. However, I laughed at her and she soon joined me. We do not mean to be extravagant with our fears. Who shall prescribe the letters of lovers to their sisters and foster-fathers? Yet there are some things their letters should be incapable of saying, and amongst them that love is not a crisis and a rebirth, but that it is common as the commonplace, a hit or miss affair which "shuffling" could not affect.

Barbara showed me your note to her. "Had I written like this of myself and Earl—"

"You could not," I objected.

"Then Herbert should have been as little able to do it," she deduced with emphasis. Here I might have told her that men and women are races apart, but no one talks cant to Barbara. So I did not console her, and it stands against you in our minds that on this critical occasion you have baffled us with coldness.

An absence of six years, broken into twice by a brief few months, must work changes. When Barbara called your letter unnatural, she forgot how little she knows what is natural to you. She and I have been wont to predetermine you, your character, foothold, and outlook, by—say by the fact that you knew your Wordsworth and that you knew him without being able to take for yourself his austere peace. Youth which lives by hope is riven by unrest.

> "I made no vows; vows were made for me,
>
> Bond unknown to me was given
>
> That I should be, else sinning gently,
>
> A dedicated spirit."

That pale sunrise seen from Mt. Tamalpais and your voice vibrant to fierceness on the "else sinning gently"—to me the splendour of rose on piled-up ridges of mist spoke all for you, so dear have you always been. It rested on the possible wonder of your life. It threw you into the scintillant Dawn with an abandon meet to a son of Waring.

Tell me, do you still read your Wordsworth on your knees? I am bent with regret for the time when your mind had no surprises for me, when the days were flushed halcyon with my hope in you. I resent your development if it is because of it that you speak prosaically of a prosaic marriage and of a honeymoon simultaneous with the Degree. I think you are too well pleased with the simultaneousness.

Yet the fact of the letter is fair. It cannot be that the soul of it is not. Hester Stebbins is a poet. I lean forward and think it out as I did some days ago when the news came. I conjure up the look of love. If the woman is content (how much more than content the feeling she bounds with in knowing you hers as she is yours), what better test that all is well? I conjure up the look of love. It is thus at meeting and thus at parting. Even here, to-night, when all is chill and hard to understand, I catch the flash and the warmth, and what I see restores you to me, but how deep the plummet of my mind needed to sound before it reached you. It is because you permitted yourself to speak when silence had expressed you better.

Show me the ideally real Hester Stebbins, the spark of fire which is she. The storms have not broken over her head. She will laugh and make poetry of her laughter. If before she met you she wept, that, too, will help the smiling. There is laughter which is the echo of a Miserere sobbed by the ages. Men chuckle in the irony of pain, and they smile cold, lessoned smiles in resignation; they laugh in forgetfulness and they laugh lest they die of sadness. A shrug of the shoulders, a widening of the lips, a heaving forth of sound, and the life is saved. The remedy is as drastic as are the drugs used for epilepsy, which in quelling the spasm bring idiocy to the patient. If we are made idiots by our laughter, we are paying dearly for the privilege of continuing in life.

Hester shall laugh because she is glad and must tell her joy, and she will not lose it in the telling. Greet her for me and hasten to prove yourself, for

"The Poet, gentle creature that he is,

Hath like the Lover, his unruly times;

His fits when he is neither sick nor well,

Though no distress be near him but his own

Unmanageable thoughts."

You will judge by this letter that I am neither sick nor well, and that I reach for a distress which is not near. If I were Merchant rather than Poet, it would be otherwise with me.

Dane.

IV. FROM HERBERT WACE TO DANE KEMPTON

The Ridge,

Berkeley, California.

October 27, 19—.

Do I still read my Wordsworth on my knees? Well, we may as well have it out. I have foreseen this day so long and shunned it that now I meet it almost with extended hands. No, I do not read my Wordsworth on my knees. My mind is filled with other things. I have not the time. I am not the Herbert Wace of six years gone. It is fair that you should know this; fair, also, that you should know the Herbert Wace of six years gone was not quite the lad you deemed him.

There is no more pathetic and terrible thing than the prejudice of love. Both you and I have suffered from it. Six years ago, ay, and before that, I felt and resented the growing difference between us. When under your spell, it seemed that I was born to lisp in numbers and devote myself to singing, that the world was good and all of it fit for singing. But away from you, even then, doubts faced me, and I knew in vague fashion that we lived in different worlds. At first in vague fashion, I say; and when with you again, your spell dominated me and I could not question. You were true, you were good, I argued, all that was wonderful and glorious; therefore, you were also right. You mastered me with your charm, as you were wont to master those who loved you.

But there came times when your sympathy failed me and I stood alone on outlooks I had achieved alone. There was no response from you. I could not hear your voice. I looked down upon a real world; you were caught up in a beautiful cloudland and shut away from me. Possibly it was because life of itself appealed to you, while to me appealed the mechanics of life. But be it as it may, yours was a world of ideas and fancies, mine a world of things and facts.

Enters here the prejudice of love. It was the lad that discovered our difference and concealed; it was the man who was blind and could not discover. There we erred, man and boy; and here, both men now, we make all well again.

Let me be explicit. Do you remember the passion with which I read the "Intellectual Development of Europe?" I understood not the tithe of it, but I was thrilled. My common sense was thrilled, I suppose; but it was all very joyous, gripping hold of the tangible world for the first time. And when I came to you, warm with the glow of adventure, you looked blankly, then smiled indulgently and did not answer. You regarded my ardour complacently. A passing humour of adolescence, you thought; and I thought: "Dane does not read his Draper on his knees." Wordsworth was great to me; Draper was great also. You had no patience with him, and I know now, as I felt then, your consistent revolt against his materialistic philosophy.

Only the other day you complained of a letter of mine, calling it cold and analytical. That I should be cold and analytical despite all the prodding and pressing and moulding I have received at your hands, and the hands of Waring, marks only more clearly our temperamental difference; but it does not mark that one or the other of us is less a dedicated spirit. If I have wandered away from the warmth of poesy and become practical, have you not remained and become confirmed in all that is beautifully impractical? If I have adventured in a new world of common things, have you not lingered in the old world of great and impossible things? If I have shivered in the gray dawn of a new day, have you not crouched over the dying embers of the fire of yesterday? Ah, Dane, you cannot rekindle that fire. The whirl of the world scatters its ashes wide and far, like volcanic dust, to make beautiful crimson sunsets for a time and then to vanish.

None the less are you a dedicated spirit, priest that you are of a dying faith. Your prayers are futile, your altars crumbling, and the light flickers and drops down into night. Poetry is empty these days, empty and worthless and dead. All the old-world epic and lyric-singing will not put this very miserable earth of ours to rights. So long as the singers sing of the things of yesterday, glorifying the things of yesterday and lamenting their departure, so long will poetry be a vain thing and without avail. The old world is dead, dead and buried along with its heroes and Helens and knights and ladies and tournaments and pageants. You cannot sing of the truth and wonder of to-day in terms of yesterday. And no one will listen to your singing till you sing of to-day in terms of to-day.

This is the day of the common man. Do you glorify the common man? This is the day of the machine. When have you sung of the machine? The crusades are here again, not the Crusades of Christ but the Crusades of the Machine—have you found motive in them for your song? We are crusading to-day, not for the remission of sins, but for the abolition of sinning, of economic and industrial sinning. The crusade to Christ's sepulchre was paltry compared with the splendour and might of our crusade to-day toward manhood. There are millions of us afoot. In the stillness of the night have you never listened to the trampling of our feet and been caught up by the glory and the romance of it? Oh, Dane! Dane! Our captains sit in council, our heroes take the field, our fighting men are buckling on their harness, our martyrs have already died, and you are blind to it, blind to it all!

We have no poets these days, and perforce we are singing with our hands. The walking delegate is a greater singer and a finer singer than you, Dane Kempton. The cold, analytical economist, delving in the dynamics of society, is more the prophet than you. The carpenter at his bench, the blacksmith by his forge, the boiler-maker clanging and clattering, are all warbling more sweetly than you. The sledge-wielder pours out more strength and certitude and joy in every blow than do you in your whole sheaf of songs. Why, the very socialist agitator, hustled by the police on a street corner amid the jeers of the mob, has caught the romance of to-day as you have not caught it and where you have missed it. He knows life and is living. Are you living, Dane Kempton?

Forgive me. I had begun to explain and reconcile our difference. I find I am lecturing and censuring you. In defending myself, I offend. But this I wish to say: We are so made, you and I, that your function in life is to dream, mine to work. That you failed to make a dreamer of me is no cause for heartache and chagrin. What of my practical nature and analytical mind, I have generalised in my own way upon the data of life and achieved a different code from yours. Yet I seek truth as passionately as you. I still believe myself to be a dedicated spirit.

And what boots it, all of it? When the last word is said, we are two men, by a thousand ties very dear to each other. There is room in our hearts for each other as there is room in the world for both of us. Though we have many things not in common, yet you are my dearest friend on earth, you who have been a second father to me as well.

You have long merited this explanation, and it was cowardly of me not to have made it before. My hope is that I have been sufficiently clear for you to understand.

Herbert.

V. FROM DANE KEMPTON TO HERBERT WACE

London,

3 a Queen's Road, Chelsea, S.W.

November 16, 19—.

You sigh "Poesy and Economics," supplying the cause and thereby admitting the fact. I wish you had shown some reluctance to see my meaning, that you had preferred to waive the matter on the ground of insufficient data, that you had been less eager to ferret out the science of the thing. Do you remember how your boy's respect rose for little Barbara whenever she cried when too readily forgiven? "She dreads a double standard," you explained to me with generous heat. You sympathised with her fear lest I demand less of her than of you, honouring her insistence on an equality of duty as well as of privilege. Is the man Herbert less proud than the child Barbara, that you speak of a temperamental difference and ask for a special dispensation?

You are not in love (this you say in not gainsaying my attack on you, and so far I understand), because you are a student of Economics. At the last I stop. What is this about economics and poesy? About your emancipation from my riotously lyric sway? The hand of the forces by which you have been moulded cannot detain you from going out upon the love-quest. The fact of your preference for Draper cannot forestall your spirit's need of love. There are many codes, but there is one law, binding alike on the economist and poet. It springs out of the common and unappeasable hunger, commanding that love seek love through night to day and through day to night.

Yet it is possible to put oneself outside the pale of the law, to refuse the gift of life and snap the tie between time and space and creature. It is possible to be too emaciated for interest or feeling. The men and women of the People know neither love nor art because they are too weary. They lie in sleep prostrate from great fatigue. Their bodies are too much tried with the hungers of the body and their spirits too dimly illumined with the hope of fair chances. It is also possible to fill oneself so full with an interest that all else is crowded out. You have done this. Like the cobbler who is a cobbler typically, the teacher who is a pedagogue, the physician and the lawyer who are pathologists merely, you are a fanatic of a text. You are in the toils of an idea, the idea of selection, as I well know, and you exploit it like a drudge. When a man finds that he cannot deal in petroleum without smelling of it, it is time that he turn to something else. Every man is engaged in the cause of keeping himself whole, in watching himself lest his man turn machine, in watching lest the outside world assail the inner. Nature spares the type, but the individual must spare himself. He is strong who is sensitive and who responds subtly to everything in his environment, but his response must be characteristic; he must sustain his personality and become more himself through the years. He alone is vital in the social scheme who lets nothing in him atrophy and who persists in being varied from all others in the scale of character to the degree of variability that was his at the beginning.

I read in your letter nothing but a decision to stop short and give over, as if you had strength for no more than your book and your theory! You have become slave to a small point of inquiry, and you call it the advance to a new time. "The crusade is on," you say. Coronation rites for the commoners and destruction to superstition. I put my hand out to you in joy. The joy is in unholy worship of a fetish, the pain that there is no joy also deference to a fetish. Your creed thunders "Thou shalt not." Love is a thing of yesterday. No room for anything that intimately concerns the self. But what are the apostles of the young thought preaching if it is not the right of men to their own, and what would it avail them to come into their own if life be stripped of romance?

I am dissatisfied because you are willing to live as others must live. You should stay aristocrat. Ferdinand Lassalle dressed with elegance for his working-men audiences, with the hope, he said, of reminding them that there was something better than their shabbiness. You are of the favoured, Herbert. It devolves upon you to endear your life to yourself. You do not agree with me. You do not believe that love is the law which controls freedom and life. Slave to your theory and rebel to the law, you lose your soul and imperil another's.

"Gently! Gently!" I say to myself. Old sorrows and wrongs oppress me and I grow harsh. My heat only helps to convince you that my position is not based on the *rational rightness* you hold so essential and that therefore it is unlivable. I will state calmly, then, that it is wrong to marry without love. "For the perpetuation of the species"—that is noble of you! So you strip yourself of the thousand years of civilisation that have fostered you, you abandon your prerogative as a creature high in the scale of existence to obey an instinct and fulfil a function? You say: "These men and women will marry, and the work of the world go on just as it did before. Shuffle them about and the work of the world would yet go on." And you are content. You feel no need of anything different from this condition.

Believe me, Herbert, these million men and women will not let you shuffle them about. There are forces stronger than force, shadows more real than reality. We know that the need of the unhungered for the one friend, one comrade, one mate, is good. We honour the love that persists in loving. More beautiful than starlight is the face of the lover when the Voice and the Vision enfold him. The race is consecrated to the worship of idea, and the lover who lays his all on the altar of romance (which is idea) is at one with the race. The arms of the unloved girl close about the formless air and more real than her loneliness and her sorrow is the imagined embrace, the awaited warm, close pressure of the hands, the fancied gaze. What does it mean? What secret was there for Leonardo in Mona Lisa's smile, what for him in the motion of waters? You cannot explain the bloom, the charm, the smile of life, that which rains sunshine into our hearts, which tells us we are wise to hope and to have faith, which buckles on us an armour of activity, which lights the fires of the spirit, which gives us Godhead and renders us indomitable. Comparative anatomy cannot reason it down. It is sensibility, romance, idea. It is a fact of life toward which all other facts make. For the flush of rose-light in the heavens, the touch of a hand, the colour and shape of fruit, the tears that come for unnamed sorrows, the regrets of old men, are more significant than all the building and inventing done since the first social compact.

Forgive my tediousness. I have flaunted these truisms before you in order to exorcise that modern slang of yours which is more false than the overstrained forms of a feudal France. To shut out glory is not to be practical. You are not adjusting your life artistically; there is too much strain, too little warmth, too much self-complacence. I see that you are really younger than I thought. The world never censures the crimes of the spirit. You are safe from the world's tongue lashings, and in that safety is the danger against which my friendship warns you.

I have been reading Hester's poems, and I know that she is like them, nervous, vibrant, throbbing, sensitive. I have been reading your letters, and I think her soul will escape yours. If you have not love like hers, you have nothing with which to keep her. This I have undertaken to say to you. It is a strange role, yet conventional. I am the father whose matrimonial whims are not met by the son. The stock measure is to disinherit. But the cause of our quarrel is somewhat unusual, and I can be neither so practical nor so vulgar as to set about making codicils. Love is of no value to financiers; there is no bank for it nor may it be made over in a will. Rather is it carried on in the blood, even as Barbara carried it on into the life of her girl-babe. Your sister keeps me strong with the faith of love. May God be good to her! It was five years ago that she came to me and whispered, "Earl." When she saw I could not turn to her in joy, she leaned her little head back against the roses of the porch and wept, more than was right, I fear, for a girl just betrothed. Earl was a cripple and poor and helpless, but Barbara knew better than we, for she knew how to give herself. Poor little one, whom nobody congratulated! She sends you and Hester her love, unfolding you both in her eager tenderness.

Dane.

VI. FROM THE SAME TO THE SAME

London.

November 19, 19——.

Metaphysics is contagious. I caught it from Barbara, and I cannot resist the impulse to pass it on, and to you of all others.

The mood leapt upon Barbara out of the pages of "Katia," a story by Tolstoy. To my mind, it is a painful tale of lovers who outlive their love, killing it with their own hands, but the author means it to be a happily ending novel. Tolstoy attempts to show that men and women can find happiness only when they grow content to give over seeking love from one another. They may keep the memory but must banish the hope. "Hereafter, think of me only as the father of your children," and the woman who had pined for that which had been theirs in the beginning of their union weeps softly, and agrees. Tolstoy calls this peace, but for Barbara and me this gain is loss, this end an end indeed, replete with all the tragedy of ending.

I found Barbara to-day on the last page of "Katia," and much disturbed. "Dear, I saw a spirit break," she said. I waited before asking whose, and when I did, she answered, "That of three-quarters of the world. The ghost of a Dream walked to-day—when after the spirit broke, I saw it—and myself and my Earl vanished in shadow. We and our love thinned away before the thought-shape."

"Your dreaming, Barbara, can scarce be better than your living."

We looked long at each other. She knew herself a happy woman, yet to-day the ghost had walked in the light, and her eyes were not held, and she saw. Even her life was not sufficient, even her plans were paltry, even her heart's love was cramped. Such times of seeing come to happy men and to happy women. Barbara was reading the opinions of the world and the acceptances of the world, and in disliking them she came to doubt herself. Perhaps she, too, should be less at peace, she too may be amongst Pharisees a Pharisee.

"In the midst of the breaking of spirit, how can I know?" she demanded. "Love is sure," I prompted, my hand on her forehead. "Earl and I are sure, dear," she laughed low, and a drift of sobbing swept through the music; "it is not that we are in doubt about ourselves, but sometimes, like to-day, you understand, one finds oneself bitten by the sharp tooth of the world, and a despair courses through the veins and blinds the eyes, and then, in the midst of the bitterest throe, comes a great visioning."

I heard her and understood, and my heart leapt as it had not done for long. Think of it, Herbert, fifty-three and still young! When was it that I last fluttered with joy? Ah, yes, that time the summer and the woods had a great deal to do with it, and a few words spoken by a boy. I think Barbara's majesty of attainment through vicarious breaking of spirit a greater cause for rejoicing.

And then, in the midst of the bitterest throe, came a great visioning. When pain is good and to be thanked for, how good life is! By this alone may you know the proportion and the value of the good of being. Three-quarters of the world are broken spirited, but from out the wreckage a thought-shape, and it is well. The Vision fastens upon us, and what was full seems shrunken, what whole and of all time a passing bit, an untraceable flash. And that is well, for the dream recalls the hope, and the heart grows hardy with hoping and dreaming.

So Barbara.

And you? You do not repine because of these things. Let the Grand Mujik mutter a thousand heresies, let three-quarters of the world accept and live them, you would not think the unaspiring three-quarters broken-spirited. You would hail them right practical. And if you held a thought as firmly as your sister holds the thought of love, and you found yourself alone in your esteem of it, you would part from it and go over to the others. You would not be the fanatic your sister is, to stay so much the closer by it that of necessity she must doubt her own allegiance, fearing in her devotion that, without knowing it, she, too, is cold and but half alive. You would not see visions that would put your best to shame. The thought-shape of the more you could be,

313

were you and the whole world finer and greater, would not walk before you. You would rest content and assured, and—I regret your assurance.

Always yours,

Dane Kempton.

VII. FROM HERBERT WACE TO DANE KEMPTON

The Ridge,

Berkeley, California.

December 6, 19——.

No, I am not in love. I am very thankful that I am not. I pride myself on the fact. As you say, I may not be adjusting my life artistically to its environment (there is room for discussion there), but I do know that I am adjusting it scientifically. I am arranging my life so that I may get the most out of it, while the one thing to disorder it, worse than flood and fire and the public enemy, is love.

I have told you, from time to time, of my book. I have decided to call it "The Economic Man." I am going over the proofs now, and my brain is in perfect working order. On the other hand, there is Professor Bidwell, who is likewise correcting proofs. Poor devil, he is in despair. He can do nothing with them. "I positively cannot think," he complains to me, his hair rumpled and face flushed. He did not answer my knock the other day, and I came upon him with the neglected proofs under his elbows and his absent gaze directed through window and out of doors to some rosy cloudland beyond my ken. "It will be a failure, I know it will," he growled to me. "My brain is dull. It refuses to act. I cannot imagine what has come over me." But I could imagine very easily. He is in love (madly in love with what I take to be a very ordinary sort of girl), and expects shortly to be married. "Postpone the book for a time," I suggested. He looked at me for a moment, then brought his fist down on the general disarray with a thumping "I will!" And take my word for it, Dane, a year hence, when the very ordinary girl greets him with the matronly kiss and his fever and folly have left him, he will take up the book and make a success of it.

Of course I am not in love. I have just come back from Hester—I ran down Saturday to Stanford and stopped over Sunday. Time did not pass tediously on the train. I did not look at my watch every other minute. I read the morning papers with interest and without impatience. The scenery was charming and I was unaware of the slightest hurry to reach my destination. I remember noting, when I came up the gravel walk between the rose-bushes, that my heart was not in my mouth as it should have been according to convention. In fact, the sun was uncomfortable, and I mopped my brow and decided that the roses stood in need of trimming. And really, you know, I had seen brighter days, and fairer views, and the world in more beautiful moods.

And when Hester stood on the veranda and held out her hands, my heart did not leap as though it were going to part company with me. Nor was I dizzy with—rapture, I believe. Nor did all the world vanish, and everything blot out, and leave only Hester standing there, lips curved and arms outstretched in welcome. Oh, I saw the curved lips and outstretched arms, and all the splendid young womanhood swaying there, and I was pleased and all that; but I did not think it too wonderful and impossible and miraculous and the rest of the fond rubbish I am sure poor Bidwell thinks when his eyes are gladdened by his ordinary sort of girl when he calls upon her.

What a comely young woman, is what I thought as I pressed Hester's hands; and none of the ordinary sort either. She has health and strength and beauty and youth, and she will certainly make a most charming wife and excellent mother. Thus I thought, and then we chatted, had lunch, and passed a delightful afternoon together—an afternoon such as I might pass with you, or any good comrade, or with my wife.

All of which rational rightness is, I know, distasteful to you, Dane. And I confess I depict it with brutal frankness, failing to give credit to the gentler, tenderer side of me. Believe me, I am very fond of Hester. I respect and admire her. I am proud of her, too, and proud of myself that so fine a creature should find enough in me to be willing to mate with me. It will be a happy marriage. There is nothing cramped or narrow or incompatible about it. We know each other well—a wisdom that is acquired by lovers only after marriage, and even then with the likelihood of it being a painful wisdom. We, on the other hand, are not blinded by love madness, and we see clearly and sanely and are confident of our ability to live out the years together.

Herbert.

VIII. FROM THE SAME TO THE SAME

The Ridge,

Berkeley, California.

December 11, 19—.

I have been thinking about your romance and my rational rightness, and so this letter.

"One loves because he loves: this explanation is, as yet, the most serious and most decisive that has been found for the solution of this problem." I do not know who has said this, but it might well have been you. And you might well say with Mlle. de Scudéri: *"Love is—I know not what: which comes—I know not when: which is formed—I know not how: which enchants—I know not by what: and which ends—I know not when or why."*

You explain love by asserting that it is not to be explained. And therein lies our difference. You accept results; I search for causes. You stop at the gate of the mystery, worshipful and content. I go on and through, flinging the gate wide and formulating the law of the mystery which is a mystery no longer. It is our way. You worship the idea; I believe in the fact. If the stone fall, the wind blow, the grass and green things sprout; if the inorganic be vitalised, and take on sensibility, and perform functions, and die; if there be passions and pains, dreams and ambitions, flickerings of infinity and glimmerings of Godhead—it is for you to be smitten with the wonder of it and to memorialise it in pretty song, while for me remains to classify it as so much related phenomena, so much play and interplay of force and matter in obedience to ascertainable law.

There are two kinds of men: the wonderers and the doers; the feelers and the thinkers; the emotionals and the intellectuals. You take an emotional delight in living; I an intellectual delight. You feel a thing to be beautiful and joyful; I seek to know why it is beautiful and joyful. You are content that it is, no matter how it came to be; I, when I have learned why, strive that we may have more beautiful and joyful things. "The bloom, the charm, the smile of life" is all too wonderful for you to know; to me it is chiefly wonderful because I may know.

Oh, well, it is an ancient quarrel which neither you nor I shall outlive. I am rational, you are romantic,—that is all there is to it. You are more beautiful; I am more useful; and though you will not see it and will never be able to see it, you and your beauty rest on me. I came into the world before you, and I made the way for you. I was a hunter of beasts and a fighter of men. I discovered fire and covered my nakedness with the skins of animals. I built cunning traps, and wove branches and long grasses and rushes and reeds into the thatch and roof-tree. I fashioned arrows and spears of bone and flint. I drew iron from the earth, and broke the first ground, and planted the first seed. I gave law and order to the tribe and taught it to fight with craft and wisdom. I enabled the young men to grow strong and lusty, and the women to find favour with them; and I gave safety to the women when their progeny came forth, and safety to the progeny while it gathered strength and years.

I did many things. Out of my blood and sweat and toil I made it possible that all men need not all the time hunt and fish and fight. The muscle and brain of every man were no longer called to satisfy the belly need. And then, when of my blood and sweat and toil I had made room, you came, high priest of mystery and things unknowable, singer of songs and seer of visions.

And I did you honour, and gave you place by feast and fire. And of the meat I gave you the tenderest, and of the furs the softest. Need I say that of women you took the fairest? And you sang of the souls of dead men and of immortality, of the hidden things, and of the wonder; you sang of voices whispering down the wind, of the secrets of light and darkness, and the ripple of running fountains. You told of the powers that pulsed the tides, swept the sun across the firmaments, and held the stars in their courses. Ay, and you scaled the sky and created for me the hierarchy of heaven.

These things you did, Dane; but it was I who made you, and fed you, and protected you. While you dreamed and sang, I laboured sore. And when danger came, and there was a cry in the night, and women and children

318

huddling in fear, and strong men broken, and blare of trumpets and cry of battle at the outer gate—you fled to your altars and called vainly on your phantoms of earth and sea and sky. And I? I girded my loins, and strapped my harness on, and smote in the fighting line; and died, perchance, that you and the women and children might live.

And in times of peace you throve and waxed fat. But only by our brain and blood did we men of the fighting line make possible those times of peace. And when you throve, you looked about you and saw the beauty of the world and fancied yet greater beauty. And because of me your fancy became fact, and marvels arose in stone and bronze and costly wood.

And while your brows were bright, and you visioned things of the spirit, and rose above time and space to probe eternity, I concerned myself with the work of head and hand. I employed myself with the mastery of matter. I studied the times and seasons and the crops, and made the earth fruitful. I built roads and bridges and moles, and won the secrets of metals and virtues of the elements. Bit by bit, and with great travail, I have conquered and enslaved the blind forces. I built ships and ventured the sea, and beyond the baths of sunset found new lands. I conquered peoples, and organised nations and knit empires, and gave periods of peace to vast territories.

And the arts of peace flourished, and you multiplied yourself in divers ways. You were priest and singer and dancer and musician. You expressed your fancies in colours and metals and marbles. You wrote epics and lyrics— ay, as you to-day write lyrics, Dane Kempton. And I multiplied myself. I kept hunger afar off, and fire and sword from your habitation, and the bondsmen in obedience under you. I solved methods of government and invented systems of jurisprudence. Out of my toil sprang forms and institutions. You sang of them and were the slave of them, but I was the maker of them and the changer of them.

You worshipped at the shrine of the idea. I sought the fact and the law behind the fact. I was the worker and maker and liberator. You were conventional. Tradition bound you. You were full bellied and content, and you sang of the things that were. You were mastered by dogma. Did the

Mediæval Church say the earth was flat, you sang of an earth that was flat, and danced and made your little shows on an earth that was flat. And you helped to bind me with chains and burn me with fire when my facts and the laws behind my facts shook your dogmas. Dante's highest audacity could not transcend a material inferno. Milton could not shake off Lucifer and hell.

You were more beautiful. But not only was I more useful, but I made the way for you that there might be greater beauty. You did not reck of that. To you the heart was the seat of the emotions. I formulated the circulation of the blood. You gave charms and indulgences to the world; I gave it medicine and surgery. To you, famine and pestilence were acts of providence and punishment of sin: I made the world a granary and drained its cities. To you the mass of the people were poor lost wretches who would be rewarded in paradise or baked in hell. You could offer them no earthly happiness of decency. Forsooth, beggars as well as kings were of divine right. But I shattered the royal prerogatives and overturned the thrones of the one and lifted the other somewhat out of the dirt.

Nor is my work done. With my inventions and discoveries and rational enterprise, I draw the world together and make it kin. The uplift is but begun. And in the great world I am making I shall be as of old to you, Dane. I, who have made you and freed you, shall give you space and greater freedom. And, as of old, we shall quarrel as when first you came to me and found me at my rude earth-work. You shall be the scorner of matter, and I the master of matter. You may laugh at me and my work, but you shall not be absent from the feast nor shall your voice be silent. For, when I have conquered the globe, and enthralled the elements, and harnessed the stars, you shall sing the epic of man, and as of old it shall be of the deeds I have done.

Herbert.

IX. FROM DANE KEMPTON TO HERBERT WACE

3a Queen's Road, Chelsea, S.W.

December 28, 19—.

The curtain is rung down on an illusion, but it rises again on another, this time, as before, with the look of the absolute Good and True upon it. It is because we are at once actor and spectator that we find no fault with blinking sight and slothful thought. We are finite branded and content, except during the shrill, undermining moments when the orchestra is tuning up. "Thus we half-men struggle."

I follow your letter and wonder whether your illusions have qualities of beauty which escape me. I give you the benefit of every doubt which it is possible for me to harbour with regard to my own system of illusions. You glorify the crowd practical. You attach yourself to the ranks that carried thought into action. You inspire yourself with rugged strength by dwelling on the achievements of ruggedness, forgetting that the progress of the world is not marshalled by those who work with line and rule. It was not his crew, but Columbus, who discovered America. The crew stood between the Old and the New, as indeed the crew always does. Between the idealist and his hope were hosts of practical enemies whom he had to subdue before he reached land. But I must not fall into your mistake of dividing men into categories. Men are not either intellectual or emotional; they are both. It is a rounded not an angular development which we follow. Feeling and thinking are not mutually exclusive, and the great personality feels deeply because he thinks highly, feels keenly because he sees widely. Common sense is not incompatible with uncommon sense, evil does not of necessity attend beauty, nor weakness the strength of genius.

I shall sing of the deeds you have done if your deeds are worthy of song. I shall sing a Song of the Sword, too, should the sword "thrust through the fatuous, thrust through the fungous brood." Whatever helps the races to better life sings itself into racial lore, and I alone shall not refuse the tribute.

When you come to see that the Iliad is as great a gift to the race as the doings of Achilles, that the Iliads are more significant than the doings they celebrate, you will cease to classify men into doers and singers. You will cease to dishonour yourself in the eyes of the singers with the hope that in so doing you gain somewhat elsewhere.

Professor Bidwell is in love and it interferes with his work. You have the advantage of him there, no doubt. However, you lose more than you gain. You have shattered the dream and have awakened. To what? What is this reality in which your universe is hung? Where shine the stars of your scientific heaven? By the beauty of your dreaming alone, Herbert, shall you be judged and known. You dream that you have learned the lesson, solved the problem, pierced the mystery, and become a prophet of matter. But matter does not include spirit, so the motif of your dream grows all confused. Your race epic omits the race. You sing the branch and the leaf rather than the sunlit and tenebral wood. Bidwell thinks his ordinary sort of girl a "lyric love, half angel and half bird, and all a wonder and a wild desire." Bidwell exaggerates, perhaps, but unless he feels this for his wife, he has no wife. Barbara obeyed the voice of her heart. That sounds sentimental, but it is none the less a courageous thing to do. I was inconsistent enough to be sorry because she loved a crippled man. Bidwell and Barbara are wiser and happier than you can be, Herbert, than you from whose hand the map of Parnassus Hill has been filched.

Is there one state of consciousness better than another? I think yes. Better to have long, youthful thoughts and to thrill to vibrant emotions than to grovel sluggishly; better to hope and dream and aspire and sway to great harmonies than to be blind and deaf and dumb—better for the type, better for the immortality of the world's soul. This to me is a vital thought, therefore life or death is in the issue. For the rest I know not. By the glimmer of light lent me, I can but guess greatness and descry vagueness. You go further and would touch the phantasmagorial veil. "Right!" I say, and I pray, "Godspeed." But there must be intensity. Are you thrilled? Do you stretch out your arms and dream the beauty? It is only when you gaze into a reality empty of the voices of life that I would wake you to bid you dream better.

Well, Herbert, I have quarrelled with you and shall to the end, I promise. I wish I could take you away, hide you from your Hester's sight, and pour my poetic spleen out on you. Oh, I shall torment you into reason and passion! Whatever you may choose to be, you are my son. I must take you and keep you as you are, of course, but I choose to tell the truth to you though I do love you and hold you mine. Disagreeable of me, but how else?

Dane.

X. FROM THE SAME TO THE SAME

London.

Sunday, January 1, 19—.

Behold, I have lived! I press your face to the breathing, stinging roses of my days, and bid you drink in the sweet and throb with the pain. What is my philosophy but a translation of the facts which have stamped me? Perhaps if I let you read these facts, you will the sooner come to share my consecration and my faith. I must teach you to know that you are the fact of my whole tangled web of facts, and that all that I have and am, and all that might have been I and mine, stretches itself out in the unmarked path which is before you.

I take you back with me to the road, white with dust, upon which like a Viking and like a feeble girl I have travelled. It is not long, but how many paths, what byways and what turns! What sudden glimpses of sea and sky, what inaccessibleness! Hark, from the wood on either side murmurings of hope and hard sobbing of despair, young laughter of joy and aged renunciations! See from amongst the pines the farewell gleam of a white hand. All of it dear—dearly bought and precious and miraculous, the heartache even as the gladness.

> "Life is worth living
>
> Through every grain of it,
>
> From the foundations
>
> To the last edge
>
> Of the cornerstone, death."

Ay, through every grain of it. Even that morning in the wood, thirty years ago, when your mother put her hand in mine and looked a great pity into my eyes. Indeed, she loved me well, but romance shone on the brow of John Wace. For her his face was sunlit, and she needs must take it between her hands and hold it forever. He was her Siegfried, her master. Thus the gods decreed, and we three obeyed. What else was there to do? We must be honest before all, and Ellen did not love me any more, and I must know it, and wipe out a past of deepest mutuality, and strengthen and console and restore the woman whose hand held mine while her eyes were turned elsewhere.

Before that bright, black summer morning which saw me woman-pitied, I knew I should have to renounce her. Their souls rushed together in their first meeting. John had been away, knocking about museums and colleges, and carrying on tempestuous radical work. He was splendidly picturesque. I was a youth of twenty-three, almost ten years his junior, a boy full of half-defined aims and groping powers, reaching toward what he had firm in his grasp. Ellen talked of his coming, and she planned that she should meet this my one friend in the environment she loved best—in my rooms, whose atmosphere, she declared, belonged to an earlier time and place. (She found in me Nolly Goldsmith and all of Grub Street.) So they met at the tea-table in my study, and a great warmth stole over your father. He spoke without looking at either of us, while Ellen looked as if her destiny had just begun.

Without, it rained. I strode to the window and in a dazed way stared at the lamp-post which was sticking out its flaming little tongue to the night. Why was I mocked? There was no mocking and there should have been no bitterness. Of that there was none either, after a while.

Ellen put her hand on my hair, and a strong primal emotion rose in me. In that moment civilisation was as if it had not been. I reverted to the primitive. The blood of forgotten ancestors, cave-men and river-men, reasoned me my ethics. I turned to her, met her flushed cheeks and moved being and the glory of dawning in her eyes. I measured my strength with hers and your father's, Herbert. Easily, great strength was mine in my passion, easily I could carry her off!

You, too, have had moments of upheaval when you heard the growling of the tiger and the bear, when the brute crowded out the man. Then your soul writhed in derision, you scoffed at that which you had held to be the nobility of the soul, and you minced words satirically over the exquisiteness of the type which we have evolved. Then the experiment of life turned farce, the heavens fell about your ears and "Fool!" was upon your lips. Oh, the hurricane that sweeps over the soul when it is cheated of its joy! In the first instant of Ellen's indifference, when I felt myself pushed out of her life, I forgot everything but my desire. I could not renounce her. I was in the throes of the passion for ownership.

Gentle girl between whom and myself there had been naught but sweetness and fellowship! How often had we talked large (we were very young!) of our sublimities and potentialities, how often had we pictured tragedies of surrender and greatened in the speaking! Ah, it should come true. For her and for me there must be miracles, and there were. So was the strength of the spirit proven, so was it shown to be "pure waft of the Will." So was I confirmed in the creed which believes that to keep we must lose, and to live we must die. So was I assured that there may be but one way, and that, the way of service.

I did not grip her passionately in my arms. I withdrew; I did much to make her task of leaving me an easy one. Were it not for my efforts, it would have been harder for her to obey a mandate which made for my pain. She could not quite drown an old, Puritan voice, speaking with the authority of tradition, which bade her hold to her vows. Yes, I made it easy for her. Harrow my soul with theories of selection and survival if you dare!

In those days the spires of the temple were golden, the shrine white. The door was seen from every point in the fog-begirt world. We who worshipped knew not of doubt. Stirred by the rumbling organ tones of causes and ideas, we immolated our lives gladly. High priests of thought, we swung the censers and rose on the breast of the incense. Ellen and John and myself glorified God and enjoyed Him forever,—God, the Type, the Final Humanity, the giant Body Soul of man. In our hearts dwelt a religion which compelled us to serve the ideal. We strove to become what organically we felt the "Human with his

326

drippings of warm tears" may become. We were the standard-bearers of the advancing margin of the world. We were the high-water mark toward which all the tides forever make. We were soldiers and priests.

And so when Ellen loved, and lacked courage for her love, I helped her. A past of kindness and ardour riveted her to my side. She knew that we were in feeling and fact divorced from each other by virtue of her stronger love for John, yet did she do battle with the rich young love. For two years we had been close; she had been so much my friend, she could not in maiden charity seal for me a so unwelcome fate. I had awakened her slumbering soul with my first look into the sphinx wonder of her eyes. For me she had become fire and dew, flame of the sun, and flower of the hill. Without me to help her do it she could not leave me.

To the master of matter this coping with spiritual abstractions must appear like juggling with intellectual phantasmagoria. Yet I protest that life is finally for intangible triumphs. Unnamed fragrances steal upon the senses and the soul revels and greatens. Unseen hands draw us to worlds afar, and we are gathered up in the dignity of the human spirit. Unknown ideas attract and hold us, and we take our place in the universe as intellectual factors. In giving up Ellen I helped her, and, sacredly better still, I sent on into a world of vague thinking and weak acting the impulse of devotion to revealed truth.

She had a sweet way of sitting low and resting her head on my knee. She sat through one whole day with me thus, and for hours I could have thought her asleep were it not for the waves of feeling which surged in her upturned face. Toward the end she raised her head, ecstasy in her eyes and on her cheek and lip. "Dane, I love you. Dane! Dane!" The whole of me was caught up in the accents of that tremulousness. She had know John three months; but her love for him was young, it had come unexpectedly, it was still unexpressed and ineffable. Her yearning for him led to softness toward me, and though she rose out of her mood as one does from a dream, the hours when we were like the angels, all love and all speech, were mine. So much was vouchsafed me.

Memories and echoes, gusts of sweet breath from the violets on your mother's grave—the prophet of matter will have none of them, and, I fear, will pity me that I am so much theirs. I am yours also, dear lad, and I wish to serve you.

Dane Kempton.

XI. FROM HERBERT WACE TO DANE KEMPTON

The Ridge,

Berkeley, California.

January 20, 19—.

I do not know whether to laugh or weep. I have just finished reading your letter, and I can hardly think. Words seem to have lost their meaning, and words, used as you use them, are without significance. You appear to speak a tongue strangely familiar, yet one I cannot understand. You are unintelligible, as, I dare say, I am to you.

And small wonder that we are unintelligible. Our difference presents itself quite clearly to the scientific mind, and somewhat in this fashion: Man acquires knowledge of the outer world through his sensations and perceptions. Sensation ends in sentiment, and perception ends in reason. These are the two sides of man's nature, and the individual is determined and ruled by whichever side in him happens to be temperamentally dominant. I have already classed you as a feeler, myself as a thinker. This is, I *think* true. You, I am confident, *feel* it to be true. I reason why it is true. You accept it on faith as true, lose sight of the argument forthwith, and proceed to express it in emotional terms—which is to say that you take it to heart and feel badly because it happens to be so.

You feign to know this modern scientific slang, and you are contemptuous of it because you do not know it. The terms I use freight no ideas to you. They are sounds, rhythmic and musical, but they are not definite symbols of thought. Their facts you do not grasp. For instance, the prehensile organs of insects, the great toothed mandibles of the black stag-beetle, the amorous din of the male cicada and the muteness of his mate—these are facts which you cannot relate, one with the other, nor can you generalise upon them. Let me add to these related characters, and you cannot discern the law which is alike to all. What to you the fluttering moth, decked in gold and crimson, brilliant, iridescent, splendid? The beauty of it bids you bend to deity, otherwise it has no worth; it is a stimulus to religion, and that is all. So with the glowing incandescence of the stickleback and its polished scales of silver. What make you of the hoarse voice of the gorilla? Is not the dewlap of the ox inscrutable? the mane of the lion? the tusks of the boar? the musk-sack of the deer? In the amethyst and sapphire of the peacock's wing you find no rationality; to you it is a manifestation of the wonder which is taboo. And so with the cock bird, displaying his feathered ruffs and furbelows, dancing strange antics and spilling out his heart in song.

I, on the other hand, dare to gather all these phenomena together, and find out the common truth, the common fact, the common law, which is generalisation, which is Science. I learn that there are two functions which all life must perform: Nutrition and Reproduction. And I learn that in all life, the performance, according to time and space and degree, is very like. The slug must take to itself food, else it will perish; and so I. The slug must procreate its kind, or its kind will perish; and so I. The need being the same, the only difference is in the expression. In all life come times and seasons when the individuals are aware of dim yearnings and blind compulsions and masterful desires. The senses are quickened and alert to the call of kind. And just as the fish and the reptile glimmeringly adumbrate man, so do these yearnings and desires adumbrate what man in himself calls "love," spelled all out in capitals. I repeat, the need is the same. From the amœba, up the ladder of life to you and me, comes this passion of perpetuation. And in yourself, refine and sublimate as you will, it is none the less blind, unreasoning, and compelling.

And now we come to the point. In the development of life from low to high, there came a dividing of the ways. Instinct, as a factor of development, had its limitations. It culminated in that remarkable mechanism, the bee-swarm. It could go no farther. In that direction life was thwarted. But life, splendid and invincible, not to be thwarted, changed the direction of its advance, and reason became the all-potent developmental factor. Reason dawned far down in the scale of life; but it culminates in man and the end is not yet.

330

The lever in his arm he duplicates in wood and steel; the lenses in his eyes in glass; the visual impressions of his brain on chemically sensitised wood-pulp. He is able, reasoning from events and knowing the law, to control the blind forces and direct their operation. Having ascertained the laws of development, he is able to take hold of life and mould and knead it into more beautiful and useful forms. Domestic selection it is called. Does he wish horses which are fast, he selects the fastest. He studies the physics of velocity in relation to equine locomotion, and with an eye to withers, loins, hocks, and haunches, he segregates his brood mares and his stallions. And behold, in the course of a few years, he has a thoroughbred stock, swifter of foot than any ever in the world before.

Since he takes sexual selection into his own hands and scientifically breeds the fish and the fowl, the beast and the vegetable, why may he not scientifically breed his own kind? The fish and the fowl and the beast and the vegetable obey dim yearnings and vague desires and reproduce themselves. "Poor the reproduction," says Man to Mother Nature; "allow me." And Mother Nature is thrust aside and exceeded by this new creator, this Man-god.

These yearnings and desires of the beast and the vegetable are the best tools nature has succeeded in devising. Having devised them, she leaves their operation to the blindness of chance. Steps in man and controls and directs them. For the first time in the history of life conscious intelligence forms and transforms life. These yearnings and desires, promptings of the "abysmal fecundity," have in man evolved into what is called "love." They arise in instinct and sensation and culminate in sentiment and emotion. They master man, and the intellect of man, as they master the beast and all the acts of the beast. And they operate in the development of man with the same blindness of chance that they operate in the development of the beast.

Now this is the law: *Love, as a means for the perpetuation and development of the human type, is very crude and open to improvement. What the intellect of man has done with the beast, the intellect of man may do with man.*

It is a truism to say that my intellect is wiser than my emotions. So, knowing the precise value and use of this erotic phenomenon, this sexual madness, this love, I, for one, elect to choose my mate with my intellect. Thus I choose Hester. And I do truly love her, but in the intellectual sense and not the sense you fanatically demand. I am not seized with a loutish vertigo when I look upon her and touch her hand. Nor do I feel impelled to leave her presence if I would live, as did Dante the presence of Beatrice; nor the painful confusion of Rousseau, when, in the same room with Madame Goton, he seemed impelled to leap into the flaming fireplace. But I do feel for Hester what happily mated men and women, after they have lived down the passion, feel in the afternoon of life. It is the affection of man for woman, which is sanity. It is the sanity of intercourse which replaces love madness; the sanity which comes upon sparrows after the ardour of mating, when they leave off wrangling and chattering and set soberly to work to build their nest for the coming brood.

Pre-nuptial love is the madness of non-understanding and part-understanding. Post-nuptial affection is the sanity of complete understanding; it is based upon reason and service and healthy sacrifice. The first is a blind mating of the blind; the second, a clear and open-eyed union of male and female who find enough in common to warrant that union. In a word and in the fullest sense of the word, it is sex comradeship. Pre-nuptial love cannot survive marriage any considerable time. It is doomed inexorably to flicker out, and when it has flickered out it must be replaced by affection, or else the parties to it must separate. We well know that many men and women, unable to build up affection on the ruins of love, do separate, or if they do not, continue to live together in cold tolerance or bitter hatred.

Now, Hester is my mate. We have much in common. There is intellectual, spiritual, and physical affinity. The caress of her voice and the feel of her mind are pleasurable to me; likewise the touch of her hand (and you know that in the union of man and woman the higher affinities are not possible unless there first be physiological affinity). We shall go through life as comrades go, hand in hand, Hester and I; and great happiness will be ours. And because of all this I say you have no right to challenge my happiness, and vex my days, and feel for me as one dead.

My dear, bewildered Dane, come down out of the clouds. If I am wrong, I have gone over the ground. Then do you go over that ground with me and show where I am wrong. But do not pour out on me your romantic and poetic spleen. Confine yourself to the Fact, man, to the irrefragable Fact.

Herbert.

Ah, your later letter has just arrived. I can only say that I understand. But withal, I am pained that I am not nearer to you. These intellectual phantasmagoria rise up like huge amorphous ghosts and hold me from you. I cannot get through the mists and glooms to press your hand and tell you how dear I hold you. Do, Dane, do let us cease from this. Let us discuss no further. Let me care for Hester in my own way so long as I do no sin and harm no one; and be you father to us, and bless us who else must go unblessed. For Hester, also, is fatherless and motherless, and you must be to her as you are to me.

Herbert.

XII. FROM DANE KEMPTON TO HERBERT WACE

London,

3a Queen's Road, Chelsea, S.W.

February 10, 19—.

So we have got into an argument! I have been poring over your last two or three letters, and they read like a set of briefs for a debate. Doubtless mine have the same forensic quality. Our letters have become rebuttals, pure and simple. This discovery gave my pen pause for a week. It occurred to me that Walt Whitman must have meant didactic letters too, when he said of the fretters of our little world, "They make me sick talking of their duty to God." Yet friend should speak to friend, should utter the word than which nothing is more sacred. "Let there be light, and there was light"—a ripple of light, and a flash, then the darkness broke and dispersed from the face of the waters. It was a trumpet-call of words bringing drama into a nebulous creation. Let the Word break up our night and let us not only grant, but avow the conviction it brings us, no matter what the consequence. Let us worship the irrefragable Fact.

You hold that marriage is an institution having for its purpose the perpetuation of the species, and that respect and affection are sufficient to bring two people into this most intimate possible relation. You also hold that the business of the world, pressing hard upon men, makes "love from their lives a thing apart," and that this is as it should be. Your letters are an exposition and a defence of what I may loosely call the practical theory. You show that the world is for work and workers, and that life is for results as seen in institutions and visible achievements. I, on the other hand, maintain that it takes a greater dowry to marry upon than affection, and that men love as intensely and with as much abandon as women. People love in proportion to the depth of their natures, and the finest man in the world has an infinite capacity for giving and receiving love store. The spell is strongest upon the finest.

This, briefly, is what we have been saying to each other. You attack my idealism, call me dreamer, and accuse me of being out of joint with the time, which itself is rigorously in joint with the laws of growth. And I class you with the Philistine because of your exaggeration of practical values. I hold that it is gross to respect the fact tangible at the expense of the feeling ineffable.

In your last letter you exploit the theory of Nutrition and Reproduction with a charm and warmth which helps me see you as I have so long known you, and which tells me again that you are worth fighting for and saving. But to trace love to its biologic beginning is not to deny its existence. Love has a history as significant as that of life. When, eons ago, the primitive man looked at his neighbour and recognised him as a fellow to himself, consciousness of kind awoke and a cell was exploded which functioned love. When, through the ages, economic forces taught men the need of mutual aid, when everywhere in life the law of development charged men with leanings and desires and outreachings, then the sway of love began in life. What was subconscious became conscious, what, back in the past, was a mere adumbration gloried out in Aurora splendours. The love of a Juliet is the outgrowth of natural processes manifesting themselves everywhere down the scale, but it is also the gift of the last evolution, and it speaks to us from the topmost notch in the scale. The charm of morning rests on a Juliet's love because its hour is young and yet old, striking the time of the past and the future. It is thus that the hunger of the race and the passion of the race become in the individual the need for happiness. The need of the race and the need of the individual are at once the same and different.

What was the point of your letter? That sexual selection obtains? I grant it. That it is incumbent upon us as intelligent men and women to call to the aid of instinct our social wisdom? I grant and avow it. But our social wisdom insists that we obey the choices of instinct; our social wisdom is only another phase of our refinement, which, in impelling us to a love of the beautiful, does not the less impel us to love. Our social wisdom educates our taste without lessening our taste for the thing. "Love a beautiful person nobly, but be sure you love her," says our social wisdom with interesting tautology. Besides, you are a heretic to your own breed, Herbert. It is you who would forsake our present social wisdom, ruling modern men by laws which obtained in primitive life. It is you who steadily hark back to the past, and to states of consciousness which were but can never be again. The early facts of biology cannot include that which transcends them. To borrow from Ernest Seton Thompson, man is evolved with the lower orders in the same way that water is changed into steam, and the nature of the change, when it is effected, is as radical. Add a number of degrees of heat to water and it is still water. Let one degree be wanting to the necessary number, and the substance is still intact. Add the last degree, and water is no longer water. From water to steam is a radical change and a transformation.

You agree to improve upon the beasts of the fields and upon our own race in the past, and in this you go farther than you have need if marriage is for nothing else than to serve the instinct for perpetuation. You shew some respect for what is natural and instinctive, yet you say that all would be as well if individual choice had not prevailed, and men and women were "shuffled about." You draw up a cold programme for action in affairs of the spirit and formulate a code of procedure in matters of the heart.

I have a programme too. Mine does not break with nature. On the contrary, it obeys every instinct and listens to every call on the senses. My love begins in my biologic self, grows with my growth, takes its hues from visioned sunsets in corn-flower skies, its grace from swaying rivers of grain seen in dreams. It is for me what it is for fish and fowl, beast and vegetable. It is my passion for perpetuation, but it is also something as different from this as I am different from beast and vegetable. My love is "blind, unreasoning, and compelling," and for that I trust it. I do not conceive myself Man-god, therefore I do not say to Nature, "Allow me." I cannot be sure that when I say it in the case of the horse, who obeys like me "dim yearning and vague desires," I do not sacrifice him to a lust of my own. The lust for owning and spoiling is hard to cope with. Perhaps a purer time is near, when, upborne by a sense of the dignity of romance and the sacredness of life, man will refrain from laying rough hands on his mute brothers.

The romance which is my proof of the good of being does not rest on passion. The unclean fires that consume the loutish and degenerate are not of love. You quote instances of the hyperphysical and hysterical. The feeling that I would have you obey for your soul's sake and without which you are but half alive, is not the blind passion of an oversexed sentimentalism. Rousseau was never in love in his life, though to say it were to accuse him of perjury.

One word more. Do you wish to know why I care? I care because I know you to be of those who are capable of love. Probably it was one little twist in your development that has turned you into alien ways of thinking and living. Yes, and more than for this I care because you are the fulfilment of a sacred past. You are the son of my sacrifice and your mother's love.

I care very much indeed. I do not wish you to awake some terrible night to find that you had ended your romance before you had begun it. I vex your days and call you dead? It is because I know the life that is by the grace of God yours, and because I cannot bear to let you coffin it. Herbert, there is misery when the blood pales, and the tears dry up, and the flame of the heart sinks, and all that is left is a memory of a thought—a memory of very long ago when one was young and might have chosen to live.

I am sorry we darken the days for each other.

Your friend always,

Dane Kempton.

XIII. FROM THE SAME TO THE SAME

London,

3a Queen's Road, Chelsea, S.W.

February 12, 19—.

Barbara and Earl celebrated their anniversary yesterday. Invitations were sent out, the guests consisting of Melville and myself. "Anniversary of what?" we asked. For answer we received inscrutable smiles. Birthdays are accidents of fate. You may regret the accident or you may be thick enough in illusion to rejoice over it, but you cannot in decency celebrate an occurrence wholly independent of personal control and yet concerning itself with you! Leave the merrymaking for appreciative friends. So rules Barbara. Not a birthday, then, nor the date of their marriage. The occasion was in some flash struck from Being, the memory of which enriches them,—in a mood that for an hour held them in strong grasp, in the utterance of a word charged with destiny, in the avowal of their love if their love awaited avowal. Whatever the cause, they honoured it with a will.

Barbara's eyes flashed, her cheeks were sweetly suffused, and her voice was vibrant. Earl, too, was at his best. My heart loved this man who had lain all his life with death. His health is at its bad worst this winter, which fact made of the "Celebration" a rather heart-rending affair. He has been obliged to abandon the *Journal*, but we hope he can stay with the school. Meanwhile, his chronic invalidism of body and purse does not too much affect him. He keeps his charm of tenderness and strength. He rivets his pupils to him almost as he riveted his Barbara.

I have discovered my proof of this couple's happiness. It is that I have always taken it for granted. Simple, is it not? And absolute. Often in their presence I catch myself imagining their mutual lives and seeing vaguely the graces that each brings to each. "How she must delight him!" I say. "How his eyes speak to her!" "They can never come to the end of each other," and so on. The ordinary married couple so often brings a sense of distressed surprise: "How can these two foot it together?" "How did it happen?" "How can it go on?"

Last night counted to me. Your father and I have had such evenings, but I did not think I could do it all over again. We spoke with the fire (and conceit) of young students, exciting ourselves with expired theories, hoping old hopes, smarting under blows that perhaps had long ceased to fall. What then? What if we were ill-read in the facts? We could not have been wrong in the feeling. For the old hope that has been proven vain, a new; for the ancient hurt, a modern wrong, as great and as crying. It was good to feel that we had not grown too wise to harbour thoughts of change and redress, or too much ironed out with doctrine to be resigned. I confess it is long since I have eaten my heart in fury, in impatience, in wildness, but last night we awoke the radical in one another. We condemned the system. We placed ourselves outside the régime, refusing aught at its hands, registering our protest, hating the inordinate scheme of things only as hotly as we loved the juster Hand of a future time.

It is curious that we, offsprings of parvenue success, should be capable of such repudiation. Barbara accepts the Management without the trouble of a question. "What do you know? What do you know?" the girl demands, a radiant little angel in white, and a conservative. "You must know yourselves in the wrong, else would you smite your way through the world."

Ah, Barbara has yet to learn that it is hard to live. It is not so hard to fight, and it is easy to rest neutral, but to be fighter and bearer both, to stand staunch, holding ever to the issue, and yet, without tameness, to take rebuff and wait, there's the true course and the heroic. It is difficult when one has been conquered to know it. It is difficult to honour an outgrown ideal, which cost us, nevertheless, comfort and prestige—prizes which youth scorns and which oncoming age, pathetically enough, holds dear. It is difficult to pull up when driving too fast and too far, when galloping towards fanaticism, and it is impossible to whip oneself into passion and martyrdom. It is difficult to live, little Barbara.

For me it is also difficult to report a social function. At this one Browning presided, for Melville took up "Caponsacchi" and read it to us. That voice of his is in itself an interpretation, but Browning needs interpreting less than any other man who wrote great poems, because he wrote the greatest. It was four in the morning when the "O great, just, good God! Miserable me!" of the soldier-saint fell upon our ears. How we had listened! Earl steadily paced the floor, Barbara leaned her cheek upon my hand. Her soul was doing battle, and so was mine. We were all fighting the gallant fight. Read "Pompilia" and you are filled with reverence, read "Caponsacchi" and you are caught up by the spirit of action. You must rise and forth to burn your way like he, though you may have been too weary in spirit before to answer to your name when opportunity called roll.

It was Earl who broke the silence caused by the inner tumult. In a dreamy voice, his eyes very eager and intent, he told us how at one time he had gone up a hill that faced the house in which he lived. A hard rain was driving, he fell at every step up the slippery steepness, but at every step the beauty of it became more and more wondrous, hardly bearable. The little village sank lower and lower, and about him were soft hills, graceful and verdant, a stretch of water lying dark under the clouded sky, and the mountain gray and watchful in the distance. It was then, in the chill of a January rain, on an oak-clad hill of a western spot, that he recognised the dear features of the Mother, knew her his as hers he was, and loved her with passion. The sea is vast and wondrous, but it is alien. It holds you apart; it is not of you. But the gentle earth with her undulating form and the growing life in her lap, soothes with wordless harmonies. It was then that he forgave the fate which deformed him. A twisted oak, that is all—no less a tree and no less beautiful in the landscape! And it was sufficient to live. In the bosom of so much beauty sufficient also to die. As he stood, thinking it out, feeling the wonder and the glory, at times sorry for those who can see no longer the slanting sheets of rain and the grass at the feet, at times feeling that since this is good, in some impalpable way oblivion to all this may be also good, as he stood there, flushed with the climbing and sad with great joy, the thought came: With whom? It cannot be lived alone. With whom? He turned at the touch of an arm at his shoulder to meet the smile and the look and the quick breath of her who had sent herself his Eve.

340

In the dawn stealing over the world of London, Earl told the story, and there and then we saw it all—the hill in the heart of the hills, the reconciled boy who had climbed its brow, the rain-drenched woman hurrying to overtake him, with the gift of all of herself in her eyes. We looked neither at Barbara nor at Earl. Possessed of the secret, we spoke a few words and left. Our host had divulged what the anniversary sought to celebrate. We understood and were glad.

Good night, lad. Would you could have shared our heyday at the dawning!

Dane.

XIV. FROM HERBERT WACE TO DANE KEMPTON

The Ridge,

Berkeley, California.

February 31, 19—.

Love is a something that begins in sensation and ends in sentiment. Thanks to beautiful and permissible hyperbole, you have begun with sensation in your description of love, and have ended with sentiment. You have told me about love, in terms of love, which is a vain performance and unscientific. Now let me make you a definition. *Love is a disorder of mind and body, and is produced by passion under the stimulus of imagination.*

Love is a phase of the operation of the function of reproduction, and it occurs solely in man. Love, adhering to the common understanding of the term, is an emotional excitement which does not obtain among the lower animals. The lower animals lack the stimulus of imagination, and with them the passion for perpetuation remains a mere passion. But man has developed imagination. The pure sexual passion is glossed over and obscured by a cloud of fancies, mistaken yearnings, and distorted dreams. And so well is the real intent of the function obscured, that it is actually lost to him, especially during the period of love madness, so that there seems an apparent divorce between the parts which go to make up love, between passion and imagination.

The romantic lover of to-day (expressing sensation in terms of sentiment, and fondly imagining that he is reasoning) cannot reconcile his soul-exaltation with bodily grossness, cannot conceive that soul can turn body, and in the embrace of body tell out all the wonder of soul. To all sensitive and spiritual men and women come times of anguish and tears and self-revolt, when they are confounded and heart-broken by the physical aspect of love. Poor men and women! they suffer keenly and sincerely through lack of something more than a sentimental concept of love. To them, body and soul appear things apart, to be kept apart, lest the one contaminate the other. And in the end, loving well and truly, they prove their love by enduring, though unable ever quite to shake off the sense of sin and shame and personal degradation. They do not understand life, that is the trouble. The beast, lacking imagination, needs no rational rightness for the various acts of living, such as they need, and which they do not possess. Because of their unchecked and unbalanced imagination they mistake the half of life for the whole, and when forced to face the whole are affrighted and shocked. They do not reason that the need for perpetuation is the cause of passion; and that human passion, working through imagination and worked upon by imagination, becomes love.

And while I am in this vein, I may as well deny that a greater spiritual dowry than affection is required for marriage. (For that matter, I fail to see anything so spiritual in erotic phenomena.) If a man may achieve affection for a woman, without undergoing pre-nuptial madness,—if a man may take the short cut, as it were,—then I see no reason why he should not marry that woman. He is certainly justified, since affection is what romantic love must evolve into after marriage. But do not mistake me, Dane. I do not intend this sweepingly. It will not do for the whole human herd; for at once enters that abhorrent thing you rightly fear, the marriage for convenience. Alas, it too often masquerades under the guise of romantic love. Certainly, every man is not capable of taking this short cut and at the same time of avoiding a violation of true sexual selection. Having little brain, the average man can only act in line with sexual selection by undergoing the romantic love malady. But for some few of us, and I dare to include myself, the short cut is permissible. This short cut I shall take, and far be it from any worldly sense of stocks and bonds and comfortable housekeeping.

Marriage means less to man than to woman? Yes, by all means, at least to the normal man or woman. As surely as reproduction is woman's peculiar function, and nutrition man's, just so surely does marriage sum up more to woman than to man. It becomes the whole life of the woman, while to the man it is rather an episode, rather a mere side to his many-sided life. Natural selection has made it so. The countless men of the past, even from before the time they swung down out of the trees, who devoted more time and energy to their love-affairs than to the winning of food and shelter, died from innutrition in various ways. Only the men, normal men, with a proper respect for the mechanism of life, survived and perpetuated their kind. The chance was large that the abnormal lover did not win a wife at all. At least it is so to-day. The abnormal lover is not a successful bidder for women, and is usually passed by.

But while we are on this topic, do not let us forget Dante Alighieri, your prince of lovers. Has a suitable explanation ever occurred to you concerning how he came to marry Gemma, daughter of Manetto Donati, who bore him seven children, and was never once mentioned in the "Divina Commedia?" You remember what he said of his first meeting with Beatrice, "At that moment I saw most truly that the spirit of life which hath its dwelling in the secretest chambers of the heart began to tremble so violently that the least pulses of my body shook therewith." And he later had seven children by Gemma, daughter of Manetto Donati, and whom, as the historian has recorded, "there was no reason to suppose other than a good wife."

As for the primitive, I hark back to it because we are still very primitive. How many thousands years of culture, think you, have rubbed and polished at our raw edges? One, probably; at the best, not more than two. And that takes us back to screaming savagery, when, gross of body and deed, we drank blood from the skulls of our enemies, and hailed as highest paradise the orgies and carnage of Valhalla. And before that time, think you, how many thousands of years of savagery did we endure? and how many myriads of thousands in the long procession of life up from the first vitalised inorganic? Two thousand years are an extremely thin veneer with which to cover the many millions.

And further, our much-vaunted two thousand years of culture is a thing of the mind, an acquired character. We are not born with it. Each must gather it for himself after he is born, from the spoken and written words of his fellow and forerunners. Isolate a babe from all of its kind and it will never learn to speak, and without speech words, it can never think save in the concretest possible way. Yet it will possess all the brute instincts and passions—the raw edges which do constantly shove through the culture varnish of the civilised man.

344

Our culture is the last to come, the first to go. I have seen it go from a man in an hour, nay, on the instant. Our culture is nothing more than the accumulated wisdom of the race. It is not part of us, not a thing or attribute handed down from father to son. It is a something acquired in varying degree by each individual for himself. Yes, I do well to hark back to the primitive. It tells me where I am to-day and describes to me the world I am living in. You, Dane, are hyper-refined, or refined beyond the times. You are like the idealistic and advanced zealots, who, when such action would mean destruction, advise these United States to disarm in the face of the war-harnessed world.

But no more of this jerky letter. Soon I shall proceed to make my contention good. I shall show the higher part intellect plays in conjugal love, the control, restraint, forbearance, sacrifice. And I shall show that conjugal love is higher and finer than romantic love.

Herbert.

XV. FROM DANE KEMPTON TO HERBERT WACE

London,

3a Queen's Road, Chelsea, S.W.

March 15, 19—.

Clyde Stebbins was here an hour after your theories and definitions reached me. The fact that I had been reading treason against his sister made me pick my subjects a little too carefully for smooth conversation. Your letter, partly open, was on the table before us, and my eyes fell upon it often as I wondered what it would mean to Hester's brother—if he could read it. I no longer think only of you.

I reject your definition of love. It is not a disorder of the mind and body, nor is it solely the instrument of reproduction. I reject and resent your distinction between the pre-nuptial and post-nuptial states of feelings. Further, I hold that marriage may not be based on affection alone, and I disagree with you that population is better than principle. Children need not be brought into the world at any cost.

Love is not a disorder, but a growth. There is spiritual as well as physical growth. Some men and women never grow up strong enough to love. Their development is arrested, or they are, from the beginning, poor creatures born of starvelings, and perhaps fated to give birth to pale, sapless beings like themselves. Others there are who love, and this is no ill chance, no disease of the mind and body calling for psychiater and physician. It is a strength, a becoming, a fulfilment. Let us reason from the effect to the cause. How does this madness manifest itself? Not in weakness. You never saw a man or woman in love who was the worse for it. The lover carries all things before him, and not for himself alone, but for a larger world than ever had been his. He who loves one must perforce love all the world and all the unborn worlds. This is the way life goes, which is another way of saying it is a scientific fact. That which makes men capable of consecration is not a disorder of the mind and body. It is the greatest of all forces, and it turns the wrangling and grabbing human creature into an inspired poet.

And the cause? The passion for perpetuation and the imagination. We agree. But there are other and more immediate needs than the need of perpetuation that call out love, needs that are peculiarly of the present, being bound up with the steady outreaching for help, for fellowship in the jerky journey through the universe. If love were no more than an instrument of reproduction, you would be right in maintaining that the fastidiousness I insist on is unnecessary and unnatural. If love were that and that alone, there would be no love, which is a paradox indeed.

"Because of our souls' yearning that we meet

And mix in soul through flesh, which yours and mine

Wear and impress, and make their visible selves,—

All which means, for the love of you and me,

Let us become one flesh, being one soul."

I dare a formula: In the beginning love arose in the passion for perpetuation; to-day, the passion for perpetuation arises in love. Just as we put ourselves in the way of natural selection, pitting the microcosm against the macrocosm in a passion of ethical feeling, just so do we reverse for ourselves processes that seem indeed to have all the force of law. This reversal is civilisation.

The lover is impelled to perpetuate himself in the Here and the Now. The law of life exacts from him the tribute of love. Imagination gives the lover the key to the object of his love. He enters and he beholds only the ideal which is hers; for him her clay self and the mere facts of her do not exist. The conditions of love are inherent in civilisation. When purpose is high and feeling rich, when "the everlasting possession of the good" is desired, then is heard the I Am of love.

Now to my definition. Negatively, love is not a disorder of the mind and body, not a madness, since it arises in the eternally most valuable, since it is the culmination of high processes, and since it makes for sanity of vision and strength and happiness. Positively, love is the awakening of the personality to the beauty and worth of some one being, caused by the passion for perpetuation and by imagination. It is a desire to hold to the good everlastingly, and to merge with it.

Aristotle proved to the satisfaction of his time that women have fewer teeth than men. Aristotle was a great man, and besides being a philosopher was the foremost scientist of his day. I cannot help thinking of this prodigious blunder. Perhaps (who knows?) the same famous fate which a sexual classification of teeth enjoys awaits a definition calling love a disorder.

I will continue to-morrow. A note has just been given me calling me to Earl, who is ill, but not seriously. Barbara has prescribed for him a game of chess. The desire to see you again has got into my blood. I think I shall be in the new West and with you before long.

Your friend always,

Dane Kempton.

XVI. FROM THE SAME TO THE SAME

London.

Sunday morning.

I must proceed with the three other points of my letter, so I shall stay here and write, though there is a sharp breeze this morning and a coquettishly escaping sunlight, and something tugs at me to go out upon the city streets. It is not restlessness, but the love of the open. I am fain to leave a walled house, and, better still, to get outside of the walls within and join the city in friendship and let the city join me. I never feel greater fellowship than when I walk—

Except when I write to you. Then do I greaten with the pride of life. My sympathies quicken and I grow young again. I constitute myself advocate of the world, and enthusiasm does not fail me in this high calling. It is but natural that in the face of scepticism which I cannot share I should feel greater faith, that in the face of revilement a sense of the glory of the thing belittled should settle upon me. I turn zealot and spend myself in long-drawn praising. I lay myself under a spell of harmony because I am serving and defending and approving what I hold to be good.

So when you insist that romantic love is pre-nuptial and that it dies at marriage as others suppose it to die at the approach of poverty, I grow glad with the knowledge that this is not true. I scrutinize facts which I hitherto took for granted, and become doubly sure. You dogmatise when you say that the lover and the husband are mutually exclusive. If there was love in the beginning, it will be at the end. Love doubles upon itself. Propinquity tightens bonds and there is a steady blossoming of the character in a radiant atmosphere. The marriages that fail are the unions which are based on liking. In these, weariness must set in, for marriage demands that men and women be all in all to each other, and unless it be so with them, the lives of the "contracting parties" are, by the laws of logic, and by the force of the laws of delicacy in the art of living, forever spoilt.

Yes, and people who truly love come to regret their married love, these too. But these have at least begun well. Their lives are infinitely richer for this fact. Their failure itself is made by it more bearable than the failure of those others who act the vulgarian and demand so little of life that even that little escapes them. No world-stains on these who are, at least, would-be lovers. They stand mistaken but irreproachable. It was neither their fault nor love's, and "life more abundant" comes to them even with the mistake.

You are consistent. Just as you maintain that love is passion, so do you think that it is no more than a preliminary thrill. You note a change; the flutter and the excitement felt in the presence of the unknown go, and you do not know that they give place to the steadier joys of the unknown, that after the promise comes the fulfilment, that the hope is not more beautiful than the realisation, that there is divinity in both, and that love does not disappoint.

Tell me, are the placid marriages of affection you are preparing to describe so very placid? Do these jog along so well? Is the control, restraint, forbearance, sacrifice, of which you speak, as readily practised for the person who is that to you which twenty others may quite as easily be, as it is for the one beyond all whom you love and deify, whom the laws of your being command that you serve, living and dying? God knows, the average marriage does not exhibit a striking picture of the practice of these virtues! Rather are such phrases ideals on stilts on which suffering marital partners attempt to hobble across their extremity. On the other hand, to some extent everybody practises restraint and sacrifice since everybody is to some extent moral. But it goes very hard with your average man and woman in your average marriage, and there is a decided setting of the mouth and narrowing of the eyes with the effort.

Whatever placidity there is is attained by means of vampirism. Diderot, the husband of a stupid seamstress, had no right to the love of a Mlle. Voland. It was vampirism and sin to take all from this woman, and to return her favour with so much less than all, as surely as cowardice and selfishness are sin. But the illicit relation will exist because custom cannot rid men and women of subtle sympathies and dear yearnings, because men and women will love though the world consider it cheap and mad. Individually, we have no difficulty in finding our happiness, but we are made advance toward it through the twisted byways of an unfrank world. "No straight road! Keep turning!" has been the scream of convention since convention began.

So for every commonplace marriage there is a canonised love, and the story is told in the old Greek civilisation by the Hetairæ. You remember how it reads in the history: "The low position generally assigned the wife in the home had a most disastrous effect upon Greek morals. She could exert no such elevating or refining influence as she casts over the modern home. The men were led to seek social and intellectual sympathy and companionship outside the family circle, among a class of women known as Hetairæ, who were esteemed chiefly for their brilliancy of intellect. As the most noted representative of this class stands Aspasia, the friend of Pericles. The influence of the Hetairæ was most harmful to social morality." And the practice persisted through many a renaissance where Lauras and Beatrices were besung, down to the brilliant encyclopædists of the eighteenth century with their avowed loves, down to our Goethe and John Stuart Mill. All of these loves rose in very different motives and environments, yet were they the same fundamentally,—strong, sweet love between man and woman, very much spoiled by the fact that custom permitted the loveless marriage at the same time, but yet love which was good since it was the best that could be had. And when the historian permits himself to say, "The influence of the Hetairæ was most harmful to social morality," it is evident that he also thinks that a marriage which compels husband or wife to seek soul's help elsewhere than in their union is bad and wrong.

To-day there is a change in attitude. Woman is new-born in strength and dignity, and the highest chivalry the world has ever known is in blossom. She is an equal, a comrade, a right regal person. She is no longer a means but an end in herself, not alone fit to mother men but fit to live in equality with men. I repeat, she is not a means but an individual, with a soul of her own to rear. Because of the greater and more general emancipation of woman the subtlety of modern love has become possible.

Now for the last point, the question of perpetuation. Just as function precedes organ, so the love of life is inherent in the living for the maintenance of life. But even the primitive man, in whom instinct is strongest, proves himself capable of death. Some men have always been able to give up their lives for some cause. (Indeed there is thought to be suicide amongst animals.) And to-day we certainly no longer say a man must live. Quite as often must he die. Men have found it wise to die at the stake or on the gallows. If this be true of our relation to the life which courses through us, how much more true is it of our instinct to perpetuate ourselves, which pertains to the love of life biologically only, which is often, in the social manifestation of that instinct, a cold intellectual concept and never a dominating thought! We are not driven to procreate. In fact, every child born into the world competes hard for its morsel. Under our unimaginable economic régime all increase in population is a menace.

I call bringing children into the world a codfish act which causes an overflux of vulgar little earthlings, if the process be not humanised and spiritualised. If the child is conceived not in lust but in love, it is rightly born. If it is the child of your ideal, the offspring of that which is your truest life, then is your progeny your immortality, and then, and then only, have you reason for pride and joy in that which you have caused to be.

My dear, dear Herbert, my love has not failed. This you must come to understand. Love never fails. The children that might have been mine are better unborn, since I could not give them a mother whom I loved. You remind me that Dante married Gemma, daughter of Manetto Donati, and she bore him seven children. Yet, Herbert, was this wife not mentioned in the "Commedia," nor in "La Vita Nuova," nor anywhere else in his writings. Dante was a Conformist. He was not in all respects above his time; witness his theology. Convention permitted the dispassionate marriage side by side with love. He was conventional, and the infinite moment of meeting in paradise with his Lady was embittered by her "cold, lessoned smiles."

"Ah, from what agonies of heart and brain,

What exultations trampling on despair,

What tenderness, what tears, what hate of wrong,

What passionate outcry of a soul in pain,

Uprose this poem of the earth and air,

This mediaeval miracle of song!"

It was for Beatrice that this man vexed his spirit with immortal effort and raised a Titan voice which yet is heard in charmed echoes. It was for Beatrice that he descended into the dead regions and climbed the hills of purgatory and soared towards the Rose of Paradise,—"And 'She, where is She?' instantly I cried."

Dante, our prince of lovers, might have lived better, but he loved well.

This in answer to your letter. To meet your argument I have found it best to employ something of your own method, but I cannot rid myself of the feeling that I have vulgarised the subject by saying so much about it. I fear my letter would provoke a smile from those who know love and the wonder of its simplicity through all the subtlety. "We, in loving, have no cause to speak so much!" would be their unanswerable criticism. It is easier to live than to argue about life.

The thought has suddenly assailed me that what I have said may sound derogatory to Hester. Know, then, that I do not think there is a woman in the world who is not capable of inspiring true and abiding love in the heart of some man. Besides, Hester to me looms up as a heroine. Not a hair's breadth of what I know of her that is not beautiful. My regret is that she, who could be "a vision eterne," should be doomed to receive episodically your considerate affection. She does not know your programme. She is a girl who takes your love for granted in the same way as she gives hers, without niggardliness. It is the woman who cannot be content with less than all that is slowly starved to death on a bread-and-water diet and who does not find it out until the end.

Until the carnival time when you and Hester come to love each other, if that time is to be, you two must be as separate in deed as you are in fact.

Forgive me and write soon.

Yours ever,

Dane.

XVII. FROM HERBERT WACE TO DANE KEMPTON

The Ridge,

Berkeley, California.

April 2, 19—.

So you have met Hester's brother? Well, I have had an outing with Hester. She loves me well, I know, and I cannot but confess a thrill at the thought. On the other hand, well do I know the significance of that love, the significance and the cause. Notwithstanding that wonderful soul of hers, she is in no wise constituted differently from her millions of sisters on the planet to-day. She loves—she knows not why; she knows—only that she loves. In other words, she does not reason her emotions.

But let us reason, we men, after the manner of men. And be thou patient, Dane, and follow me down and under the phenomena of love to things sexless and loveless. And from there, as the proper point of departure, let us return and chart love, its phases and occurrences, from its first beginnings to its last manifestations.

Things sexless and loveless! Yes, and as such may be classed the drops of life known as unicellular organisms. Such a creature is a tiny cell, capable of performing in itself all the functions of life. That one pulsating morsel of matter is invested with an irritability which, as Herbert Spencer says, enables it "to adjust the inner relations with outer relations," to correspond to its environment—in short, to live. That single cell contracts and recoils from the things in its environment uncongenial to its constitution, and the things congenial it draws to itself and absorbs. It has no mouth, no stomach, no alimentary canal. It is all mouth, all stomach, all alimentary canal.

But at that low plane the functions of life are few and simple. This bit of vitalised inorganic has no sex, and because of that it cannot love. Reproduction is growth. When it grows over-large it splits in half, and where was one cell there are two. Nor can the parent cell be called *mother* or *father*:

and for that matter, the parent cell cannot be determined. The original cell split into two cells; one has as much claim to parenthood as the other.

It lives dimly, to be sure, this mote of life and light; but before it is a vast evolution, Dane, on the pinnacle of which are to be found men and women, Hester Stebbins, my mother, you!

A step higher we find the cell cluster, and with it begins that differentiation which has continued to this day and which still continues. Simplicity has yielded to complexity and a new epoch of life been inaugurated. The outer cells of the cluster are more exposed to environmental forces than are the inner cells; they cohere more tenaciously and a rudimentary skin is formed. Through the pores of this skin food is absorbed, and in these food-absorbing pores is foreshadowed the mouth. Division of labour has set in, and groups of cells specialise in the performance of functions. Thus, a cell group forms the skinny covering of the cluster, another cell group the mouth. And likewise, internally, the stomach, a sac for the reception and digestion of food, takes shape; and the juices of the body begin to circulate with greater definiteness, breaking channels in their passage and keeping those channels open. And, as the generations pass, still more groups of cells segregate themselves from the mass, and the heart, the lungs, the liver, and other internal organs are formed. The jelly-like organism develops a bony structure, muscles by which to move itself, and a nervous system—

Be not bored, Dane, and be not offended. These are our ancestors, and their history is our history. Remember that as surely as we one day swung down out of the trees and walked upright, just so surely, on a far earlier day, did we crawl up out of the sea and achieve our first adventure on land.

But to be brief. In the course of specialisation of function, as I have outlined, just as other organs arose, so arose sex-differentiation. Previous to that time there was no sex. A single organism realised all potentialities, fulfilled all functions. Male and female, the creative factors, were incoherently commingled. Such an individual was both male and female. It was complete in itself,—mark this, Dane, for here individual completeness ends.

356

The labour of reproduction was divided, and male and female, as separate entities, came into the world. They shared the work of reproduction between them. Neither was complete alone. Each was the complement of the other. In times and seasons each felt a vital need for the other. And in the satisfying of this vital need, of this yearning for completeness, we have the first manifestation of love. Male and female loved they one another—but dimly, Dane. We would not to-day call it love, yet it foreshadowed love as the food-absorbing pore foreshadowed the mouth.

As long and tedious as has been the development of this rudimentary love to the highly evolved love of to-day, just so long and tedious would be my sketch of that development. However, the factors may be hinted. The increasing correspondence of life with its environment brought about wider and wider generalisations upon that environment and the relations of the individual to it. There is no missing link to the chain that connects the first and lowest life to the last and the highest. There is no gap between the physical and psychical. From *simple reflex action*, on and up through *compound reflex action*, *instinct*, and *memory*, the passage is made, without break, to *reason*. And hand in hand with these, all acting and reacting upon one another, comes the development of the imagination and of the higher passions, feelings, and emotions. But all of this is in the books, and there is no need for me to go over the ground.

So let me sum up with an analysis of that most exquisite of poets' themes, a maiden in love. In the first place, this maiden must come of an ancestry mastered by the passion for perpetuation. It is only through those so mastered that the line comes down. The individual perishes, you know; for it is the race that lives. In this maiden is incorporated all the experience of the race. This race experience is her heritage. Her function is to pass it on to posterity. If she is disobedient, she is unfruitful; her line ceases with her; and she is without avail among the generations to come. And, be it not forgotten, there are many obedient whose lines *will* pass down.

But this maiden is obedient. By her acts she will link the past to the future, bind together the two eternities. But she is incomplete, this maiden, and being immature she is unaware of her incompleteness. Nevertheless she is the creature of the law of the race, and from her infancy she prepares herself for the task she is to perform. Hers is a certain definite organism, somewhat different from all other female organisms. Consequently there is one male in all the world whose organism is most nearly the complement of hers; one male for whom she will feel the greatest, intensest, and most vital need; one male who of all males is the fittest, organically, to be the father of her children. And so, in pinafores and pigtails, she plays with little boys and likes and dislikes according to her organic need. She comes in contact with all manner of boys, from the butcher's boy to the son of her father's friend; and likewise with men, from the gardener to her father's associates. And she is more or less attracted by those who, in greater or less degree, answer to her organic demand, or, as it were, organic ideal.

And upon creatures male she early proceeds to generalise. This kind of man she likes, that she does not like; and this kind she likes more than that kind. She does not know why she does this; nor, with the highest probability, does she know she is doing it. She simply has her likes and dislikes, that is all. She is the slave of the law, unwittingly generalising upon sex-impressions against the day when she must identify the male who most nearly completes her.

She drifts across the magic borderland to womanhood, where dreams and fancies rise and intermingle and the realities of life are lost. A dissatisfaction and a restlessness come upon her. There seems no sanity in things, and life is topsy-turvy. She is filled with vague, troubled yearnings, and the woman in her quickens and cries out for unity. It is an organic cry, old as the race, and she cannot shut out the sound of it or still the clamour in her blood.

But there is one male in all the world who is most nearly her complement, and he may be over on the other side of the world where she may not find him. So propinquity determines her fate. Of the males she is in contact with, the one who can more nearly give her the completeness she craves will be the one she loves.

All of which is well and good in its way, but let us analyze further. What is all this but the symptoms of an extreme over-excitation and nervous disorder? The equilibrium of the organism has been overthrown and there is a wild scrambling for the restoration of that equilibrium. The choice made may be good or ill, as chance and time may dictate, but the impelling excitement forces a choice. What if it be ill? What if to-morrow a male who is a far better complement should appear? The time is now. Nature is not neglectful, and well she knows the disaster of delay. She is prodigal of the individual and is satisfied with one match out of many mismatches, just as she is satisfied that of a million cod eggs one only should develop into a full-grown cod. And so this love of the human in no wise differs from that of the sparrow which forgets preservation in procreation. Thus nature tricks her creatures and the race lives on.

For the lesser creatures the trick serves the purpose well. There is need for a compelling madness, else would self-preservation overcome procreation and there be no lesser creatures. And man is content to rest coequal with the beast in the matter of mating. Notwithstanding his intelligence, which has made him the master of matter and enabled him to enslave the great blind forces, he is unable to perpetuate his species without the aid of the impelling madness. Nay, men will not have it otherwise; and when an individual urges that his reason has placed him above the beast, and that, without the impelling madness, he can mate with greater wisdom and potency, then the poets and singers rise up and fling potsherds at him. To improve upon nature by draining a malarial swamp is permitted him; to improve upon nature's methods and breed swifter carrier-pigeons and finer horses than she has ever bred is also permitted; but to improve upon nature in the breeding of the human, that is a sacrilege which cannot be condoned! Down with him! He is a brute to question our divine Love, God-given and glorious!

Ah, Dane, remember the first dim yearning of divided life, and the soils and smirches and frenzies put upon it by the spawn of multitudinous generations. There is your love, the whole history of it. There is no intrinsic shame in the thing itself, but the shame lies in that we are not greater than it.

Herbert.

XVIII. FROM THE SAME TO THE SAME

The Ridge,

Berkeley, California.

April 4, 19—.

There were several things in your letter which I forgot to answer. Much of beauty and wonder is there in what you have said, and unrelated facts without end. Many of those facts I endorse heartily, but it seems to me you fail to embody them in a coherent argument.

I have stated, in so many words, that there are two functions common to all life—nutrition and reproduction. Of this you have missed the significance in your rejection of my definition of love, so I must explain further. Unless these two functions be carried on, life must perish from the planet. Therefore they are the most essential concerns of life. The individual must preserve its own life and the life of its kind. It is more prone to preserve its own life than the life of its kind, less prone to sacrifice itself for its species. So natural selection has developed a passion of madness which forces the individual to make the sacrifice. In all forms of life below man the struggle for existence is keen and merciless. The least weakness in an individual is the signal for its destruction. Therefore it is counter to the welfare of the individual to do aught that will tend to weaken it. On the other hand, the law is that the individual must procreate. But procreation means a weakening and a temporary state of helplessness. Problem: How may the individual be brought to procreate? to do that which is inimical to its welfare? Answer: It must be forced by something deeper than reason, and that something is unreasoning passion. Did the individual reason on the matter, it would certainly abstain. It is because the passion is not rational that life has persisted to this day. Man, coming up from the walks of lower life, brought with him this most necessary passion. Developing imagination, he commingled the two; love was the product.

Now, because of our imagination, do not let us confuse the issue. The great task demanded of man is reproduction. He is urged by passion to perform this task. Passion, working through the imagination, produces love. Passion is the impelling factor, imagination the disturbing factor; and the disturbance of passion by imagination produces love.

Stripped of all its superfluities, what function does love serve in the scheme of life? That of reproduction. Nay, now, do not object, Dane; for you state the same thing, though less clearly, in your own definition of love. You say, "Love is the awakening of the personality to the beauty and worth of some one being" and is a desire to merge the life with that of the beloved being. In other words, your definition tells that the passion for perpetuation is the cause of love, and perpetuation the end to be accomplished. Thus nature tricks her creatures and the race lives on.

Then you say negatively, "Love is not a disorder of mind and body, not a madness, since it arises in the eternally most valuable, since it is the culmination of high processes, and since it makes for strength and sanity of vision and happiness." I have shown the value of passion, and the processes of which love is the culmination, and I have shown that both are unreasoning and why they are unreasoning. Do you demonstrate where I am wrong.

Then again, you dare a formula: "In the beginning love arose in the passion for perpetuation; to-day the passion for perpetuation arises in love." It is clever, but is it true? Yes, as true as this formula I dare to pattern after yours: In the beginning man ate because he was hungry; to-day he is hungry because he eats.

There are many things more I should like to answer, but I am writing this 'twixt breakfast and lecture hour, and time presses and students will not wait.

Herbert.

XIX. FROM DANE KEMPTON TO HERBERT WACE

London,

3a, Queen's Road, Chelsea, S.W.

April 22, 19—.

Nature tricks her creatures and the race lives on, and I, overcivilised, decadent dreamer that I am, rejoice that the past binds us, am proud of a history so old and so significant and of an heritage so marvellous. Nature tricks her creatures and the race lives on, and I am prayerfully grateful. The difference between us is that you are not. You are suffering from what has been well called, the sadness of science. You accept the thesis of a common origin only to regret it. You discover that romance has a history, and lo! romance has vanished! You are a Werther of science, sad to the heart with a melancholy all your own and dropping inert tears on the shrine of your accumulated facts.

In this you are with your generation. Just as every age has its prevailing disease of the body so has it its characteristic spiritual ailment. To-day we are in the throes of travail. In our arms is the child of our ever-delving intellect, but another deliverance is about to be and the suffering is great. After science comes the philosophy of science. Our eyes are bathed in Revelation, but upon our ears the music of the Word has not yet fallen. Until that time when the meaning of it all shall flash out upon the world, the race will be hidebound in callousness and in faint-hearted melancholy. As yet we do not know what to do with all which we know, and we are afflicted with the pessimism of inertia and the pessimism of dyspepsia. Intellectually, we have been living too high the last hundred years or so. In this is the secret of our difference. You insist upon cheapening life for yourself because it has become evident to you that the phenomenon is common, and I, on the other hand, shout its glory because it is universal. To myself I am breathless with wonder, but to you and in my work I needs must shout it.

Here let me be clear. I take it that you are under the sway of a contemporary mood, that your position is an accidental phase of to-day's materialism. Broadly, our quarrel is that of pessimism and optimism, only your pessimism is unconscious, which makes it the more dangerous to yourself. You are too sad to know that you are not happy or to care. Does my diagnosis surprise you? Analyze the argument of your last letter. You trace the growth of the emotion of love from protoplasm to man. You follow the progress of the force which is stronger than hunger and cold and swifter and more final than death, from its potential state in the unicellular stage where life goes on by division, up through the multifarious forms of instinctive animal mating, till you reach the love of the sexes in the human world. And the exploring leads you to the belief that nothing has been reserved for the human worth his cherishing, to the conviction that the plan of life is simple and unvaried and therefore unacceptable.

You raise the wail of Ecclesiastes, "All is vanity and a striving after wind, and there is no profit under the sun." The Preacher and Omar and Swinburne are pathetically human, and we who are also human respond to their finality, to their quizzical indifference and their stinging resentment. We also say, "Vanity of vanities," and bow our heads murmuring "Ilicet," and stretch out our hands to "turn down an empty glass," but all this in twilight moods when a dimness as of dying rests upon the soul. There are a few with whom it is always morning, and others who remember something of the radiance of the young day even in the heart of midnight. These disprove the postulates of sameness and satiety, these are not smitten by the seen fact as are you of the microscopic retina, these "see life steadily and see it whole."

We need not fear the label of an idea. When I say that your position is that of the pessimist, it is not more of an accusation than if I said it was that of the optimist. The thing to concern oneself with is the question, "which of these makes the nearer approach to the truth?" You have been asking me, "What is love worth?" And you have answered your question often enough and to your satisfaction, "In itself it is worth nothing, being but the catspaw to scheming forces." With your denial of any intrinsic beauty in the emotion, with your acceptance of it as an unfortunate incident in human affairs, comes a vague hope that the race will outgrow this force. Here is your rift in the cloud. You picture a scientific Utopia where there are no lovers and no back-harkings to the primitive passion, and you appoint yourself pioneer to the promised land of the children of biology.

Ah! I speak as if I were vexed instead of simply being sure I am in the right. I wish to help you to see that there is another reading to your facts. If love is essentially the same from protoplasm to man, it does not for this reason become worthless. By virtue of being universal it is enhanced and most divinely humanly binding. You tell me that love is involuntary, compelled by external forces as old as time and as binding as instinct, and I say that because of this, life is finally for love. What! The cavemen, and the birds, too, and the fish and the plants, forsooth! What! The inorganic, perhaps, as well as the organic, swayed by this force which is wholly physical and yet wholly psychical! And does it not fire you? You are not caught up and held by this giant fact? You find that love is not sporadic, not individual, that it does not begin with you or end with you, that it does not dissociate you, and you do not warm to the world-organic kinship, you do not hear the overword of the poets and philosophers of all times, you do not see the visions that gladdened the star-forgotten nights of saints?

The same surprise sweeps over the mind in reading Ecclesiastes. Is it a sorry scheme of things that one generation goes and another comes and the world abides forever? If the same generation peopled the earth for a million years, the dignity of life would not be increased. It is not necessary to have the assurance of eternal life as the dole for having come to be, in order to live under the aspect of eternity. It is larger to be short-lived, to be but a wave of the sea rolling for one sunful day and starry night towards a great inclusiveness. It is a higher majesty to be inalien and a part—a ringed ripple in the Vastness—than to lie broad and smiling in meaningless endlessness.

So it is a strange thing that men who are schooled by evolution to relate themselves to all that exists, and to seek for new kinships, should lament that there is no new thing under the sun. And whose eye would be satisfied with seeing and whose ear with hearing? Who would rather have the truth than the power to seek it? There is a way of reading Ecclesiastes and Schopenhauer with a triumphant lilt in the voice. After all, it is the modulation that carries the message of the text. When you write the history of love, I find it fair reading. When you tell me love is primal and engrossing, I hold it the more a sin to crouch away from its fires.

"Love is the assertion of the will to live as a definitely determined individual." This is Schopenhauer's thesis and (unnecessarily enough) he apologises for it, as if it belittled love to say that it affects man in his *essentia æterna*. The genius of the race takes the lover conscript and makes him a soldier in life's battalions.

"The genius of the race," a metaphysical term, but meaning what you do when you speak of the function of love. Schopenhauer is a pessimist consciously, you, unconsciously; and you have both missed the living value of your facts. "Love is ruled by race welfare," says Schopenhauer. "It (the race welfare) alone corresponds to the profoundness with which it is felt, to the seriousness with which it appears, to the importance which it attributes even to the trifling details of its sphere and occasion." Love concerns itself with "The composition of the next generation," therefore you find it common as the commonplace, therefore Schopenhauer regards it as a force treacherous to happiness, since to live is to be miserable. "These lovers are the traitors who seek to perpetuate the whole want and drudgery which would otherwise speedily reach an end; this they wish to frustrate as others like them have frustrated it before."

Because love frustrates the death of the race, it is the joy of my senses and the goal of my striving.

Says Schopenhauer: "Through love man shows that the species lies closer to him than the individual, and he lives more immediately in the former than in the latter. Why does the lover hang with complete abandon on the eyes of his chosen one, and is ready to make every sacrifice for her? *Because it is his immortal part that longs after her, while it is merely his mortal part that desires everything else.*" Because this is so, love is the God of my faith.

You see where our subject takes us! And all the while I care nothing for the points of argument except where they prick you from your position. One

365

must scale the skies and swim the seas in order to reach you. Well, have I approached within your hearing?

I was sitting amongst the fennel in Barbara's garden when your letter was brought, and I read it twice to make sure I understood. When the sun lies warm on waving fennel and a city is before you, mysterious in a veil of mist, it is easier to feel love than to think about it. For a while, it was difficult to see the bearing of the data which you marshalled so well in defence of your denial. You went far in order to answer why you are content to marry a woman you do not love. Your methods are not the methods of the practical mind. I am glad for that. You idealise your attitude, you go far back in time, you enmesh yourself in theories and generalisations, you ride your imagination proudly, in order to reconcile yourself to something which suggests itself as more ideal than that for which the unreasoning heart hungers. You are sad, but you are not practical and you are not blasé.

Of Barbara, of myself, and of London doings, this is no time to write. Tell Hester your friend thinks of her.

Yours with great memories and greater hopes,

Dane Kempton.

XX. FROM HERBERT WACE TO DANE KEMPTON

The Ridge,

Berkeley, California.

May 18, 19—.

I stand aloof and laugh at myself and you. Oh, believe me, I see it very clearly myself in the heyday and cocksureness of youth, flinging at you, with much energy and little skill, my immature generalisations from science; and you with an elderly beneficence and tolerance, smiling shrewdly and affectionately upon me, secure in the knowledge that sooner or later I am sure to get through with it all and join you in your broad and placid philosophy. It is the penalty age exacts from youth. Well, I accept it.

So I am suffering from the sadness of science. I had been prone to ascribe my feelings to the passion of science. But it does not matter in the least— only, somehow, I would rather you did not misunderstand me so dreadfully. I do not raise the wail of Ecclesiastes. I am not sad, but glad. I discover romance has a history, and in history I am quicker to read the romance. I accept the thesis of a common origin, not to regret it, but to make the best of it. That is the key to my life—to make the best of it, but not drearily, with the passiveness of a slave, but passionately and with desire. Invention is an artifice man employs to overcome the roundabout. It is the short cut to satisfaction. It makes man potent, so that he can do more things in a span. I am a worker and doer. The common origin is not a despair to me; it has a value, and it strengthens my arm in the work to be done.

The play and interplay of force and matter we call "evolution." The more man understands force and matter, and the play and interplay, the more is he enabled to direct the trend of evolution, at least in human affairs. Here is a great and weltering mass of individuals which we call society. The problem is: How may it be directed so that the sum of its happiness greatens? This is my work. I would invent, overcome the roundabout, seek the short cut. And I consider all matter, all force, all factors, so that I may invent wisely and justly. And considering all factors, I consider romance, and I consider you. I weigh your value in the scheme of things, and your necessity, and I find that you are both valuable and necessary.

But the history of progress is the history of the elimination of waste. One boy, running twenty-five machines, turns out a thousand pairs of socks a day. His granny toiled a thousand days to do the same. Waste has been eliminated, the roundabout overcome. And so with romance. I strive not to be blinded by its beauty, but to give it exact appraisal. Oftentimes it is the roundabout, the wasteful, and must needs be eliminated. Thus chivalry and its romance vanished before the chemist and the engineer, before the man who mixed gunpowder and the man who dug ditches.

I melancholy? Sir, I have not the time—so may I model my answer after the great Agassiz. I am not a Werther of science, but rather you are a John Ruskin of these latter days. He wept at the profanation of the world, at the steam-launches violating the sanctity of the Venetian canals and the electric cars running beneath the shadow of the pyramids; and you weep at the violation of like sanctities in the spiritual world. A gondola is more beautiful, but the steam-launch takes one places, and an electric car is more comfortable than the hump of a camel. It is too bad, but waste romance, as waste energy, must be eliminated.

Enough. I shall go on with the argument. I have drawn the line between pre-nuptial love and post-nuptial love. The former, which is the real sexual love, the love of which the poets sing and which "makes the world go round," I have called romantic love. The latter, which in actuality is sex comradeship, I call conjugal affection or friendship. To be more definite, I shall call the one "love," the other "affection" or "friendship." Now love is not affection or friendship, yet they are ofttimes mistaken, one for the other, for it so happens that the friendship, which is akin to conjugal affection, is in many instances pre-nuptial in its development—a token, I take it, of the higher evolution of the human, an audaciousness which dares to shake off the blind passion and evade nature's trick as man evaded when he harnessed steam and rested his feet. It is of common occurrence that a man and woman, through long and tried friendship, reach a fine appreciation of each other and marry; and the run of such marriages is the happiest. Neither blinded nor frenzied by the unreasoned passion of love, they have weighed each other,—faults, virtues, and all,—and found a compatibility strong enough to withstand the strain of years and misfortune, and wise enough to compromise the individual clashes which must inevitably arise when soul shares never ending bed and board with soul. They have achieved before marriage what the love-impelled man and woman must achieve after marriage if they would continue to live together; that is, they have sought and found compatibility before binding themselves, instead of binding themselves first and then seeking if there be compatibility or not.

Let me apparently digress for the moment and bring all clear and straight. The emotions have no basis in reason. We smile or are sad at the manifestation of jealousy in another. We smile or are sad because of the unreasonableness of it. Likewise we smile at the antics of the lover. The absurdities he is guilty of, the capers he cuts, excite our philosophic risibility. We say he is mad as a March hare. (Have you ever wondered, Dane, why a March hare is deemed mad? The saying is a pregnant one.) However, love, as you have tacitly agreed, is unreasonable. In fact, in all the walks of animal life no rational sanction can be found for the love-acts of the individual. Each love act is a hazarding of the individual's life; this we know, and it is only impelled to perform such acts because of the madness of the trick, which, though it strikes at the particular life, makes for the general life.

So I think there is no discussion over the fact that this emotion of love has no basis in reason. As the old French proverb runs, "The first sigh of love is the last of wisdom." On the other hand, the individual not yet afflicted by love, or recovered from it, conducts his life in a rational manner. Every act he performs has a basis in reason—so long as it is not some other of the emotional acts. The stag, locking horns with a rival over the possession of a doe, is highly irrational; but the same stag, hiding its trail from the hounds by taking to water, is performing a highly rational act. And so with the human. We model our lives on a basis of reason—of the best reason we possess. We do not put the scullery in the drawing-room, nor do we repair our bicycles in the bedchamber. We strive not to exceed our income, and we deliberate long before investing our savings. We demand good recommendations from our cook, and take letters of introduction with us when we go abroad. We overlook the petulant manner of our friend who rowed in the losing barges at the race, and we forgive on the moment the sharp answer of the man who has sat three nights by a sick-bed. And we do all this because our acts have a basis in reason.

Comes the lover, tricked by nature, blind of passion, impelled madly toward the loved one. He is as blind to her salient imperfections as he is to her petty vices. He does not interrogate her disposition and temperament, or speculate as to how they will coördinate with his for two score years and odd. He questions nothing, desires nothing, save to possess her. And this is the paradox: *By nature he is driven to contract a temporary tie, which, by social observance and demand, must endure for a lifetime.* Too much stress cannot be laid upon this, Dane, for herein lies the secret of the whole difficulty.

But we go on with our lover. In the throes of desire—for desire is pain, whether it be heart hunger or belly hunger—he seeks to possess the loved one. The desire is a pain which seeks easement through possession. Love cannot in its very nature be peaceful or content. It is a restlessness, an unsatisfaction. I can grant a lasting love just as I can grant a lasting satisfaction; but the lasting love cannot be coupled with possession, for love is pain and desire, and possession is easement and fulfilment. Pursuit and possession are accompanied by states of consciousness so wide apart that they can never be united. What is true of pursuit cannot be true of possession, no more than the child, grasping the bright ball, can deem it the most wonderful thing in the world—an appraisement which it certainly made when the ball was beyond reach.

Let us suppose the loved one is as madly impelled toward the lover. In a few days, in an hour, nay, in an instant—for there is such a thing as love at first sight—this man and woman, two unrelated individuals, who may never have seen each other before, conceive a passion, greater, intenser, than all other affections, friendships, and social relations. So great, so intense is it, that the world could crumble to star-dust so long as their souls rushed together. If

370

necessary, they would break all ties, forsake all friends, abandon all blood kin, run away from all moral responsibilities. There can be no discussion, Dane. We see it every day, for love is the most perfectly selfish thing in the universe.

But this is easily reconcilable with the scheme of things. The true lover is the child of nature. Natural selection has determined that exogamy produces fitter progeny than endogamy. Cross fertilisation has made stronger individuals and types, and likewise it has maintained them. On the other hand, were family affection stronger than love, there would be much intermarriage of blood relations and a consequent weakening of the breed. And in such cases it would be stamped out by the stronger-breeding exogamists. Here and there, even of old time, the wise men recognised it; and we so recognise it to-day, as witness our bars against consanguineous marriage.

But be not misled into the belief that love is finer and higher than affection and friendship, that the yielding to its blandishments is higher wisdom on the part of our lovers. Not so; they are puppets and know and think nothing about it. They come of those who yielded likewise in the past. They obey forces beyond them, greater than they, their kind, and all life, great as the great forces of the physical universe. Our lovers are children of nature, natural and uninventive. Duty and moral responsibility are less to them than passion. They will obey and procreate, though the heavens roll up as a scroll and all things come to judgment. And they are right if this is what we understand to be "the bloom, the charm, the smile of life."

Yet man is man because he chanced to develop intelligence instead of instinct; otherwise he would to this day have remained among the anthropoid apes. He has turned away from nature, become unnatural, as it were, disliked the earth upon which he found himself, and changed the face of it somewhat to his liking. His trend has been, and still is, to perform more and more acts with a rational sanction. He has developed a moral nature, made laws, and by the sheer force of his will and reason curbed his lyings and his lusts.

However, our lovers are natural and uninventive. They get married. Pursuit, with all its Tantalus delights, its sighings and its songs, is gone, never to return. And in its place is possession, which is satisfaction, familiarity, knowledge. It heralds the return of rationality, the return to duty of the weighing and measuring qualities of the mind. Our lovers discover each other to be mere man and woman after all. That ethereal substance which the man took for the body of the loved one becomes flesh and blood, prone to the common weaknesses and ills of flesh and blood. He, on the other hand, betrays little petulancies of disposition, little faults and predispositions of which she never dreamed in the pre-nuptial days, and which she now finds eminently distasteful. But at first these things are not openly unpleasant. There are no scenes. One or the other gives in on the instant, without self-betrayal, and one or the other retires to have a secret cry or to ruminate about it over a cigar—the first faint hints, I may slyly suggest, of the return of rationality. *They are beginning to think.*

Ah, these are little things, you say. Precisely; wherefore I lay emphasis upon them. The sum of the innumerable little things becomes a mighty thing to test the human soul. Moreover, many a home has been broken because of disagreement as to the uses or abuses of couch cushions, and more than one divorce induced by the lingering of tobacco odours in the curtains.

If the marriage of our lovers conform to the majority of marriages, the first year of their wedded life will determine whether they are able to share bed and board through the lengthening years. For this first year—often the first months of it—marks the transition from love to conjugal affection, or witnesses a rupture which nothing less than omnipotence can ever mend. In the first year a serious readjustment must take place. Unreason, as a basis for the relation, must give way to reason; blind, ignorant, selfish little love must flutter away, so that friendship, clear-eyed and wise, may step in. There will come moments when wills clash and desires do not chime; these must be moments of sober thought and compromise, when one or the other sacrifices self on the altar of their nascent friendship. Upon this ability to compromise depends their married happiness. Returning to the rationality which they forsook during mating-time, they cannot live a joint rational existence without compromising. If they be compatible, they will gradually grow to fit, each with the other, into the common life; compromise, on certain definite points, will become automatic; and for the rest they will exhibit a tacit and reasoned recognition of the imperfections and frailties of life.

All this reason will dictate. If they be incapable of rising to compromise, sacrifice, and unselfishness, reason will dictate separation. In such cases, when they will have become rational once more, they will reason the impossibility of a continued relation and give it up. In which case the true-love disciple may contend that there was no real love in the beginning. But he is wrong. It was just as real as that of any marriage, only it failed in the post-nuptial quest after compatibility. In all marriages love—passionate, romantic love—must disappear, to be replaced by conjugal affection or by nothing. The former are the happy marriages, the latter the mistaken ones.

As I close, the saying of La Bruyère comes to me, "The love which arises suddenly takes longest to cure." This generalisation upon all the love-affairs within the scope of a single lifetime cannot but be true, and it is quite in line with the general argument. I have shown that the love (so called) which grows slowly is akin to friendship, that it is friendship, in fact, conjugal friendship. On the other hand, the more sudden a love the more intense it must be; also the less rationality can it have. And because of its intensity and unreasonableness, the longer period must elapse ere its frenzy dies out and cool, calm thought comes in.

Herbert.

P.S.—My book is out—"The Economic Man." I send it to you. I cannot imagine you will care for the thing.

XXI. FROM THE SAME TO THE SAME

The Ridge,

Berkeley, California.

May 26, 19—.

"Pretty nineteen-year-old Louisa Naveret, because her slower-minded fiancé, Charles J. Johnson, could not understand a joke, is dying with a bullet in her brain, and he, her murderer, lies dead at the morgue. They were to have been married to-day."

From to-day's paper I quote the above introduction to a column murder-sensation in simple life. Simple it was, and elemental—the man loving steadily and doggedly and madly, after the manner of the male before possession; the woman fluttering, and teasing, and tantalising, after the manner of the female courting possession. They had been engaged for some time. The woman loved the man and fully intended to marry him. The engagement neared its close, and on the day before that of the wedding, the man, slow minded, loving intensely, procured the marriage licence. The woman read the document, and with the last coy flutter before surrender told him that she would not marry him.

"I meant it as a jest," she said as she lay on a cot at the receiving hospital; but four bullets were in her body, and Charles J. Johnson, clumsy and natural lover, lay dead in an adjoining room with the fifth bullet in his brain.

In this pitiful little tragedy appear two of the most salient characteristics of love; namely, madness and selfishness. Let us analyze Charles J. Johnson's condition. He was a lineman for a telegraph company, healthy and strong, used to open-air life and hard work. He had steady employment and good wages. Can't you see the man, content with a good digestion, unailing body, and mild pleasures, and enjoying life with bovine placidity? But pretty Louisa Naveret entered his life. The "abysmal fecundity" was stirred and life clamoured to be created. Peacefulness and content vanished. All the forces of his existence impelled him to seize upon and possess "nineteen-year-old" Louisa Naveret. He was afflicted with a disorder of mind and body, a madness so great, a delusion so powerful, a pain and unrest so pressing, that the possession of that particular "nineteen-year-old" woman became the dearest thing in the world, dearer than life itself and more potent than the "will to live."

I do well to call love a madness. Any departure from rationality is madness, and for a man of Charles J. Johnson's calibre, suicide is an extremely irrational act. But he also killed Louisa Naveret, wherein he was as selfish as he was mad. Convinced that he was not to possess her, he was determined that no other man should possess her.

While on this matter of love considered as a disorder of mind and body, I recall a recent magazine article of Mr. Finck's, in which he analyzes Sappho's conception of love. "In that famous poem of Sappho," he says, "that has been so often declared a compendium of all the emotions that make up love, I have not been able to find anything but a comic catalogue of such feelings as might overwhelm a woman if she met a bear in the woods—'deadly pallor,' 'a cold sweat,' 'a fluttering heart,' 'tongue paralyzed,' 'trembling all over,' 'a fainting fit.'"

Dante suffered similarly from the disorder of love, if you will recollect. In this connection may be cited the following passage from Diderot's "Paradox of Acting ":—

"Take two lovers, both of whom have their declarations to make. Who will come out of it best? Not I, I promise you. I remember that I approached the beloved object with fear and trembling; my heart beat, my ideas grew confused, my voice failed me, I mangled all I said; I cried *yes* for *no*; I made a thousand blunders; I was illimitably inept; I was absurd from top to toe, and the more I saw it the more absurd I became. Meanwhile, under my very eyes, a gay rival, light hearted and agreeable, master of himself, pleased with himself, losing no opportunity for the finest flattery, made himself entertaining and agreeable, enjoyed himself; he implored the touch of a hand which was at once given him, he sometimes caught it without asking leave, he kissed it once and again. I, the while, alone in a corner, avoided a sight which irritated me; stifling my sighs, cracking my fingers with grasping my wrists, plunged in melancholy, covered with a cold sweat, I could neither show nor conceal my vexation."

Oh, the clamour of life to be born is a masterful thing, and so far as the individual is concerned, a most irrational thing; and so far as the world of beasts and emotional men and women is concerned, it is a most necessary thing. That life may live and continue to live, a driving force is needed that is greater than the puny will of life. And in the disorder produced by the passion for perpetuation, whether or not assisted by imagination, is found this driving force. As Ernest Haeckel, that brave old hero of Jena, explains:—

"The irresistible passion that draws Edward to the sympathetic Otillia, or Paris to Helen, and leaps all bounds of reason and morality, is the same *powerful, unconscious*, attractive force which impels the living spermatozoon to force an entrance into the ovum in the fertilisation of the egg of the animal or plant—the same impetuous movement which unites two atoms of hydrogen to one atom of oxygen for the formation of a molecule of water."

But with the advent of intellectual man, there is no longer need for obeying blind and irresistible compulsion. Intellectual man, changing the face of life with his inventions and artifices, performing telic actions, adjusting himself and his concerns to remote ends and ultimate compensations, will grapple with the problem of perpetuation as he has grappled with that of gravitation. As he controls and directs the great natural forces so that, instead of menacing, they are made to labour for his safety and comfort, so will he control and direct the operation of the reproductive force so that life will not only be perpetuated but developed and made higher and finer. This is not more impossible than is the steam-engine impossible or democracy impossible.

Herbert.

XXII. FROM DANE KEMPTON TO HERBERT WACE

London,

3a, Queen's Road, Chelsea, S.W.

June 12, 19—.

Please remember that these letters are written to you alone. I do not think that there is less love in the world than ever before. I make you representative of a class, which, in turn, is characteristic of the modern scientific type, but I do not make you representative of all that to-day's world has lived up to and lived down. So I do not join my Ruskin in lamenting the past. To be sure, you are contemporary and you are parvenu. What then? You are few, nevertheless, and like the parvenu rich, you must pass into something quite unlike yourself. It is the law of growth. I ask you to account for yourself as an individual. The thing is fiercely personal. But you choose the roundabout method of answering me. For a view of what in your eyes is pertinent to this matter, you stretch a canvas wide as the world. You are resolved that your course should dramatise the whole play and interplay of force and matter. It is ideally ambitious of you and I am glad. It puts you in the ranks with the students of the ideal tendencies. It shows that you are not always impatient for short cuts, and that you begin to be of those who harness "horses of the sun to plough in earth's rough furrows."

Your letter sounds conclusive. Romance is waste, love is unreasoning; compatibility alone is worth while. You think this, and are ready to encrust yourself with what is conventional and practical. Ah, no, it is not even decently conventional! The formal world pretends, at least, to love. It also reaches for the fires that thrill and thaw, whereas you stand before a cold hearth and think the chill well and welcome, since you understand its cause. You have grasped part of a truth, and though my mind complete your arc into the perfection of a circle, I cannot place it about your head as a halo. My confusion comes from thinking of you more than of my creed. A pregnant factor in our debate is the debater. The Hafiz of the Hafiz maxims, the philosopher of your philosophy happens to interest me. You have been building yourself up before my eyes, and for watching I cannot speak.

With what does romance interfere? If it implied a waste of vital force, a giving up, a postponement of life, it were a roundabout path to development and happiness. But we live most when we are most under its sway, and it is for such self-promised sparks that we live at all. Romance quickens and controls as does nothing else, and because of this it is not only a means but an end in itself. It is stirred-up life. We live most when we love most. The love of romance and the romance of love is the only coin for which the heart-hurt sell their death. A trick? Perhaps. The love of life is a trick to save the races from self-murder. Nature makes legitimate her tricks. Let the Genius of the Race lure us with passion and dreaming! We are not the losers by it. And if the dream fades and we grow gray despite what has been lived, then it is something to remember that soul and sense have leapt and pulsed. I am thankful that romance has an aftermath, and that old men and women can prattle about days that were robust. I am thankful that the soldiers of life are at the end given a furlough in which to fondle the arms they wielded with clumsiness and with spirit, and in which to pass themselves in review before their pension expires and their days are over. Youth has the romance of loving, and age the romance of remembering.

Lovers are not always compatible, you say, and, before all, you insist upon good partnership. How will you insure yourself against unfitness? Surely not by a registering and weighing of qualities, not by bargaining and speculating. We do not choose our wives as we do our saddle-horses; we do not plan our marriages as we plan our houses. It may sound paradoxical, but there is a higher compatibility than that of quality and degree. It is not whether people can live together, but whether they should live together. "It is an awkward thing to play with souls,"—you override the fastidiousness of the soul in marrying your companion. Unless you are an automaton, you cannot rest happy in the fact that you and she do not disagree. For comfort's sake you would have a negative dimension to your cosmos, forgetting that your longings and your needs and, it may be, your dreams, are positive. If sex-comradeship and affection were not as accidental and as dependent on mood as love itself, your position would have much in its favour. You could then arrange for compatibility in marriage.

You speak of the methods in economics that conserve energy and capital, such as the employ of the machine-guiding boy, which saves the labour power of a hundred men, and you hold that in the realm of personal life like methods may obtain with value and dignity. I can see how natural it has become for you to take this viewpoint. One can be a zealot in matters frigid. The law behind the fact has you in its coil, and your passion goes to ice. You burn for that cold thing, compatibility. You, too, are in the market-place bound to a stake—it is not for such as you to escape the fire. If you look to compatibility and want it intensely, as others want love, then you suffer, and from your standpoint (not mine) you raise a vain cry; for compatibility, like everything else, is illusory. The illusions of love are a strength, and the ways of love are divine; through them we come to that feeling of completion which is compatibility and which is as ineffable as the white-lipped promise of waves heard by those who have also listened to weeping. Love is not responsible for institutionalism. There would be no fewer marriages if people married for convenience, nor would the law make such unions less binding. It is not the fault of love that the great social paradox exists. In the precipitancy of feeling, you say, the lover fastens upon an unsuitable mate, and, with possession, love dies. Here I attack your facts. If an awakening comes, it is not for either of these reasons. Love is not essentially rational, but then it is love. There is some consistency in affairs natural, and the esoteric draught that enchanted at one time cannot poison at another.

Love is not essentially rational, and it will not of a sudden become so at the possession of the loved one. People who marry from convenience may wake to find their union most inconvenient. "There are more things in heaven and earth," and there are more intricacies of feeling and more sloughs and depths, than are dreamed of in your philosophy. A definite understanding as to sofa cushions and tobacco smoke does not always insure unwearied forbearance and devotion. With love, on the other hand, disappointment is very much less likely to spring up, for the reason that it is free from calculation. Love is a sympathy. It takes hold, it grows upon the soul and the senses, and it does not flee before argument and explanation.

Still less can I admit that possession kills love. Do we give up living because the world is based on Will and Idea? Yet to will is to want, Schopenhauer tells us, and to want is to be in pain. Do we know ourselves in pain every minute of our lives? Hardly. This applies. You hold that, with the fulfilled hope and the appeased hunger, indifference takes the place of desire. It reads so in logic, but not in life. If what is in our possession be good, we prize it more highly for its being within reach. The good in our keeping does not sate; it pains with divine hungers. We do not tire of what we have; we rise to it. We do not know the sweetness of being steadfast until we are so impelled by the love with which we have grown great. The lover may well say: "She was not my ideal; before I knew her I was not great enough to think her. She taught me."

Besides, an acquaintance with your wife's faults does not kill your love. You cannot turn from your brother or your friend if he commit even a lurid act; you cannot turn from a stranger; much less can you turn from your beloved. Herbert, when men set themselves to judge, they are invariably ridiculous and an offence to high heaven. Believe me, it is artificial. The true judge cares not for the fact of the deed, but for its motive. And the lover knows the motive. He has the key to the life. He knows his beloved, not as she is, but "as she was born to be." His lips press and his arms enfold not her so much as the ideal of her, and unless she unmake herself, he cannot unlove her. "To judge a man by the fruit of his actions," says Professor Edward Howard Griggs, "it is necessary to know all of the fruit, which is impossible. You can only know what he eternally must be if you catch the aspect of his soul and grow to understand his aspirations and his loves." To idealise, therefore, is not to be blind, but to be far-seeing.

There is another way of looking on this question of the paradox. Granted that it is caused by romantic love, romantic love is still exclusively the best thing in the world. You cannot pay too dearly for the good of life. I know that the misery of being in the intimacy of wedlock with one who is not loved is unutterable. It is to become degraded and unrecognisable, it is to wear the brand of liar before God! The man whose outer life belies the inner is an enforced suicide. There is something of majesty on "laying one's self down with a will," and there is something of strength in cloistering the body for the spirit's health's sake, but to die when all within is warm and clamorous for life is terrible. Such a death they die who are held together, not by the bonds of the spirit, but by those of convention. They who would go from each other and dare not, die the ignominious death of fear. The suicide is contemptible, besides being pitiable, when he is hounded out of life despite himself, when he is a little embezzler of a clerk who rushes from the music hall to the Thames and thinks of the unfinished glass with his last breath. No, I do not underestimate the tragedy of the paradox. Yet I say that if love were accountable for it (which it is not), it would still be folly to forswear love. Do you ask why? Because its dangers are the dangers common to all life, and we are so made that we cannot be frightened away from our portion of experience. We are as loth to give up our nights as our days. The winters as the summers, all the seasons and all the climes, the fears as the hopes, all the travail of deepest, fullest living, we claim as our own forever. We guard jealously our heritage of feeling. Would you for all the world sleep rather than wake, forget rather than remember? Then cease the requiem of your speech about the dangers of disillusion!

Madness and selfishness were the cause of Louisa Naveret's death, and the man who was mad and selfish was her lover. The poor man had not the strength to renounce when he thought he found himself face to face with the necessity of renouncing. But all lovers are not too weak to cope with love. John Ruskin, if you remember, loved his wife, and he shot neither himself, nor her, nor Millais. Charles J. Johnson is not a Ruskin, and Ruskin's love was not a madness.

And, Herbert, to me there is nothing comic in a stress of feeling. Let the lover pale and flutter and faint; in the presence of his deity it is an acceptable form of worship. The very self-possessed lover is more preposterous!

Your book has not yet reached me. To-morrow I shall write again, providing I remember how to write a natural letter.

Yours,

Dane Kempton.

381

XXIII. FROM THE SAME TO THE SAME

London.

June 20, 19—.

There are impersonal hours when the things of the day drop below consciousness and the spirit grows devotional and wends a pilgrimage to larger spheres, there to sit apart. Such a respite was mine to-day. There had been a call to rouse and put forth work, and I wrought with all the puniness of my might (woe is me!), and earned my post at the window that looks out upon the large things. The best of nights and days of toil is that there comes a twilight in which fatigued eyes see clear. I said it did not matter how you do about your marriage. Time may right you in a way I cannot know. I said it did not matter if you are not righted in this, there being so much that never rights itself. Both hope and despair were followed by a calm of neutrality. The inquiry waited no solution. The stress no longer touched me, and my twilight became luminous. I saw things as from a height and forms dropped out of my range, when Barbara came tugging at me, and my pale while of abstraction was at an end.

She wanted to know what troubled me. She made her way to me, hurried but resolved, and stated her demand. "You catechised me yesterday; to-night you shall answer."

She had come to defend herself. My talk having of late taken on the sameness of that of the man of one idea, Barbara was aroused. I was gauging her because she distressed me, was her thought. (I had been trying to find whether it is possible to live differently from her and live happily and well.) "You think I am not close enough to Earl, because I mourn for my little one, perhaps. You think me not sufficiently happy to be wifely." Could I suppose aught else from such an utterance but that there was an estrangement and hidden pain? How, unless there were sorrow, could the woman see herself sorrowed for? My mind leapt to possibilities. Little Barbara on the rack was more than I could bear. I groped for her hands. It was a fault in her to be so much on her guard. She had no sorrow to confess, and spoke—only to ward off what was not directed toward her.

"The tenour of your talk led me on to believe—" she stammered with hot cheeks. It is a standing offence of hers to imagine herself accused, and she admits it is a weakness born of lack of poise. "But I took all for granted, I thought you fortunate beyond any other woman," I protested. At this the radiance broke forth. I forgave the chill that her first words on entering the room struck to my heart, and she forgot what she had imagined.

There is nothing more important than the play and interplay of feeling. Were Barbara "unwifely," I could not blame her, but neither could I have at hand my proof of dear miracles. My proof remained to me, for there she stood, her face lifted toward mine, her mouth tremulous, her grey eyes swimming. The mate woman was stirred. Barbara is twenty-six and has been married seven years, and she still vibrates with the old wonder to find herself loving and beloved.

I meant to tell you of what we spoke later, in the hope that I could show you a little better what I hold dear and why. But my hand grows nerveless. The twilight of abstraction has set in. A little while ago this hand was quick to rest on Barbara's as I called her my heroine. She is that, not alone because she is pure and good and strong, but because she can accept the test of her instincts. It takes both faith and strength to obey oneself. "When shows break up, what but one's Self remains?" asks Whitman. The shows are but shows for Barbara. Will I look into your eyes on the morrow and find them, like hers, clear? Grant that it be!

Dane.

XXIV. FROM HERBERT WACE TO DANE KEMPTON

The Ridge,

Berkeley, California.

July 1, 19—.

Somewhere in Ward you may read, "It must constantly be borne in mind that all progress consists in the arbitrary alteration, by human efforts and devices, of the normal course of nature, so that civilisation is wholly an artificial product." Why, Dane, this is large enough to base a sociology upon. And I must ask you first, is it true? Second, do you understand, do you appreciate, the tremendous significance of it? And third, how can you bring your philosophy of love in accord with it?

Romantic love is certainly not natural. It is an artifice, blunderingly and unwittingly introduced by man into the natural order. Is this audacious? Let us see. In a state of nature the love which obtains is merely the passion for perpetuation devoid of all imagination. The male possesses the prehensile organs and the superior strength. Beyond the ardour of pursuit the female has no charms for him. But he is driven irresistibly to pursuit. And by virtue of his prehensile organs and superior strength he ravishes the females of his species and goes his way. But life creeps slowly upward, increasing in complexity and necessarily in intelligence. When some forgotten inventor of the older world smote his rival or enemy with a branch of wood and found that it was good and thereafter made a practice of smiting rivals and enemies with branches of wood, then, and on that day, artificiality may be said to have begun. Then, and on that day, was begun a revolution destined to change the history of life. Then, and on that day, was laid the cornerstone of that most tremendous of artifices, CIVILISATION!

Trace it up. Our ape-like and arboreal ancestors entered upon the first of many short cuts. To crack a marrow-bone with a rock was the act which fathered the tool, and between the cracking of a marrow-bone and the riding down town in an automobile lies only a difference of degree. The one is crudely artificial, the other consummately artificial. That is all. There have been improvements. The first inventors grasped that truthful paradox, "the longest way round is the shortest way home," and forsook the direct pursuit of happiness for the indirect pursuit of happiness. If the happiness of a savage depended upon his crossing an extensive body of water, he did not directly proceed to swim it, but turned his back upon it, selected a tree from the forest, shaped it with his rude tools and hollowed it out with fire, then launched it in the water and paddled toward where his happiness lay.

Now concerning love. In the state of nature it is a brutal passion, nothing more. There is no romance attached. But life creeps upward, and the gregarious human forms social groups the like of which never existed before. Consider the family group, for instance. Such a group becomes in itself an entity. By means of the group man is better enabled to pursue happiness. But to maintain the group it must be regulated; so man formulates rules, codes, dim ethical laws for the conduct of the group members. Sexual ties are made less promiscuous and more orderly. A greater privacy is observed. And out of order and privacy spring respect and sacredness.

But life creeps upward, and the family group itself becomes but a unit of greater and greater groups. And rules and codes change in accordance, until the marriage tie becomes possessed of a history and takes to itself traditions. This history and these traditions form a great fund, to which changing conditions and growing imagination constantly add. And the traditions, more especially, bear heavily upon the individual, overmastering his natural expression of the love instinct and forcing him to an artificial expression of that love instinct. He loves, not as his savage forebears loved, but as his group loves. And the love method of his group is determined by its love traditions. Does the individual compare his beloved's eyes to the stars—it is a trick of old time which has come down to him. Does he serenade under her window or compose an ode to her beauty or virtue—his father did it before him. In his lover's voice throb the voices of myriads of lovers all dead and dust. The singers of a thousand songs are the ghostly chorus to the song of love he sings. His ideas, his very feelings are not his, but the ideas and feelings of countless lovers who lived and loved and whose lives and loves are remembered. Their mistaken facts and foolish precepts are his, and likewise their imaginative absurdities and sentimental philanderings. Without an erotic literature, a history of great loves and lovers, a garland of love songs and ballads, a sheaf of spoken love tales and adventures—without all this, which is the property of his group, he could not possibly love in the way he does.

To illustrate: Isolate a boy babe and a girl babe of cultured breed upon a desert isle. Let them feed and grow strong on shell-fish and fruit; but let them see none other of their species; hear no speech of mouth, nor acquire knowledge in any way of their kind and the things their kind has done. Well, and what then? They will grow to man and woman and mate as the beasts mate, without romance and without imagination. Does the woman oppose her will to that of the man—he will beat her. Does he become over-violent in the manifestation of his regard, she will flee away, if she can, to secret hiding-places. He will not compare her eyes to the stars; nor will she dream that he is Apollo; nor will the pair moon in the twilight over the love of Hero and Leander. And the many monogamic generations out of which he has descended would fail to prevent polygamy did another woman chance to strand on that particular isle.

It is the common practice of the man of the London slum to kick his wife to death when she has offended him. And the man of the London slum is a very natural beast who expresses himself in a very natural manner. He has never heard of Hero and Leander, and the comparison of the missus' eyes to the stars would to him be arrant bosh. The gentle, tender, considerate male is an artificial product. And so is the romantic lover, who is fashioned by the love traditions which come down to him and by the erotic literature to which he has access.

And now to the point. Romantic love being an artificial product, you cannot base its retention upon the claim that it is natural. Your only claim can be that it is the best possible artifice for the perpetuation of life, or that it is the only perfect, all-sufficient, and all-satisfying artifice that man can devise. On the one hand, for the perpetuation of life, man demonstrates the inefficiency of romantic love by his achievements in the domestic selection of animals.

And on the other hand, the very irrationality of romantic love will tend to its gradual elimination as the human grows wiser and wiser. Also, because it is such a crude artifice, it forces far too many to contract the permanent marriage tie without possessing compatibility. During the time romantic love runs its course in an individual, that individual is in a diseased, abnormal, irrational condition. Mental or spiritual health, which is rationality, makes for progress, and the future demands greater and greater mental or spiritual health, greater and greater rationality. The brain must dominate and direct both the individual and society in the time to come, not the belly and the heart. Granted that the function romantic love has served has been necessary; that is no reason to conclude that it must always be necessary, that it is eternally necessary. There is such a thing as rudimentary organs which served functions long since fallen in disuse and now unremembered.

The world has changed, Dane. Sense delights are no longer the sole end of existence. The brain is triumphing over the belly and the heart. The intellectual joy of living is finer and higher than the mere sexual joy of living. Darwin, at the conclusion of his "Origin of Species," experienced a nobler and more exquisite pleasure than did ever Solomon with his thousand concubines and wives. And while our sense delights themselves have become refined, their very refinement has been due to the increasing dominion over them of the intellect. Our canons of art are not founded on the heart. No emotion elaborated the laws of composition. We cannot experience a sense of delight in any art object unless it satisfies our intellectual discrimination. "He is a *natural* singer," we say of the poet who works unscientifically; "but he is lame, his numbers halt, and he has no knowledge of technique."

The intellect, not the heart, made man, and is continuing to make him— ah, slowly, Dane, for life creeps slowly upward. The "Advanced Margin" is a favourite shibboleth of yours. And I take it that the Advanced Margin is that portion of our race which is more dominated by intellect than the race proper. And I, as a member of that group, propose to order my affairs in a rational manner. My reason tells me that the mere passion of begetting and the paltry romance of pursuit are not the greatest and most exquisite delights of living. Intellectual delight is my bribe for living, and though the bargain be a hard one, I shall endeavour to exact the last shekel which is my due.

Wherefore I marry Hester Stebbins. I am not impelled by the archaic sex madness of the beast, nor by the obsolescent romance madness of later-day man. I contract a tie which my reason tells me is based upon health and sanity and compatibility. My intellect shall delight in that tie. My life shall be free and broad and great, and I will not be the slave to the sense delights which chained my ancient ancestry. I reject the heritage. I break the entail. And who are you to say I am unwise?

Herbert Wace.

XXV. FROM THE SAME TO THE SAME

The Ridge,

Berkeley, California.

July 5, 19—.

I had not intended to answer your letter critically, but, on re-reading, find I am forced to speak if for no other reason than your epithet "parvenu." The word has no reproach. It was ever thus that the old and perishing recognised the vigorous and new. Parvenu, upstart—the term is replete with significance and health. I doubt not Elijah himself was dubbed parvenu when he fluttered with his golden harp into that bright-browed throng, pride-swollen for that they had fought with Michael when Lucifer was hurled into hell.

"We do not choose our wives as we buy our saddle-horses; we do not plan our marriages as we do the building of our houses,"—so you say, and it is said excellently. No better indictment of romantic love do I ask. And oh, how many good men and women have I heard bitterly arraign society in that in the begetting of children it does not exercise the judgment which it exercises in breeding its horses and its dogs! Marriage is something more than the mere pulsating to romance, the thrilling to vague-sweet strains, the singing idly in empty days, the sating of self with pleasure—what of the children?

"Never mind the children," says selfish little Love. "It has been our wont never to give any thought to the children; they were incidental. Always have we sought our own pleasure; let us continue to seek our own pleasure." So Society continues to breed its horses and dogs with judgment and forethought and to trust to luck for its children.

But it won't do, Dane. Life, in a sense, is living and surviving. And all that makes for living and surviving is good. He who follows the fact cannot go astray, while he who has no reverence for the fact wanders afar. Chivalry went mad over an idea. It idealised, if you please. It made of love a fine art, and countless knights-errant devoted themselves to the service of the little god. It sentimentalised over ladies' gloves and forgot to make for living and surviving. And while chivalry committed suicide over its ladies' gloves, the stout, wooden-headed burghers, with an eye to the facts of life, dickered and bickered in trade. And on the wreck and ruin of chivalry they flaunted their parvenu insolence. God, how they triumphed! The children and cobblers and shop-keepers buying with the yellow gold the "thousand years old names!" buying with their yellow gold the proud flesh and blood of their lords to breed with them and theirs! patronising the arts, speaking a kind word to science, and patting God on the back! But they triumphed, that is the point. They reverenced the fact and made for living and surviving.

Love is life, you say, and you seem to hold it the achievement of existence. But I cannot say that life is love. Life? It is a toy, i' faith, given to us, we know not why, to play with as we chance to please. Some elect to dream, some to love, and some to fight. Some choose immediate happiness, and some ultimate happiness. One stakes the Here and Now upon the Hereafter; another takes the Here and Now and lets the Hereafter go. But each grasps the toy and does with it according to his fancy And while none may know the end of life, all know that life is the end of love. Love, poor little, crude little, love, is the means to life—and so we complete the circle. Life? It is a toy, i' faith, given us, we know not why, to play with as we chance to please.

But this we know, that love is the means to life, and it is subject to inevitable improvement. By our intellect will we improve upon it. Life abundant! finer life! higher life! fuller life! When we scientifically breed our race-horses and our draught-horses, we make for life abundant. And when we come scientifically to breed the human, we shall make for life abundant, for humanity abundant.

You say an acquaintance with the petty vices of one's wife does not kill one's love. Oh yes, it does, and out of the ashes of that love rises affection, comradeship, in kind somewhat similar to the affection and comradeship which I have for my brother. I do not *love* my brother, and it is because I do not love him, and because I do have *affection* and *comradeship* for him, that I do not turn away when he commits even a lurid act. Love, you will remember, takes its rise in the emotions, and is unstable and wanton and capricious. But affection takes its rise in the intellect, is based upon judgment of the brain. Love is unyielding tyranny; affection is compromise. Love never compromises, no more than does the mad little mating sparrow compromise.

My brother?—I played with him as a boy. His weaknesses and faults incensed and hurt me, as mine incensed and hurt him. Many were our quarrels. But he had also good qualities which pleased me, and at times performed gracious acts and even sacrifices. And I likewise. And with my brain I weighed his weaknesses and faults against his gracious acts and sacrifices, and I achieved a judgment upon him. The ethics of the family group also contributed to this judgment. The duties of kinship and the responsibilities of blood ties were impressed upon me. We grew up at our mother's knee, and she and our father became factors in determining what my conduct should be. They, too, taught me that my brother was my brother, and that in so far as he was my brother, my relations with him must be different from my relations with those who were not my brothers. And all went to crystallise an intellectual judgment, or a set of criteria, as it were, to guide all sane, unemotional acts and even to control and repress any emotional acts. These criteria, I say, became crystallised, became automatic in my thought processes.

And now, in manhood, my brother commits a lurid act, an act repulsive to me, one capable of arousing emotions of anger, of bitterness, of hatred. I experience an emotional impulse to pour my wrath upon him, to be bitter toward him, to hate him. Then I experience an intellectual impulse. Whatever way I may act, I must first settle with my crystallised criteria. The personal bonds of my boyhood and manhood press upon me—the gracious acts and sacrifices and compromises, our father and our mother, the duties of kinship and the responsibilities of blood. Thus two counter-impulses strive with me. I desire to do two counter things. Heart and head the fight is waged, and heart or head I shall act according to which is the stronger impulse. And if my affection be stronger, I shall not turn away, but clasp my brother in my arms.

I fear I have not made myself clear. It is difficult to write hurriedly of things psychological, when the extreme demand is made upon intellect and vocabulary; but at least you may roughly catch my drift. What I have striven to say is, that I forgive my brother, not because I *love* him, but because of the *affection* I bear him; also that this affection is the product of reason, is the sum of the judgments I have achieved.

Herbert.

XXVI. FROM DANE KEMPTON TO HERBERT WACE

London,

3a, Queen's Road, Chelsea, S.W.

July 21, 19—.

"Progress is an arbitrary alteration, by human efforts and devices, of the normal course of nature, so that civilisation is wholly an artificial product." You ask me to consider this refracted bit of sociology and by its light to cast out my exalted notion of love. As if you have proven that love is incompatible with civilisation! We make over life with each successive step, but we do not give over living. In developing new forms and in establishing more and more subtle social relations we are only building upon what we find ready to hand. The paradox of creature and creator does not exist. When your sociologist speaks of arbitrary alterations, he has reference to polities and governments and criteria, to the material and ideal forces which a progressive society may wield for itself. He cannot include under progress an alteration of those needs of existence which make up the quality of existence. Speak of a community which equally distributes the products of labour and I will grant that there has been an arbitrary alteration, the normal course of nature being that the stronger, openly, and even with the common assent, takes to the repletion of his desire from the weaker. But speak of a condition so progressive that it subverts the need, so that where in the one case hunger was equitably gratified, in the other, hunger was done away with, and I will say that you are giving an Arabian Nights' entertainment.

Love is of a piece with life, like hunger, like joy, like death. Your progress cannot leave it behind; your civilisation must become the exponent of it.

Your last letter is formal and elaborate, and—equivocal. In it you remind me, menacingly, of the possibilities of progress, you posit that love is at best artificial, and you apotheosise the brain. As an emancipated rationality, you say you cut yourself loose from the convention of feeling. Progress cannot affect the need and the power to love. This I have already stated. "How is it under our control to love or not to love?" Life is elaborate or it is simple (it depends upon the point of view), and you may call love the paraphernalia of its wedding-feast or you may call it more—the Blood and Body of all that quickens, a Transubstantiation which all accept, reverently or irreverently, as the case may be.

I can more readily conceive the existence of a central committee elected for the purpose of regulating the marriages of a community, than of a community satisfied with such a committee. There is no logic in social events. The world persists in not taking the next step, and what to the social scout looked a dusty bypath may prove to be the highway of progress for the hoboing millions. Side issues are constantly cropping up to knock out the main issues of the stump orator; so let us be humble. For this reason I refuse to discuss possibilities in infinity. You and I cannot have become products of an environment which is not in existence. It is safe to suppose that our needs are like those of the race and that in us nothing is vestigial that is active in others. You cannot have become too rational to love. The device has not yet been formed.

You think I should take your word for it? But why? Have you never found yourself in the wrong, never disobeyed your best promptings never meant to take the good and grasped the bad? Is it not possible that you are not yet awake, or, God pity you, that you are hidebound in the dogmatism of your bit of thinking.

It is for the second point of your letter that I called you equivocal. Earlier in our discussion, I remember, you laid stress on the fact that love is an instinct common to all forms of life; now you go to great lengths in order to show that it is artificial.

How do you differentiate between the artificial and nature? Surely a development is not artificial because it is recent! Surely man is as integral to life as his progenitors! When we come to civilisation, we are face to face with the largest and subtlest thing in life, and the civilisation of human society is not artificial. It is the fulfilment of the nature of man, the promise made

394

good, the career established, the influence sent out. A universe of mind-stuff and a civilising force constantly causing change, for change is growth, constantly compelling expression of that change—to conceive it is to conceive infinitude. And the purpose? Development, always development. To that end the individual perishes, to that end the race is conserved, to that end the peril and the sacrifice, and the agony of triumph in the overcharged heart at its last bound. And what is this refining of the type, this goal for which we all make with such tragic directness, but the gaining in the power to love? We begin with love to end with greater love, and that is progress. To write the epic of civilisation is a task for some giant artist who shall combine in himself Homer and Shakespeare, and the work will be a love story.

We do not throw away the grain and keep the chaff, nor do we transmit the "absurdities" and "philanderings" alone. If in the lover's voice throb the voices of myriads of lovers, it is because he is stirred even as they. If a ballad wakes a response in him, it is because its motif has been singing itself of its own accord in his heart, and its rhythm was the dream nightingale to which he bade Her hearken. Behind the tradition lies the fact. The expression may be ephemeral, the song flat, the motto conventional, but the feeling which prompted it is true. Else it could not have survived. And it has more than survived. It has grown with growth. For centuries it lodged in the nature of man, lulled in acquiescence, then, when the sense of recognition awoke, back in those wondrous young days, it wakened to pale life, and now the feeling is man's whole support, giving him courage to work and purpose to live.

But the half brute of the London slums kicks his wife when she offends him and knows nothing of love. Well for the honour of love that it is so! The half brute of the London slums had not food enough when a child, and malnutrition is deadly. Later, he stole and lied in order to eat, and he was bullied and kicked for it out of human shape. The trick was passed on to him. The unfortunate of the London slums will push us all from heaven's gate, because we do not do battle with the conditions that make him. It is not such as he that should lead you to scorn love, for he is a mistake and a crime.

In your example of the isolated boy babe and girl babe we meet with a different condition. The individual repeats the history of the race, and as these have been left out by the civilising forces, they revert to past racial states. For these it is natural to live stolidly—is it therefore natural for us? The point I make is that our refinement, crying in us with great voice, is as much a part of us as are the simple few hungers of the racial infant. We are not the less natural for being subtle. And can it not be that the face of romance reveals itself even to savage eyes? According to the need is the power, and the early man needs must hope and desire; he is curbed by waiting and taught by loss in the hunting, he is hungry, and he dreams that he is feasting. This dream is his romance—a red flicker in the dawn, then still the gray. To suppose this is not to be unscientific, for what is true of us must have had a beginning, and feeling, as well as being, cannot have been spontaneously generated.

There is an absolute gravitation to justice in nature. This was the creed preached by Huxley to Kingsley a week after his boy's death. Grief had turned the mind upon itself, and in the upheaval he formulated a philosophy of faith and joy!

Our reward is meted out according to our obedience to all of the law, spiritual and physical. Nature keeps a ledger paying glad life's arrears each minute of time. And the creed rises to my lips when I hear you cry shame upon the delight of love. It must be good, this thing which is so fraught with joy! You brand it sense delight, but all delight is of the senses, and Darwin at the conclusion of "The Descent of Man," if he was not overtaken by a feeling of incompleteness in the work and a consuming fever for the further task, was glad in a human way, with the senses and through the emotions. Darwin's supreme moment may have come at quite a different time. What can we know of the moments of repletion that fall into another's life? With Huxley we may only know that our hearts bound high when we strike a chord of harmony and prove ourselves obedient to "all of the law," and our hearts bound high when we love. It is nature's way of showing her approval. Oh, the strength of love and the miracles of its compensations! The sense of becoming that it gives, even in its defeats, the gladness that ripples in its sob-strangled throat!

The day for asceticism is gone, or shall we say the night? We are not afraid of sense delights. We are intent upon living on all sides of our natures, roundly and naturally. You have a fine gospel of work and I congratulate you upon it, but you make no mention of the purpose of it all. It must not be work for work's sake. "When I heard the learned astronomer—" says Whitman. Do you remember? He caught in one hour the whole majesty, caught to himself the wonder that was unseen by the watching astronomers. Somehow you feel the learned ones had made a mistake in calculating so long that they had no time to see with personal eyes the glory of the stars, and that Whitman had been philosopher and had gained where they failed. The inspiration of the poet, of the painter, of the economist, and biologist, is in the revelation which they receive of what to do and why to do. For this reason philosophy, which treats of the life and works of man, is in the highest sense sociological. The generalisations of philosophy go to improve our methods so that we may have greater proneness for sense of delight and greater possibility for sense delight. Why, what else is there? You are a poet, and you give an unrestorable day, when the sun is shining and the hills lie purple in the distance, to writing a sonnet. If you do so merely to employ yourself, it must be that the wolf of despair is at your being's door. You have come to the end, and the sun and the hills do not matter. You and they have parted company. But if you write, impelled by the wish that others should read and recognise, read and remember, and grow to know and feel better, and perhaps to love the sun and hills better, then is yours a work of love, and it will be made good to you, so that for the day which you have not seen, your night shall be instinct with light. And if your labours are more especially in the service of art, then, also, with each approach toward expression, you are warmed through with the delight of achievement.

Is my meaning quite dashed away by this torrent of speech? It is simply this: Before we think we feel, and the end of thinking is feeling. The century of Voltaire and Dr. Johnson held that man is rational, the century of James, Ribot, Lange, and Wundt is thrilled to the heart with the doctrine that first, last, and always man is emotional. To speak loosely, the dimensions of the human cosmos are feeling, emotion, and sensation.

Build your fine structures. We like to see the foundations laid well and the thick walls go up. Keep to your wizard inventions. We like to live in a magic world. And ah, the indomitable machines with their austere promise of free days for weary hands, and ah, the locomotives and the ships steaming their ways toward intercourse, toward comity, toward fellowship! We like the intricacy and the vastness of the world in which we live. But "an unconsidered life is not fit to be lived by any man," says Aristotle. We must consider the phenomenon, civilisation, searching down for the nucleus of its worth. We will find that the stone structure without hope were a pitiable thing, that the making of compacts and the banking of capital, without hope, were pitiable. This hope that is the life germane, the immortal flash of mortality, the most keenly human point in all humanity, is the hope for greater and greater social happiness. Our world is an ever unfinished house which we are employed in building. If we are imbued with the spirit of the architect and not of the hod-carrier, we will hope sweetly for the work. The house beautiful will begin to mean our life, and each night we will consult our drawings, looking to it that on the house built of our days the sun shall wester, and that within shall be intimacy, and laughter, great speech and close love, looking to it that the home be such as to better to-day's tenant so that he be more loving and lovable than the one of yesterday.

We are wrong, perhaps. Long ago we were no less than now. When we reached a hand in the darkness and grasped that of our fellow, the love and the strongly frail human abandon were no less. We have not grown in heart's munificence, perhaps. It is one of the illusions only. But the hope is ours. For what do you hope?

Dane.

XXVII. FROM THE SAME TO THE SAME

London.

July 22, 19—.

Your birthday, Herbert, and for greeting I state that I walk your length with you. A truce to quarrelling! It is now a year since you informed me you were going to be married, and since then the gods have thundered their laughter at the sight of two muttering men who sat themselves on the axes of earth to dangle their legs into orbit vastness. Chronic somnambulists that they are, they took their monopolist way thither in their sleep.

I cannot tell you how full of vagary the correspondence we have fallen into seems to me. I deliberately attempted to write you into passion and for months you deliberately continued to convict yourself out of your own mouth, and we did not see that it was tragic and comic and preposterous. Could we personify this our dealing, we would do well to call it a kind of Caliban. And the tentacles we threw out, clawing at everything, stealing for prop to our little theory all of man and God! It is the conceit of us that I find utterly hopeless of grace. So I drop my rôle of omniscience. I take my form off the hub, believing the system will maintain its gravity though I go my private way, and I promise to let you alone. Forgive me, and God bless you. Ah, yes, and many happy returns of the day. All my heart in the blessing and the wish.

I did some remembering to-day, dear lad. When you were born, I was five years younger than you are now, yet I felt myself old. "If we were as old as we feel, we would die of old age at twenty-one." My life seemed all behind me, long, turbulent, packed with pain, useless. I spoke of myself as if all were over. "It had been full of purpose, but what came of it? A few rhymes and a spoilt hope." To my morbid fancy your having come to be was a signal for me to go. I had no thought of dying, yet I accepted you as the proof of my failure. In the exacting eyes of the genius of the race I was insolvent. You were not mine. I looked into Time, and saw none of me there.

Yet the letter I wrote to your parents was sincere,—how else? And that night and the next and the next, I wrote "Gentleman Adventurers," which the critics called the epitome of all that is balladesque. One pitied the dead because they could go forth no more on water and under sky. This poem, written in a mood which beneficent nature sends on the too-sick spirit, has served for more than a quarter of a century as the complete and accepted catalogue of the reasons for living. Well, I must not laugh at it. It may be true that the passion of my heart incarnated itself in it beyond the rest, that my one song sang itself out those first three days of your life. If so, it is true that love is never cheated of its fruit, and that the joy which might have been for the individual oozes out of him to the race, that the strength which would have settled upon itself in the calm of satisfied hope, filters through him outwards.

Good night, lad. My hand is on your shoulder and I am loath to take it off. For a while I would like what cannot be, to travel with you the red-brown country-roads fragrant with hay, to cross the stiles and knock upon the cabin doors, and enter where sorrow and where gladness is, big with greeting and sure of welcome. I have often pleased myself with the fancy that the outer aspects of life are patterned after the inner, so that in the map of the spirit are to be found city and country, wood, desert, and sea, so that we know these outer worlds through having travelled the worlds within. Though I stay behind, my eyes can follow you from this night's landmark along the stretch, on to the city avenues, up the highways, tracing the twists of the bypaths, clambering untrod trails of wilderness and mountain, on, on, till out upon the sea.

In one of the near turnings a woman with waiting face smiles subtly. Her hands beckon you to the tryst. Godspeed, my son.

Dane.

XXVIII. FROM HERBERT WACE TO DANE KEMPTON

The Ridge,

Berkeley, California.

August 6, 19—.

As I have constantly insisted, our difference is temperamental. The common words we lay hold of mean one thing to you and another thing to me. I do not equivocate when I say that love is instinctive, and that the latter-day expression of love is artificial. "Art," as I understand the term in its broadness, contradistinguishes from nature. Whatever man contrives or devises is an artifice, a thing of art not of nature, and therefore artificial.

As for ourselves, among animals we are the only real inventors and artificers. Instead of hair and hide, we have soft skins, and we weave cunning textures and wear wondrous garments. In cold weather, in place of eating much fat meat, we keep ourselves warm by grate fires and steam heat. We cut up our blood-dripping meat chunks with pieces of iron hardened by fire and sharpened by stone, and we eat fish with a fork instead of our fingers. We put a roof over our heads to keep out storm and sunshine, sleep in pent rooms, and are afraid of the good night air and the open sky. In short, we are consummately artificial.

As I recollect, I have shown that the natural expression of the love instinct is bestial and brutal and violent. I have shown how imagination entered into the development of the expression of this love instinct till it became *romantic*. And, in turn, I have shown how artificial was the romantic expression of this love instinct, by isolating a boy babe and a girl babe in a natural state wherein they expressed their love instinct bestially and brutally and violently. As you say, they have simply been "left out by the civilising force." And this civilising, or socialising force is simply the sum of our many inventions. The isolated pair merely expressed their instincts in the unartificial, natural way. They had not been taught a certain particular fashion in which to express those instincts as have you and I and all artificial beings been taught.

As Mr. Finck has said, "Not till Dante's 'Vita Nuova' appeared was the gospel of modern love—the romantic adoration of a maiden by a youth—revealed for the first time in definite language."

Dante, and the men who foreshadowed and followed him, were inventors. They introduced an artifice for protracting one of our most vital pleasures. Well, they succeeded. And what of it? There are artifices and artifices, and some are better than others. The automobile is a more cunning artifice than the ox-cart, the subway than a palanquin. Devices come and devices go. Change is the essence of progress. All is development. The end of rapes and romances is the same—perpetuation. There may be head love as well as heart love. And in the time to come, when the brain ceases to be the servant of the belly, the head the lackey of the heart, in that time stirpiculture, which is scientific perpetuation, will take the place of romantic love. And in the present there may be men ready for that time. There must be a beginning, else would we still be jolting in ox-carts. And I am ready for that time now.

You say, "Love is of a piece with life, like hunger, like joy, like death." Quite true. And civilisation is merely the expression of life—a variform utterance which includes love, and hunger, and joy, and death. Else what is this civilisation for? How did it happen to be? And I answer: It is the sum of the many inventions we have made to aid us in our pursuit of life and love and joy. It helps us to live more abundantly, to love more fruitfully, to joy more intelligently, and to get grim old Death by his knotty throat and hold him at arm's length as long as possible.

I stated that "all progress consists in the arbitrary alteration, by human efforts and devices, of the normal course of nature." This sociological concept comes inevitably into accord with my philosophy of love. It is the law of development, and all things of human life (which includes love) come inside of it. Wherefore, certainly, I am not outside our province when I demand of you to bring your philosophy of love into like accord.

Incidentally, I will state that I *have* fallen in love. I have grown feverish with desire, gone mad with dumb yearning. I have felt my intellect lose dominion, and learned that I was only a garmented beast, for all the many inventions very like the other beasts ungarmented. Nay, I am no cold-blooded theorist, no thick-hided dogmatist; nor am I a chastely simple young man mooning in virginal innocence. My generalisations have been tempered in the heats of passion, and what I know I know, and without hearsay.

I have seen a learned man, drunk with wine, interrogate the new states of consciousness of his unwonted condition, and so doing, gain a more comprehensive psychological insight. So I, with my loves. I was impelled toward the women I shall presently particularise. I asked why the impulsion. I reasoned to see if there were a difference between these illicit passions of mine and the illicit passions of my respectable and respected friends. And I found no difference. Separated from codes and conventions, shorn of imagination, divested of romance, stripped naked down to the core of the matter, it was old Mother Nature crying through us, every man and woman of us, for progeny. Her one unceasing and eternal cry—Progeny! Progeny! Progeny!

Just as little girls, instinctively foreshadowing motherhood, play with dolls, so children feel vague sex promptings, and in sweetly ridiculous ways love and quarrel and make up after the approved fashion of lovers. You loved little girls in pigtails and pinafores. We all did. And in our lives there is nothing fairer and more joyful to look back upon than those same little pigtails and pinafores. But I shall pass the child loves by, and instance first my calf love.

Do you remember the incident of the torn jacket and the blackened eyes?—so inexplicable at the time. Try as you would, neither you nor Waring could get anything out of me. Oh, believe me, it was tragic! I was fifteen. Fifteen, and athrill with a strange new pulse; flushed, as the dawn, with the promise of day. And, of course, I thought it was the day, that I loved as a man loved, and that no man ever loved more. Well, well, I laugh now. I was only fifteen—a young calf who went out and butted heads with another calf in the back pasture.

She was a demure little coquette, Celia Genoine, Professor Genoine's daughter, if you will recollect. "Ah," I hear you remonstrate, "but she was a woman." Just so. Fifteen and twenty-two is usually the way of calf loves. I invested her with all the glow and colour of first youth, and in her presence became a changed being. I blushed if she looked at me; trembled at the touch of her hand or the scent of her hair. To be in her presence was to be closeted with the awfulness and splendour of God. I read immortality in her eyes. A smile from her blinded me, a gentle word or caressing look and I went faint and dizzy, and I was content to lurk in some corner and gaze upon her secretly with all my soul. And I took long, solitary walks, with book of verse beneath my arm, and learned to love as lovers had loved before me.

Sufficient romance was engendered for me to pass more than one night worshipping beneath her window. I mooned and sentimentalised and fell into a gentle melancholy, until you and Waring began to worry over an early decline, to consult specialists, and by trick and stratagem to entice me into eating more and reading less. But she married—ah, I have forgotten whom. Anyway, she married, and there was trouble about it, too, and I bade adieu to love forever.

Then came the love of my whelpage. I was twenty, and she a mad, wanton creature, wonderful and unmoral and filled with life to the brim. My blood pounds hot even now as I conjure her up. The ungarmented beast, my dear Dane, the great primordial ungarmented beast, mighty to procreate, indomitable in battle, invincible in love. Love? Do I not know it? Can I not understand how that splendid fighting animal, Antony, quartered the globe with his sword and pillowed his head between the slim breasts of Egyptian Cleopatra while that hard-won world crashed to wrack and ruin?

As I say, This was the love of my whelpage, and it was vigorous, masterful, masculine. There was no sentimentalising, no fond foolishness of youth; nor was there that cool, calm poise which comes of the calculation and discretion of age. Man and woman, we were in full tide, strong, simple, and elemental. Life rioted in our veins; we were a-bubble with the ferment; and it is out of such abundance that Mother Nature has always exacted her progeny. From the strictly emotional and naturalistic viewpoint, I must consider it, even now, the perfect love. But it was decreed that I should develop into an intellectual animal, and be something more than a mere unconscious puppet of the reproductive forces. So head mastered my heart, and I laid the grip of my will over the passion and went my way.

And then came another man's wife, a proud-breasted woman, the perfect mother, made pre-eminently to know the lip clasp of a child. You know the kind, the type. "The mothers of men," I call them. And so long as there are such women on this earth, that long may we keep faith in the breed of men. The wanton was the Mate Woman, but this was the Mother Woman, the last and highest and holiest in the hierarchy of life. In her all criteria were satisfied, and I reasoned my need of her.

And by this I take it that I was passing out of my blind puppetdom. I was becoming a conscious selective factor in the scheme of reproduction, choosing a mate, not in the lust of my eyes, but in the desire of my fatherhood. Oh, Dane, she was glorious, but she was another man's wife. Had I been living unartificially, in a state of nature, I would certainly have brained her husband (a really splendid fellow), and dragged her off with me shameless under the sky. Or had her husband not been a man, or had he been but half a man, I doubt not that I would have wrested her from him. As it was, I yearned dumbly and observed the conventions.

Nor are these experiences heart soils and smirches. They have educated me, fitted me for that which is yet to be. And I have written of them to show you that I am no closet naturalist, that I speak authoritatively out of adequate understanding. Since the end of love, when all is said and done, is progeny; and since the love of to-day is crude and wasteful; as an inventor and artificer I take it upon myself to substitute reasoned foresight and selection for the short-sighted and blundering selection of Mother Nature. What would you? The old dame would have made a mess of it had I let her have her way. She tried hard to mate me with the wanton, for it was not her method to look into the future to see if a better mother for my progeny awaited me.

And now comes Hester. I approach her, not with the milk-and-water ardours of first youth, nor with the lusty love madness of young manhood, but as an intellectual man, seeking for self and mate the ripe and rounded manhood and womanhood which comes only through the having of children—children which must be properly born and bred. In this way, and in this way only, can we fully express ourselves and the life that is in us. We shall utter ourselves in the finest speech in the world, and, our children being properly born and bred, it shall be in the finest terms of the finest speech in the world. To do this is to have lived.

Herbert.

XXIX. FROM DANE KEMPTON TO HERBERT WACE

London,

3a, Queen's Road, Chelsea, S.W.

August 26, 19—.

You insist that the question is not on the value of love but on the significance of the artificial. Be that as it may. To me love is integral with life, and to speak of civilising it away, seems, in point of fact, as preposterous and as anomalous as a Hamletless play of Hamlet. You forget that in developing you carry yourself along; you change, yet you remain racial and natural. Else there were too many missing links in all your departments. We read Homer to-day—telling proof that the chain of sympathy stretches unbroken through epochs of inventions and discoveries and revolutions. Truism that it is, it presents itself with particular force at this stage.

With how much force? We stand in danger of exaggerating these vociferous thoughts. This question of naturalness as opposed to artificiality is not immediately pertinent to our problem, nor is the matter of optimism and pessimism, nor the biologic idea of survival. We should have looked more to the way of love in the lives of men and women and become historians of the method and conduct of the force. There would have been less confusion. So I write, "Be that as it may," and go back to more immediate considerations. And yet we were not far wrong! The little flower in the crannied wall could tell what God and man is. This is of all thoughts the most charged with truth. Let me understand one of your conclusions, root and all, and all in all, and such is the gracious plan of oneness in the branching and leafage and uptowering, that I must know and name the tree. Your winding bypath, could I but follow it to the end, must bring me to the highway of your thought, every step tell-tale of the journey's destination. But soon I shall be with you (the fifth of next month, after all; the arrangements as planned). Then we will begin to know each other, and we will no longer be tormented by the irksomeness of writing. Therefore, until easier and more fluent times, to the heart of the subject straight.

Your love-affairs—how well you have outgrown them and how ably you criticise them! They have not withstood the test of time, for you bear them no loyalty. Calfdom and whelpage, vagaries of adolescence, you call them. You do not show them much respect! For this reason your examples lose what weight they might have borne. They belong so wholly to the past, they are mere wraiths of bygone stirrings, they cannot clothe you with knowledge of love. Cold now, what boots it that you have been afire? You cannot be taught by what is utterly over.

You are catching what I aim to say, I hope, for I aim to say much. Put it that instead of a girl whom you idealised, it was a principle—some scheme of reform which you honoured with all the passion of young hope and dream, and which knit your alert being into a Laocoon of striving. Your maturer eyes see this ideal impossible and narrow. In no wise can it satisfy your bolder reach and larger sympathy. But you do not laugh at what has been. If you strove for it sincerely at any time, no matter how remote, you could never again deride it. Because once you loved it you are eternal keeper of the key to its good. What has been wholly yours you never quite desert. Nothing has remained to you of your love-affairs, therefore your recital of them is empty of meaning. If you were in love to-day, and because of your philosophy you determined to do battle with your feeling, your experience would be more authoritative.

You have known love, and having known you refuse it. Henceforth, it must be reason and not feeling. "What is your objection?" you ask. This merely, that the thing cannot be. Marriage to be marriage must come through love, through the reddest romance of love, through fire of the spirit, yes, even through the love of calfdom and whelpage. Else it is a mockery. Where is the woman of character who would sell the be-all and end-all of her existence for a neat catalogue of possible advantages? Where is the man who would frankly and without embellishment dare make such proposal? You point to yourself. But you have never explained yourself to Hester, and even to me you are embellishing the matter with all the might in your persuasive pen.

The ardours of calfdom and whelpage that you smile at I would have you throb with. You underrate the firstlings of the heart, the rose and white blossoming, the call upon the senses and the readiness to respond and to fulfil, to give and to take, to be and make happy—the great pride and utter abandon which is young love. At fifteen, fortunately for the development of mind and character, hope is placed where hope must pine. Love, then, is doomed to be tragic. The youth "attains to be denied." But he sounds his depth. Thereafter, he knows what to expect of himself. He has a precedent. After this he will count it a sin to forget, and to accept the solace of mediocrity. In this lies the value of the tragedy.

I sometimes think that whatever is youngest is best. It is the young that, timid and bold, pay greatest reverence to knowledge, receiving without chill of prejudice and shameful cowardice of quibbling the brave new thought. Wisdom may be of age, but passion for scholarships, trail-breaking, and hardy prospecting in the treasure mines of research, is of young pioneerhood alone. It is a youth who dares be radical, who dares, in splendid largess, build mistake upon mistake, bleeding his life out in service. And it is a youth, standing tiptoe upon the earth, now waiting in unperturbed ease, now searching with unbridled zeal, who is lover and mystic. "The best is yet to be," says Rabbi Ben Ezra, "the last of life, for which the first is made." Yes, the last of life will be good, but only if it is like youth, beating with its pulse and instinct with its spirit.

The unhappy youth is left on the battle-field but not to die. The sword-thrusts challenge him to put forth greater strength in fiercer wars. He learns hard and well.

Indeed, I cannot leave this subject of first love. How do you know it was not good for you to love as you did? It is strange you should resolve to love no more because at one time you loved deeply enough almost to remain in love. It cannot be that you have grown old and that nature is resolving for you. You tell me of your experiences in order that I may be convinced that you know whereof you speak and I listen in wonder. Your conclusions are unwonted.

Then something was amiss, for you have outgrown and forgotten, but how is it with you in the present when your indifference waits not upon time? You approach your future wife clothed in indifference as in mail, and you do violence. How can I show you? I speak as I would to a child to whom it is necessary to explain that it is bad to abandon an education. Life is a school, and to me it seems that you are about to resign long before diploma and degree, so I interpose. I was taught by first love, and I honour that time beyond any other. I was Ellen's. I have been lonely. For the mere human need, for the sake of that which to the lonely is very dear, I have thought of marriage, but I remembered and I refused to do violence to myself remembering. Long ago my standard was established. I learned how deeply I could feel, and I refuse to acknowledge myself bankrupt, I refuse to approach an honourable human being with less than my all. Until my soul flower out again, until suns flame about my head as in that dear yoretime, I shall keep teeming with dreams and make no affront. I who have seen love, dare not live without love.

I would not give in to fate, Herbert. I would assert my manhood. I would abide in the strength of the first output, going with the flush of the first glow into the gloom. I would spurn the calm of compromise and mediocrity and register a high claim. I would keep the peace with Romance and fly her colours to the last. You have lived? It is well, and it might have been better, but do not give over and talk of stirpiculture. You are not wiser than the laws which made you.

Dane.

XXX. FROM HERBERT WACE TO DANE KEMPTON

The Ridge,

Berkeley, California.

September 18, 19—.

How abominable I must seem to you, Dane! For certainly a creature is abominable that lays rough hands on one's dearest possessions. I doubt if even you realise how deeply you are stirred by my conduct towards love. My marriage with Hester, considering the quality and degree of the contracting parties, must appear as terrible to you as the sodomies that caused God's ancient wrath to destroy cities. You see, I take your side for the time, see with your eyes, live your thoughts, suffer what you suffer; and then I become myself again and steel myself to continue in what I think is the right.

After all, mine is the harder part. There are easier tasks than those of the illusion-shatterer. That which is established is hard to overthrow. It has the nine points of possession, and woe to him who attempts its disestablishment; for it will persist till it be drowned and washed away in the blood of the reformers and radicals.

Love is a convention. Men and women are attached to it as they are attached to material things, as a king is attached to his crown or an old family to its ancestral home. We have all been led to believe that love is splendid and wonderful, and the greatest thing in the world, and it pains us to part with it. Faith, we will not part with it. The man who would bid us put it by is a knave and a fool, a vile, degraded wretch, who will receive pardon neither in this world nor the next.

This is nothing new. It is the attitude of the established whenever its conventions are attacked. It was the attitude of the Jew toward Christ, of the Roman toward the Christian, of the Christian toward the infidel and the heretic. And it is sincere and natural. All things desire to endure, and they die hard. Love will die hard, as died the idolatries of our forefathers, the geocentric theory of the universe, and the divine right of kings.

So, I say, the rancour and warmth of the established when attacked is sincere. The world is mastered by the convention of love, and when one profanes love's Holy of Holies the world is unutterably shocked and hurt. Love is a thing for lovers only. It must not be approached by the sacrilegious scientist. Let him keep to his physics and chemistry, things definite and solid and gross. Love is for ardent speculation, not laboratory analysis. Love is (as the reverend prior and the learned bodies told brother Lippo of man's soul):—

"—a fire, smoke ... no, it's not ...

It's vapour done up like a new-born babe—

(In that shape when you die it leaves your mouth)

It's ... well, what matters talking, it's the soul!"

I thoroughly understand the popular sentimental repugnance to a scientific discussion of love. Because I dissect love, and weigh and calculate, it is denied that I am capable of experiencing love. It is too radiant and glorious a thing for a dull clod like me to know. And because I cannot experience love and be made mad by it, my fitness to describe its phenomena is likewise denied. Only the lover may describe love. And only the lunatic, I suppose, may compose a medical brochure on insanity.

Herbert.

XXXI. FROM DANE KEMPTON TO HERBERT WACE

London,

October 7, 19—.

It is true that you have a hard task before you, but it is not because you are fighting convention and shattering illusion; it is because you are assailing a good. Love has never acquired the prestige of the established, and the run of marriages are prompted by advantage, routine, or passion. So you are no innovator, Herbert. The idolatry of love will not be overthrown by a drawn battle between those of the Faith and those of the Reformation. Nothing so spectacular awaits us.

I have a friend who has undertaken to translate "Inferno" into English, keeping to the *terza rima*. "It is like climbing the Matterhorn," he says gravely. "I get to places where I feel I can go neither forward nor back. The task is prodigious." And it is. But whom will it concern if he succeeds in going forward? There are few who will read his book. The translation is of more importance to the translator than to anyone else. Yet the professor's *magnum opus* confers a degree upon us all. Because a standard is upheld and a man is willing and able to climb a Matterhorn of thought, we can ourselves stride forward with better courage. The work will be an output of heroism, and it will ennoble even those who will not know of it.

I have another friend who ruined his life for love, so says the world that you think steeped in the idolatry of love. A priest, who by a few strokes was able to quell in America a strong and bitter movement, a gifted orator, a man of giant powers, and who was won away at the age of forty from his career by a mere girl. The girl planned nothing. She found herself a force in his life almost despite herself. The mere fact that she lived was enough to wrest this Titan from the arms of the Church. He told me that she criticised him with the directness of a simple nature, and that he came to understand her truths better than she herself. I think she must have loved him at first, but she did not go to him when all grew calm. I wish it could have been otherwise, and that she could have brought him a woman's heart.

The priest, as the professor, is a hero. Both made great outputs.

There are few who can live like these. But because there are a few who can love and work, the game is saved. And because there are a few of these, we must ever quarrel with the many who are not like them.

"Give all to love;

Obey thy heart;

Friends, kindred, days,

Estate, good fame,

Plans, credit, and the Muse,—

Nothing refuse."

Does this really seem such poor philosophy to you? And when, Herbert, will you marry?

Dane Kempton.

XXXII. FROM THE SAME TO THE SAME

Stanford University.

November 20, 19—.

Hester met me at the station, and we walked through the Arboretum to her home on the campus. Then followed an evening together in the dormitory parlour. I have just left her. Her face was tumultuously joyous when I murmured my "At last!" Her tearful excitement was like Barbara's. You did not tell me she is so young. You must have made her feel our closeness, or she may have found a bit of my verse that all expressed her, and presto, the whole-hearted one is my friend. Her poet is now her father, brother, comrade,—what she chooses, and all she chooses.

At one time, before we were well out of the Arboretum, our eyes met, and there was something so sad and mild and strange in the burn of her gaze that I felt her frank spirit was unveiling itself in an utterness of speech. But I have become too much spoilt by mere length of living to be able to remember back and recognise what young eyes mean when they look like that. From London to Palo Alto is a short trip, if at the end of it you meet a Hester. Yet I am sad. The mood crept on me the moment we grew aware that evening had come, and we stopped a little in front of the arch to observe the night-look of the foot-hills. Lights had begun to appear in the corridors of the quadrangle, and here and there in a professor's office, while Roble and Encina looked like lit-up ferries. There was a spell of mystery and promise in the quiet which was deeper for being suggestive of the seething student-life just subsided. It was a silence that seemed to echo with bells and recitations, and babble and laughter and heartache. I fell into thought. One generation cometh and another passeth away. There is no respite. March with time and find death, mayhap, before it has found you. As years ago the flamelet of the street-lamp, so now these outposts of the colossal embryo of a world derided me and seemed to point me out and away. The evening grew chill with "a greeting in which no kindness is."

"Your coming has been announced in every class, and your lecture is on the bulletin-boards. After that, can you be depressed?"

The light words were spoken low, as if doubtful whether they could be taken in good part, and they came with something that was like music. Was it the voice or some inexplicable feeling? I turned in wonder. Her head was raised, and in the indistinctness I caught that sweet look of hers which besought me, and which I answered without knowing to what question.

I owe you a great happiness. Good-night.

Dane Kempton.

XXXIII. FROM THE SAME TO THE SAME

Stanford University.

Wednesday.

Last night I delivered my address to the student body. Behold the chapel crowded to the doors, aisles and window-seats crammed, and faces peering in from without, those of boys and girls who had perched themselves on the outer sills. A student audience is at the same time most critical and the most generous. I spoke on Literature and Democracy.

Hester approved my effort. "How does it feel to be great?" she laughed. "How does it feel to be cruel?" I retorted. "But think, Mr. Kempton, when you visited the English classes you were just so much text for us. It should count us a unit merely to have seen you."

A memory stood up and had its revenge on me. It taunted me for the half-expressed thought, for the fled insight, for the swelling note that midmost broke. Praise the artist, and he feels himself betrayer. Blear-eyed, the poet recalls the poem's sunrise, straightens himself with the old pride, is held again by the splendour which forecasts the about-to-be-steadier glory of day, and even with the recalling he shrinks together before what he knows was a false dawn. There was never a day. The song's note never sang itself at all.

Hester looked up with that wistfulness which so draws me. Her look said: "I pity you. I wish you were as happy as I." And a thought leaped out in answer to her look which would have smote her had it spoken. It was, "You, too, are awakened by a false dawning." Why is she so sure of herself and of you? Is she sure? The puny bit of writing had a vigorous rising. The ragged author was clad in it as in ermine. So the seeming love makes a strong call, for a while holding the girl intent upon a splendour of unfolding, her nature roused, her being expectant. But later, for poet and lover, the failure and the waste! Were it otherwise with your feeling for your betrothed, the comparison would not hold.

Hester does not think these things, and she is beautiful and happy.

Yours devotedly,

Dane Kempton.

XXXIV. FROM THE SAME TO THE SAME

Stanford University.

Saturday.

Her happiness wrung it from me. Before I could intervene, the question asked itself, "How will it be with you in after years?"

Straight the answer came, "There will be Herbert."

Hester is proud. To-night I saw it in the lift of her chin, in the set of her neck, in the brilliance of her cheek. She knows herself endowed. So when she prattled with abandon of all you both meant to be and do, her form erect before me, her hands eloquent with excitement, her voice pleading for the right to her very conscious self-esteem, I asked her to look still further. Further she saw you, and was content.

That was before dinner. Later we were walking. "I have a friend in Orion," she said. The witchery of starshine played in her eyes and about her mouth. Where were you, Herbert? This night will never return. Yet what has been was for you—the more, perhaps, that you seemed away. So it is with lovers. She thinks you love her.

"I am sorry for your mood," she said. "You are holding yourself to account these days in a way I know." Then she spoke, and I learned with new heaviness of spirit that she does know the way of it. You never thought Hester had much to struggle with?

"I am difficult," she said. And again, "There are times when no power can hold me." Then she quoted Browning:—

"Already how am I so far

Out of that minute? Must I go

Still like the thistle-ball, no bar,

Onward, whenever light winds blow,

Fixed by no friendly star?"

"Are you unhappy, Hester?" I asked.

"Yes, but with no more reason than you for your unhappiness. Since you have come here, you have renewed your demands upon yourself. You wish to go to school with the youngest and find you cannot. You suffer because more seems behind you than before." Her voice rose as if she were fighting tears. It was different with her, I told her. Nothing was behind her.

"You test your work and I test my love. When you are sad, it is because the soul of the song spent itself to gain body—" She did not finish. Why is she sad? Because the soul of her love is narrower than she hoped?

On our return from our walk she sank on the seat under the '95 oak. "Did you think I meant I was always unhappy?" she asked. Her words seem always to say more than her meaning. She imparts something of her own elaborateness to them. I laughed.

"How could I with the 'Herbert is' in my ears?" Then her love became voluble. I forgot what I knew of your theories and grew aflame with her ardour. I anticipated as largely as she. She was again possessed by her hopes.

There, under the shadow of the quadrangle which her young strides measured, she spoke of what, with you in her life, the years must be. Beyond words you are blessed, Herbert. But if she mistakes?

D.K.

XXXV. FROM THE SAME TO THE SAME

Stanford University.

November 27, 19—.

Be outspoken! What will happen I can only surmise, but you must tell her what she is to you. Set her right.

This is the fourth letter in seven days about Hester. I am endeavouring to make you acquainted with her. I had no need if you loved her. How she loves you! Yet she thinks that your calm is depth, your silence prayer. Her pride protects her, but she strains for the word which does not come. She has never been quite sure, and I thank God for that. Hester has been fearing somewhat, and she has been doubting, and it is this that may save her when the night sets in and the storm breaks over her head.

You, too, are thankful that her instincts served her true and that she never quite accepted the gift that seemed to have been proffered?

You have a right to demand the reason for my renewed attack. It is because I have learned the strength of her love. "You are blessed beyond words," I said two days ago, but as you reject the blessing, Hester must know it and you must tell her. Herbert, I am your friend.

Dane Kempton.

XXXVI. FROM HERBERT WACE TO DANE KEMPTON

The Ridge,

Berkeley, California.

November 29, 19—.

What a flutter of letters! And what a fluttery Dane Kempton it is! The wine of our western sunshine has bitten into your blood and you are grown over-warm. I am glad that you and Hester have found each other so quickly and intimately; glad that you are under her charm, as I know her to be under yours; but I am not glad when you spell yourself into her and write out your heart's forebodings on her heart. For you are strangely morbid, and you are certainly guilty of reading your own doubts and fears into her unspoken and unguessed thoughts.

Believe me, rather than the soul of her love seeming narrower than she hopes, the truth is she gives her love little thought at all. She is too busy—and too sensible. Like me, she has not the time. We are workers, not dreamers; and the minutes are too full for us to lavish them on an eternal weighing and measuring of heart throbs.

Besides, Hester is too large for that sort of stuff. She is the last woman in the world to peer down at the scales to see if she is getting full value. We leave that to the lesser creatures, who spend their courtship loudly protesting how unutterable, immeasurable, and inextinguishable is their love, as though, forsooth, each dreaded lest the other deem it a bad bargain. We do not bargain and chaffer over our feelings, Hester and I. Surely you mistake, and stir storms in teacups.

"Be outspoken," you say. If my conscience were not clear, I should be troubled by that. As it is, what have I hidden? What sharp business have I driven? And who is it that cried "cheated!"? Be outspoken—about what, pray?

You bid me tell her what she is to me. Which is to bid me tell her what she already knows, to tell her that she is the Mother Woman; that of all women she is dearest to me; that of all the walks of life, that one is pleasantest wherein I may walk with her; that with her I shall find the supreme expression of myself and the life that is in me; that in all this I honour her in the finest, loftiest fashion that man can honour woman. Tell her this, Dane. By all means tell her.

"Ah, I do not mean that," I hear you say. Well, let me tell you what you mean, in my own way, and bid you tell her for me. In the lust of my eyes she is nothing to me. She is not a mere sense delight, a toy for the debauchery of my intellect and the enthronement of emotion. She is not the woman to make my pulse go fevered and me go mad. Nor is she the woman to make me forget my manhood and pride, to tumble me down doddering at her feet and gibbering like an ape. She is not the woman to put my thoughts out of joint and the world out of gear, and so to befuddle and make me drunk with the beast that is in me, that I am ready to sacrifice truth, honesty, duty, and purpose for the sake of possession. She is not the woman ever to make me swamp honour and poise and right conduct in the vortex of blind sex passion. She is not the woman to arouse in me such uncontrolled desire that for gratification I would do one ill deed, or put the slightest hurt upon the least of human creatures. She is not the most beautiful woman God Almighty ever planted on His footstool. (There have been and are many women as true and pure and noble). She is not the woman for whose bedazzlement I must advertise the value of my goods by sweating sonnets to her, or shivering serenades at her, or perpetuating follies for her. In short, she is not anything to me that the woman of conventional love is to the man.

And again, what *is* she to me? She is my other self, as it were, my good comrade, and fellow-worker and joy-sharer. With her woman she complements my man and makes us one, and this is the highest civilised sense of union. She is to me the culmination of the thousands of generations of women. It took civilisation to make her, as it takes civilisation to make our marriage. She is to me the partner in a marriage of the gods, for we become gods, we half brutes, when we muzzle the beast and are not menaced by his growls. Under heaven she is my wife and the mother of my children.

Tell her, then, tell her all you wish, you dear old fluttery, mothery poet father—as though it made any difference.

Herbert.

XXXVII. FROM DANE KEMPTON TO HERBERT WACE

Stanford University.

December 3, 19—.

Not three weeks ago you were sitting opposite me and speaking of Hester. You admitted many things that night, amongst them that the girl never carried you off your feet. You stated over again with precision all you had written. You betrothed yourself, not because Hester is different from everybody else in the world, but because she is like. You took her for what is typical in her, not for what is individual. You preferred to walk toward her before your steps were impelled, because you feared that impulsion would preclude rational choice. With the hope of out-tricking nature, you reached for Hester Stebbins, in order that there might be a wall between your heart's fancy and yourself, should your heart become rebellious. I was to understand that this is the new school, that so live the masters of matter and of self.

And as you spoke, I wondered about the woman Hester and the form of love-making which existed between you, and whether she was simple and without any charm despite her culture and her gift of song. "She either loves him too well to know or to have the strength to care, or she is, like him, of the new school," I thought. I sat and watched you, noting your youth, surprised by the scorn in your eyes and the sadness on your lips. You seemed hopeless and helpless. I closed my eyes. "What has he left himself?" I kept asking. "How will he tread 'The paths gray heads abhor?'" My own head bowed itself as before an irreparable loss. I had rejoined the child of my care only to find him blasted as by grief, the first sunshine smitten from his face and his heart weighted. One word, one ray lighting your looks in a wonted way, one uncontrolled movement of the hand, one little silence following the mention of her, would have led me to believe that I had not understood and that all was well. The night grew old with your plans and analyses. We parted with a sense of shame upon us that we should have written and spoken so long and with such heat, and to such little purpose.

You do not see how this answers your last letter. I will tell you. It shows you that you have explained yourself fully the night we spoke face to face.

You say that Hester is the woman to complement your man. This sounds like a lover, only I happen to know that she is not the irresistible woman. I found it out quite by accident—a few words dropped into a letter, a corroboration of the fact and further committal, a protracted defence of your position, running through a correspondence of over a year, and, finally, a face-to-face declaration. What boots it now that you write prettily? You do not love Hester. You want her to mother your children, and you install her in your life for the purpose before the need.

Love is not lust, and it is good. The irresistible marriage, alone, is the right one. Upon it, alone, does the sacrament rest. The chivalry of your last letter refers less to the girl than to your own ends. It is not because Hester is what she is, that "of all the walks in life that one is pleasantest wherein you may walk with her," but because that walk is the one you choose beyond any other for your wife to follow. The mother woman is legion, and you refuse to specialise.

Hester does not peer down at the scales to see if she is getting full value, yet she does look to her dignity, and, being poor, will not account herself rich. Hester has felt since you made known to her that you wished her to be yours, that she counted punily in your scheme, that you placed little of yourself in charge of her. She loved you and avowed it, but she has never been happy. The tragedy of love is not (what it is thought to be) the unreciprocated love, but the meagerly returned love. It is better to be rejected, equal turned from equal, than to be held with slim desire for slight purpose. Can you see this, Herbert? You are hurting the girl's life. She will ask for what you withhold, though not a word rise to her lips; will thirst for it through the years, will herself grow cramped with your denial till her own love seem a thing of dream, unstable and vague and illusive. And all the time you are gentle. You are devoted to her interests, furthering her happiness to the best in your power; but your power cannot touch her happiness. It is not what you do; it is the motive to your acts, and Hester would know that she has left you unmoved. You respect the function of motherhood, but you do not love Hester. Tell her this, and

426

prevent her from entering a union in which she must feel herself half useful, half wifely, half happy, and therefore all unhappy.

It is not Hester's fault that you cannot love her, and perhaps it is not her misfortune. There is no need for panic. Of two persons, one loving and one loath, the indifferent one is in the right. Can a tree defend itself from the hewer's axe? What would avail it, then, to feel pain at the blows? It is beyond our control to love or not to love, and no effort that we may put forth can draw love to us when it is denied. It does not avail us to suffer from unrequited love.

This which I have just said is an article of faith which the doctrine of experience often contradicts, for there may be mistake, and the one who does not love may be in the wrong. If only you could wait to see the beauty which is she before you call her! A year later and Hester may flower for you in a passionate blossoming; her face may challenge you to live. A year later and you may find that she is indeed the woman to guide you and to follow you; her voice a song; her eyes a light in the day. As yet, you have not gauged her, and you would put her to small uses. Stand aside, dear Herbert. It will be better.

I have played a surly part. I may be accused of having been to you both a Dmitri Roudin and an Iago. I beg you to believe that it has not been easy for me. I have uttered the earnest word, have driven you on by the goad of friendship, which drives far. I looked upon the days that came tripping toward you out of the blue-white horizon of time and saw them gray for a dear woman, gray and silent as the tomb over a dead love, and heavy hearted for a man who is my son.

Ever wholly yours,

Dane Kempton.

XXXVIII. FROM HESTER STEBBINS TO HERBERT WACE

Stanford University.

December 15, 19—.

Over and ended. It shall be as I said last night. Herbert, there is no call for anger; believe me, there is not. I am doing what I cannot help doing. You have not changed, but my faith in you has, and I cannot pretend to a happiness I do not feel.

Oh, but I laugh, my very dear one, I laugh that I could seem to choose to wrest myself from you. Did you at one time love me? That morning of wild sunshine when you took my hand and asked me to be your wife seems very long ago. I should have understood—the blame is all mine—I should have known you did not love me, I should have been filled with anger and shame instead of happiness. The blame is all mine.

Last night, while you were speaking, I was standing in the window wondering what all the trouble was about. I could afford to be calm since I knew I was not hurting you very deeply. At most I was disappointing a very self-sufficient man. How do women find courage, O God, to take from men who love them the love they gave? No such ordeal mine?

Farewell, Herbert. Let us think calmly of each other since we have helped each other for so long a stretch of life. Farewell, dear.

Always your friend,

Hester Stebbins.

XXXIX. FROM HESTER STEBBINS TO DANE KEMPTON

Stanford University.

December 18, 19—.

Herbert has analyzed the situation and has arrived at the conclusion that my dissatisfaction arises in an inordinate desire for happiness. You should not care so much about yourself, he says. Poor, dear, young Herbert! He is very young and cannot as yet conceive how much there is about oneself that demands care. I thought it out in the hills to-day. It was gray and there was a fitful wind. What is this selfishness but a prompting to make much of life? You and I and people of our kind are old before our time, that is the reason we are not reckless. Our dreams mature us. I was a mere girl when Herbert said he wished to marry me, but I was old enough to grasp the full meaning of the pact, as he could not grasp it. In a moment I had travelled my way to the grave and back. I looked at the sheer, quick clouds that flitted past the blue, and I felt that I had caught up with life; I had overtaken the wonders that hung in the sky of my dreaming. Then I looked at him and the sunshine got in my face and made me laugh (or cry)—I was so more than happy, being so much too sure of his need of me. I am glad I walked to-day. The view from the hills was beautiful. (You see I am not unhappy!) I stood on a rock and looked about me, thinking of you, of Barbara,—I feel I know her,—and of Herbert. He and I had often come to these spots. Oh, the hungry memories! Yet what were we but a young man and a young woman, who, without being battered into apathy by misfortune, without being wearied or ill, were taking each other for better or for worse because they seemed compatible? We were doing just that, to Herbert's certain knowledge! I failed him; he hoped for more complaisance. Marriage is a hazard, Mr. Kempton, confess it is, and a man does much when he binds himself to make a woman the mother of his children—nay, the grandmother of theirs, even that. What else and what more? I would never have been wholly in my husband's life, comrade and fellow to it. Herbert knew this clearly, and I vaguely but I acted with clearness on my vagueness. It was hard to do. It has left me breathless and a little afraid to be myself,—as if I had killed a dear thing,—and tearful, too, and spasmodic for your sympathy and sanction.

I told him that for a long time I did not understand, supposing myself beloved and desired and chosen for him by God, thinking he yearned for the subtlety and mystery of me, thinking all of him needed me and cleaved earths and parted seas to come to me. Later, when I became oppressed by a lack and was made to hear the stillness that followed my unechoed words, I became grave and still myself. He had unloved me, I said, and I waited. Something seemed pending, and meanwhile I could love! I made much of every word of comfort that he dropped me, and dwelt with hope on the future. All this I told Herbert the night when I explained, and he turned pale. "You people fly away with yourselves. I cannot follow you. What is wrong, Hester?" He smiled in his distress. Yet was there in his softness an imperiousness, commanding me to be other than I am, forbidding me the right to crave in secret what I had made bold to ask for openly. His man was stronger than my woman, and I leapt to him again. "My husband," I whispered, my hands in his. This, even after I understood, dearest Mr. Kempton.

It is a sorry tangle. If only one could suit feeling to theory! It is not for a theory that I refuse to be Herbert's wife. Yet if I loved him enough, I could give up love itself for him. He hinted it, looking as from a distance at me in my attitude of protest and restraint. If I loved him enough, I could forego love itself for him. Somewhere there is a fault, it would seem, somewhere in my abandon is restraint, in my love, self-seeking. Remorse overcame me just as he was about to leave, and I schooled myself to think that there had been no affront, that it honours a woman to be wanted no matter for what end, that every use is a noble use, that we die the same, loved or used. If Herbert Wace wants a wife and thinks me fitting, why, it is well. I thought all this and aged as I thought. Nevertheless, my hand did not put itself out a second time to detain the man who had forced me to face this.

There is a youth here who loves me. If Herbert's face could shine like his for one hour, I believe I would be happier than I have ever been. And it would not spoil that happiness if this love were toward another than myself. Say you believe me. You must know it of me that before everything else in the

430

world I pray that knowledge of love come to the man over whom the love of my girlhood was spilled.

Do you ask what is left me, dear friend? Work and tears and the intact dream. Believe me, I am not pitiable.

Hester.

About Author

John Griffith London (born **John Griffith Chaney**; January 12, 1876 – November 22, 1916) was an American novelist, journalist, and social activist. A pioneer in the world of commercial magazine fiction, he was one of the first writers to become a worldwide celebrity and earn a large fortune from writing. He was also an innovator in the genre that would later become known as science fiction.

His most famous works include The Call of the Wild and White Fang, both set in the Klondike Gold Rush, as well as the short stories "To Build a Fire", "An Odyssey of the North", and "Love of Life". He also wrote about the South Pacific in stories such as "The Pearls of Parlay", and "The Heathen".

London was part of the radical literary group "The Crowd" in San Francisco and a passionate advocate of unionization, workers' rights, socialism, and eugenics. He wrote several works dealing with these topics, such as his dystopian novel The Iron Heel, his non-fiction exposé The People of the Abyss, The War of the Classes, and Before Adam.

Family

Jack London's mother, Flora Wellman, was the fifth and youngest child of Pennsylvania Canal builder Marshall Wellman and his first wife, Eleanor Garrett Jones. Marshall Wellman was descended from Thomas Wellman, an early Puritan settler in the Massachusetts Bay Colony. Flora left Ohio and moved to the Pacific coast when her father remarried after her mother died. In San Francisco, Flora worked as a music teacher and spiritualist, claiming to channel the spirit of a Sauk chief, Black Hawk.

Biographer Clarice Stasz and others believe London's father was astrologer William Chaney. Flora Wellman was living with Chaney in San Francisco when she became pregnant. Whether Wellman and Chaney were legally married is unknown. Stasz notes that in his memoirs, Chaney refers to London's mother Flora Wellman as having been his "wife"; he also cites an advertisement in which Flora called herself "Florence Wellman Chaney".

According to Flora Wellman's account, as recorded in the San Francisco Chronicle of June 4, 1875, Chaney demanded that she have an abortion. When she refused, he disclaimed responsibility for the child. In desperation, she shot herself. She was not seriously wounded, but she was temporarily deranged. After giving birth, Flora turned the baby over for care to Virginia Prentiss, an African-American woman and former slave. She was a major maternal figure throughout London's life. Late in 1876, Flora Wellman married John London, a partially disabled Civil War veteran, and brought her baby John, later known as Jack, to live with the newly married couple. The family moved around the San Francisco Bay Area before settling in Oakland, where London completed public grade school.

In 1897, when he was 21 and a student at the University of California, Berkeley, London searched for and read the newspaper accounts of his mother's suicide attempt and the name of his biological father. He wrote to William Chaney, then living in Chicago. Chaney responded that he could not be London's father because he was impotent; he casually asserted that London's mother had relations with other men and averred that she had slandered him when she said he insisted on an abortion. Chaney concluded by saying that he was more to be pitied than London. London was devastated by his father's letter; in the months following, he quit school at Berkeley and went to the Klondike during the gold rush boom.

Early life

London was born near Third and Brannan Streets in San Francisco. The house burned down in the fire after the 1906 San Francisco earthquake; the California Historical Society placed a plaque at the site in 1953. Although the family was working class, it was not as impoverished as London's later accounts claimed. London was largely self-educated.

In 1885, London found and read Ouida's long Victorian novel Signa. He credited this as the seed of his literary success. In 1886, he went to the Oakland Public Library and found a sympathetic librarian, Ina Coolbrith, who encouraged his learning. (She later became California's first poet laureate and an important figure in the San Francisco literary community).

434

In 1889, London began working 12 to 18 hours a day at Hickmott's Cannery. Seeking a way out, he borrowed money from his foster mother Virginia Prentiss, bought the sloop Razzle-Dazzle from an oyster pirate named French Frank, and became an oyster pirate himself. In his memoir, John Barleycorn, he claims also to have stolen French Frank's mistress Mamie. After a few months, his sloop became damaged beyond repair. London hired on as a member of the California Fish Patrol.

In 1893, he signed on to the sealing schooner Sophie Sutherland, bound for the coast of Japan. When he returned, the country was in the grip of the panic of '93 and Oakland was swept by labor unrest. After grueling jobs in a jute mill and a street-railway power plant, London joined Coxey's Army and began his career as a tramp. In 1894, he spent 30 days for vagrancy in the Erie County Penitentiary at Buffalo, New York. In The Road, he wrote:

> Man-handling was merely one of the very minor unprintable horrors of the Erie County Pen. I say 'unprintable'; and in justice I must also say undescribable. They were unthinkable to me until I saw them, and I was no spring chicken in the ways of the world and the awful abysses of human degradation. It would take a deep plummet to reach bottom in the Erie County Pen, and I do but skim lightly and facetiously the surface of things as I there saw them.

> — Jack London, The Road

After many experiences as a hobo and a sailor, he returned to Oakland and attended Oakland High School. He contributed a number of articles to the high school's magazine, The Aegis. His first published work was "Typhoon off the Coast of Japan", an account of his sailing experiences.

As a schoolboy, London often studied at Heinold's First and Last Chance Saloon, a port-side bar in Oakland. At 17, he confessed to the bar's owner, John Heinold, his desire to attend university and pursue a career as a writer. Heinold lent London tuition money to attend college.

London desperately wanted to attend the University of California, located in Berkeley. In 1896, after a summer of intense studying to pass certification exams, he was admitted. Financial circumstances forced him to leave in 1897 and he never graduated. No evidence has surfaced that he ever wrote for student publications while studying at Berkeley.

While at Berkeley, London continued to study and spend time at Heinold's saloon, where he was introduced to the sailors and adventurers who would influence his writing. In his autobiographical novel, John Barleycorn, London mentioned the pub's likeness seventeen times. Heinold's was the place where London met Alexander McLean, a captain known for his cruelty at sea. London based his protagonist Wolf Larsen, in the novel The Sea-Wolf, on McLean.

Heinold's First and Last Chance Saloon is now unofficially named Jack London's Rendezvous in his honor.

Gold rush and first success

On July 12, 1897, London (age 21) and his sister's husband Captain Shepard sailed to join the Klondike Gold Rush. This was the setting for some of his first successful stories. London's time in the harsh Klondike, however, was detrimental to his health. Like so many other men who were malnourished in the goldfields, London developed scurvy. His gums became swollen, leading to the loss of his four front teeth. A constant gnawing pain affected his hip and leg muscles, and his face was stricken with marks that always reminded him of the struggles he faced in the Klondike. Father William Judge, "The Saint of Dawson", had a facility in Dawson that provided shelter, food and any available medicine to London and others. His struggles there inspired London's short story, "To Build a Fire" (1902, revised in 1908), which many critics assess as his best.

His landlords in Dawson were mining engineers Marshall Latham Bond and Louis Whitford Bond, educated at Yale and Stanford, respectively. The brothers' father, Judge Hiram Bond, was a wealthy mining investor. The Bonds, especially Hiram, were active Republicans. Marshall Bond's diary mentions friendly sparring with London on political issues as a camp pastime.

London left Oakland with a social conscience and socialist leanings; he returned to become an activist for socialism. He concluded that his only hope of escaping the work "trap" was to get an education and "sell his brains". He saw his writing as a business, his ticket out of poverty, and, he hoped, a means of beating the wealthy at their own game. On returning to California in 1898, London began working to get published, a struggle described in his novel, Martin Eden (serialized in 1908, published in 1909). His first published story since high school was "To the Man On Trail", which has frequently been collected in anthologies. When The Overland Monthly offered him only five dollars for it—and was slow paying—London came close to abandoning his writing career. In his words, "literally and literarily I was saved" when The Black Cat accepted his story "A Thousand Deaths", and paid him $40—the "first money I ever received for a story".

London began his writing career just as new printing technologies enabled lower-cost production of magazines. This resulted in a boom in popular magazines aimed at a wide public audience and a strong market for short fiction. In 1900, he made $2,500 in writing, about $77,000 in today's currency. Among the works he sold to magazines was a short story known as either "Diable" (1902) or "Bâtard" (1904), two editions of the same basic story; London received $141.25 for this story on May 27, 1902. In the text, a cruel French Canadian brutalizes his dog, and the dog retaliates and kills the man. London told some of his critics that man's actions are the main cause of the behavior of their animals, and he would show this in another story, The Call of the Wild.

In early 1903, London sold The Call of the Wild to The Saturday Evening Post for $750, and the book rights to Macmillan for $2,000. Macmillan's promotional campaign propelled it to swift success.

While living at his rented villa on Lake Merritt in Oakland, California, London met poet George Sterling; in time they became best friends. In 1902, Sterling helped London find a home closer to his own in nearby Piedmont. In his letters London addressed Sterling as "Greek", owing to Sterling's aquiline nose and classical profile, and he signed them as "Wolf". London was later to depict Sterling as Russ Brissenden in his autobiographical novel Martin Eden (1910) and as Mark Hall in The Valley of the Moon (1913).

In later life London indulged his wide-ranging interests by accumulating a personal library of 15,000 volumes. He referred to his books as "the tools of my trade".

First marriage (1900–04)

London married Elizabeth "Bessie" Maddern on April 7, 1900, the same day The Son of the Wolf was published. Bess had been part of his circle of friends for a number of years. She was related to stage actresses Minnie Maddern Fiske and Emily Stevens. Stasz says, "Both acknowledged publicly that they were not marrying out of love, but from friendship and a belief that they would produce sturdy children." Kingman says, "they were comfortable together... Jack had made it clear to Bessie that he did not love her, but that he liked her enough to make a successful marriage."

London met Bessie through his friend at Oakland High School, Fred Jacobs; she was Fred's fiancée. Bessie, who tutored at Anderson's University Academy in Alameda California, tutored Jack in preparation for his entrance exams for the University of California at Berkeley in 1896. Jacobs was killed aboard the USAT Scandia in 1897, but Jack and Bessie continued their friendship, which included taking photos and developing the film together. This was the beginning of Jack's passion for photography.

During the marriage, London continued his friendship with Anna Strunsky, co-authoring The Kempton-Wace Letters, an epistolary novel contrasting two philosophies of love. Anna, writing "Dane Kempton's" letters, arguing for a romantic view of marriage, while London, writing "Herbert Wace's" letters, argued for a scientific view, based on Darwinism and eugenics. In the novel, his fictional character contrasted two women he had known.

London's pet name for Bess was "Mother-Girl" and Bess's for London was "Daddy-Boy". Their first child, Joan, was born on January 15, 1901, and their second, Bessie (later called Becky), on October 20, 1902. Both children were born in Piedmont, California. Here London wrote one of his most celebrated works, The Call of the Wild.

438

While London had pride in his children, the marriage was strained. Kingman says that by 1903 the couple were close to separation as they were "extremely incompatible". "Jack was still so kind and gentle with Bessie that when Cloudsley Johns was a house guest in February 1903 he didn't suspect a breakup of their marriage."

London reportedly complained to friends Joseph Noel and George Sterling:

> [Bessie] is devoted to purity. When I tell her morality is only evidence of low blood pressure, she hates me. She'd sell me and the children out for her damned purity. It's terrible. Every time I come back after being away from home for a night she won't let me be in the same room with her if she can help it.

Stasz writes that these were "code words for fear that was consorting with prostitutes and might bring home venereal disease."

On July 24, 1903, London told Bessie he was leaving and moved out. During 1904, London and Bess negotiated the terms of a divorce, and the decree was granted on November 11, 1904.

War correspondent (1904)

London accepted an assignment of the San Francisco Examiner to cover the Russo-Japanese War in early 1904, arriving in Yokohama on January 25, 1904. He was arrested by Japanese authorities in Shimonoseki, but released through the intervention of American ambassador Lloyd Griscom. After travelling to Korea, he was again arrested by Japanese authorities for straying too close to the border with Manchuria without official permission, and was sent back to Seoul. Released again, London was permitted to travel with the Imperial Japanese Army to the border, and to observe the Battle of the Yalu.

London asked William Randolph Hearst, the owner of the San Francisco Examiner, to be allowed to transfer to the Imperial Russian Army, where he felt that restrictions on his reporting and his movements would be less severe. However, before this could be arranged, he was arrested for a third time in four months, this time for assaulting his Japanese assistants, whom he accused of stealing the fodder for his horse. Released through the personal intervention of President Theodore Roosevelt, London departed the front in June 1904.

Bohemian Club

On August 18, 1904, London went with his close friend, the poet George Sterling, to "Summer High Jinks" at the Bohemian Grove. London was elected to honorary membership in the Bohemian Club and took part in many activities. Other noted members of the Bohemian Club during this time included Ambrose Bierce, Gelett Burgess, Allan Dunn, John Muir, Frank Norris, and Herman George Scheffauer.

Beginning in December 1914, London worked on The Acorn Planter, A California Forest Play, to be performed as one of the annual Grove Plays, but it was never selected. It was described as too difficult to set to music. London published The Acorn Planter in 1916.

Second marriage

After divorcing Maddern, London married Charmian Kittredge in 1905. London had been introduced to Kittredge in 1900 by her aunt Netta Eames, who was an editor at Overland Monthly magazine in San Francisco. The two met prior to his first marriage but became lovers years later after Jack and Bessie London visited Wake Robin, Netta Eames' Sonoma County resort, in 1903. London was injured when he fell from a buggy, and Netta arranged for Charmian to care for him. The two developed a friendship, as Charmian, Netta, her husband Roscoe, and London were politically aligned with socialist causes. At some point the relationship became romantic, and Jack divorced his wife to marry Charmian, who was five years his senior.

Biographer Russ Kingman called Charmian "Jack's soul-mate, always at his side, and a perfect match." Their time together included numerous trips, including a 1907 cruise on the yacht Snark to Hawaii and Australia. Many of London's stories are based on his visits to Hawaii, the last one for 10 months beginning in December 1915.

The couple also visited Goldfield, Nevada, in 1907, where they were guests of the Bond brothers, London's Dawson City landlords. The Bond brothers were working in Nevada as mining engineers.

London had contrasted the concepts of the "Mother Girl" and the "Mate Woman" in The Kempton-Wace Letters. His pet name for Bess had been "Mother-Girl;" his pet name for Charmian was "Mate-Woman."Charmian's aunt and foster mother, a disciple of Victoria Woodhull, had raised her without prudishness.every biographer alludes to Charmian's uninhibited sexuality.

Joseph Noel calls the events from 1903 to 1905 "a domestic drama that would have intrigued the pen of an Ibsen.... London's had comedy relief in it and a sort of easy-going romance." In broad outline, London was restless in his first marriage, sought extramarital sexual affairs, and found, in Charmian Kittredge, not only a sexually active and adventurous partner, but his future life-companion. They attempted to have children; one child died at birth, and another pregnancy ended in a miscarriage.

In 1906, London published in Collier's magazine his eye-witness report of the San Francisco earthquake.

Beauty Ranch (1905–16)

In 1905, London purchased a 1,000 acres (4.0 km2) ranch in Glen Ellen, Sonoma County, California, on the eastern slope of Sonoma Mountain.He wrote: "Next to my wife, the ranch is the dearest thing in the world to me." He desperately wanted the ranch to become a successful business enterprise. Writing, always a commercial enterprise with London, now became even more a means to an end: "I write for no other purpose than to add to the beauty that now belongs to me. I write a book for no other reason than to add three or four hundred acres to my magnificent estate."

Stasz writes that London "had taken fully to heart the vision, expressed in his agrarian fiction, of the land as the closest earthly version of Eden ... he educated himself through the study of agricultural manuals and scientific tomes. He conceived of a system of ranching that today would be praised for its ecological wisdom." He was proud to own the first concrete silo in California, a circular piggery that he designed. He hoped to adapt the wisdom of Asian sustainable agriculture to the United States. He hired both Italian and Chinese stonemasons, whose distinctly different styles are obvious.

The ranch was an economic failure. Sympathetic observers such as Stasz treat his projects as potentially feasible, and ascribe their failure to bad luck or to being ahead of their time. Unsympathetic historians such as Kevin Starr suggest that he was a bad manager, distracted by other concerns and impaired by his alcoholism. Starr notes that London was absent from his ranch about six months a year between 1910 and 1916 and says, "He liked the show of managerial power, but not grinding attention to detail .... London's workers laughed at his efforts to play big-time rancher the operation a rich man's hobby."

London spent $80,000 ($2,280,000 in current value) to build a 15,000-square-foot (1,400 m2) stone mansion called Wolf House on the property. Just as the mansion was nearing completion, two weeks before the Londons planned to move in, it was destroyed by fire.

London's last visit to Hawaii, beginning in December 1915, lasted eight months. He met with Duke Kahanamoku, Prince Jonah Kūhiō Kalaniana'ole, Queen Lili'uokalani and many others, before returning to his ranch in July 1916. He was suffering from kidney failure, but he continued to work.

The ranch (abutting stone remnants of Wolf House) is now a National Historic Landmark and is protected in Jack London State Historic Park.

Animal activism

London witnessed animal cruelty in the training of circus animals, and his subsequent novels Jerry of the Islands and Michael, Brother of Jerry included a foreword entreating the public to become more informed about this practice. In 1918, the Massachusetts Society for the Prevention of Cruelty to Animals and the American Humane Education Society teamed up to create the Jack London Club, which sought to inform the public about cruelty to circus animals and encourage them to protest this establishment. Support from Club members led to a temporary cessation of trained animal acts at Ringling-Barnum and Bailey in 1925.

Death

London died November 22, 1916, in a sleeping porch in a cottage on his ranch. London had been a robust man but had suffered several serious illnesses, including scurvy in the Klondike. Additionally, during travels on the Snark, he and Charmian picked up unspecified tropical infections, and diseases, including yaws. At the time of his death, he suffered from dysentery, late-stage alcoholism, and uremia; he was in extreme pain and taking morphine.

London's ashes were buried on his property not far from the Wolf House. London's funeral took place on November 26, 1916, attended only by close friends, relatives, and workers of the property. In accordance with his wishes, he was cremated and buried next to some pioneer children, under a rock that belonged to the Wolf House. After Charmian's death in 1955, she was also cremated and then buried with her husband in the same spot that her husband chose. The grave is marked by a mossy boulder. The buildings and property were later preserved as Jack London State Historic Park, in Glen Ellen, California.

Suicide debate

Because he was using morphine, many older sources describe London's death as a suicide, and some still do. This conjecture appears to be a rumor, or speculation based on incidents in his fiction writings. His death certificate gives the cause as uremia, following acute renal colic.

The biographer Stasz writes, "Following London's death, for a number of reasons, a biographical myth developed in which he has been portrayed as an alcoholic womanizer who committed suicide. Recent scholarship based upon firsthand documents challenges this caricature." Most biographers, including Russ Kingman, now agree he died of uremia aggravated by an accidental morphine overdose.

London's fiction featured several suicides. In his autobiographical memoir John Barleycorn, he claims, as a youth, to have drunkenly stumbled overboard into the San Francisco Bay, "some maundering fancy of going out with the tide suddenly obsessed me". He said he drifted and nearly succeeded in drowning before sobering up and being rescued by fishermen. In the dénouement of The Little Lady of the Big House, the heroine, confronted by the pain of a mortal gunshot wound, undergoes a physician-assisted suicide by morphine. Also, in Martin Eden, the principal protagonist, who shares certain characteristics with London, drowns himself.

Plagiarism accusations

London was vulnerable to accusations of plagiarism, both because he was such a conspicuous, prolific, and successful writer and because of his methods of working. He wrote in a letter to Elwyn Hoffman, "expression, you see—with me—is far easier than invention." He purchased plots and novels from the young Sinclair Lewis and used incidents from newspaper clippings as writing material.

In July 1901, two pieces of fiction appeared within the same month: London's "Moon-Face", in the San Francisco Argonaut, and Frank Norris' "The Passing of Cock-eye Blacklock", in Century Magazine. Newspapers showed the similarities between the stories, which London said were "quite different in manner of treatment, patently the same in foundation and motive." London explained both writers based their stories on the same newspaper account. A year later, it was discovered that Charles Forrest McLean had published a fictional story also based on the same incident.

Egerton Ryerson Young claimed The Call of the Wild (1903) was taken from Young's book My Dogs in the Northland (1902). London acknowledged using it as a source and claimed to have written a letter to Young thanking him.

In 1906, the New York World published "deadly parallel" columns showing eighteen passages from London's short story "Love of Life" side by side with similar passages from a nonfiction article by Augustus Biddle and J. K. Macdonald, titled "Lost in the Land of the Midnight Sun". London noted the World did not accuse him of "plagiarism", but only of "identity of time and situation", to which he defiantly "pled guilty".

444

The most serious charge of plagiarism was based on London's "The Bishop's Vision", Chapter 7 of his novel The Iron Heel (1908). The chapter is nearly identical to an ironic essay that Frank Harris published in 1901, titled "The Bishop of London and Public Morality". Harris was incensed and suggested he should receive 1/60th of the royalties from The Iron Heel, the disputed material constituting about that fraction of the whole novel. London insisted he had clipped a reprint of the article, which had appeared in an American newspaper, and believed it to be a genuine speech delivered by the Bishop of London.

Views

Atheism

London was an atheist. He is quoted as saying, "I believe that when I am dead, I am dead. I believe that with my death I am just as much obliterated as the last mosquito you and I squashed."

Socialism

London wrote from a socialist viewpoint, which is evident in his novel The Iron Heel. Neither a theorist nor an intellectual socialist, London's socialism grew out of his life experience. As London explained in his essay, "How I Became a Socialist", his views were influenced by his experience with people at the bottom of the social pit. His optimism and individualism faded, and he vowed never to do more hard physical work than necessary. He wrote that his individualism was hammered out of him, and he was politically reborn. He often closed his letters "Yours for the Revolution."

London joined the Socialist Labor Party in April 1896. In the same year, the San Francisco Chronicle published a story about the twenty-year-old London's giving nightly speeches in Oakland's City Hall Park, an activity he was arrested for a year later. In 1901, he left the Socialist Labor Party and joined the new Socialist Party of America. He ran unsuccessfully as the high-profile Socialist candidate for mayor of Oakland in 1901 (receiving 245 votes) and 1905 (improving to 981 votes), toured the country lecturing on socialism in 1906, and published two collections of essays about socialism: The War of the Classes (1905) and Revolution, and other Essays (1906).

Stasz notes that "London regarded the Wobblies as a welcome addition to the Socialist cause, although he never joined them in going so far as to recommend sabotage." Stasz mentions a personal meeting between London and Big Bill Haywood in 1912.

In his late (1913) book The Cruise of the Snark, London writes about appeals to him for membership of the Snark's crew from office workers and other "toilers" who longed for escape from the cities, and of being cheated by workmen.

In his Glen Ellen ranch years, London felt some ambivalence toward socialism and complained about the "inefficient Italian labourers" in his employ. In 1916, he resigned from the Glen Ellen chapter of the Socialist Party, but stated emphatically he did so "because of its lack of fire and fight, and its loss of emphasis on the class struggle." In an unflattering portrait of London's ranch days, California cultural historian Kevin Starr refers to this period as "post-socialist" and says "... by 1911 ... London was more bored by the class struggle than he cared to admit."

Race

London shared common concerns among many European Americans in California about Asian immigration, described as "the yellow peril"; he used the latter term as the title of a 1904 essay. This theme was also the subject of a story he wrote in 1910 called "The Unparalleled Invasion". Presented as an historical essay set in the future, the story narrates events between 1976 and 1987, in which China, with an ever-increasing population, is taking over and colonizing its neighbors with the intention of taking over the entire Earth. The western nations respond with biological warfare and bombard China with dozens of the most infectious diseases. On his fears about China, he admits, "it must be taken into consideration that the above postulate is itself a product of Western race-egotism, urged by our belief in our own righteousness and fostered by a faith in ourselves which may be as erroneous as are most fond race fancies."

By contrast, many of London's short stories are notable for their empathetic portrayal of Mexican ("The Mexican"), Asian ("The Chinago"), and Hawaiian ("Koolau the Leper") characters. London's war correspondence from the Russo-Japanese War, as well as his unfinished novel Cherry, show he admired much about Japanese customs and capabilities. London's writings have been popular among the Japanese, who believe he portrayed them positively.

In "Koolau the Leper", London describes Koolau, who is a Hawaiian leper—and thus a very different sort of "superman" than Martin Eden—and who fights off an entire cavalry troop to elude capture, as "indomitable spiritually—a ... magnificent rebel". This character is based on Hawaiian leper Kaluaikoolau, who in 1893 revolted and resisted capture from forces of the Provisional Government of Hawaii in the Kalalau Valley.

An amateur boxer and avid boxing fan, London reported on the 1910 Johnson–Jeffries fight, in which the black boxer Jack Johnson vanquished Jim Jeffries, known as the "Great White Hope". In 1908, London had reported on an earlier fight of Johnson's, contrasting the black boxer's coolness and intellectual style, with the apelike appearance and fighting style of his Canadian opponent, Tommy Burns:

> [What won] on Saturday was bigness, coolness, quickness, cleverness, and vast physical superiority ... Because a white man wishes a white man to win, this should not prevent him from giving absolute credit to the best man, even when that best man was black. All hail to Johnson. ... superb. He was impregnable ... as inaccessible as Mont Blanc.

Those who defend London against charges of racism cite the letter he wrote to the Japanese-American Commercial Weekly in 1913:

> In reply to yours of August 16, 1913. First of all, I should say by stopping the stupid newspaper from always fomenting race prejudice. This of course, being impossible, I would say, next, by educating the people of Japan so that they will be too intelligently tolerant to respond to any call to race prejudice. And, finally, by realizing, in industry and

government, of socialism—which last word is merely a word that stands for the actual application of in the affairs of men of the theory of the Brotherhood of Man.

In the meantime the nations and races are only unruly boys who have not yet grown to the stature of men. So we must expect them to do unruly and boisterous things at times. And, just as boys grow up, so the races of mankind will grow up and laugh when they look back upon their childish quarrels.

In 1996, after the City of Whitehorse, Yukon, renamed a street in honor of London, protests over London's alleged racism forced the city to change the name of "Jack London Boulevard"[failed verification] back to "Two-mile Hill".

Eugenics

London supported eugenics, including forced sterilization of criminals or those deemed feeble minded. His novel Before Adam(1906–07) has been described as having pro-eugenic themes.

London wrote to Frederick H. Robinson of the periodical Medical Review of Reviews, stating, "I believe the future belongs to eugenics, and will be determined by the practice of eugenics."

Works

Short stories

Western writer and historian Dale L. Walker writes:

London's true métier was the short story ... London's true genius lay in the short form, 7,500 words and under, where the flood of images in his teeming brain and the innate power of his narrative gift were at once constrained and freed. His stories that run longer than the magic 7,500 generally—but certainly not always—could have benefited from self-editing.

London's "strength of utterance" is at its height in his stories, and they are painstakingly well-constructed. "To Build a Fire" is the best known of all his stories. Set in the harsh Klondike, it recounts the haphazard trek of a new arrival who has ignored an old-timer's warning about the risks of traveling alone. Falling through the ice into a creek in seventy-five-below weather, the unnamed man is keenly aware that survival depends on his untested skills at quickly building a fire to dry his clothes and warm his extremities. After publishing a tame version of this story—with a sunny outcome—in The Youth's Companion in 1902, London offered a second, more severe take on the man's predicament in The Century Magazine in 1908. Reading both provides an illustration of London's growth and maturation as a writer. As Labor (1994) observes: "To compare the two versions is itself an instructive lesson in what distinguished a great work of literary art from a good children's story."

Other stories from the Klondike period include: "All Gold Canyon", about a battle between a gold prospector and a claim jumper; "The Law of Life", about an aging American Indian man abandoned by his tribe and left to die; "Love of Life", about a trek by a prospector across the Canadian tundra; "To the Man on Trail," which tells the story of a prospector fleeing the Mounted Police in a sled race, and raises the question of the contrast between written law and morality; and "An Odyssey of the North," which raises questions of conditional morality, and paints a sympathetic portrait of a man of mixed White and Aleut ancestry.

London was a boxing fan and an avid amateur boxer. "A Piece of Steak" is a tale about a match between older and younger boxers. It contrasts the differing experiences of youth and age but also raises the social question of the treatment of aging workers. "The Mexican" combines boxing with a social theme, as a young Mexican endures an unfair fight and ethnic prejudice to earn money with which to aid the revolution.

Several of London's stories would today be classified as science fiction. "The Unparalleled Invasion" describes germ warfare against China; "Goliath" is about an irresistible energy weapon; "The Shadow and the Flash" is a tale about two brothers who take different routes to achieving invisibility; "A

Relic of the Pliocene" is a tall tale about an encounter of a modern-day man with a mammoth. "The Red One" is a late story from a period when London was intrigued by the theories of the psychiatrist and writer Jung. It tells of an island tribe held in thrall by an extraterrestrial object.

Some nineteen original collections of short stories were published during London's brief life or shortly after his death. There have been several posthumous anthologies drawn from this pool of stories. Many of these stories were located in the Klondike and the Pacific. A collection of Jack London's San Francisco Stories was published in October 2010 by Sydney Samizdat Press.

Novels

London's most famous novels are The Call of the Wild, White Fang, The Sea-Wolf, The Iron Heel, and Martin Eden.

In a letter dated December 27, 1901, London's Macmillan publisher George Platt Brett, Sr., said "he believed Jack's fiction represented 'the very best kind of work' done in America."

Critic Maxwell Geismar called The Call of the Wild "a beautiful prose poem"; editor Franklin Walker said that it "belongs on a shelf with Walden and Huckleberry Finn"; and novelist E.L. Doctorow called it "a mordant parable ... his masterpiece."

The historian Dale L. Walker commented:

> Jack London was an uncomfortable novelist, that form too long for his natural impatience and the quickness of his mind. His novels, even the best of them, are hugely flawed.

Some critics have said that his novels are episodic and resemble linked short stories. Dale L. Walker writes:

> The Star Rover, that magnificent experiment, is actually a series of short stories connected by a unifying device ... Smoke Bellew is a series of stories bound together in a novel-like form by their reappearing

protagonist, Kit Bellew; and John Barleycorn ... is a synoptic series of short episodes.

Ambrose Bierce said of The Sea-Wolf that "the great thing—and it is among the greatest of things—is that tremendous creation, Wolf Larsen ... the hewing out and setting up of such a figure is enough for a man to do in one lifetime. "However, he noted, "The love element, with its absurd suppressions, and impossible proprieties, is awful."

The Iron Heel is an example of a dystopian novel that anticipates and influenced George Orwell's Nineteen Eighty-Four. London's socialist politics are explicitly on display here. The Iron Heel meets the contemporary definition of soft science fiction. The Star Rover (1915) is also science fiction.

Apocrypha

Jack London Credo

London's literary executor, Irving Shepard, quoted a Jack London Credo in an introduction to a 1956 collection of London stories:

> I would rather be ashes than dust!
>
> I would rather that my spark should burn out in a brilliant blaze than it should be stifled by dry-rot.
>
> I would rather be a superb meteor, every atom of me in magnificent glow, than a sleepy and permanent planet.
>
> The function of man is to live, not to exist.
>
> I shall not waste my days in trying to prolong them.
>
> I shall use my time.

The biographer Stasz notes that the passage "has many marks of London's style" but the only line that could be safely attributed to London was the first. The words Shepard quoted were from a story in the San Francisco Bulletin, December 2, 1916, by journalist Ernest J. Hopkins, who visited the ranch just weeks before London's death. Stasz notes, "Even more so than today journalists' quotes were unreliable or even sheer inventions," and says no direct source in London's writings has been found. However, at least one line, according to Stasz, is authentic, being referenced by London and written in his own hand in the autograph book of Australian suffragette Vida Goldstein:

Dear Miss Goldstein:–

Seven years ago I wrote you that I'd rather be ashes than dust. I still subscribe to that sentiment.

Sincerely yours,

Jack London

Jan. 13, 1909

In his short story "By The Turtles of Tasman", a character, defending her "ne'er-do-well grasshopperish father" to her "antlike uncle", says: "... my father has been a king. He has lived .... Have you lived merely to live? Are you afraid to die? I'd rather sing one wild song and burst my heart with it, than live a thousand years watching my digestion and being afraid of the wet. When you are dust, my father will be ashes."

"The Scab"

A short diatribe on "The Scab" is often quoted within the U.S. labor movement and frequently attributed to London. It opens:

After God had finished the rattlesnake, the toad, and the vampire, he had some awful substance left with which he made a scab. A scab is a two-legged animal with a corkscrew soul, a water brain, a combination backbone of jelly and glue. Where others have hearts, he carries a tumor of rotten principles. When a scab comes down the street, men turn their backs and Angels weep in Heaven, and the Devil shuts the gates of hell to keep him out....

In 1913 and 1914, a number of newspapers printed the first three sentences with varying terms used instead of "scab", such as "knocker","stool pigeon"or "scandal monger"

452

This passage as given above was the subject of a 1974 Supreme Court case, Letter Carriers v. Austin, in which Justice Thurgood Marshall referred to it as "a well-known piece of trade union literature, generally attributed to author Jack London". A union newsletter had published a "list of scabs," which was granted to be factual and therefore not libelous, but then went on to quote the passage as the "definition of a scab". The case turned on the question of whether the "definition" was defamatory. The court ruled that "Jack London's... 'definition of a scab' is merely rhetorical hyperbole, a lusty and imaginative expression of the contempt felt by union members towards those who refuse to join", and as such was not libelous and was protected under the First Amendment.

Despite being frequently attributed to London, the passage does not appear at all in the extensive collection of his writings at Sonoma State University's website. However, in his book The War of the Classes he published a 1903 speech entitled "The Scab", which gave a much more balanced view of the topic:

> The laborer who gives more time or strength or skill for the same wage than another, or equal time or strength or skill for a less wage, is a scab. The generousness on his part is hurtful to his fellow-laborers, for it compels them to an equal generousness which is not to their liking, and which gives them less of food and shelter. But a word may be said for the scab. Just as his act makes his rivals compulsorily generous, so do they, by fortune of birth and training, make compulsory his act of generousness.
>
> [...]
>
> Nobody desires to scab, to give most for least. The ambition of every individual is quite the opposite, to give least for most; and, as a result, living in a tooth-and-nail society, battle royal is waged by the ambitious individuals. But in its most salient aspect, that of the struggle over the division of the joint product, it is no longer a battle between individuals, but between groups of individuals. Capital and labor apply

themselves to raw material, make something useful out of it, add to its value, and then proceed to quarrel over the division of the added value. Neither cares to give most for least. Each is intent on giving less than the other and on receiving more.

Legacy and honors

Mount London, also known as Boundary Peak 100, on the Alaska-British Columbia boundary, in the Boundary Ranges of the Coast Mountains of British Columbia, is named for him.

Jack London Square on the waterfront of Oakland, California was named for him.

He was honored by the United States Postal Service with a 25¢ Great Americans series postage stamp released on January 11, 1986.

Jack London Lake (Russian), a mountain lake located in the upper reaches of the Kolyma River in Yagodninsky district of Magadan Oblast.

Fictional portrayals of London include Michael O'Shea in the 1943 film Jack London, Jeff East in the 1980 film Klondike Fever, Aaron Ashmore in the Murdoch Mysteries episode "Murdoch of the Klondike" from 2012, and Johnny Simmons in the 2014 miniseries Klondike. (Source: Wikipedia)

NOTABLE WORKS

<u>NOVELS</u>

The Cruise of the Dazzler (1902)

A Daughter of the Snows (1902)

The Call of the Wild (1903)

The Kempton-Wace Letters (1903) (published anonymously, co-authored with Anna Strunsky)

The Sea-Wolf (1904)

The Game (1905)

White Fang (1906)

Before Adam (1907)

The Iron Heel (1908)

Martin Eden (1909)

Burning Daylight (1910)

Adventure (1911)

The Scarlet Plague (1912)

A Son of the Sun (1912)

The Abysmal Brute (1913)

The Valley of the Moon (1913)

The Mutiny of the Elsinore (1914)

The Star Rover (1915) (published in England as The Jacket)

The Little Lady of the Big House (1916)

Jerry of the Islands (1917)

Michael, Brother of Jerry (1917)

Hearts of Three (1920) (novelization of a script by Charles Goddard)

The Assassination Bureau, Ltd (1963) (left half-finished, completed by Robert L. Fish)

SHORT STORIES

"An Old Soldier's Story" (1894)

"Who Believes in Ghosts!" (1895)

"And 'FRISCO Kid Came Back" (1895)

"Night's Swim In Yeddo Bay" (1895)

"One More Unfortunate" (1895)

"Sakaicho, Hona Asi And Hakadaki" (1895)

"A Klondike Christmas" (1897)

"Mahatma's Little Joke" (1897)

"O Haru" (1897)

"Plague Ship" (1897)

"The Strange Experience Of A Misogynist" (1897)

"Two Gold Bricks" (1897)

"The Devil's Dice Box" (1898)

"A Dream Image" (1898)

"The Test: A Clondyke Wooing" (1898)

"To the Man on Trail" (1898)

"In a Far Country" (1899)

"The King of Mazy May" (1899)

"The End Of The Chapter" (1899)

"The Grilling Of Loren Ellery" (1899)

"The Handsome Cabin Boy" (1899)

"In The Time Of Prince Charley" (1899)

"Old Baldy" (1899)

"The Men of Forty Mile" (1899)

"Pluck and Pertinacity" (1899)

"The Rejuvenation of Major Rathbone" (1899)

"The White Silence" (1899)

"A Thousand Deaths" (1899)

"Wisdom of the Trail" (1899)

"An Odyssey of the North" (1900)

"The Son of the Wolf" (1900)

"Even unto Death" (1900)

"The Man with the Gash" (1900)

"A Lesson in Heraldry" (1900)

"A Northland Miracle" (1900)

"Proper "GIRLIE"" (1900)

"Thanksgiving on Slav Creek" (1900)

"Their Alcove" (1900)

"Housekeeping in the Klondike" (1900)

"Dutch Courage" (1900)

"Where the Trail Forks" (1900)

"Hyperborean Brew" (1901)

"A Relic of the Pliocene" (1901)

"The Lost Poacher" (1901)

"The God of His Fathers" (1901)

""FRISCO Kid's" Story" (1901)

"The Law of Life" (1901)

"The Minions of Midas" (1901)

"In the Forests of the North" (1902)

"The "Fuzziness" of Hoockla-Heen" (1902)

"The Story of Keesh" (1902)

"Keesh, Son of Keesh" (1902)

"Nam-Bok, the Unveracious" (1902)

"Li Wan the Fair" (1902)

"Lost Face"

"Master of Mystery" (1902)

"The Sunlanders" (1902)

"The Death of Ligoun" (1902)

"Moon-Face" (1902)

"Diable—A Dog" (1902), renamed Bâtard in 1904

"To Build a Fire" (1902, revised 1908)

"The League of the Old Men" (1902)

"The Dominant Primordial Beast" (1903)

"The One Thousand Dozen" (1903)

"The Marriage of Lit-lit" (1903)

"The Shadow and the Flash" (1903)

"The Leopard Man's Story" (1903)

"Negore the Coward" (1904)

"All Gold Cañon" (1905)

"Love of Life" (1905)

"The Sun-Dog Trail" (1905)

"The Apostate" (1906)

"Up the Slide" (1906)

"Planchette" (1906)

"Brown Wolf" (1906)

"Make Westing" (1907)

"Chased by the Trail" (1907)

"Trust" (1908)

"A Curious Fragment" (1908)

"Aloha Oe" (1908)

"That Spot" (1908)

"The Enemy of All the World" (1908)

"The House of Mapuhi" (1909)

"Good-by, Jack" (1909)

"Samuel" (1909)

"South of the Slot" (1909)

"The Chinago" (1909)

"The Dream of Debs" (1909)

"The Madness of John Harned" (1909)

"The Seed of McCoy" (1909)

"A Piece of Steak" (1909)

"Mauki" (1909)

"The Whale Tooth" (1909)

"Goliath" (1910)

"The Unparalleled Invasion" (1910)

"Told in the Drooling Ward" (1910)

"When the World was Young" (1910)

"The Terrible Solomons" (1910)

"The Inevitable White Man" (1910)

"The Heathen" (1910)

"Yah! Yah! Yah!" (1910)

"By the Turtles of Tasman" (1911)

"The Mexican" (1911)

"War" (1911)

"The Unmasking of the Cad" (1911)

"The Scarlet Plague" (1912)

"The Captain of the Susan Drew" (1912)

"The Sea-Farmer" (1912)

"The Feathers of the Sun" (1912)

"The Prodigal Father" (1912)

"Samuel" (1913)

"The Sea-Gangsters" (1913)

"The Strength of the Strong" (1914)

"Told in the Drooling Ward" (1914)

"The Hussy" (1916)

"Like Argus of the Ancient Times" (1917)

"Jerry of the Islands" (1917)

"The Red One" (1918)

"Shin-Bones" (1918)

"The Bones of Kahekili" (1919)

SHORT STORY COLLECTIONS

Son of the Wolf (1900)

Chris Farrington, Able Seaman (1901)

The God of His Fathers & Other Stories (1901)

Children of the Frost (1902)

The Faith of Men and Other Stories (1904)

Tales of the Fish Patrol (1906)

Moon-Face and Other Stories (1906)

Love of Life and Other Stories (1907)

Lost Face (1910)

South Sea Tales (1911)

When God Laughs and Other Stories (1911)

The House of Pride & Other Tales of Hawaii (1912)

Smoke Bellew (1912)

A Son of the Sun (1912)

The Night Born (1913)

The Strength of the Strong (1914)

The Turtles of Tasman (1916)

The Human Drift (1917)

The Red One (1918)

On the Makaloa Mat (1919)

Dutch Courage and Other Stories (1922)

AUTOBIOGRAPHICAL MEMOIRS

The Road (1907)

The Cruise of the Snark (1911)

John Barleycorn (1913)

NON-FICTION AND ESSAYS

Through the Rapids on the Way to the Klondike (1899)

From Dawson to the Sea (1899)

What Communities Lose by the Competitive System (1900)

The Impossibility of War (1900)

Phenomena of Literary Evolution (1900)

A Letter to Houghton Mifflin Co. (1900)

Husky, Wolf Dog of the North (1900)

Editorial Crimes — A Protest (1901)

Again the Literary Aspirant (1902)

The People of the Abyss (1903)

How I Became a Socialist (1903)

The War of the Classes (1905)

The Story of an Eyewitness (1906)

A Letter to Woman's Home Companion (1906)

Revolution, and other Essays (1910)

Mexico's Army and Ours (1914)

Lawgivers (1914)

Our Adventures in Tampico (1914)

Stalking the Pestilence (1914)

The Red Game of War (1914)

The Trouble Makers of Mexico (1914)

With Funston's Men (1914)

POETRY

A Heart (1899)

Abalone Song (1913)

And Some Night (1914)

Ballade of the False Lover (1914)

Cupid's Deal (1913)

Daybreak (1901)

Effusion (1901)

George Sterling (1913)

Gold (1915)

He Chortled with Glee (1899)

He Never Tried Again (1912)

His Trip to Hades (1913)

Homeland (1914)

Hors de Saison (1913)

If I Were God (1899)

In a Year (1901)

In and Out (1911)

Je Vis en Espoir (1897)

Memory (1913)

Moods (1913)

My Confession (1912)

My Little Palmist (1914)

Of Man of the Future (1915)

Oh You Everybody's Girl (19)

On the Face of the Earth You are the One (1915)

Rainbows End (1914)

Republican Rallying Song (1916)

Sonnet (1901)

The Gift of God (1905)

The Klondyker's Dream (1914)

The Lover's Liturgy (1913)

The Mammon Worshippers (1911)

The Republican Battle-Hymn (1905)

The Return of Ulysses (1915)

The Sea Sprite and the Shooting Star (1916)

The Socialist's Dream (1912)

The Song of the Flames (1903)

The Way of War (1906)

The Worker and the Tramp (1911)

Tick! Tick! Tick! (1915)

Too Late (1912)

Weasel Thieves (1913)

When All the World Shouted my Name (1905)

Where the Rainbow Fell (1902)

Your Kiss (1914)

PLAYS

Theft (1910)

Daughters of the Rich: A One Act Play (1915)

The Acorn Planter: A California Forest Play (1916)